ISAAC ASIMO[

ROBOT CITY

VOLUME ONE

MICHAEL P. KUBE-McDOWELL

Michael P. Kube-McDowell was raised in Camden, New Jersey. He attended Michigan State University as a National Merit Scholar, holds a master's degree in science education, and was honored for teaching excellence by the 1985 White House Commission on Presidential scholars. Kube-McDowell's stories have appeared in such magazines as *Analog, Asimov's, Amazing,* and *Fantasy* and *Science Fiction,* as well as in various anthologies published in the U. S. and Europe. Three of his stories were adapted as episodes for the TV series *Tales from the Darkside.* He is the author of a highly praised future-history trilogy consisting of the novels *Emprise, Enigma,* and *Empery.*

MICHAEL McQUAY

The late Michael McQuay began his writing career in 1975 while a production line worker at a factory. Before that he had worked at a variety of jobs, including musician, airplane mechanic, banker, retail story owner, bartender, Club Med salesman, and film pirate. Following the publication of his first novel, *Lifekeeper,* in 1980, McQuay published over 22 novels and short story collections in a variety of fields: science fiction, children's, horror, mainstream thriller, and adventure.

ISAAC ASIMOV'S
ROBOT CITY

VOLUME ONE

Book One by
MICHAEL P. KUBE-McDOWELL

Book Two by
MIKE McQUAY

ibooks
new york
www.ibooksinc.com

DISTRIBUTED BY SIMON & SCHUSTER, INC

An Original Publication of ibooks, inc.

Pocket Books, a division of Simon & Schuster, Inc.
1230 Avenue of the Americas, New York, NY 10020

An ibooks, inc. Book

ibooks, inc.
24 West 25th Street
New York, NY 10010

The ibooks World Wide Web Site Address is:
http://www.ibooksinc.com

You can visit the ibooks web site for a free read and
download the first chapters of all the ibooks titles:
http://www.ibooksinc.com

ISBN 0-671-03893-1
First Pocket Book Printing November 1999

10 9 8 7 6 5 4 3 2 1

Cover art and interior illustrations by Paul Rivoche
Cover design by Claude Goodwin
Interior design by Michael Mendelsohn at MM Design 2000, Inc.

Printed in the U.S.A.

For all the students
who made my seven years of teaching time well spent,
but especially for:

Wendy Armstrong, Todd Bontrager, Kathy Branum,
Jay & Joel Carlin, Valerie Eash, Chris Franko, Judy Fuller,
Chris & Bryant Hackett, Kean Hankins, Doug Johsnson,
Greg LaRue, Julie Merrick, Kendall Miller, Matt Mow,
Amy Myers, Khai & Vihn Pham, Melanie & Laura Schrock,
Sally Sibert, Stephanie Smith, Tom Williams,
Laura Joyce Yoder, Scott Yoder

And for
Joy Von Blon,
who made sure they always had something good to read.
— MICHAEL P. KUBE McDOWELL

For
Brian Shelton
and the bruised banana
— MIKE McQUAY

MY ROBOTS

by ISAAC ASIMOV

I wrote my first robot story, "Robbie," in May of 1939, when I was only nineteen years old.

What made it different from robot stories that had been written earlier was that I was determined *not* to make my robots symbols. They were *not* to be symbols of humanity's over-weening arrogance. They were *not* to be examples of human ambitions trespassing on the domain of the Almighty. They were *not* to be a new Tower of Babel requiring punishment.

Nor were the robots to be symbols of minority groups. They were *not* to be pathetic creatures that were unfairly persecuted so that I could make Aesopic statements about Jews, Blacks or any other mistreated members of society. Naturally, I was bitterly opposed to such mistreatment and I made that plain in numerous stories and essays—but *not* in my robot stories.

In that case, what *did* I make my robots?—I made them engineering devices. I made them tools. I made them machines to serve human ends. And I made them objects with built-in safety features. In other words, I set it up so that a robot *could not* kill his creator, and having outlawed that heavily overused plot, I was free to consider other, more rational consequences.

Since I began writing my robot stories in 1939, I did not mention computerization in their connection. The electronic computer had not yet been invented and I did not foresee it. I did foresee, however, that the brain had to be electronic in some fashion. However, "electronic" didn't seem futuristic enough. The positron—a subatomic particle exactly like the electron but of opposite electric charge—had been discovered only four years before I wrote my first robot story. It sounded very science fictional indeed, so I gave my robots "positronic brains" and imagined their thoughts to consist of flashing streams of positrons, coming into existence, then going out of existence almost immediately. These stories that I wrote were therefore called "the positronic robot series," but there was no greater significance than what I have just described to the use of positrons rather than electrons.

At first, I did not bother actually systematizing, or putting into words, just what the safeguards were that I imagined to be built into my robots. From the very start, though, since I wasn't going to have it possible for a robot to kill its creator, I had to stress that robots could not harm human beings; that this was an ingrained part of the makeup of their positronic brains.

Thus, in the very first printed version of "Robbie" (it appeared in the September 1940 *Super Science Stories*, under the title of "Strange Playfellow"), I had a character refer to a robot as follows: "He just can't help being faithful and loving and kind. He's a machine, *made so.*"

After writing "Robbie," which John Campbell, of *Astounding Science Fiction*, rejected, I went on to other robot stories which Campbell accepted. On December 23,

1940, I came to him with an idea for a mind-reading robot (which later became "Liar!") and John was dissatisfied with my explanations of why the robot behaved as it did. He wanted the safeguard specified precisely so that we could understand the robot. Together, then, we worked out what came to be known as the "Three Laws of Robotics." The concept was mine, for it was obtained out of the stories I had already written, but the actual wording (if I remember correctly) was beaten out then and there by the two of us.

The Three Laws were logical and made sense. To begin with, there was the question of safety, which had been foremost in my mind when I began to write stories about *my* robots. What's more I was aware of the fact that even without actively attempting to do harm, one could quietly, by doing nothing, allow harm to come. What was in my mind was Arthur Hugh Clough's cynical "The Latest Decalog," in which the Ten Commandments are rewritten in deeply satirical Machiavellian fashion. The one item most frequently quoted is: "Thou shalt not kill, but needst not strive/Officiously to keep alive."

For that reason I insisted that the First Law (safety) had to be in two parts and it came out this way:

1. A robot may not injure a human being, or, through inaction, allow a human being to come to harm.

Having got that out of the way, we had to pass on to the second law (service). Naturally, in giving the robot the built-in necessity to follow orders, you couldn't forfeit the overall concern of safety. The second law had to read as follows, then:

2. A robot must obey the orders given it by human beings except where such orders would conflict with the First Law.

And finally, we had to have a third law (prudence). A

robot was bound to be an expensive machine and it must not needlessly be damaged or destroyed. Naturally, this must not be used as a way of compromising either safety or service. The Third Law, therefore, had to read as follows:

3. A robot must protect its own existence, as long as such protection does not conflict with the First or Second Laws.

Of course, these laws are expressed in words, which is an imperfection. In the positronic brain, they are competing positronic potentials that are best expressed in terms of advanced mathematics (which is well beyond my ken, I assure you). However, even so, there are clear ambiguities. What constitutes "harm" to a human being? Must a robot obey orders given it by a child, by a madman, by a malevolent human being? Must a robot give up its own expensive and useful existence to prevent a trivial harm to an unimportant human being? What is trivial and what is unimportant?

These ambiguities are not shortcomings as far as a writer is concerned. If the Three Laws were perfect and unambiguous there would be no room for stories. It is in the nooks and crannies of the ambiguities that all one's plots can lodge, and which provide a foundation, if you'll excuse the pun, for *Robot City*.

I did not specifically state the Three Laws in words in "Liar!" which appeared in the May 1941 *Astounding*. I did do so, however, in my next robot story, "Runaround," which appeared in the March 1942 *Astounding*. In that issue on line seven of page one hundred, I have a character say, "Now, look, let's start with the three fundamental Rules of Robotics," and I then quote them. That, incidentally, as far as I or anyone else has been able to tell, represents the first appearance in print of the word "robotics"—which, apparently, I invented.

Since then, I have never had occasion, over a period of over forty years during which I wrote many stories and novels dealing with robots, to be forced to modify the Three Laws. However, as time passed, and as my robots advanced in complexity and versatility, I did feel that they would have to reach for something still higher. Thus, in *Robots and Empire*, a novel published by Doubleday in 1985, I talked about the possibility that a sufficiently advanced robot might feel it necessary to consider the prevention of harm to humanity generally as taking precedence over the prevention of harm to an individual. This I called the "Zeroth Law of Robotics," but I'm still working on that.

My invention of the Three Laws of Robotics is probably my most important contribution to science fiction. They are widely quoted outside the field, and no history of robotics could possibly be complete without mention of the Three Laws. In 1985, John Wiley and Sons published a huge tome, *Handbook of Industrial Robotics*, edited by Shimon Y. Nof, and, at the editor's request, I wrote an introduction concerning the Three Laws.

Now it is understood that science fiction writers generally have created a pool of ideas that form a common stock into which all writers can dip. For that reason, I have never objected to other writers who have used robots that obey the Three Laws. I have, rather, been flattered and, honestly, modern science fictional robots can scarcely appear without those Laws.

However, I have firmly resisted the actual quotation of the Three Laws by any other writer. Take the Laws for granted, is my attitude in this matter, but don't recite them. The concepts are everyone's but the words are mine.

But, then, I am growing old. I cannot expect to live for very much longer, but I hope that some of my brainchildren can. And to help those brainchildren attain something approaching long life, it is just as well if I relax my rules and allow others to make use of them and reinvigorate them. After all, much has happened in science since my first robot stories were published four decades ago, and this has to be taken into consideration, too.

Therefore, when Byron Preiss came to me with the notion of setting up a series of novels under the overall title of *Robot City*, in which "Asimovian" robots and ideas were to be freely used, I felt drawn to the notion. Byron said that I would serve as a consultant to make sure that my robots *stay* "Asimovian," that I would answer questions, make suggestions, veto infelicities, and provide the basic premise for the series as well as challenges for the authors. (And so it was done. Byron and I sat through a series of breakfasts in which he asked questions and I—and sometimes my wife, Janet, as well—answered, thus initiating some rather interesting discussions.)

Furthermore, my name was to be used in the title so as to insure the fact that readers would know that the project was developed in conjunction with me, and was carried through with my help and knowledge. It is, indeed, a pleasure to have talented young writers devote their intelligence and ingenuity to the further development of my ideas, doing so each in his or her own way.

The first novel of the series, *Robot City Book 1: Odyssey*, is by Michael P. Kube-McDowell, the author of *Emprise*, and I am very pleased to be connected with it. The prose is entirely Michael's; I did none of it. In saying this, I am not trying to disown the novel at all; rather I want to make sure that Michael gets all the credit from those who like the writing. It is my role, as I have indicated, only to supply robotic concepts, answer (as best I can) questions posed by Byron and Michael, and suggest solutions to problems raised by the Three Laws. In fact, Book Two of this series will introduce three interesting new laws concerning the way robots would deal with humans in a robotic society, a relationship which is the underpinning of *Robot City.*

In nearly half a century of writing I have built up a name that is well known and carries weight and I would like to use it to help pave the way for young writers by way of their novels and to preserve the names of older writers by the editing of anthologies. The science fiction field in general and a number of science fiction practitioners in particular have, after all, been very good to me over the years, and the best repayment I can make is to do for others what it and they have done for me.

Let me emphasize that this is the first time I have allowed others to enter my world of robots and to roam about freely there. I am pleased with what I've seen so far, including the captivating artwork of Paul Rivoche, and I look forward to seeing what is done with my ideas and the concepts I have proposed in the books that follow. The books may not be (indeed, are bound not to be) exactly as I would have written them, but all the better. We'll have other minds and other personalities at work, broadening, raising, and refocusing my ideas.

For you, the reader, the adventure is about to begin.

BOOK ONE

ODYSSEY

MICHAEL P. KUBE-McDOWELL

CHAPTER 1

AWAKENING

The youth strapped in the shock couch at the center of the small chamber appeared to be peacefully sleeping. The muscles of his narrow face were relaxed, and his eyes were closed. His head had rolled forward until his chin rested on the burnished metal neck ring of his orange safesuit. With his smooth cheeks and brush-cut sandy blond hair, he looked even younger than he was—young enough to raise the doorman's eyebrow at the least law-abiding spaceport bar.

He came to consciousness slowly, as though he had been cheated of sleep and was reluctant to give it up. But as the fog cleared, he had a sudden, terrifying sensation of leaning out over the edge of a cliff.

His eyes flashed open, and he found himself looking down. The couch into which the five-point harness held him was tipped forward. Without the harness, he would have awakened in a jumbled heap on the tiny patch of sloping floorplate, wedged against the one-ply hatch that faced him.

He raised his head, and his darting eyes quickly took in

the rest of his surroundings. There was little to see. He was alone in the tiny chamber. If he unstrapped himself, there would be room for him to stand up, perhaps to turn around, but nothing more ambitious. A safesuit helmet was cached in a recess on the curving right bulkhead. On the left bulkhead was a dispensary, with its water tube and delivery chute.

None of what he saw made sense, so he simply continued to catalog it. Above his head, hanging from the ceiling, was some sort of command board with a bank of eight square green lamps labeled "PI," "P2," "F," and the like. The board was in easy reach, except that there appeared to be no switches or controls for him to manipulate. In one corner of the panel the word MASSEY was etched in stylized black letters.

Apart from the slight rasp of his own breathing, the little room was nearly silent. From the machinery which filled the space behind his shoulders and under his feet came the whir of an impeller and a faint electric hum. But there was no sound from outside, from beyond the walls.

Thin as it was, the catalog was complete, and it was time to try to make something of it. He realized that, although he did not recognize his surroundings, he was not surprised by them. But then, since he could not remember where he had fallen asleep, he had carried no expectations about where he should be when he awoke.

The simple truth was he did not know where he was. Or why he was there. He did not know how long he had been there, or how he had gotten there.

But at the moment none of those things seemed to matter, for he realized—with rapidly growing dismay and disquiet—that he also did not know who he was.

He searched his mind for any hint of his identity—of a

place he had known, of a face that was important to him, of a memory that he treasured. There was nothing. It was as though he was trying to read a blank piece of paper. He could not remember a single event which had taken place before he had opened his eyes and found himself here. It was as though his life had begun at that moment.

Except he knew that it had not. He was not a crying newborn child, but a man—or near enough to one to claim the title until challenged. He had existed. He had had an identity and a place in the world. He had had friends—parents—a home. He had to have had all of that and more.

But it was gone.

It was a different feeling than merely forgetting. *At least when you forget something, you have a sense that you once knew it—*

"Are you all right?" a pleasant voice inquired, breaking the silence and making him suddenly tense all his muscles.

"Who are you?" he demanded. "Where are you? Where am I?"

"I am Darla, your Companion. Please try to remain calm. We're in no immediate danger." The voice, coming from the command panel before him, was more clearly female now. "You are inside a Massey Corporation Model G-85 Lifepod. Massey has been the leader in space safety systems for more than . . ."

While Darla continued on with her advertisement, he twisted his head about as he reexamined the compartment. I should have known that, he thought. Of course. A survival pod. Even the name *Massey* was familiar. "Why are there no controls?"

"All G-series pods have been designed to independently evaluate the most productive strategy and respond appropriately."

Of course, he thought. You don't know who's going to climb into a pod, or what kind of condition they'll be in. "You're not a person. What are you, then? A computer program?"

"I am a positronic personality," Darla said cheerfully. "The Companion concept is the Massey Corporation's unique contribution to humane safety systems."

Yes. Someone to talk to. Someone to help him pass hours of waiting without thinking about what it would mean if he weren't found. The full picture dawned on him. All survival pods were highly automated. This one was more. It was a robot—presumably programmed as a therapist and charged with keeping him sane and stable.

A robot—

A human had a childhood. A robot did not. A human learned. A robot was programmed. A robot deprived of the core identity which was supposed to be integrated before activation might "awake" and find he had knowledge without experience, and wonder who and what he was—

Suddenly he bit down on his lower lip.

How does a robot experience sensor overload? As pain?

When he tasted blood, he relaxed his jaw. He would take the outcome of his little experiment at face value. He was human. In some ways, that was the more disturbing answer.

"Why have you done harm to yourself?" Darla intruded.

He sighed. "Just to be sure I could. Do you know who *I* am?"

"Your badge identifies you as Derec."

He looked down past the neck ring and saw for the first time that there was a datastrip in the badge holder on the right breast of the safesuit. The red printing, superimposed on the fractured black-and-white coding pattern, indeed read DEREC.

He said the name aloud, experimentally: "Derec." It seemed neither familiar nor foreign to his tongue. His ear heard it as a first name, even though it was more likely a surname.

But if I'm Derec, why does the safesuit fit so poorly? The waist ring and chest envelope would have accommodated someone with a much stockier build. And when he tried to straighten his cramped legs, he found that the suit's legs were a centimeter or two short of allowing him to do so comfortably.

I certainly was shorter once—maybe I was heavier, too. It could be my old suit—one I wouldn't have used except in an emergency. Or it could be my ID, but someone else's suit.

"Can you scan the datastrip on the badge?" he asked hopefully. "There should be a photograph—a citizenship rec-ord—kinship list. Then I'd know for sure."

"I'm sorry. There's no data reader in the pod, and my optical sensors can't resolve a pattern that fine."

Frowning, he said, "Then I guess I'll be Derec, for now."

He paused and collected his thoughts. To know his name—if it was his name—did nothing to relieve his feelings of emptiness. It was as though he had lost his internal com-pass, and with it, the ability to act on his own behalf. The most he could do now was react.

"All of the pod's environmental systems are working well," Darla offered brightly. "Rescue vessels should be on their way here now."

Her words reminded him that there was a problem more important in the short run than puzzling out who he was. Survival had to come first. In time, perhaps the things he did know would tell him what he had forgotten.

He was in a survival pod. His mind took that one fact and began to build on it. When he shifted position in his harness, he noted how the slightest movement set the pod to rocking, despite the fact that its mass could hardly be less than five hundred kilograms. He extended an arm and let the muscles go limp. It took a full second to fall to his side.

A hundredth of a gee at best. I'm in a survival pod on the surface of a low-gravity world. I was in a starcraft, on my way somewhere, when something happened. Perhaps that's why I can't remember, or perhaps the shock of landing—

There was no window or port anywhere in the pod, not even a hatch peephole. But if he couldn't see, perhaps Darla could.

"Where are we, Darla?" he asked. "What kind of place did you land us on?"

"Would you like me to show you our surroundings? I have a limpet pack available."

Derec knew the term, though he wondered where he had learned it. A limpet pack was a disc-shaped sensor array capable of sliding across the outer surface of a smooth-hulled space craft—a cheaper but more trouble-prone substitute for a full array of sensor mounts. "Let's see."

The interior lights dimmed, and the central third of the hatch became the background for a flatscreen projection directed down from the command board overhead. Derec looked out on an ice and rock landscape that screamed its wrongness to him. The horizon was too close, too severely curved. It had to be a distortion created by the camera, or a false horizon created by a foreground crater.

"Scan right," he said.

But everywhere it was the same: a jumble of orange-tinged ice studded with gray rock, merging at the horizon into the velvet curtain of space. He could see no distinct stars in the sky, but that was likely to be due to the limited resolving power of the limpet, and not because of any atmosphere. The planetoid's gravity was too slight to hold even the densest gases, and the jagged scarps showed no signs of atmospheric weathering.

In truth, it looked like a leftover place, the waste of star- and planet-making, a forgotten world which had not changed since the day it was made. It was a cold world, and a sterile one, and, in all probability, a deserted one.

Formerly deserted, he corrected himself. "Moon or asteroid?" he asked Darla.

"No matter where we are, we are safe," Darla said ingenuously. "We must trust in the authorities to locate and retrieve us."

Derec could foresee quickly growing weary of that sort of evasion. "How can I trust in that when I don't know where we are and what the chances are that we'll be found? I know that this pod doesn't have a full-recycle environmental system. No pod ever does. Do you deny it?" He waited a moment for an answer, then plunged on. "How much of a margin did the Massey Corporation decide was enough? Ten days? Two weeks?"

"Derec, maintaining the proper attitude is crucial to—"

"Save the therapist bit, will you?" Darren sighed. "Look, I know you're trying to protect me. Some people cope better that way—what they don't know and all that. But I'm different. I need information, not reassurance. I need to know what you know. Understand? Or should I start digging into your guts and looking for it myself?"

Derec was puzzled when Darla did not answer. It dawned on him slowly that he must have presented her with a dilemma which her positronic brain was having difficulty resolving—but there should have been no dilemma. Darla was obliged by the Second Law of Robotics to answer his questions.

The Second Law said, "A robot must obey the orders given it by human beings except where such orders would conflict with the First Law."

A question was an order—and silence was disobedience. Which could only be if Darla was following her higher obligation under the First Law.

The First Law said, "A robot may not injure a human being, or, through inaction, allow a human being to come to harm."

Darla had to know how small the chance of rescue was, even within a star system, even along standard trajectories. And Darla knew as well as any robot could what sort of harm that fact could do to the emotional balance of a human being. The typical survivor, already terrorized by whatever events brought him into the lifepod, would respond with despair, a loss of the will to live.

It made sense to him now. Of course Darla would try to protect him from the consequences of his own curiosity—unless he could make her see that he was different.

"Darla, I'm not the kind of person you were told to expect," he said gently. "I need something to do, something to think about. I can't just sit here and wait. I can deal with bad news, if that's what you're hiding. What I can't take is feeling helpless."

It seemed as though she were prepared for his kind too, after all, but had only needed convincing that he was one. "I understand, Derec. Of course I'll be happy to tell you what I know."

"Good. What ship are we from?" he asked. "There's no shipper's crest or ship logo anywhere in the cabin."

"This is a Massey Corporation G-85 Lifepod—"

"You told me that already. What ship are we from?"

Darla was silent for a moment. "Massey Lifepods are the primary safety system on six of the eight largest general commercial space carriers—"

"You don't know?"

"My customization option has not been initialized. Would you care for a game of chess?"

"No." Derec mused for a moment. "So all you know how to do is shill for the manufacturer. Which means that we probably came from a privately owned ship—all the commercial carriers customize their gear."

"I have no information in that area."

Derec clucked. "In fact, I think you do. Somewhere among your systems there has to be a data recorder, activated the moment the pod was ejected. It should tell you not only what ship we came from and where it was headed, but what's happened since. It's time to find out how smart you really are, Darla," he said. "We need to find that recorder and get into it."

"I have no information about such a recorder."

"Trust me, it's there. If it wasn't, there'd be no way to do postmortems after a ship disaster. Are you in control of the pod's power bus?"

"Yes."

"Look for an uninterruptible line. That'll be it."

"Just a moment. Yes, there are two."

"What are they called?"

"My system map labels them 1402 and 1632. I have no further information."

Derec reached for the water tube again. "That's all right. One will be the recorder, and the other is probably the locator beacon. We're making progress. Now find the data paths that correspond with those power taps. They should tell us which one is which."

"I'm sorry. I can't."

"They have to be there. The recorder will be taking data from your navigation module, from the environmental system, probably even an abstract of this conversation. There ought to be a whole forest of data paths."

"I'm sorry, Derec. I am unable to do what you ask."

"Why?"

"When I run a diagnostic trace in that portion of the system, I am unable to find any unlabeled paths."

"Can you show me your service schematic? Maybe I can find something."

The icescape vanished and was replaced by a finely detailed projection of the lifepod's logic circuits. Scanning it, Derec quickly found the answer. A smart data gate—a Maxwell junction—was guarding the data line to the recorder. The two systems were effectively isolated. Similar junctions stood between Darla and the inertial navigator, the locator beacon, and the environmental system.

This is all very odd, Derec thought. It wasn't surprising that there was a lower-level autonomous system regulating routine functions. What was strange was how Darla was locked out of getting any information from it.

Coddling frightened survivors required tact and discretion. But robots were strongly disposed toward an almost painful honesty. Perhaps it had proven too difficult to program a Companion to put on a happy face while keeping grim secrets. Lying did unpredictable things to the potentials inside a positronic brain.

And there were Third Law considerations as well. The Third Law went, "A robot must protect its own existence, as long as such protection does not conflict with the First or Second Laws."

How would a robot balance its responsibility to preserve itself with the increasing probability of its demise? It was as though the designers had concluded that there were things Darla was better off not knowing, and thrown up barriers to prevent her from finding out. They had kept her ignorant of herself, and even of her ignorance.

There was a disturbing parallel in that to Derec's own situation. *Is that what happened to me?* he wondered. He had hoped almost from the first that his loss of memory was the consequence of whatever disaster had put him in the lifepod, perhaps along with the shock of a hard landing on this world.

Now he had to ask whether such selective amnesia could be an accident. He had read the schematic easily, but he could not remember where or why he had acquired that skill. Obviously he had some technical training, a fact which—if he survived—might prove a useful clue to his identity. But why would he remember the lessons, but not the teacher? Could his brain have been that badly scrambled?

Yet reading the schematic was a complex task which clearly required that his mind and memory be unimpaired. As well as he could judge, his reasoning was measured and clear. If he were in shock or suffering from a concussion, wouldn't all his faculties be affected?

Perhaps this wasn't something that had happened to him. Perhaps, as with Darla, it was something that had been done to him.

Derec grimaced. It was unsettling enough looking at the blank wall of his past, but more unsettling to think that hiding behind that wall might be the reason why it had been built.

By this time Darla had grown impatient. "Have you found anything?" Darla asked with a note of anxiety.

Blinking, Derec looked up at the status board. "The recorder's tied in through a Maxwell junction. The junction won't pass through to the recorder anything it doesn't recognize, which is why you can't find it with a trace. And why we're not going to be able to read it through you. But there has to be a data port somewhere, probably on the outer hull—"

At that moment, the whole pod lurched and seemed to become buoyant. Derec had the sensation that it was no longer in contact with the frozen surface of the asteroid. "What's going on?" he demanded.

"Please stay calm," Darla said.

"What is it? Have we been found?"

"Yes. I believe we have. But I am unable to say by whom."

Derec gaped openmouthed for a moment. "Put the exterior deo up again! Quickly!"

"I am becoming concerned about your level of agitation, Derec. Please close your eyes and take several deep breaths."

"I'll do no such thing," he said angrily. "I want to see what's going on."

There was a moment's hesitation, and then Darla acquiesced. "Very well."

The sight that greeted Derec's eyes made his breath catch in his throat. The limpet's cameras were no longer trained on the horizon, but down at the ground. A half-dozen machines, each different from the next, were arrayed around the pod. The largest was taller than a man, the smallest barely the size of a safesuit helmet. The tiny ones hovered on tiny jets of white gas, while the larger ones were on wheels or articulated tracks.

He could also see a portion of some sort of cradle or deck which seemed to be centered below the pod. And all of them—the machines, the cradle, and the pod—were moving, proceeding along together toward some unknowable destination like some sort of ice-desert caravan.

"What's going on?" he demanded of Darla. "Can you identify them? Did they make any contact with us?"

"The device below us appears to be a cargo sled. I have no information on the other mechanisms."

Derec reached for his helmet and unsnapped the catch holding it in place. "I'm going out. I'm not going to let us be hijacked like this with no explanation."

"Leaving the pod would be too dangerous," Darla said. "In addition, you will lose a minimum of four hours' oxygen opening the hatch."

"It's worth it to find out what's going on."

"I can't allow that, Derec."

"It's not your decision," he said, reaching for the harness release with his free hand.

"I am sorry, Derec. It is," Darla said.

Too late, Derec realized that a Massey Companion was equipped to calm a distraught survivor not only verbally, but chemically. The dual jets of mist from either side of the headrest caught him full in the face, and he inhaled the sickly sweet droplets in the gasp of surprise.

Derec had barely enough time to be astonished at how quickly the drug acted. Both his arms went limp, the right falling well short of the harness release, the left losing its grasp on the helmet. His vision rapidly grayed. As though from a distance, he heard dimly the sound of the helmet hitting the floor. But between the first bounce and the second, he drifted away into the silent darkness of unconsciousness, and saw and heard nothing more.

CHAPTER 2

UNDER THE ICE

For the second time in one day, Derec awoke in strange surroundings.

This time, he was lying flat on his back staring up at the ceiling. There was a sour taste in his mouth and an empty, growly sensation in his stomach. He lay there for a moment, remembering, then sat up suddenly, his muscles tensed defensively as he looked about him.

As before, Derec was alone. But this time he found himself in more domestic surroundings—a four-man efficiency cabin, three meters wide by five meters long. The bed he had been lying in was a fold-down bunk, one of four mounted on the side walls. To his right as he sat on the edge of the bunk was a bank of storage lockers of assorted sizes. To his left was a closed door.

That damned Darla, he thought fiercely.

Though what he saw around him struck a vaguely familiar chord, Derec dismissed it as meaningless—there was a tedious sameness to all modular living designs. A more important question was whether the cabin was part of a work camp on the surface of the asteroid, tucked away somewhere inside a speeding spacecraft, or somewhere else he couldn't imagine. The cabin itself offered no clue. Nor could it tell him whether he had been rescued or captured.

Glancing down at himself, he saw that he was no longer wearing the safesuit. His torso and legs were covered by a formfitting white jumpsweat, the sort of garment a space worker would wear inside his work jitney or augment. It was clean and relatively new, but there was some wear on the abrasion pads at heel and knee and waist. It might have been what he was wearing under the safesuit, or—

"The suit," he said with sudden dismay.

He jumped to his feet and looked around wildly. There was only one locker large enough to hold a safesuit. It was unlocked, but it was also empty. He went through the other lockers mechanically. All were empty.

No, they were more than empty, he decided. They looked as though they'd never been used.

Derec felt a twinge of panic. If he didn't find the suit, he would never learn whatever information the datastrip on its name badge had to offer. And he had to find Darla as well, or lose the irreplaceable data stored in her event recorder.

Half afraid that he would find it locked, Derec crossed to the door and touched the keyplate. The door slid aside with a hiss. Outside was a short corridor flanked by four doors. The corridor was deserted, the other doors all closed.

To Derec's left, the corridor terminated in a blank wall. The other end was sealed by an airlock, suggesting that the four rooms formed a self-contained environmental cell. Through the small window in the inner pressure door he caught a glimpse of another corridor lying beyond.

"Hello?" Derec called. There was no answer.

The door facing him was labeled WARDROOM. Inside, he found a table large enough to seat eight for a meeting or a meal, a compact autogalley, and a sophisticated computer terminal and communications center.

Derec ran his fingertips across the surface of the table, and they came away clean, without even a coating of dust. The status lights on the galley told him that the unit was in Extended Standby, which meant that its food stores had been irradiated and deep-frozen. No one had eaten here for some time.

Was it all for him? Was that why it was unused? Or was he a surprise visitor in an empty house?

He switched the galley to Demand status, and a timer began counting down the two hours it would take to bring it on line. But when he tried to activate the com center, it demanded a password.

"Derec," he offered.

INVALID PASSWORD, the screen advised him.

He had only the most infinitesimal chance of guessing a truly random password. His only chance was if a lazy systems engineer had left one of the classic wild-card passwords in the security database. "Test," he suggested.

INVALID PASSWORD.

"Password," Derec said.

INVALID PASSWORD. ACCESS DENIED.

From that point on, the center ignored him. The silent-entry keypad was disabled, and nothing he said evoked any response. Apparently the center had not only rejected his passwords, but blacklisted him as well. The systems engineer had not been lazy.

Returning to the corridor, Derec briefly checked the other two rooms. One was another cabin, mirror-image to the one in which he had woken up. The other, labeled ME-CHANICAL, contained several racks of lockers and what appeared to be maintenance modules for environmental subsystems. Both rooms were as tidy and deserted as everything else Derec had seen since waking.

That left only the airlock and the mysteries beyond it to explore. The inner door bore the sonograph-in-a-circle emblem which meant VoiceCommand. "Open," he said, and the inner door of the hatch cracked open with the ripping sound of adhesion seals separating.

Derec stepped into the tiny enclosure and the door closed behind him. Peering through the window of the outer door, Derec could see no reason why the airlock was even there. The corridor beyond looked little different than the one he was leaving. "Cycle," he said.

The inner door closed behind him, the momentary surge of pressure on his eardrums telling him it had sealed. "Warning. There is a reduced-pressure nitrogen atmosphere beyond this point," the hatch advised him. "Please select a breather."

"Nitrogen?"

Only then did Derec notice the small delivery door in the side wall. Inside he found several gogglelike masks made of gray plastic. Selecting one, he saw that the mask was meant to fit over the middle third of his face, like a pair of wraparound sunglasses that had slipped down his nose. The breather's "straps" were hollow elastic tubes that met behind his neck. A flexible gas delivery tube led from there to the cartridge pack, which was small enough to strap to the upper arm.

When he put the breather on, however, he could not make the bottom edge of the mask seal against his upper lip to keep out the outside air. With the gap, the breaths he drew would be a mixture of free nitrogen and oxygen from the breather.

Belatedly, Derec realized that that was intentional. It was an arrangement that not only reduced the size of the cartridge pack, but also left his sense of smell unimpeded. A clever bit of engineering, with a minimalist flavor.

"Ready," Derec said.

"Warning: reduced gravity beyond this point," the hatch advised him.

"I hear you," he said as the outer door began to open. Nitrogen? Low-G? he wondered as he stepped out. Where am I? What's going on?

There were no immediate answers. It was cold—cold enough to bring a flush of color to his cheeks. The chill seemed to radiate equally from the ceiling and floor, though they were both made of an insulating synthetic mesh.

Standing there just outside the pressure hatch, Derec could hear a cacophony of machine noises—hissing, rumbling, grinding, squealing. But the drop in pressure, which distended his eardrums, made it seem as though he were trying to hear through a pillow. Aside from the fact that there was activity somewhere, he got nothing useful out of what he heard. He could not tell what kinds of machines he was hearing, or what they were doing.

Determined to follow the sounds to their source, he started down the corridor—or tried to. He ended up flat on his face on the cold decking, uninjured but chastened. Collecting himself, he tried again, this time pulling himself along the corridor by the center handrail.

Thirty meters ahead, the corridor opened into an enormous low-ceilinged chamber. Derec gaped as he took in its dimensions. It suggested armories, playing arenas, open-plan factories. He forced a yawn and swallowed hard, and the pressure in his left ear equalized. Yes, those were definitely machine noises. But what kind of machines, doing what kind of work?

Between the cold and low gravity, Derec concluded that he was still on the asteroid where his lifepod had crashed. From the structure of the chamber, he concluded that he was most probably underground.

More important, he was not alone. There were robots moving among the stacks and aisles—dozens of them, of a half-dozen varieties. But in another sense, he was alone, for there were no other people. There were not even any handrails in the aisles to make the chamber human-accessible. The chamber belonged to the robots by default. What task they were so busily attending to, he could not divine.

The nearest of the robots, a squat boxlike unit with a single telescoping arm, was only a few dozen meters from Derec. As Derec watched, it plucked a fist-sized component from a rack, stowed it in a cargo basket, and retracted its manipulator arm. Its mission apparently accomplished, the robot started away, coasting on a cushion of air from under its venturi skirt.

"Stop!" Derec called out.

But the robot continued on, seemingly deaf to Derec's command. On impulse, Derec released the handrail and went in pursuit. But in the asteroid's minimal gravity field, it was like trying to run with both legs asleep. He was perpetually off-balance, his slippered feet failing to give him the traction he expected. When he came to his first ninety-degree turn, he went sprawling, scattering a rack of small chromium cylinders.

Not even the racket from his spill slowed the robot's retreat. It continued on toward what appeared to be a lift shaft—a circular black pit in the floor and a matching one in the ceiling, linked by four chrome guide rods.

"How am I supposed to catch you?" he complained, climbing to his feet. "*I* can't fly."

There had to be a better way, and looking more closely at two robots heading down the aisle toward him, Derec saw what it was. Unlike the picker, the man-sized robots were built on standard three-point ball-drive chassis—like three marbles under a bottle cap. Ball-drive chassis were standard in clean environments because they offered complete freedom of movement. The drawback: here, with the reduced friction due to the low gravity, the drive balls should do more spinning than pushing.

But each large robot had a second ball-drive chassis mounted at the top of a telescoping rod. Pushing against the ceiling, the second chassis provided the necessary pressure for the dual drives to grab. Like the bumper cars at a revival carnival, each robot needed to be in constant contact with both surfaces to operate.

Derec realized that he could use that trick, too. The ceiling was low enough that he could push against it with his fingertips while standing flat-footed. "Hand-walking," as he dubbed the technique, he could have caught the picker.

Now he waited to see what the two approaching robots would do about him. They stopped short of where he stood and began to restore order where he had fallen down, deftly using their three-fingered grapples to replace the cylinders on the shelving. He waited, wondering if they would notice him. They did not.

"I'm in danger," he called to them. "I need your help."

The two robots continued their housekeeping, apparently oblivious to his presence. He drew closer and examined the nearer of the two as it worked. It had normal audio sensors, but no evidence of a vocalizer. In short, it was mute. It could not answer.

But there had to be some higher-level robots in the complex, ones capable of recognizing him for what he was and responding to his needs. The pickers and custodians he'd crossed paths with could hardly be working without supervision.

Likewise, the E-cell he awoke in couldn't be the only structure for humans within the complex. Somewhere there was a management team, programmers, supervisors. There was no such thing as a completely autonomous robot community.

Thinking that there had to be a way to call the control room from the E-cell, Derec started back. As he did, he saw a sight that brought him up short. A tall humanoid robot was standing at the end of the corridor to the E-cell, studying him.

They stared at each other for a long moment. The robot's skin was a gleaming pale blue, a vivid declaration of its machine nature. Its optical sensors were silver slits in its helmet-like head, lacking the customary red tracking marker which telegraphed when the robot was looking in your direction. Even so, there was no doubt in Derec's mind that he was the object of the robot's rapt and unnaturally focused attention.

The robot was the first to move, turning away and disappearing into the corridor, hand-walking with easy coordination. Derec followed as quickly as he was able, but by the time he reached the corridor, the robot was already inside the airlock. It took no more than fifteen seconds for Derec to reach the outer hatch and pass through into the E-cell. Even so, when he stepped out into the inner corridor, the robot was already emerging from the wardroom, its business apparently finished.

"I'm in danger," Derec said. "I need your help."

"False assessment: you are not now in danger," the humanoid robot said. "Should you be in danger, help will be provided."

The robot took one step toward the pressure hatch, and Derec moved to place himself in its path.

"I'm not letting you leave here until you tell me where I am and what I'm doing here," Derec said sharply.

The robot's answer was nonverbal but perfectly clear. Stepping closer, it grasped his shoulders firmly but gently and moved him out of the way. Then it walked with smooth strides past him to the hatch.

"Open," it said.

Feeling helpless, Derec let the robot go, then turned to see if he could discover what it had been doing in the wardroom. Only two things had changed since Derec had left. The galley was still counting down to full Demand status, but the selector was now showing a short list of selections that were already available. Derec himself had set that change in motion.

It was the other change that the robot was responsible for. The screen of the com center was no longer blank. In bright red letters, it reported: MESSAGE TRANSMITTED.

It was then that Derec knew for certain that he was alone on the asteroid. The fact that there was an environmental cell deep under the surface implied that there had once been at least a temporary human presence here. But this little world was in the hands of the robots now, and he was a trespasser. What message they had sent about him, and to whom they had sent that message, there was no telling.

CHAPTER 3

THE ROBOTS' MISSION

Derec took the time for a meal, which he needed, and a shower, which he did not. But the shower provided him with something to do while thinking, and he had a lot to think about. His presence, his identity, the cause and reason for his memory impairment were as troublesome as ever. And after his excursion, he had a new mystery. Why were the robots behaving so strangely?

Derec asked himself under what circumstances a robot might refuse to answer his question, which amounted to refusing to obey his orders. Within his understanding of the Laws of Robotics, Derec could think of only two, both illustrated by his experience with Darla: because it did not know the answers, or because it had been instructed previously not to reveal them.

Precedence did count for something with robots. A robot ordered by its owner to service a flyer would not leave that job to search for a neighbor child's missing cat—unless it was the owner, not the child, who made the request. A carefully worded command would hold up against anything but a counterorder rooted in a First Law situation. If the robots had been told not to talk about what they were doing, nothing Derec could do would make them disobey.

Before he dressed, he searched his body for clues to who he was. He found no scars large enough that he would expect to remember when and how he acquired them. He bore no tattoos or skin ornaments, wore no rings or jewelry.

The only distinctive mark he seemed to bear was inside, in the things that he knew. Somewhere, sometime, he had received advanced training in microelectronics. He had more than a passing understanding of robotics and computers. Was that commonplace, a standard curriculum for someone his age? He thought not. And if not, it might be the trail that he could follow to rediscover himself.

The com center was continuing its intransigence, still ignoring his input, still mockingly displaying the words MESSAGE TRANSMITTED. But there was one door that hadn't yet been slammed in his face. Donning a breather and a spare cartridge pack, Derec left the E-cell to explore the rest of the complex.

Derec began by creating a mental map of the great chamber, assigning arbitrary compass points with the E-cell as his reference for south. The chamber seemed to be roughly rectangular, longer north to south than east to west by a factor of two or more. He started hand-walking northward down the same corridor the custodian robots had used, counting his paces as he went.

Five hundred paces later, his arms were tired and the north wall seemed no closer. Stopping to rest, he surveyed the robot population of the chamber. He tallied seventeen of the humanoid robots, none of which were nearby. Among the nonhumanoid robots, he identified five different types:

the pickers, the custodians, a large cargo handler Derec dubbed a porter, some multi-armed micro-assemblers, and an armored robot with oversized grapples whose function he could not guess.

Most of the robots he encountered were moving purposefully through the aisles, carrying out their assignments. But toward the north end of the chamber, Derec spotted a small army of robots standing inert and de-energized, waiting to be called into action. All the varieties were represented among the reserves except for the humanoid robots.

The robot stockpile was Derec's clue to understanding where he was. The chamber seemed to be primarily a collection of spare parts. True, he had spotted a cluster of injection and extrusion machines in one area, a battery of laser welders in another, a chip-burning shop in a third, all apparently in full-time use. But all those operations were apparently maintenance related.

Whatever they're doing here, they're on a very heavy duty cycle—possibly even continuous operations, he told himself. Zero down-time could only be bought with a large-scale repair and maintenance operation. And that high price was only worth paying when time mattered more than money.

There was a steady stream of robot traffic on the lifts located at intervals through the chamber, and the obvious next step was to find out where they were going. Giving up his plan to walk the length of the chamber, Derec headed for the nearest lift.

Like the breather, the lifts were clearly the product of a unique approach to engineering. To Derec, they looked like something either unfinished or nonfunctional. They were also more proof that the complex had been designed with robots alone in mind. No human would have ridden one voluntarily.

The shaft was a vertical boring three meters in diameter, its sides lined with the same synthemesh as the chamber ceiling. Peering out over the edge and down, Derec glimpsed a deep shaft lit at regular intervals by stationary blue glows, which he assumed marked other levels. The shaft seemed to extend much farther down than up. Above the great chamber—which he had begun to think of as the warehouse—he counted only seven levels, while below it he could see at least twenty levels before the traffic in the shaft obscured what might lie beyond.

A descending lift platform on the nearest guide rod obliged Derec to duck back out of the way. The platform, a square grid a meter on a side, reached the floor level and stopped as though waiting for him.

While it waited there, traffic kept moving on the other three guide rods. Watching the robots board and disembark, Derec saw that while the lift was in operation, the robots were clamped to the platforms magnetically. He wondered how he would be able to keep his balance and footing without that assistance. There were no railings to grab on to, and the guide rod itself appeared to be electrically live.

Personal considerations aside, he could not help but admire the engineering aesthetics of the lift. It was a clean and focused solution to the problem of moving the maximum amount of traffic in the minimum time and space, a solution fully integrated with the requirements of the colony.

But clever as the system was, Derec was not eager for a ride in the dark on an open platform above a seemingly bottomless pit. Still, it was that or go back to the E-cell. He swallowed hard once and stepped carefully out onto the waiting platform.

"Up," he said.

"Level, please?"

"Uh—Level Two."

Singing a high-pitched song, the car began to climb swiftly. He stood with his arms crossed over his chest and his legs spread wide. Keeping his vision focused upward toward the nearest of the blue glows, he tried not to look at the shaft walls sliding swiftly by.

The platform flashed through several other levels before gradually slowing to let him off. The glimpses he caught of them prepared him for what awaited him on Two. When he stepped off the lift, he was standing at the crossroads of two low-ceilinged tunnels, each six meters wide. The walls, floor and ceiling were covered with the ubiquitous off-white syn-themesh. The air was colder than ever, cold enough to make him hunch his shoulders and bury his hands under his arms.

Though the immediate vicinity of the lift was brightly lit by the blue floodlights, the tunnels themselves were il-luminated only by dim yellow lamps set at intervals in the ceiling. Each was barely bright enough to mark its own po-sition and make a tiny pool of yellow light on the floor of the tunnel.

The distant ends of the intersecting tunnels were invis-ible, the lines of ceiling lamps receding into infinity in both directions. The tunnels could be kilometers long, even tens of kilometers for all he could tell.

Have they honeycombed this entire asteroid? Derec won-dered. *Thousands of levels—shafts a hundred kilometers deep—could this be a mining operation?*

But he could not understand why anyone would go to the trouble to mine an asteroid from the inside. The cutters on a prospecting ship could slice all but the densest nickel-iron asteroids into bite-sized chunks for the leviathan proc-essing centers. No ore Derec knew of was worth the expense of tunnel-and-shaft mining on this scale. Even with the energy-and-raw-materials economics which applied with robot labor, it would have to be something a hundred times more precious than the rarest element—unless the value of secrecy was part of the equation.

Who am I dealing with? Derec wondered. Newly so-bered, he stepped back onto the lift.

"Level Three," he said.

The next two levels were just as silent and finished-looking as Two. Derec could not decide whether they were finished-waiting-to-be-used, like the spare parts in the great chamber, or finished-and-abandoned.

But Level Five was another story. The rumble of heavy machinery assaulted his ears even before the platform reached the lighted zone. When he stepped off the lift, he could feel rolling, low-frequency vibrations in the floor and ceiling of the tunnel.

I'm getting closer, he thought. Now—which way? The sound surrounded him, offering no clue as to which of the tunnels had the most promise.

While he stood there equivocating, a double platform arrived and disgorged a porter robot. On impulse, Derec climbed onto its half-full cargo pad. He was counting on its ignoring him, as the picker had. He was not disappointed. Neither cradling him in its arms nor trying to dislodge him, the porter started down the south tunnel.

For the first two minutes of the ride, wind noise and the whine of the robot's own mechanisms masked the distant work noise. But before long Derec could sort the separate elements: irregular thumping sounds like muffled explo-sions, a highpitched grinding that made his skin crawl, and a steady background rumble that suggested great masses of rock and ice being moved about.

Presently the end of the tunnel came in sight as a black patch in the distance. Shortly after, Derec began to detect a whiff of ammonia in the air. The moment he did, another piece of the puzzle fell into place.

He had wondered from the start why the complex outside the E-cell was filled with nitrogen. The robots did not require it. Strictly speaking, robots did not require an atmosphere at all. And keeping the complex sealed and pressurized had to be more complicated than simply opening it to space.

But maintaining a standard two-gas atmosphere in the proper proportions through the vast complex was even more complicated. Derec had concluded that the nitrogen atmosphere and "open" breathers were a compromise between the inconvenience of full pressure suits and the complexity of a dual-gas E-system. The nitrogen allowed humans to speak and hear normally and to move about without safesuits, without the fire and explosion risk posed by free oxygen.

But Derec had overlooked something important. The ices which made up a large fraction of the asteroid's bulk were not water, but compounds like methane and ammonia. The mining processes would inevitably release them as gases into the work area, where they might react with the high energies and circuits of the mining machinery or with each other.

I should have seen it sooner, he thought. Without an atmosphere comprised of some relatively inert gas, there would be no way to dilute the unwelcome compounds or efficiently flush them out. So of course, an atmosphere. Of course, nitrogen. The atmosphere accommodated a human presence, but was not primarily for human convenience.

The porter slowed as they neared the end of the tunnel, and Derec took that opportunity to jump off. Ahead of him were several robots, gathered near the end of the tunnel, and the gateway to what he presumed was the work chamber.

Through the gateway he caught glimpses of a ragged rock wall, equipment booms, and an occasional flash of bright light.

The gateway itself was an enormous boxlike machine which filled the tunnel flush to the walls, floor, and ceiling. The only path through to the work chamber was a narrow walkway between columns of bright green chemical storage tanks. That was where he had to go.

As Derec drew closer, he saw that the gateway was actually crawling slowly forward. Like some mechanical larva, the gateway was burrowing through the asteroidal mass and leaving a finished tunnel in its wake. Everything—the raw material of the walls, the covering of reinforcing synthe-mesh, even the overhead lamps—was being handled in one continuous operation. The gateway was a four-surface paving machine.

But Derec's real interest was in the excavation beyond. He stepped up onto the gateway and threaded his way between the shoulder-high cylinders, aware as he did that one of the humanoid robots was following him. There was a strong draft through the walkway, from the tunnel to the chamber beyond. Even so, the odor of ammonia was almost strong enough to make him gag.

At the forward end, the narrow walkway widened into a control cabin, where two humanoid robots sat behind a bank of transparent panels looking out into the excavation chamber that surrounded the gateway on three sides. Derec stopped a few steps short of the ramp into the excavation and tried to sort out the functions of the equipment that filled it.

The uncut face of the asteroidal material was some thirty meters away. A two-headed boom cutter was working it, one boom bearing rotary grinders, the other microwave lasers. They moved back and forth like weaving cobras, and the ice and rock wall crumbled before them.

The lasers seemed to be doing most of the damage. Suddenly released from its icy glue, loose rock sloughed off the face with a cracking sound. More resistant deposits were gouged off by the rotating teeth of the grinder. The gases boiling off the face were being sucked into the wide-mouthed exhaust vents that loomed over the work face.

As he studied the work rig, a metallic hand touched his shoulder.

"You may not enter the processing zone during operations," the robot said.

The robot's edict stirred a flash of annoyance. "I will if I want to," Derec snapped back over his shoulder.

The robot tightened its grip pointedly. "You may not enter the processing zone during operations," the robot repeated. "Untrained personnel are to be considered at risk."

Shrugging off its touch, Derec turned his back on the robot and looked once more into the excavation. Like the gateway, the mining unit was slowly advancing toward an ever-receding rock face. The motion brought the jumble of loose rock within reach of scuttling scooper arms, which funneled it up a ramp to an enormous hopper. A pair of high-sided conveyors carried material away from the hopper, one to the left and one to the right. While on the conveyor it passed through an N-ray station, an X-ray station, and a magnetometer.

From that point on, things got confusing. It was as though after having gone to all that trouble to mine the asteroid, the robots had forgotten to sort out the part of it they wanted to keep.

Some of the tailings were diverted to a spur conveyor,

run through a crusher, and then used as the raw material for the fifteen-centimeter thick walls of the tunnel. To Derec's astonishment, the rest was carried to the back wall of the work chamber, reunited with the captured methane and ammonia, and built up into a wall of ice and rock again. The excavation never got any larger.

But what about the tunnel? Derec wondered. They have to be taking something out—

Closer study showed him otherwise. The empty volume of the ever-lengthening access tunnel meant only that the asteroidal material surrounding it was being replaced in a more compressed state than it was in when mined. Nothing was being extracted. Nothing was being carried away for later refining or shipment.

It just didn't make sense.

The depletion alarm on Derec's first cartridge pack began to sound, and he transferred the delivery tube to the backup. He would have to leave soon or risk dying of nitrogen poisoning before he could return to the E-cell. But it was hard to tear himself away from the incomprehensible sight of a dozen robots and a few million dollars worth of heavy equipment engaged in a task as senseless as trying to dig a hole in water. And how many other excavations just like this were underway elsewhere in the complex? Ten? Fifty? Five hundred?

Trying to understand, Derec focused his attention on the robots. Three of the armored type patrolled the hopper, breaking up snags with their grapples. A fourth stood on a small platform under the booms of the cutter, shattering oversized rocks as they fell from the face with blasts from its chestmounted laser. Two humanoids stood at the N-ray stations, intently studying the scanning screen.

Derec's guardian angel was still standing within arm's reach behind him, and he turned and sought the robot's eyes. "What are you mining here?" he demanded. "What's the point of all this?"

But the robot said nothing, gazing back with its expressionless eyes.

"Get out of the way," Derec said disgustedly, and the robot stepped aside into the control booth to let him pass.

His annoyance spilling over into anger, Derec stalked down the narrow walkway and jumped down to the tunnel. It was then he realized his mistake: there were no porter robots there to carry him back to the lift.

"I need a ride," Derec said sharply to the nearest humanoid robot. "Can you tell me when the next porter robot will be making a delivery?"

"What is your need?"

"I need a ride."

"That is not an approved allocation of resources."

Derec did not even bother to argue. Turning away, he stalked away northward, his mind unsettled, churning with unconnected thoughts. He felt as though the answer to all his questions was already in his grasp, except he couldn't recognize it. How did it all add up? What was wrong with the picture?

As he hand-walked along the tunnel, his thoughts kept carrying him back to the robots. There was something about the way they behaved, the way they worked together. Throughout the complex, all the routine, repetitive jobs were being done by the nonhumanoid robots. The blue-skinned humanoid robots were supervisors, trouble-shooters, technicians, repair specialists. But they could have just as easily done the repetitive jobs as well, even tending the front line

in the excavation. Instead, there were a half-dozen specialized varieties, porters and pickers and miners that didn't act
like robots at all—

Derec stopped short and turned to stare back down the
tunnel toward the excavation. Of course. Of course. The
picker and the custodians, the tenders and the porters *weren't*
specialized robots working with the blue robots. They were
tools being *used* by the blue robots. Their intelligence was
limited—perhaps not even positronic in nature. The real intelligence resided in the humanoid robots, which might well
be more sophisticated than any Derec had previously known
of.

But why were they all here?

Derec thought of all the levels, all the tunnels that had
already been bored out, all the mass of the asteroid still
waiting undisturbed. Could he have stumbled on an industrial test site? It might explain much—the secrecy, the distinctive stamp of the unknown designer, the unending but
pointless excavation.

Focus on the robots, Derec told himself. The tasks they're
handling themselves are the ones they consider critical—

In a flash of memory, he saw the two humanoid robots
tending the scanning instruments on the conveyor line, and
suddenly Derec knew. The realization staggered him, and
yet there was no pushing the notion away once it had
formed in his mind.

The robots weren't mining the asteroid at all. They were
sifting it. They were searching for something, something lost
or buried or hidden, something so unique and valuable that
it was worth any price, any effort.

What that something was, Derec could not imagine. And
just at that moment, he was not sure that he ever wanted
to find out.

CHAPTER 4

YOU CAN'T GET THERE FROM HERE

It was a very long way back to the lift. How fast had the porter gone when carrying him to the excavation? Forty kilometers per hour? Then the shaft lay ten kilometers away. Sixty? Then a fifteen-kilometer hike awaited him, at a thousand strides, a thousand arm-swings to a kilometer. Even in a gravity field this weak, that was asking a lot from his body.

He did not turn back only because he was sure that the Supervisors, as he had begun to think of the humanoid robots, knew where he was and how much oxygen he had. At some point the two changing variables would intersect at a value which said that he was in danger, and they would send a porter to fetch him and whisk him back to the E-cell.

Each time he saw a robot coming toward him, or heard one closing on him from behind, he began to anticipate relief for his weary arms and legs. But each time, the robot sped past without even slowing. He considered trying to stop a porter by blocking the tunnel, but the only porters that came by were burdened with a full load of chemical tanks or machine parts. There was no room for him.

Because there was no choice, Derec pressed on. For a time he tried counting the yellow ceiling lamps to prove to himself that he was making progress, but his mind wandered and he lost count. There was a terrible sameness to the tunnel, with its unrelieved stretches of white. It seemed as though he were caught in limbo, trapped on a subterranean treadmill.

As it turned out, he was not wrong in thinking that the Supervisors were aware of him. But he was quite wrong about the form their help would take.

He had sat down to rest, his back against the west wall, when a picker came racing up and stopped half a meter away. From its cargo basket it plucked a pair of fresh cartridge packs, laying them at his feet. Before he could react, it backed up, pivoted, and raced away. The timing was so perfect that the pack Derec was using began to sound its depletion alarm just as the picker vanished from sight in the distance.

"Consistent," he said crossly, addressing the absent Supervisors as he swapped the depleted packs for the new ones. "You've done as little as possible to help me right from the start. And this really is the very least you could do."

Hours later, he reached the E-cell with barely enough energy to fold down one of the bunks before he collapsed in it. He was asleep in minutes, his body claiming its rest. But his troubles pursued him even in his dreams, which were full of silent blue robots moving through dark places ripe with the cold scent of danger.

When he awoke, Derec began to think about escaping. For it was clear now that the most likely message for the Supervisor to have sent was something on the order of, "We have an intruder. What shall we do with him?" And Derec did not like most of the possible answers to that question.

He did not think the Supervisor robots, independent as

they might be, were capable of killing him. The First Law was too deeply rooted in the basic structure of a positronic brain. To remove it or tamper with it was to guarantee trouble, up to and including complete intellectual disintegration.

But the recipient of the message was probably human, and therefore quite capable of using violence in service of his or her self-interest. They would want to know how he had discovered the installation, and what he had wanted there, and he would have nothing to tell them.

Perhaps they would accept that at face value, and help him return to wherever he had come from. But considering the circumstances, the stronger possibility was that they would insist on answers. Derec sensed that it would take a long time to convince them he had none. Even so, afterward they would want to make sure that he could never tell anyone what he had stumbled on.

No, he did not want to wait around for the Supervisors' masters to arrive. The key to escaping was Darla. The pod's thrusters were almost certainly rated for a much stronger gravity field than the one the asteroid boasted. If so, then there should be more than enough fuel remaining to lift off the asteroid again and put some distance between it and himself—if only he could convince Darla of the wisdom of that act.

But first, he had to find her. Measuring from memory, Derec suspected that the pod was too large to have been brought down the lift. The robots must have removed him from the pod somewhere on the surface—inside an entry dome, perhaps—and left the pod behind.

So he began by riding the lift in search of the place where he had been brought into the asteroid. It turned out to be called Level Zero. At the top of the lift shaft a disclike pressure door scissored out of the way to allow the platform to pass, and the lift carried Derec up into a high-ceilinged circular room a hundred meters across.

Most of the chamber was filled with neatly aligned rows of machines—buglike augers and borers, tracked carriers, and flying globes like the one Derec had seen when the robots were carrying him and his pod away. On the far side of the room, a steep ramp enclosed by a transparent material led up and out onto the surface.

There was a Supervisor there as well, seated at a control station with its back to Derec. Though it gave no such sign, Derec was sure the robot was aware of his presence.

Stepping off the lift, Derec began to wander among the idle machines. This must be some of the equipment that was used to survey the outer crust of the asteroid, he thought. The flying globes were probably scanning platforms, while the other machines could be used to dig up any promising sites.

It seemed just as obvious to Derec that the surface survey was complete. It was not only the appearance of the machines that led to that conclusion. Searching the surface first made sense. Why even begin the underground excavation before you were sure that the object of your search wouldn't be turned up by a much faster and far less complicated aerial survey?

But Derec was less interested in sorting out the remaining mysteries about this world than he was in finding Darla and saying good-bye to it. A quick catalog of the chamber turned up no sign of the pod or of his safesuit. But he did find a rack with three pearl-white augmented worksuits. They were too large for use in the lower levels or to allow him to climb into the pod if he found it, but he could still use one for an excursion to the surface.

Moving behind the nearest suit, Derec grabbed the

crossbar and vaulted himself feet first through the access door on the back. As he settled in the saddlelike seat, he felt the feedback pads snugging up against his feet. He inserted his arms into the suit's arms, and the controllers for the external manipulator came into his hands. A sloping display screen reflected the status of the suit's systems on the bubblelike canopy before him.

"Close and pressurize," he said, and the access door began to swing shut. He tried raising his arms, and the suit stirred in smooth response. At last, a little power, he thought.

But when he turned to head for the ramp, he found a Supervisor barring his way. "The surface is a restricted area," the robot said.

Derec heard the words through a speaker at his ear and halted his advance. Probably the augmented suit was more than a match for a Supervisor, or would be in the hands of a skilled operator. But Derec did not want a fight. He only wanted answers.

"Tell me where I can find the survival pod I came here in," Derec said.

"You do not have authorization to leave the community."

"That's where it is, isn't it? On the surface. That's where you hid it. What did you do, put my suit back in it after you took it off me?" Derec demanded. "I'm going out. If you don't want to be damaged you'd better get out of the way."

The robot did not move. "The survival pod is not on the surface," it said.

Considering the way the Supervisors had been treating him, that was a generous answer. But Derec wanted more. "Either I go looking on the surface, or you show me where the pod is. Those are the only choices."

There was a brief pause before the robot responded. When the answer came, it was a welcome surprise. "I will show you the pod."

"Are we going outside, or down below?"

"Down."

Derec still wanted to go to the surface. He had hopes of being able to use the stars and sky to determine at least in general terms where the planetoid was located—what kind of star it was orbiting, and whether the planetoid was independent or part of a planetary system. But until he found the pod, none of that mattered, so Derec could afford to be a gracious victor.

"Thank you," he said. "If you'll wait just a moment, I'll put this suit back."

But Derec did not get to enjoy his victory for long. The Supervisor took him back down to the warehouse level and led him through the maze toward the east wall. As they swung around the molding section and its high rack supply cache, the robot stopped short.

"Here."

But Derec could see no pod. All he could see was a large open area with rows of assorted components neatly arrayed on the floor. "Where?"

With a sweeping motion of his arm, the Supervisor repeated, "Here."

That was when Derec took a closer look at the hardware laid out before him and realized the truth. The pod was there, just as the Supervisor said. But it was in a thousand pieces, lying on the floor like a giant jigsaw puzzle. The robots had disassembled it down to fundamental components. Derec could recognize but a few—curved plates that had been part of the hull, several thruster bells, and, a few meters from where Derec stood, the lenses from the seven green lamps on the command console.

"No," he cried out despairingly. "Why did you do it?"

"It was necessary to determine that the search objective was not concealed within the pod."

"And my safesuit? Did they tear that apart, too?"

In answer, the Supervisor led Derec into the maze and showed him his suit, lying in several dozen pieces. The fabric had been separated from the binding rings, the environmental systems stripped out of the chest unit. Even the helmet had been disassembled.

"I'm surprised that you didn't tear me apart, too," he said bitterly as he looked at it.

"Please explain the reason for your surprise," the robot said. "It is impossible for a robot to harm a human. Have you not been informed of this fact?"

"Nevermind," Derec said with a sigh. "I was being sarcastic."

"Sir?"

"Humans don't always mean what they say. Haven't you been informed of that fact?" After a moment, he added, "But you did search me, didn't you?"

"Yes. While you were unconscious, you were subjected to a full-body magnetic resonance scan," the robot replied.

Derec almost laughed at the absurdity of it. "It figures," he said. "I suppose having you put the suit and pod back together is out of the question."

"Nothing may take priority over the primary directive."

"What about all those spare robots sitting up north doing nothing? You could activate a few of them."

"The tasks would require not only Assemblers but the supervision of a Systemist. All Systemists are fully scheduled under the current duty cycle."

"I guess that means no," Derec said. He looked across the expanse of parts that once was a spacecraft and sighed. "Do you have a name of some kind?"

"I am Monitor 5."

"Why are you talking to me, Monitor 5?"

"I perceived that you were stressed. While stressed, humans frequently derive benefit from communication."

Derec snorted. "I guess that's one way to say it. Then tell me, Monitor 5—do you robots know what you're looking for?"

"I may not reveal any information about my mission here."

"What about me? Are you allowed to tell me what you know about me?"

"What do you wish to know?"

"The event recorder in the survival pod—did they find it?"

"I was not part of that work unit. I will consult Analyst 3." The robot paused. "Yes. A data recorder was located."

"Did it tell you what ship I came from? How I got here? Anything?"

"The recorder had not been initialized. The recording disk was blank."

Stunned, Derec looked down and away to hide his expression from the robot. His gaze fell on the pile of fabric from his suit, and he knelt down and began to sift through it. "There was a datastrip on my suit—"

"Yes. It was a test strip. It contained no personal data."

Letting the fabric fall from his hands back to the floor, Derec slowly stood. "A test strip?"

"They are quite common. They are used in calibrating a data reader's scanner."

"But it said Derec—"

44

"Yes. The leading manufacturer of such readers is Derec Data Systems."

Derec felt the strength go out of his legs. "Then you don't know who I am, either."

"No. We do not know who you are."

"And that message you sent about me? What did it say?"

"I did not send the message. One moment while I consult Analyst 17." The robot paused. "Analyst 17 believed that due to your irrational behavior, you would come to harm or endanger the primary objective unless continually supervised. Therefore he sent a message requesting that you be rescued."

"He made that decision on his own?"

"Analyst 17 felt that the threat was of sufficient magnitude to transcend the prohibition regarding communications."

"Prohibition from who? Who's in charge here? And who'd he send the message to?"

"I may not—"

"—reveal any information about your mission here, yes." Grimacing, Derec closed his eyes and tried to shut out the world.

"Are you ill?" Monitor 5 asked, concerned.

"No," Derec said in an unsteady voice. "I'm just back to square one again, that's all."

CHAPTER 5

REPLY

Dispirited, Derec retreated to the E-cell, his illusion of being even partially in control of his own fate destroyed. There was no chance of his reconstructing the pod himself. He might leave the community using one of the augmented worksuits, but there was no way he could leave the asteroid. It seemed that all he could do was stay out of the robots' way and wait for whoever Analyst 17 had signalled to respond.

As though the robots had decided that he needed something to keep him occupied and safely out of their way, Derec found the wardroom com center unlocked and displaying the word "READY." When Derec touched the "Help" key, a short menu popped up on the screen. It offered him a choice between something called Scratchpad and a library index.

Scratchpad proved to be a cross between a notebook and an engineer's sketch pad. He amused himself for a while with its graphics capabilities by drawing a map of the part of the complex he knew firsthand. The system made it easy for him, converting his unsteady movements with the tracer into straight lines, copying duplicate sections, performing fills and rotations.

When drawing deteriorated into doodling, Derec shifted mental gears and decided to make a diary of what had happened since he had awoken in the pod. But his first entry was self-conscious and self-indulgent, and he ended his log with a short sarcastic note:

Dear Mom,
　　　　I got no friends here. Can I come home?

Embarrassed by his own self-pity, Derec purged the Scratchpad memory and pushed his chair away from the terminal. But the terrible feeling of separateness which underlay the thought was not so easily banished. Without family, friends, an ally of any sort, Derec's little world was a lonely place.

The book-film library was Derec's last defense against maudlin thoughts. Scanning the directory, he was struck by the unusual mix of entries. There was a whole subdirectory of texts from Earth's Classical Age, including a few whose authors or titles Derec was intrigued to discover he recognized: Lucretius' *De Rerum Natura*, Newton's *Principia*, Darwin's *The Origin of Species*.

Another large subdirectory consisted of architectural drawings and photographs. Again, a few names struck chords in Derec's memory—Mies van der Rohe, Buckminster Fuller, Frank Lloyd Wright. But when he asked the system to sample those files at one image every few seconds, he found the images were of places that he could not remember ever being and structures he could not remember seeing. It left him wondering why he knew the names in the first place.

Conspicuously absent was any sort of current technical reference on such topics as microelectronics, robotics, process design, and the like. Derec assumed that they were in a separate technical library not available to him.

But there were other sections which under other circumstances would probably have appealed to him—a biography of robotics pioneer Susan Calvin; *Genesis*, Marvin Eller's anecdotal history of twentieth-century computer science; a screenful of titles on astronomy and astrography.

But Derec was not interested in being educated, or in anything that required thinking. He wanted to be a spectator to someone else's problems, to disengage his mind and surrender himself to the spell of the storyteller.

Yet when he turned to the fiction subdirectory, he found the pickings sparse. Aside from a few interactive mysteries and a half-dozen text novels, all of which would require too much work on his part, Derec's choice was limited to the world of theater. *Faust, Waiting for Godot, Daedalus and Icarus, Sweeney Todd*—the titles meant nothing to Derec. But Shakespeare he knew, and Shakespeare was well represented on the list.

Feeling a need for laughter, Derec chose the comedy *A Midsummer Night's Dream.* Then he retreated to a comfortable chair, propped his feet up on the conference table, and let the recording carry him away to ancient Greece, to a woods near the city of Athens, where he might amuse himself with the love-crossed confusion of human and fairy kings, and the pranks of the devilish sprite Puck.

"Up and down, up and down," Puck vowed. "I will lead them up and down. I am feared in field and town. Goblin, lead them up and down—"

In the middle of Puck's declamation, Derec heard the

unmistakable sound of the inner door of the airlock opening. He came to his feet as a Supervisor entered the wardroom and crossed toward the com center.

"What do you want?" Derec demanded, following.

The robot ignored Derec. "Priority interrupt," the robot said to the com center. The screen went black and the speakers silent.

PASSWORD?

The robot's fingers flew over the keypad in a blur, but nothing appeared on the screen except the instruction PROCEED.

Without hesitation, the robot began to hammer at the keys again. Even standing only an arm's length away, Derec had no clue to what the robot was entering. The steady staccato of keyclicks lasted perhaps twenty seconds—three or four hundred characters. Then the robot raised his hand and stepped back.

MESSAGE TRANSMITTED, the screen acknowledged.

"Resume," the robot said, and turned to go.

"Cancel," Derec said, moving quickly to place his body between the robot and the door. "Identify yourself."

"I am Analyst 9."

"What's happening? What did you just do?"

"Please stand aside," Analyst 9 said. "I have urgent duties elsewhere."

"The last time one of you was in here, it was to send a distress message. What's up now? Is a ship here? Is that it? I have a right to know what's going on—"

For an answer, Analyst 9 raised his arm and pushed Derec firmly out of the way. He stumbled back toward the conference table and sat down hard in one of the chairs.

"Do not interfere," the Supervisor said, and left the room.

Though his shock at the robot's physical treatment of him slowed him for an instant, Derec scrambled to his feet and followed.

Out in the chamber, Derec found frenzied activity bordering on chaos. Dozens of porter and picker robots were streaming off the lifts, as if some massive exodus were underway. Scores more were scurrying through the aisles gathering up components and carrying them toward the west wall and the recycling smelter located there.

To Derec's astonishment, instead of depositing what they held and turning back to get more, the pickers and porters queued up at the smelter carried their burdens directly into the heart of the smelter and never appeared again. For some reason, the robots were systematically destroying selected items in their storehouse—and themselves at the same time.

Distracted by the parade of suicidal robots, Derec had lost track of Analyst 9. Now, as he scanned the chamber to try to find it, he saw something else extraordinary. There were no Supervisors anywhere in the warehouse. The various manufacturing centers were standing silent and abandoned.

On a hunch, Derec fought his way through to the lift and commandeered a platform to carry him up to Level Zero. There he found a gathering of twenty Supervisors. They were standing motionless in a circle, with hands linked as though in some sort of direct conference.

They took no notice of his arrival, and so Derec crossed the room to where two other Supervisors sat at the giant command console.

"Monitor 5?"

"Yes, Derec," one of the robots said with a nod of acknowledgment.

"Can you tell me what's happening?"

"Surface sensors have detected a large spacecraft approaching. The trajectory and velocity profile indicate that it will match orbit with this planetoid."

"I'm going to get off this rock?" Derec exulted. "Praise the stars!"

"There is a sixty-eight percent probability that the ship intercepted the distress signal. However, there is only a nine percent probability that the ship is here to rescue you."

That news jolted Derec back to earth. "Intercepted? They aren't the people you were calling?"

"No, Derec."

"Who are they, then? What do they want?"

"The ship is currently unidentified."

"Is that why all the robots downstairs are going crazy?"

"I cannot answer that question now," Monitor 5 said. "I may be able to tell you more shortly."

"What should I do?"

"Wait."

"Great. How long?"

"Not long," Monitor 5 said, standing. "Excuse me. The Analysts are calling for me."

Crossing the room, Monitor 5 joined the conference circle. He stood there with them for perhaps two minutes, then the circle broke apart. Most of the Supervisors headed for the lift. Two of them, including Monitor 5, came to where Derec stood.

"I have been appointed to communicate with you," Monitor 5 said.

"Appointed?" The robot's choice of word confused Derec.

"By default," the robot admitted. "None of the Analysts feel comfortable dealing with a human."

"Are you telling me that they haven't been talking to me because they don't want to? They don't know how?"

"With few exceptions, their experience has been exclusively with other robots. I have been chosen because of my previous success in communicating with you," Monitor 5 said.

"Is that another exception?" Derec said, indicating the robot standing just behind Monitor 5.

"I am accompanied by Analyst 17."

"Ah—we've met—sort of."

"Analyst 17 is here to assist me," Monitor 5 said. "Please, Derec. There are important matters to discuss, and there is very little time."

"Then get started."

"Thank you. The Analysts are agreed that the approaching ship is a threat to the security of our operation. The possibility of discovery was anticipated by those who placed us here. Our instructions for such a circumstance are to destroy ourselves and this facility. Certain preliminary steps are already underway—"

"The robots at the smelter."

"Yes. All proprietary technology must be destroyed and the excavation rendered unusable. This directive was impressed on us at the highest level of necessity and urgency. We must comply. However, your presence was *not* anticipated."

"What do I have to do with it?"

"As long as you are present, we are not able to fulfill our directive, since to destroy the complex would kill you. Even to destroy ourselves would leave you unprotected. Therefore, for us to carry out our directive, it is necessary for you to leave."

"I've been ready to leave since I got here. Just show me the way."

Analyst 17 spoke up at that point. "Unfortunately, since leaving the community also represents a significant risk to your life, we are unable to assist you in doing this and are in fact obliged to prevent it."

"So you're not going to put my pod back together? My safesuit?"

"No."

"This is crazy."

"On the contrary, it is fundamentally logical," Analyst 17 said. "If we protect you, you will almost certainly die, which we cannot allow. If we fail to protect you, you may survive, but you will be placed in grave danger, which we cannot allow."

Derec looked from Monitor 5 to the Analyst in disbelief, then back again. "So what *are* you going to do with me?"

"Nothing," Monitor 5 said. "No action is possible. If we help you to escape, we will be placing you in danger. But if we prevent your escape, we will also be placing you in danger."

Derec was starting to get lost in the convolutions of the conversation. "Is that what you want me to do? Escape?"

The robot hesitated. "We want you to remain safe and unharmed."

It seemed as though the robot were tiptoeing through a logical minefield. "What if I do leave?"

"When we discover that you are gone, we will have to pursue you." It hesitated again. "However, until you are returned to our care the remainder of the community will be free to pursue the next highest priority directive."

"In other words, if I escape, the First Law is no longer

a factor. You can go ahead and destroy yourselves in good conscience."

"That is essentially correct," said Analyst 17, "though I must warn you there is a danger if you continue to discuss it."

Derec ignored the warning. "Escape to where?"

"We cannot consider that question," Monitor 5 said.

"Well, I can, and I don't like the answer!" Derec snapped. "I'll tell you what I intend to do—as soon as that ship is close enough to pick up the signal from a suit transmitter, I'm getting into one of those augments over there and going up to the surface to ask them to save me from you."

"We could not allow that."

"So what am I supposed to do? Go wander around on the surface until my air runs out? This is nuts. How can you even ask me to do such a thing?"

"Derec, I must repeat, there is a danger—," Analyst 17 began.

"We have not asked you to do anything," Monitor 5 said. "We have simply outlined for you the consequences of actions you may choose to take."

"You may not be asking, but you're dropping some loud hints," Derec said. "You're telling me that if I want to go kill myself, you'll look the other way. I don't understand how this whole conversation can even be taking place. What's wrong with all of you?"

Monitor 5 answered. "I am following a highly conditional logic path proposed by Analyst 17—"

"So that's why he's really here."

"—in which the uncertainty of your fate is modified by your own volitional acts to a positive value weighed against the high probability of harm due to inaction."

"In other words, you talked yourself into it," Derec said. "Well, you haven't talked me into it. Your prime objective and your security don't mean a thing to me. Do you think it's important to me if you can't destroy yourselves? I don't care if that ship belongs to your worst enemy.

"In fact, I'm beginning to think that if they're your enemy, that makes them my friend. I'm not going anywhere. And I'm sure as hell not going to go kill myself to get you off the hook."

The robots were apparently not willing to let it go at that. When Derec left Level Zero, Analyst 17 followed. It took a different lift, and when they reached the warehouse level, it studiously trailed several steps behind him. But there was no question that he was under surveillance.

It did not make sense that immediately after asking him to escape, the robots would set a bloodhound to dog his heels. But since he had no intention of doing what the robots wanted, it hardly mattered if he understood. He could safely ignore his shadow.

The warehouse was still a hive of chaotic activity, and Derec retreated from it to the quiet of the E-cell. He thought Analyst 17 might content itself to watch and wait outside, since the cell had only one exit. But the robot came inside as well, and when Derec entered the wardroom, it followed him in and took a seat at the opposite end of the conference table.

At first, however, Derec barely noticed the robot's entry. The video from a sky camera somewhere on the surface was being displayed on the com center screen. It showed a small, distant orange sun and a field of dim stars in which Derec saw no immediately recognizable patterns. A dark backlit hulk was moving across the star background, growing perceptibly larger as it closed on the asteroid. It was still too far away to show a distinctive profile, but it was clearly a massive spaceship of some kind.

"More propaganda?" Derec asked.

"The Analysts agreed that you have a right to know the source and current status of the threat."

"Do you think I'm going to see that thing up there and panic? It won't work. This isn't much, but it's home. I'm not leaving."

The robot made no reply, and remained silent while Derec went to the autogalley and assembled a lunch. When he came back with it and sat down, he soon became painfully conscious of the robot patiently watching him.

"Whose side are you on, anyway?" Derec asked between mouthfuls.

"Clarify."

"What are you doing here? I thought you wanted me to skip out. But I couldn't make a move without you knowing about it."

"Your conversation with Monitor 5 forced him into recognizing a First Law conflict."

"You mean his little self-deception fell apart?"

"Monitor 5 is now deeply concerned that you may attempt to escape and harm yourself in the process or as a consequence. To relieve that potential and allow Monitor 5 to return to his duties, I offered to watch you."

"What about you? Did I make your logic bomb blow up, too?"

"No."

"So you're not here to stop me," Derec said, pushing his plate away. "You're here to make sure no one else stops me."

"Your observations are irrelevant to the situation. You have stated your intention to remain in our care."

"Right." Derec glanced up at the screen. The ship was still a dark shape without texture, but it now filled fully a third of the frame. "But I still think you expect me to start getting worried and make a move. Well, to show you just how worried I am, I'm going to go in the other room to take a nap," Derec said, standing. "If you decide to come along, all I ask is that you pick out your own bunk. There isn't room in mine for two."

CHAPTER 6

A ROCK AND
A HARD PLACE

Analyst 17 did not follow, and Derec did not nap. He lay on his bunk and stared at the ceiling, trying to regain perspective.

The robots' predicament was real and substantial. It was not only the matter of being frustrated in their attempt to fulfill their Second Law obligations to their master. They were tiptoeing along the edge of a First Law chasm, a paradox capable of paralyzing not only individual robots, but the entire community. He was their first obligation, and yet there was nothing they could do for him but beg him to save himself.

If it were not so serious, it would be laughable. It was as though a person suffering from hiccups had asked a friend, "Please surprise me." How could he catch the robots off guard, even with Analyst 17's collaboration?

On top of which, the whole idea of escaping was absurd. Without help from the robots, he couldn't possibly reassemble the pod before the ship arrived. And even if he could, there was no way it could run from the approaching ship.

If he continued to think of both the robots and the strangers as enemies, there were no solutions to the equation. Only by assuming that the strangers were coming to help him, or would be willing to help him even if they had other purposes there, could he envision a way out. He could wait until the ship was in orbit, then go to the surface in an augment and radio to them for help.

Just then the bunk shuddered under him, and he sat bolt upright. He thought for a moment that he hadn't felt it, or experienced the sudden start which sometimes comes just before dozing off. But then another tremor shook the room, and he could no longer think it was an illusion. He jumped to his feet and ran across to the wardroom.

Analyst 17 was still sitting there as Derec had left him. "What's happening?" Derec demanded.

"We are under attack," the robot said, gesturing toward the com center.

Derec stared at the screen. The ship had tacked to a position where half of its sunward side was visible, allowing Derec to see details for the first time. What he saw confused him. The ship seemed to have been not designed, but collected. It looked more like a space junkyard than a dangerous raider. But raider it was.

Just in the part Derec could see clearly, there were eleven distinct hulls, as well as a tangled matrix of connecting structures. There were ships old enough to be in a museum and others new enough to be a shipwright's showpiece. Sleek transatmospheric profiles nestled against the cylinders and grips of deep-space haulers. All across the mass of the ship, small red and orange lights were blinking on and off.

"Who are they?" Derec whispered.

"Unknown."

"Well, didn't they hail us? What do they want?"

"There was no signal on any frequency commonly used for communication."

Derec felt another vibration through the floor. "What kind of weapons are they using?"

"The ship's armament appears to consist primarily of phased microwave lasers."

"And what do we have to fight back?"

"The community has no weapons."

"What?" Derec demanded.

The robot's answer was patient and calm. "It is highly probable that the ship contains humans. We would not be permitted to use weapons against them."

Derec stared at the robot, then at the screen. Unlike in careless fictions, there were no stabbing beams of brilliant light to betray the energies pouring down from the radar ship. There were only the winking lights, and the ground moving under Derec's feet. "Are we in danger?"

"Yes."

"How much?"

"The ship began its attack in the area of our only permanent surface installation, the antenna farm located 170 degrees east of the primary shaft—"

"These vibrations we're feeling are from that far away?"

"Yes. The primary assault was successful and communications are out. A number of tunnels in the region have apparently collapsed. Firing pattern now appears to be random. The ship is currently in a nearly synchronous orbit with a slippage of two degrees per minute."

"So in less than ninety minutes they'll be overhead."

"That is correct."

It was obvious to Derec that he could wait no longer to act. If the ship breached the complex's pressure envelope while he was still in the E-cell, he would never get out. The breathers couldn't keep him alive in a vacuum.

And there was another danger, just as acute—that the power would be interrupted or the lifts disabled, and he would be trapped on the warehouse level. Even in low gravity he did not think he could climb up a lift shaft by hand.

Not that running about on the surface in an augment was as attractive a proposition as it had been a short time ago. The chances were that he would be taken not for a prisoner trying to escape but for an enemy to be destroyed. Even so, dying buried in the icy heart of the asteroid was infinitely less appealing than dying out in the open.

"This logic path that you devised—am I correct in thinking that you and Monitor 5 are the only Supervisors who were able to follow it without hitting a First Law conflict?"

"Yes."

"Why? Why you?"

"My experience with human beings has provided me with a more sophisticated perspective on their nature and behavior."

"You've had contact with other humans? Besides me?"

"Yes."

"Who?"

"I am not permitted to say,"

Dead end. "Are the other robots even aware of what you asked me to try to do?"

"No."

"How were you going to destroy the complex?"

"The material used to line all the tunnel walls contains an explosive. Once all the other Supervisors have been destroyed, the last Monitor and Analyst will together transmit the trigger signal. The resulting explosion should cause the entire excavated portion of the asteroid to subside."

"I see," Derec said. Great, he thought to himself. If I stay in the complex, the raiders will bring it down on my head. If I leave, the robots will blow it up under my feet.

Unless—

Unless there was some way to get off the surface, some source of thrust adequate to give him and his augment escape velocity. Considering the weakness of the asteroid's gravity, escape velocity did not amount to much. He could probably put a ball in orbit just by throwing it as hard as he could. The leg servos of the augmented suit were likely powerful enough to permit him to literally jump clear.

Unfortunately, the safety regs on augment design required governors on the leg servos to prevent someone from trying exactly that. But what engineers had joined together, tinkerers could tear asunder—

At that moment, a bright flare seemed to appear on the body of the ship, and an instant later the energy beam burned out the eyes of the camera unit relaying the picture. Another camera some distance away took over, and the low angle at which it was focused showed not only the ship but the bilious clouds boiling off the surface where its weapons were trained.

The sight spurred Derec to action. "There doesn't seem to be any escape for any of us," he lied, wearing his best look of resignation. "I guess there's nothing else for me to do but go prepare to die. I would be grateful if you could grant me privacy while I carry out the appropriate rituals."

The lie passed. "I do not fully understand the purpose of such rituals," the robot said, "but I will respect your privacy."

Derec did not need long to put his rapidly developing plan in motion. Returning to his cabin, he swept up the pillows off two of the bunks, then ran to the airlock with them cradled in his arms.

"Open."

The sound of the inner seal opening brought Analyst 17 out of the wardroom, but by then it was too late. Derec stepped inside the lock, and the door closed behind him.

"Cycle," he said, fumbling with the straps of a breather.

When the outer door opened, he draped the pillows over the bottom sill of the hatch and then stepped out over them. Just as Derec had expected, the pillows kept the outer door from sealing, interrupting the cycle and imprisoning the robot inside. He did not know how long it would hold, whether there was some way for the robot to override the lock system, and he did not wait around to find out.

The line at the smelter included Supervisors, but they took no notice of him as he passed by. He rode the lift up to Level Zero, where he discovered that Monitor 5 had been busy taking precautions against his return. Two of the augments were missing, vanished as though they had never been there. The third was wedged against the wall by one of the tracked carriers, which in turn was barricaded in place by a four-legged auger unit.

He did not think the suit was damaged—tampering with safety equipment would almost certainly invoke the First Law—but it was going to take a little getting to. And part of the problem would be Monitor 5. The robot was seated at the console when Derec arrived, and rose and started for Derec the moment he stepped off the lift and placed it on standby.

Their paths intersected when Derec was a few meters short of the carrier. "The surface is a restricted area," the robot said.

"I know that," Derec said, circling and staying out of

reach of the robot's hands. "This equipment is improperly stored. I'm going to take care of it."

But Monitor 5 was not going to be put off that easily.

"You may not leave. You are in no danger here," it said, reaching for him.

Derec backed away and scrambled up the steps into the enclosed operator's station. "Wrong. If I stay here, I'll be killed when the ship destroys the station."

"We will protect you."

Derec wasted no time or breath arguing the point. "You can't even protect yourselves," he said, and slammed and locked the door.

The operator's interface was standard, and the functions of those few controls which weren't were clear at a glance. He touched the power switch, and the display came alive with information on the vehicle's status. The most important item was near the bottom:

POWER CELL . . . . . . 100,000 Kw . . . OK

The robot was politely knocking on the window and trying to attract Derec's attention, but Derec ignored it. With a touch on one of two small joysticks in the armrest at his right hand, Derec unshipped the small crane which lay crosswise behind the control cab.

Since the controls had been designed primarily for robots with their fine motor control, Derec found them a little touchy. But the crane was semi-automatic, so when he had managed to swing the boom out over the back end of the carrier and bring the auger in range of the crane's camera, all he had to do was say, "Pick it up." The crane handled the rest.

Monitor 5 seemed slow to realize what was happening.

Derec couldn't decide if that was because it was still experiencing some internal conflict, or if he was just seeing the difference between a Monitor and an Analyst. But when Derec lifted the auger off the floor of the chamber and began to swing it out of the way, the robot suddenly became agitated.

"Analyst 17 was in error," it said, grasping the door latch and shaking violently. "Derec—you cannot escape. You cannot leave. I am required to protect you. I am responsible."

Saying nothing, Derec used the dangling mass of the auger to brush the robot away from the side of the carrier and back it toward the wall. The robot's protestations went up in volume, but Derec did not stop until he had gently pinned the robot against the wall ten meters to the left of where it had done the same to the augment.

"Reverse slow," Derec said, and the carrier crawled away from the wall. "Stop. Standby."

He jumped out and ran to the augment. As he wrestled the suit away from the wall, Monitor 5 was struggling to extricate itself. It was a race Derec had to win.

Finally the access door was clear, and Derec levered himself inside. At that moment, Monitor 5 clambered to the top of the auger, free from its makeshift prison. But it was too late to stop him. The access door was closing to seal Derec in the suit.

"Power on," he said.

His next objective was the open control cab on the other side of the carrier, meant for use by workers in augments. But before he could reach it, Monitor 5 was again trying to block his way.

"I don't want to harm you," Derec said. "You can't stop me. You've done your duty by trying. Now stand aside."

"You are attempting to commit suicide. I am not required to comply with your orders under these circumstances."

"I'm trying to save myself," Derec said. "If you really want me to live, you'll step aside and give me a chance."

"I will take you to a safe place within the community—"

"There are no safe places here!" Derec shouted. "Don't you understand?"

"I cannot allow—"

"I can't stand here and debate it," Derec said. "I'm sorry."

As he spoke, he swung the right grapple of the suit in a sweeping arc that caught the robot in the neck and sent it sprawling. But Derec had barely taken three steps when it was back again, clawing at the suit's emergency panel.

This time Derec reached down and grabbed the robot's right leg, upending it and dropping it on its back. Catching its ankle with the other grapple, Derec pinched down hard until he heard the sounds of metal crumpling. When he released his grip, the robot's leg was crippled, the foot frozen at an odd angle.

Derec climbed into the open cab unimpeded. As he backed the carrier away from the wall and turned it toward the ramp, he saw Monitor 5 still lying on the floor where he had left it, vainly trying to repair the damage Derec had done. It's slitlike scanners followed Derec and the carrier across the chamber.

It was still watching him, its gaze somehow forlorn and somehow accusing, when Derec drove the carrier up through the lock and out onto the surface.

CHAPTER 7

FRIEND OR FOE

After his time underground, it seemed strange to have the infinite open sky of space overhead. The sun, a tiny orange disk, hung low in the sky. Barely twenty degrees above the horizon, it cast long shadows into the depressions. The sky was bright with stars, but no planets declared themselves to Derec's eye.

He did not know how long it would take to make the modifications to the augment. He only knew that the raider ship's orbit was bringing it closer, and he had to be done before it arrived. He knew too that the robots would be pursuing him in a short-sighted effort to protect him. It was as though the jaws of a vise were closing on him. Somehow he had to squirm away or die.

He only drove far enough over the rugged, frozen terrain to separate himself from the potential target of the complex entrance. Then he parked the carrier half in shadow on a valley floor and started off on foot across the frozen wastes. Though he was sacrificing speed in giving up the carrier, the vehicle almost certainly contained a tracking transponder that would lead the robots right to him.

As soon as he was on foot, he began looking for the right place to hole up while working on the suit. He did not need sunlight for what he had to do, since the augment had its own worklamps. A shadowed hollow, a darkened crevice, a pitch-black ice cave—any of those would hide him without hindering his efforts. But the better hidden he was, the less warning he would have about the approach of the robots or the raiders. There was no having it both ways.

While Derec hiked across the frozen terrain and equivocated, he used the augment's omnidirectional radio to send a series of distress calls. Derec did not know if the signals would carry over the horizon to the raider, and he feared that they would lead the robots to him. But he had to try, had to give the raiders a chance and a reason to save him.

"Clear channel, code 1. To all ships: pilot marooned, requires pickup. Respond if in range. To all ships—"

Eventually Derec settled on a fissure in an ice cliff that faced back the way he had come. From there, he had a fair view of the terrain, except for what was blocked by the larger crags and mounds. And he had a clear view of the sky from the horizon on the northwest to the horizon on the northeast.

"Diagnostic library," he said.

The lower half of the bubblelike viewport turned opaque and a list of subsystems appeared on it in bright yellow letters. He scanned down the list quickly.

"Motive systems."

One of the items near the middle of the list flashed twice, and then the entire list was replaced by another. In the same manner, Derec worked his way through the help screens until the circuit and logic paths of the subcontroller filled the half-display with a maze of fine tracings. Derec studied the system carefully, his lips pursed into a frown.

"Frost," he muttered finally.

It was as he had feared. The governor was not a physical device that could be readily disconnected. It was a feedback loop in the leg servo circuits. The loop told the suit controller, "Do not allow the force applied by the drivers to exceed a force of x number of dynes per second." Small forces applied quickly were acceptable, as were large forces applied slowly. But large forces applied quickly, which was what he needed, were forbidden.

If he had had more time, there might have been a chance to reprogram the subcontrollers. But under the circumstances, it would have to be radical surgery. Fortunately, augments were designed to be field-repairable, a practice which had saved more than one laborer's life.

The various "hands" which the augment could use were located in bulging closures on the suit's thighs. Derec selected an illuminated micromanipulator for the right, and a spotweld laser for the left.

Just then the ground under and around him shook suddenly, bringing a minor avalanche of slow-falling particles down on the crown of the suit. "Clear," he ordered. The bubble became a window again, revealing to Derec a chilling sight. The attacking spacecraft had climbed above the western horizon. It was still firing randomly, still carving out a path of destruction on the asteroid's surface. Time was running out.

"Shut down subsystem twenty-four." That was it: he was committed. With the leg controllers powered down, Derec could no longer walk.

The modifications included burning through three circuit traces and fusing a fourth to a neighboring circuit as a shunt. Accuracy with the tiny laser was absolutely critical. A misfire could destroy enough circuits to cripple the augment permanently.

With the help of the augment's pointing guide, Derec completed the work on the right leg without mishap. But by the time he was ready to start on the left, the vibrations from the more powerful explosions were more than strong enough to disturb his aim. As he stood trying to outguess the shaking ground, a familiar voice intruded:

"Derec, please listen. Derec, you must stop. This is madness—"

Two hundred meters away on the slope of the mound due north of him was a robot. It was Monitor 5, waving its arms and advancing directly toward where Derec stood. It was walking easily, with no sign of the damage Derec had inflicted on its leg.

In the same glance, Derec saw that the reason the shaking was stronger was that the raider ship was much closer, more nearly overhead than he had expected. Once again he was trapped between the raiders, who would rescue him by killing him, and the robots, who would kill him by rescuing him.

"Go away!" Derec hissed.

"Derec, you must return to the compound. You are in danger here."

The raider ship seemed to have taken notice of the robot, for the plain between Monitor 5 and the cliff where Derec stood suddenly came under a barrage of pinpoint laser impacts.

These were not the high-intensity weapons which were shaking the ground, and mercifully, the gunners did not seem to be targeting Derec. But the surface in this area was nearly all ice, and volatile. One blast boiled away the top of the mound behind the robot. Another gouged a deep trench between the robot and Derec.

Derec did not think that would stop Monitor 5, and he was right. The robot scrambled down into the trench before the billow of gas could even dissipate, and Derec lost sight of it.

He could not afford to worry about the robot. Setting his jaw determinedly, Derec went back to work on the left subcontroller. Using the body rigidity and autocontrol of the augment to the fullest, he made short work of it. The three unwanted circuits vaporized in tiny puffs of atomic metal. The two parallel traces melted and merged into one.

"Derec!" Monitor 5 called suddenly. "It's here! In the ice! I've found it!"

Derec looked up. The firing had stopped, and there was no sign of the robot. "Close the panels," he said, then tongued the radio switch. "Monitor 5, go back to the installation. There's nothing you can do for me out here."

Just then, a metallic arm appeared above the lip of the trench, the hand clutching a small silver object. A moment later Monitor 5 struggled out of the trench. Starting toward Derec, Monitor 5 raised the silver object triumphantly overhead in one hand.

"The key is here, Derec. You must take it—"

The robot's triumph did not last long. The raider ship was now a great ominous mass directly overhead. Monitor 5 had barely taken a step when the laser fire started up again. Red targeting beams danced like spotlights on a stage on the ice around it.

For a moment it seemed as though the robot was going to escape destruction. Then, a dozen strides from the foot of the cliff, a laser tracked a fiery line across the robot's torso. An instant later, Monitor 5 disappeared in a silent explosion, all blue-green flame and disintegrating metal.

Disappeared—but not completely. The explosion sent pieces flying in all directions. One of the largest, spinning so rapidly Derec could not tell what it was, came cartwheeling toward him. As it struck the ground and skidded to a stop, Derec saw what it was: Monitor 5's right arm, from the shoulder joint to the fingers.

And still gripped tightly in those fingers was the shining silver object—a rectangle perhaps five centimeters by fifteen centimeters, the size of a remote controller or a memory cartridge.

Could this be the object that the robots were so obsessively searching for all this time? If so, then why had Monitor 5's last act been to try to give it to Derec?

For a moment Derec hesitated. To retrieve the object was an additional risk in an enterprise which was already too risky. But he knew that it was impossible for him to simply leave it lying there. Ripping the specialized end effectors from the augment's arms, Derec slapped the general-purpose grapples back in place.

"Power up system twenty-four," he snapped, and the sole red lamp on the augment's status board turned to green.

His descent down the slope to where the arm rested was a controlled fall at best. With the leg servos jimmied, Derec could not control a walking gait. But he got there all the same, seizing the arm and the artifact in his right hand and locking the grapple.

Gathering his feet under himself, Derec glanced upward to gauge the distance and angle to the raider ship. He lifted his feet on the control pads, and the suit went into a crouch. He jammed his feet down hard, and the powerful legs of the augment kicked out with all their unrestrained might. Like a tiny spacecraft, the augment launched itself from the surface, carrying Derec toward a rendezvous with the raider ship.

One way or another, I'm coming aboard—

Suddenly the entire surface of the asteroid seemed to shudder and rise up in a convulsion. The robots had triggered their self-destruct at last, and the explosion sent a hailstorm of fragments blasting outward like space shrapnel.

Almost immediately, the weapons pods of the raider ship sprang to life. At first Derec thought that they were aiming at him, trying to get him before he was lost in the deluge of ice and rock boulders which had erupted from the asteroid. Then it seemed as though the gunners were targeting the debris itself, the smaller and faster-moving bits of which were already overtaking him.

Whichever was their goal, the net effect was the same: when he was within about a hundred meters of the nearest part of the ship and beginning to scan for a place to latch on with his free hand, the entire bubble faceplate of the augment lit up with a blue light that crawled in all directions like something alive.

Derec's limbs went numb and his senses went wild. He had only enough time to think *Not again!* before the light faded and darkness took him away once more.

Despite all the tumult which had surrounded him as he had lost consciousness, Derec came back to awareness calmly and easily. He could not say how long he had been unconscious, but it had to have been more than a few minutes. He was no longer outside the alien ship. For that matter, he was no longer in the augment. Instead, he was lying on his back on hard decking, staring up at a ceiling filled with small doors.

Propping himself up on his elbows, Derec surveyed his surroundings. He was in a narrow room, almost a corridor. The long walls were covered with more doors—storage bins?—and there was an exit at each end—or at least a tall metal ellipse which might be an exit.

Derec did not spend much time wondering about the exits or the contents of the storage bins. A large animal covered with mottled brown and gold fur squatted on its haunches nearby, watching Derec. It reminded Derec of a dog, like an undersized Saint Bernard with the alert eyes of a wolf. But the face was too flat, the ears too high and pointed, and the forelegs ended not in paws but in gray-skinned sausagelike fingers.

Whatever it was, he had never seen anything like it before. Moving slowly so as not to alarm the creature, Derec sat up. When he did, the creature sidled forward a step and cocked its head.

"Arr 'u aw right?" it asked in a guttural voice.

Derec could not have been more surprised if the creature had suddenly molted and turned into a butterfly. Not only speech, but Standard—however curiously accented—

"I—I think so," he stammered.

"That iss good," the creature said. "Aranimas will be pleased. 'Ee did not want 'u 'armed."

"The best way to guarantee that is not to shoot at people."

"Eff we 'ad been shooting at 'u, we would 'ave 'it 'u," the alien said with a tooth-bearing grimace that might have been a smile or a threat display.

Though that message was garbled, other body language was coming through more clearly. The alien's crouch struck Derec as a posture from which it could spring quickly.

Seated, he was at a disadvantage both in agility and reach, a fact which he felt keenly when he met the alien's gaze. Their eyes were on the same level, but Derec felt threatened, intimidated.

Still moving slowly, Derec felt for the wall behind him and hauled himself to his feet. The alien's only reaction was to rise with him. When both were standing, the tips of the alien's ears reached only to Derec's chest, and the psychological comfort that went with being the taller shifted to Derec.

"What are you?" he demanded.

" 'Urr friend," the alien said. "What morr do 'u need to know?"

"There's a hundred forty colonized worlds, and there's nothing like you on any of them."

"Wherr I come from therr arr two 'undred colonized worlds, and nothing like 'u on any of them," the alien said, grimacing again. This time, the circumstances seemed to call more clearly for a smile, and Derec decided that's what it was. "Come. Aranimas iss waiting."

"Who is Aranimas?"

"Aranimas iss ship's boss. 'Ull see," the alien said, turning away and starting toward the far door.

"Wait," Derec called. "What's your name?"

The alien stopped and turned. It opened its mouth and out poured a torrent of sounds not in any human alphabet—like a growl punctuated with a sibilant hiss and sounds like bubbles popping. Then the alien smiled-grimaced. "Can say?"

Derec shook his head sheepishly. "No."

"Thought not. Come, then. Not wise to keep Aranimas waiting."

Taking a brisk loping pace, the alien led Derec through three more compartments identical to the one he had awakened in. Derec wondered briefly about the mismatch between his escort and the design of the ship they were in. The overhead storage bins were far above Derec's head; he doubted if he could reach them even by jumping. Unless the caninoid alien were as agile a climber as a terrestrial primate, it would need a ladder to get to their contents.

Efficient use of space—terrible ergonomic design, Derec thought critically.

They came to a tiny hexagonal room barely large enough for both of them to stand in. It seemed to be a hub between intersecting corridors, since each wall framed an identical door. The alien paused for Derec to catch up, then continued on through.

"Where do the other doors lead?"

"Can't tell 'u," the alien said cheerfully.

Beyond the hub, the interior of the ship had a different character. There were just as many walls and small spaces, but the walls were either of a coarse mesh, almost more like fencing, or had large windowlike cutouts. Together the mesh and the cutouts provided long lines of sight and the feeling not of small spaces but of a large busy one.

The largest space within this deck seemed to be straight ahead. Peering over the alien's shoulder, Derec caught glimpses of what seemed to be a control center, and of a figure seated at the console with its back to them. There was something familiar and human about the figure, and something wrong and disturbing at the same time.

As soon as the caninoid led him into the control center, Derec knew why he was getting mixed messages, and who—or what—the storage corridors had been designed for. The alien sitting at the console was decidedly humanoid, and Derec could describe him in very human terms—a slender build, thin neck, almost hairless head, pale skin.

But even sitting down, Aranimas was as tall as Derec, and he had the arm span of a condor. The entire horseshoe-shaped console, easily three human arm spans wide, was within his comfortable reach.

Beyond and above Aranimas was a huge curved viewing screen on which eight different views of the asteroid's surface were being projected. Superimposed on most of them were blue-lined targeting grids and small characters Derec took to be numbers. Some of the characters were changing constantly, and others seemed to change in response to Aranimas's hands moving over the console and to the endless pattern of explosions and groundslides on the surface.

"Praxil, denofah, praxil mastica," he was saying, apparently into a microphone. "Deh feh opt spa, nexori."

Derec took a step forward. "Aranimas?"

The alien turned his head slightly to the left, and a chill went through Derec. The lizardlike eye that peered back at him was set in a raised socket on the side of Aranimas's head. From behind, Derec had mistaken the eye bumps for ears.

"Sssh!" the caninoid alien said nervously, grasping Derec's hand and pulling him back. "Don't interrupt the boss. 'E'll talk to 'u when 'e's ready."

Aranimas turned back to his work and resumed speaking. Derec had the impression that he was issuing orders, chiding, prodding, reprimanding, assigning targets and grading gunners. There was nothing moving on the surface and nothing stirring below, and yet the carnage went on.

After a few minutes of watching, Derec could no longer restrain himself. "There's nothing down there anymore,"

Derec blurted. "They blew it all up. What are you doing this for?"

"Prrractice," Aranimas said. His voice was high-pitched and he trilled the "r" sound.

It went on for another ten minutes that way, millions of watts of energy expended uselessly against an inert and lifeless world. Then Aranimas ran a fingertip along a row of switches, and the screens went blank.

"Rijat," he said, and turned his chair to face them. "What is your name?"

"Derec." Only one of Aranimas's eyes was trained on him; the other glanced around randomly. Derec could not imagine what it would be like to view the world that way. Did the alien's brain switch back and forth between the two inputs, like a director choosing a camera shot? Or did it somehow integrate the two images into one?

"This device you used to attack my ship," Aranimas continued. "What was it?"

"An augmented worksuit—altered to allow the leg servos to operate at full power. But I wasn't attacking you. I was escaping."

Aranimas's other eye pivoted forward and focused on Derec. "Were you a prisoner?"

"I was stranded on the asteroid in a survival pod. The robots found me and then wouldn't let me go. I had to steal that equipment from them to get away."

"And where did you come from before you were stranded?"

"I don't know," Derec said, frowning. "I can't remember anything before that."

"Don't lie to 'im," the caninoid whispered. "It makes 'im angry."

"I'm not lying," Derec said indignantly. "As far as I can

tell, five days ago I didn't exist. That's how much I know about who I am."

While Derec spoke, Aranimas reached inside the folds of his clothing and extracted a small golden stylus. Seeing it, the caninoid cringed and turned half away.

"Oh, no," it whined. "Too late."

Aranimas pointed the stylus at Derec's side, and a pale blue light began to dance over the entire surface of Derec's hand. He screamed in pain and dropped to his knees. It was as though he had trust his hand into a raging furnace, except that no skin was being destroyed and no nerve endings deadened. The pain just went on and on, sapping his strength until even the screams caught in his throat, too feeble to free themselves.

"I know something of the rules of governing robots and humans," Aranimas said calmly while Derec writhed on the floor. "Humans build robots to serve them. Robots follow human direction. If you were the only human on this asteroid, then it follows that the robots here were under your command, and serving your purpose."

Aranimas tipped the stylus ceilingward, and the blue glow vanished. The pain vanished with it, except for the memory. Derec lay on his side and sucked in air in great gasping breaths.

"I will know who you are and what you know about the object you brought aboard," Aranimas said quietly. "To end the pain, you need only tell me the truth."

His face as emotionless as his trilling voice, Aranimas pointed the stylus at Derec once more.

CHAPTER 8

TEST OF LOYALTY

At some point, it ended. But by that time Derec was in no condition to know clearly why Aranimas had interrupted his torture. He had only a vague awareness of Aranimas's going away, and of being dragged away from the control center by the caninoid.

Unable to either resist or help, he was taken to another section of the subdivided compartment and laid on a thinly padded board. He lay there drifting in and out of consciousness, sometimes aware of the caninoid crouching solicitously beside him, sometimes aware of nothing but his own confusion and fatigue.

In one of his lucid moments he became aware that the alien was holding a cup of clear liquid for him, and struggled up on one elbow.

" 'U bettrr tell Aranimas what 'e wants to know," the caninoid whispered as it offered the cup.

Derec tipped his head forward and reached for the cup. His right hand trembled uncontrollably, so he had to use his left to steady the cup as he sipped at the cool liquid. It was sweet, like a thin honey, and bathed his ravaged throat with relief.

"How tough do you think humans are?" he croaked. "If I knew anything I'd have told him in the first five minutes. If he keeps this up he's going to kill me. Why won't he believe me?"

The caninoid glanced nervously around before answering. "Do 'u know Narwe?"

Derec could not tell if the name was of a species or an individual, but it did not matter to his answer. "No."

"Aranimas knows Narwe. Narwe 'ass to be forced to be honest. If 'u ask Narwe a question, it will lie or pretend it doesn't understand or hass forgotten. Hurt Narwe enough and it always tell."

"I'm not a Narwe!" Derec protested weakly. "Is he too stupid to see that?"

"Aranimas thinks 'u use the Narwe trick," the caninoid said. "Besides, Aranimas iss very angry."

"Why is he angry at me? I didn't do anything to him."

"When Aranimas iss angry, everyone in trouble," the alien said. "Gunners werr not supposed to destroy robot nest."

"They didn't. The robots did it themselves."

"Doesn't matter. Aranimas wanted to capture robots to work forr 'im."

Derec closed his eyes and laid back. "I'm afraid there won't be much to capture."

"Aranimas went to see what salvage team brought back," the alien said. "Eff truly not much, 'e'll be worse when 'e comes back."

"Can't you help me?" Derec pleaded. "You believe me, don't you?"

"Not my job to believe or not believe," the caninoid shrugged. "Can't 'elp."

With a sigh, Derec lowered himself back to a reclining position and closed his eyes. "Then he is going to kill me, because I don't have anything to tell him. And maybe that's just as well."

The caninoid reclaimed the cup from Derec's hand and stood up. "Perfect Narwe thought. Don't let Aranimas 'ear 'u."

Dozing, the first Derec knew of Aranimas's return was when the alien seized him by the arm and hauled him roughly to a sitting position.

"It's time to stop playing," Aranimas said. "I grow impatient."

"That was playing?" Derec said lightly. "You people have some funny ideas about games. Remind me not to play cutthroat eight-card with you."

At that, the caninoid, crouching in a doorway a few meters away, closed its eyes and began to shake its head. Aranimas's answer was to reach inside his clothing for the stylus.

"Wait," Derec said quickly, holding up a hand palm out. "You don't need that."

"Have you decided to share your knowledge after all?"

"I always was willing to. You just didn't want what I had to offer."

"I will know who you are and what you know about the object you brought aboard," Aranimas said.

Derec slid off the edge of the bench and found his feet. Aranimas still dwarfed him, but even so, he felt better standing. "The fact is, you know as much as I do about who I am, and I wouldn't be surprised if you knew more than I do about the silver box. But there is something I know more about than you do, and that's robots. How did your prospecting go?"

One of Aranimas's eyes cast a baleful glance in the direction of the caninoid, which hunched its shoulders and retreated from the doorway. "They brought back fragments only," Aranimas said. "Your robots were very efficient about destroying themselves."

"They weren't my robots," Derec said. "But why don't you show me what you have?"

Aranimas lowered his arms to his side and slowly massaged his knees with his hands while he weighed Derec's proposition. "Yes," he said finally. "That will be a good test of your intentions and usefulness. I will have you build me a robot."

Derec's face paled. "What?"

"If you truly do not know who you are, then you have no loyalties or obligations to any other master. When you have built me a robot servant I will know that you have accepted your place serving me."

Derec knew better than to pick that moment to make a noble speech about freedom and choice, but he still could not simply accept Aranimas's terms. "What if I can't build you a robot out of what you have? I said I knew a lot about them. I didn't say I could manufacture one out of good intentions. I need certain key parts—"

"If you fail, I will know that you are either unreliable or have no usefulness to me at all," Aranimas said, "and that I should not waste valuable consumables keeping you alive."

Derec swallowed hard. "What are we waiting for? Show me your inventory."

• • •

Aranimas had not been minimizing the problem when he termed what the scavengers had recovered from the asteroid "fragments." I would have said scrap, he thought as he stood in the ship's hold surveying the raiders' paltry booty. The largest intact piece was the one Derec himself had brought aboard—Monitor 5's arm. The next largest was a Supervisor's knee joint. Chances were that it was from Monitor 5 as well.

No other piece was bigger than the palm of Derec's hand: a badly scorched regulator, an optical sensor with a cracked lens, bits of structural forms like shards of broken pottery. There were no positronic brains and no microfusion powerpacks—the two absolutely indispensable items.

And all the Crown's horses and all the Crown's men couldn't put the robots together again, he thought. "Is this all you have?" he asked with a heavy heart.

Mercifully, it was not. In one of the storage corridors, he was shown two tall lockers, each of which contained a nearly intact robot.

"I see this isn't a new hobby of yours," Derec said, stepping forward to examine the collection. The new robots were of a familiar domestic design. He would know more about where they had come from and what they had been used for when he used a microscanner on the serial number plates found at various sites on the robots' bodies. Clearly, though, he was not the first human the raiders had encountered.

There seemed to be enough good parts to make about one and a half robots. One of the robots was headless, and the mounting circle on the neck was twisted and deformed. That told Derec something about the circumstances under which the robots had been acquired.

More important at the moment, it meant there was only

one positronic brain. But there was no guarantee that it was functional. The upper torso of the other robot was torn open at the chest as though by some sort of projectile weapon, and the right shoulder area was rippled as though it had been seared by intense heat. Not only did that hold out little hope for the key components located in the torso, but it also virtually guaranteed that the brain's powerdown had been anything but orderly.

But at least there was something to work with, and an outside chance, at least, of success. Derec stepped back from the lockers and turned to look up at Aranimas.

"So what do you have in the way of an engineering lab around here?" he asked with a breeziness that was more show than real. "I'm ready to get to work."

Aranimas nodded gravely. "I will give you that opportunity."

Answering Derec's query about a place to work meant going deeper into the confusing maze of the raider ship. Unlike when he had been inside the asteroid, Derec found it impossible to retain any sense of direction. There were too many turns, too short sight lines, and too few absolute references. Once he lost track of where he was in relation to the command center, it was over.

Despite being lost, Derec was still collecting useful information with every step. He learned that different parts of the ship had slightly different atmospheres, and the storage corridors acted as interlocks between them. In one section, something in the air made Derec feel as though a furry ball were caught in his throat. In another, yellowish tears ran from Aranimas's eyes. Only the caninoid seemed at home in all the atmospheres.

The ship was not only a maze, but a zoo as well, featuring at least four species. Derec saw five of Aranimas's kin, all of high rank to judge by the activities Derec saw them engaged in. Curiously, the caninoid seemed to be the only one of his kind aboard.

Most numerous were the gaunt-faced Narwe, several of whom had been recruited by Aranimas to carry the robot parts. The Narwe were short bald-headed bipeds with gnarled skull ridges like false horns, which made them look fierce and formidable. But it was clearly only protective coloring, for Aranimas and the caninoid alike cuffed and bullied the Narwe without fear.

The fourth species was the most interesting and the most elusive. Inside the compartment where Aranimas's eyes began to tear, Derec caught a glimpse of a strange five-limbed wall-clinging creature not unlike a giant sea star. It retreated as they approached, and was gone from sight by the time they reached the spot.

Fascinated as Derec was by the parade of alien biologies, he was also concerned about having so casual a contact with them. He knew that his own body was host to a rich biotic community: bacteria, viruses, fungi, and parasites. He did not know just how different the aliens were from him. He hoped they were wildly different. The more similar their fundamental structure was to his, the greater the risk that his symbiotes could endanger them or theirs endanger him.

He could only hope that Aranimas had either taken precautions or determined that no precautions were necessary. He based that hope on the fact that the raiders had evidently had some previous contact with humans. The scavenged robots and the aliens' command of Standard proved that.

But that was another mystery for his lengthening list. Derec was positive that human beings had never crossed paths with even one intelligent alien lifeform, much less with four of them. To understand interplanetary politics, he had to know history and economics, but not xenobiology.

Did the raiders' presence mean that he was far out on the fringes of human space? Or had knowledge of the contacts been made a state secret, meant only for those with a need to know? Were the raiders pirates, prospectors, or pioneers? Had they perhaps come looking for the same thing the robots had been looking for? And having found it, were they carrying him toward their home, or his?

They were questions with serious consequences. Tensions were high enough between Earth and the Spacers without any random factors to jumble the picture. An attack of the sort Derec had already witnessed, directed against one of the many human worlds with no planetary defense net, could bring on war.

Which brought Derec back to the silver artifact. If it was as important as the robots' search for it implied, if it was powerful enough or important enough for the raiders to come after it, then it was too important and too powerful to be left in the raiders' hands. As much as he hated to be thinking about anyone's problems but his own, Derec had an obligation to try to reclaim it for humanity.

Mercifully, the lab was located in a section with a normal atmosphere, though the air was a bit warm and dry. While Aranimas settled into a chair and supervised the Narwe's arrangement of the robot parts on the open areas of the floor, Derec browsed the workbench and wall racks with the caninoid at his elbow to answer questions. By the time he finished, the Narwe were gone.

"Explain each step as you perform it," Aranimas said, crossing his arms as though settling in.

"Do you intend to sit there and watch?"

"I intend to learn what you know."

"Then I hope you're a patient sort," Derec said.

"According to your story, it took you only a short time to convert an article of clothing into an escape propulsion system," Aranimas said. "This should require even less time, since you only need to turn a robot into a robot."

"You've got to be kidding," Derec said, throwing his hands in the air. "I'm not sure I'm going to be able to do it at all, much less in an hour or two."

"Explain the problem," Aranimas said.

Derec bit back a laugh. In the hopes of loosening the noose Aranimas had around his neck, Derec had been rehearsing complaints that the equipment in the lab was ill suited, too crude, anything to lower Aranimas's expectations.

But his dismay was real, not manufactured. He had prepared himself for instruments designed for nonhuman hands, to having to have one of the raiders at his elbow coaching him. But he had not been prepared to do without what he thought of as the basics.

"The problem is you don't have the right tools," Derec said. "I need a diagnostic bench, an etcher, micromanipulators—There's nothing in here that would even pass for a chip mask or circuit tracer—"

Even as he spoke, he realized that he should not have been surprised. Aranimas would not be so curious about robots, would not need to have Derec repair them, if the culture which he represented were capable of making them. The fact that the raiders employed gunners instead of autotargeting systems should have tipped him off that their computer technology was deficient.

Aranimas stood. "Such tools as are available will be brought to you. Describe what you need to Rrullf"—Aranimas's shortened version of the caninoid's name was almost pronounceable—"and she will bring them to you or take you to them."

She? Derec cast a surprised glance at the caninoid. *Interesting.*

"Thank you," he said to Aranimas, and started to turn away. As he did, a thousand bees settled between his shoulder blades and began to sting him wildly. Gasping, his knees buckling, he grabbed for the edge of the workbench to keep from collapsing on the floor. He did not need to see to know that Aranimas had the stylus trained at the middle of his back.

"Do not make the mistake of trying to deceive me," Aranimas said coldly as the pain held Derec firmly in its grip. "I may be ignorant of your art, but I am not foolish."

"I–I–"

"Save your words of apology," Aranimas said as the bees flew away. "Show me results."

Doubled over the workbench, Derec turned his head in time to see Aranimas return the stylus to whatever hidden pocket was reserved for it. Clearing the phlegm from his throat, he nodded weakly. "Right, boss."

When Aranimas was gone, the caninoid's face twisted into its macabre grin. " 'Urr lucky Aranimas wants robots so bad. Otherwise I guess 'u be dead now."

"Thanks for the cheery thought," Derec said. "What exactly does he want them for?"

"Can't 'u figure? Aranimas wants to replace Narwe with robots. Aranimas iss sick of Narwe crying scenes."

"Do the Narwe know what he has in mind?"

"Narwe been on best behavior since the boss told them," the caninoid said cheerfully. "What 'u need to work?"

But Derec had been thinking about something else. The caninoid was treating him in a way that could only be called friendly, and was the best prospect for an ally aboard the raider ship besides. If they were going to be working together, it was time for Derec to stop thinking of the alien as *it*. Or even *she*.

"First things first. I can't say your name even as well as Aranimas does—"

"Thass pretty low standard."

"—but I have to call you something. Can you live with Wolruf?"

"Iss not my name, but I know who 'u mean when 'u say it."

"That's all I wanted. Wolruf, I've got some fine print to read. What can you find me to read it with?"

"I get 'u something," she promised.

The magnifying scanner that Wolruf came up with was an inspection instrument of some sort. It had a display screen rather than an eyepiece, a fixed focus, and a tiny field of view. But the incident lighting at the aperture highlighted perfectly the fine grooves of the serial number engraving, making up for all the other shortcomings.

With Wolruf peering over his shoulder, Derec scanned the fifteen lines of data. "Do you read Standard, too?"

"No," Wolruf said. "Tell 'u a secret—I learn Standard so I not 'ave to lissen to Aranimas mangle my language."

Derec laughed, and the sound startled Wolruf. "What I'm looking at is one of the robot's identification gratings. It'll tell me several things that will help me fix the damage— the manufacturer, the model, the date of initialization, any customization parameters," he said breezily.

He went on like that awhile longer, loading his explanation with as many technical terms as he could in the hopes of appearing to be open and cooperative while actually explaining nothing. He did not mention that if the robot were from Earth, the grating would also tell who owned it, or that the three cryptic lines of symbols at the bottom of the screen were the programming access codes and the initialization sequence, the keys that would allow him to do more than merely repair the robot, but to alter its programming.

"What does it say?"

"This one is a Ferrier Model EG," Derec said, scanning. "Customized for valet service." And personal defense, he added silently. A bodyguard robot. "Initialization date, Standard Year '83—"

Then he scanned a few words ahead and was struck dumb.

"What is it?" Wolruf asked. "Is something wrong?"

"No," Derec managed to say. "The robot was registered on Aurora."

"That iss one of 'urr worlds?"

"Yes."

"Iss that important?"

"No," Derec said. "Let's look at the other one."

But it *was* important, and his hands were trembling as he took the scanner in them and rose from his seat. He remembered Aurora. He *remembered* the World of the Dawn. Not the things that everyone knew—that it was the first Spacer world and long the preeminent one, that it was home to the highly regarded Institute of Robotics from which most advances in robotic science had emerged.

No, like a ray of light sneaking past the black curtain, Derec remembered Aurora as a place he had been: glimpses of a spaceport, a parklike city, a pastoral countryside. He was connected with it in some way, some way strong enough that the word alone had the power to break through the wall separating him from his past.

At last, he knew something about himself. He had been to Aurora. It was not much of a biography, but it was a beginning.

CHAPTER 9

ALLY

Without a diagnostic board or even a computer at his disposal, Derec had no choice but to activate the robot and rely on its own self-diagnostic capabilities. But before he could get even that far, he had a jigsaw puzzle to assemble.

The headless robot was an EX series, but the differences did not affect the parts Derec needed to borrow to make the EG whole. The active systems—as opposed to the merely structural—of any mass-produced robot were modular and standardized. It would not have been possible to produce them economically any other way. So the kidney-sized microfusion powerpack of the EX was a plug-compatible replacement for the damaged one inside the EG.

But the powerpack's mounting cradle, which contained the interface for the primary power bus, had also been damaged by the fight which had downed the robot. Regrettably, the cradle had not been designed for field replacement, and it seemed to be attached to every other component inside the EG's torso—and not by convenient micromagnetic fields.

The manufacturer had settled for the less costly alternative of sonic welds.

Lacking the proper tools, swapping the cradles was a challenge. He practiced on the damaged cradle inside the EG, then used his hard-won expertise to transfer the undamaged one into the vacancy. That alone took more than two hours. But when he was done, it took less than two minutes to swap powerpacks.

Unfortunately, that did not end the matter. In all Ferrier models, the basic data library used by the robot was contained in removable memory cubes placed in a compartment just behind its "collarbone." The robot's extensive positronic memory was reserved completely for the business of learning from experience.

From the manufacturer's standpoint, that arrangement meant that the positronic brains did not have to be specialized according to the robot's function. From the owner's viewpoint, it meant that their investment was protected against obsolescence or changing needs.

But from Derec's perspective, it meant trouble. The headless robot had five cube slots, four of them occupied. For the EG, the numbers were seven and five. But the two empty slots and three of the occupied ones had been caught in the same blast that had damaged the power cradle.

There was no repairing them and no replacing them. But what was worse was that Derec was bound to use one of the two functional slots for the standard Systems cube, without which the robot would know nothing about its own structure and operation. He had five cubes packed full of data and logic routines, and he could only use one of them at a time. Eventually he settled on the Mathematics cube, concealing the Personal Defense cube for possible use at some future time.

Derec's inventory of visible damage to the robot included severed cables that would render the right arm paralyzed and a frozen gimbal on one of the dual gyroscopes. But with power and the working library restored, there was only one truly critical part left to see to: the positronic brain.

In appearance, the brain was a three-pound lump of platinum-iridium. In function, it was the repository for the fundamental positromotive potentials governing the robot's activity, for the temporary potentials which represented thought and decision, and for the pathways which represented learning.

What Derec was hoping was that the fundamental pathways had not been randomized, as could happen if the brain had been exposed to hard radiation. There was no hope for the robot's experience base. The backup microcell, used to refresh the pathways while the robot was being serviced, had long since been exhausted and the pathways had long ago decayed. The robot would remember nothing of its previous service. But if the brain was undamaged, it should function normally when reinitiated.

Just like me—

Given the equipment available, the only way to test the condition of the positronic brain was to activate the robot and test it. For obvious reasons, that was dangerous. At one point in the history of robotics, robots had been designed to shut down when they detected any internal error conditions. But several hundred years of progress in robotics design had produced a different philosophy built around fault-tolerance and self-maintenance. He could not be sure what would happen.

By the time he was ready to find out, Wolruf had either grown bored or was obliged to go tend to some other duty.

That was a fortunate turn, since when the robot was activated, it would be facing a situation that no robot had ever faced before. It would have to decide whether Aranimas and Wolruf were "human" enough that it was required to protect them and obey their orders.

Since robots were as a rule literal-minded to a fault, it should not have been a problem. Aranimas was clearly an alien, despite his superficially humanoid appearance. Wolruf was even more so.

Those who manufactured robots did not ordinarily limit the definition of a human being, but left it as broad as possible. A power plant worker in a max suit did not look human, but a robot would obey its order. Robots were not, could not be, completely literal. They did not judge merely on appearance. A three-year-old child was human, yet a robot would frequently decline its orders.

It was possible that the programming which permitted those distinctions would find some fundamental identity between the aliens and Derec. If there was any way of preventing that, Derec was determined to do so. Because of the First Law, the robot could not be used against him. But if the robot could be persuaded that the aliens were not entitled to protection under the First Law, he might be able to use the robot against Aranimas.

With some trepidation, Derec pressed the power reset. A moment later, all of the robot's joints except those in the damaged arm stiffened. Its eyes lit up with a red glow that pulsed rhythmically.

"Alpha alpha epsilon rho," Derec said, repeating the sequence of Greek letters which had appeared on the ID grating. "Sigma tau sigma."

There was a brief pause, and then the robot's eyes began to glow steadily. "My default language is Galactic Standard,

Auroran dialect," it said. "No other language banks are currently available. Is that acceptable, sir?"

Derec broke into a smile. After his frustrations with the robots on the asteroid, it was a pleasure to be addressed civilly again. "Auroran Galactic is fine."

"Yes, sir. Who is my owner, sir?"

"I am," Derec said. "You are never to acknowledge that to anyone. But if you ever receive conflicting orders from myself and another, my orders are always to take precedence."

"Yes, sir. By what name may I call you, sir?"

For some reason, Derec resented having to supply the robot with his meaningless, casually adopted name. "Derec," he said finally, unable to think of an alternative.

"Yes, sir. To what name would you like me to respond?"

Derec suppressed a bitter laugh. Who am I to tell you your name, when I can't even tell myself mine? "So long as you are the only one on this ship, Alpha is name enough."

"Thank you, Derec. During my power-on self-test I detected a number of error states. Would this be a convenient time to review them?"

"In a moment," Derec said. "Can you scan this compartment?"

"Yes, sir."

"Are there any spyeyes here with us?"

"I detect no active sensors of any sort, Derec."

"Good. Listen closely. I need to tell you something about what's happening. You and I are on board a spaceship populated by hostile lifeforms. These lifeforms are a potential threat to both of us. Until I tell you otherwise, you are to immediately enter a passive wait-state any time we have company or I leave the lab."

"I understand. You do not wish them to know that I am functional."

"That's right."

"Is it possible that these wait-states will be of extended duration, sir?"

"It is."

"Then may I ask if there are any problems to which I may devote myself during those periods?"

"I'm sure we'll find some," Derec said. "Right now, the problem is getting you in shape. Let's have the first anomaly off your error list."

The first that Derec knew of Wolruf's return was when the robot stiffened suddenly and its eyes went black. A few seconds later, the caninoid entered the lab and crossed to where Derec was seated. She stood at Derec's elbow and peered briefly into the exposed inner mechanisms of the robot, then turned to him. She seemed less animated than she had been earlier.

"Aranimas would like a report on 'urr progress."

"You can tell Aranimas that I have reason to hope I'll have a robot for him in a few days."

" 'Ow many days?"

"I don't know," Derec said, laying down the pen he had been using as a probe. "I also don't know how much it'll be able to do. I've replaced a few damaged components. Right now I'm trying to do something with the servo linkages for the right arm, which are really a mess. Was it you people who roughed up these robots, or did you find them this way?"

"Can't say," Wolruf said, and headed for the door. "I tell Aranimas."

"Hold on a moment," Derec said, standing. "You can also tell him that I don't work around the clock. I need time to rest and a place to do it."

"Rest 'ard to get on Aranimas's ship," Wolruf said, gesturing toward the floor. "Sleep 'ere."

That was not an entirely unhappy prospect, since Derec had already determined that he had some privacy there. "What about a pillow, some kind of cushion?"

The caninoid made a sort of whistling sound that Derec read as a sigh. "I get 'u something," she said, and started to go.

"Am I going to be allowed to eat?" he called after her.

The sigh was a wheeze this time. "I get 'u something."

"Tell you what, Wolruf," Derec said, drawing closer. "Why don't you show me where the food is kept, so I can get it myself when I'm hungry? That'll save you some running around on my account."

Wolruf wrinkled her cheeks in surprise, then frowned. "Aranimas wants 'u working, not running errands. Thass my job."

"You've got enough things to do without all the extra work I'm creating," Derec said on a hunch. "If Aranimas makes a fuss, I'll tell him I insisted. If I'm going to do my best work, I'm going to need to get out of that lab from time to time just to clear my mind."

Cocking her head, Wolruf considered. "Okay. I show 'u."

"Great. Ah—one more thing." The thought of an alien Personal was an unpleasant one, but he was suddenly aware that there was some urgency. "I have—um—excretory needs. Do you also—ah—is there—"

Wolruf laughed, a sound like purring. "Of course. Come, I show 'u that, too."

• • •

There seemed to be fewer aliens afoot in the ship at that hour, which started Derec wondering about the sleep cycles observed by the various species aboard. The curiosity stayed in his mind while Wolruf showed him the Personal, identified to him the three foods in the pantry considered safe for him, and escorted him back to the lab. By that time, he was certain that she was fatigued, and when she left him, he was certain that it was for an appointment with a bed.

There was no lock on the lab door. There was no Narwe guard to note his comings and goings. The opportunity was there, if he wanted it. Wolruf would not disturb him. Perhaps Aranimas was now sleeping as well. Derec could scout the layout of the ship, snoop in some of the hundreds of storage bins he had seen.

Or perhaps Aranimas was waiting for a report from Wolruf, and might soon be coming to check Derec's progress personally. Or perhaps he never slept. Perhaps his mind was structured in a way that he did not need the periodic "dumpings" dreams represented, his metabolism clocked at a steady pace rather than cycling through active and passive periods.

The uncertainty stilled Derec's impulse to go exploring, at least for a time. Turning to the food he had carried back with him, he gnawed at a few of the thick crackerlike biscuits, ate most of the fatty mottled-blue paste, sipped at the honey juice. Though his taste buds regarded it all with suspicion, none of it alarmed his stomach.

When he was done, his own fatigue was pressing in on him. He placed Alpha in a wait-state, then unrolled the thin cushion in an open spot of floor and stretched out. The cushion did little to make the floorplates less hard. He supposed that Aranimas, slender as he was, would have found it entirely suitable. But Derec turned restlessly from back to side to stomach in a fruitless quest for a comfortable position.

How long had it been since he had slept? Thirty hours? Forty? He had started the day a reluctant prisoner of the robots, and now he was an even more reluctant prisoner of the raiders. *I really should go snooping*, he thought. He could not let the opportunity pass. Perhaps the absence of a guard was an oversight that would be corrected tomorrow.

I'll just lie here for an hour or so, he told himself, make sure that Aranimas isn't going to show up, give Wolruf a chance to settle in. Then it'll be safe. I can rest a little while. This poor excuse for a bed is too hard to sleep on anyway—

He was wrong. One moment he was closing his eyes against the uncomfortably bright light which he had not been told how to douse. The next, he was rubbing sleep out of those eyes, gingerly stretching sore muscles, and bemoaning his own foul breath. The room was in semidarkness, but Wolruf was crouching in the doorway, silhouetted against the well-lit corridor.

"Iss it done yet?" Wolruf asked brightly.

"Eat space and die," Derec growled, and threw the nearest rock-sized bit of robot scrap in Wolruf's direction. The caninoid snatched it neatly out of the air and threw it back in one motion.

"No thanks," she said with a curled-lip grin. "I already 'ad breakfast."

Though there was running water in the Personal, there was no provision for a shower or bath. Derec settled for sponging himself off, though there were no blowers and the only toweling available was harsh and scratchy. By the time he emerged, Wolruf was nowhere in sight. Derec wondered if she had perhaps stopped by only to waken him and would not be coming back.

Thinking that it wouldn't take him long to get tired of the fare, he carried another meal of biscuits, cheese, and honey back to the lab. Settling at the workbench, he resumed work on the robot's right arm. The electrical connections were sound, but the servo linkages were damaged beyond Derec's ability to repair. His efforts to do so only made things worse. Whatever skill he had was cybernetic, not electromechanical.

"Alpha, I don't think I can fix your arm. I'm wondering if you can, with your good arm. I could get a mirror so you could see inside—"

"I am sorry. Without a Robotech cube in my library, my abilities in this area are limited to diagnosis only, sir."

"I figured as much," Derec said. "But it never hurts to ask."

"Sir, I detect a deactivated robot in the room. Perhaps it would be possible to salvage the appropriate parts from its mechanism to repair me."

"That's what I've been trying to do," Derec said gruffly. "I can't do it, not without micromanipulators. Besides, there's some structural damage in the shoulder mount, which isn't replaceable."

Sighing, Derec pushed himself back from the bench and crossed to where his paltry inventory of robot parts lay spread out on the floor. As it had many times before, his gaze fell on Monitor 5's arm. For the first time, he picked it up and examined it closely.

"I guess you're just going to have to make do with one wing," he said. "There's a lot of it going around."

The robot made no reply. Derec turned the Monitor's arm over and tried to flex the elbow. It resisted—consistent with the fact that the hand had been locked in a literal death grip on the silver artifact.

Consistent, Derec realized with a sudden shock, except that the arm contained no joints. Not at the elbow, not at the wrist, not at the knuckle. Oh, the elbow was bent at an obtuse angle, the wrist twisted slightly, the fingers curled. But insofar as he could tell from looking at it, the arm was incapable of movement.

There were any number of syntheskin coverings which would flex and wrinkle realistically while masking joints. But this was no covering. It was rigid to the touch and absolutely seamless, like a plastic casting. Puzzled, Derec carried it back to where the robot sat.

"What magnification are your optical sensors capable of?"

"Only a limited amount, sir—one hundred power."

"At what resolution?"

"That would vary with the distance of the object being observed, sir. The maximum resolution is approximately ten micrometers."

"That's better than I can do with that thing," Derec said, nodding toward the inspection scanner. "See what you can tell me about the structure of this arm."

"Sir, I am not knowledgeable in this area."

"You can see and you can describe. I'll settle for that at the moment."

"Yes, sir. May I hold the limb?"

Derec surrendered the arm, and the robot held it at eye level in its rock-steady grip. "At ten power, the surface is undifferentiated. Increasing magnification now. Granularity becoming evident. There seems to be a regular pattern. Pattern resolving now into hexagonal planar surfaces. Maximum magnification." The robot paused for a fraction of a second. "The surface appears to consist of twelve-sided solids in close association."

"What?"

"The surface appears—"

"I heard you. Look at another spot."

The robot turned his head slightly to the left. "I observe the same pattern."

"The end," Derec snapped. "Look at the end, where it broke off."

"The surface is much more irregular, but it is made up of the same dodecahedral units."

"All the way through?"

"Yes, Derec."

Derec stood staring, dumbfounded. What the robot had described suggested a completely new approach to robotic design—not an evolution, but a revolution. It sounded as though the Supervisor robots had been built—no, it couldn't be.

"Kill your right shoulder control bus," Derec snapped.

"The circuits are now inert," the robot said.

Derec separated the three-conductor control wire from the damaged right arm and threaded it out through the opening where he had been working. He touched the connector to the stump end of the Supervisor arm, and it clung there as though it belonged.

"Activate the control circuit. Send a command to bend the elbow."

Almost instantly, the disembodied Supervisor arm slowly began to flex. "Look at the joint," Derec demanded. "Tell me what's happening."

"The changes are taking place more quickly than my scan rate allows me to observe," the robot said. "However,

I infer that the dodecahedrons are undergoing some type of directed rearrangement."

"Flowing into a new shape. The material of the arm is transforming itself."

"Those descriptors are imprecise but consistent with my observations. The technical term for such reorganization is morphallaxis."

Derec felt for his chair and sat down shakily. The Supervisors had been built out of billions of tiny crystal-shaped modules—a cellular structure. Each had to contain kilometers of circuit connections, megabytes of programming. It was the cells that were the robots. The robots were more like organisms.

What a feat of engineering they represented—the essence of a robot in a package a few microns in diameter. Properly programmed, they could take on any shape. A Supervisor was an infinity of specialized forms held within one generalized package.

As he marveled, Derec was reminded of something he had not thought about for several days. The cellular design bore the same distinctive stamp that the asteroid colony's lifts and environmental system had. Superficial simplicity—achieved on the strength of hidden complexity. Elegance of design, novelty of approach. It was another brush with the minimalist designer, and it gave Derec one more reason to seek to escape from the raiders.

Because somehow, somewhere, he had to meet the designer.

CHAPTER 10

MORE THAN SEMANTICS

After a short break for a late lunch of the same monotonous foods, Derec set about installing the cellular arm in place of the robot's original limb.

It was not an easy task, requiring both structural and functional marriages between two wildly divergent technologies. Derec worried about the functional link first, and not only because he expected it to be the tougher challenge. If the robot could not control the new arm, there was no point in going to the trouble of attaching it.

But the cellular arm apparently used the standard command set and carrier voltages. Though there was no evidence of any contacts or wiring in the stump end, the arm responded no matter where Derec attached the control bus.

Experimenting, he found that the arm responded even if he attached the control bus to the skin of the forearm, the palm of the hand, even the tips of two fingers. It seemed as though the cellular microrobots were smart enough to accept the command input from any location and channel it to the appropriate sites.

Once attached, the arm responded not only to all the robot's basic motor commands, but even to some novel commands. With coaching from Derec, the robot was able to "think" an additional joint onto his arm between the elbow and wrist. In another test, Derec asked the robot to try to modify the cellular thumb and forefinger into long, slender microclamps. To his delight and amazement, it could. With the right command codes, the material of the arm seemed to be infinitely malleable.

But no matter how Derec prepared the mounting ring the arm was connected to, the right shoulder joint remained weaker than the left was or the original had been. At one point, the cellular arm broke loose completely when the robot tried to lift an object weighing less than twenty kilos. Even after he reattached it, Derec had doubts it would withstand the stresses of, for instance, a brawl.

"Looks like you're going to have one strong arm and one smart one," he told the robot. "Try not to forget which is which."

"It is not possible for me to forget, sir."

"This isn't an off-the-shelf replacement," Derec said sternly. "Until you've burned what it can do and can't do into your pathways, you be careful with it. And never let anyone but me see you doing tricks with it, understand?"

While Derec was talking, the robot went rigid and its eyes dimmed. Derec knew what that meant, and fell silent. A moment later her heard the soft padding of Wolruf's footsteps in the corridor. It was becoming a familiar sound, for it was Wolruf's third visit to the lab that day. Aranimas, apparently occupied with the duties of "ship's boss," had managed only two.

Like the previous visits, this one was casual. Wolruf had no messages for him and no burning curiosity about what he was doing with the robot. It was almost as though she was using checking on him as an excuse to avoid other work, or trying to cultivate his friendship. But Derec kept up his guard. Wolruf was Aranimas's lieutenant, no matter how sympathetic she might seem. Even her concern for him while he was being tortured, he had decided, was nothing more than a good cop, bad cop stage show meant to speed his surrender.

As before, Wolruf stayed but a few minutes, then continued on to some other task. As soon as she was out of earshot, the robot reanimated.

"I understand, sir," it said, as though there had been no interruption.

"The next time you have to go down like that, you might spend your time trying to analyze the arm's command set. Can you do that?"

"I can try, sir. It should be possible to separate those command codes which are valid from those which are nulls. However, I will have to be fully functional to test the valid codes and determine their function."

"Let's wait on that until we know we're going to have some privacy." He paused a moment to decide what he needed doing next. There was still the matter of reprogramming the robot, but that was also a job which required some assurance of privacy. The best opportunity seemed to be during shipboard night, which was also the best time to explore the ship.

Too much to do, too little time, Derec thought. But if he was going to make better use of the night hours than he had last night, he needed to be better rested. "Alpha."

"Yes, Derec."

"What time is it?"

"I do not know what time it is, since my temporal register has not been reset since I was deactivated. However, it has been fourteen decads since reinitialization."

Decads were units of Auroran decimal time, Derec recalled. "I'm going to take a nap. Wake me in a Standard hour."

"Yes, sir."

But it was Aranimas, not the robot, who woke him.

"Are you finished? Is my servant ready?" he demanded, looming over Derec like some long-limbed water bird.

"Not yet," Derec said sleepily, sitting up. He noted with satisfaction that the robot was standing inert by the workbench. It, at least, had not been taken by surprise.

"Then why do you rest? To keep me waiting?"

"I rest so I don't get so tired that I make a mistake that'll damage the robot," Derec said. "Maybe your kind doesn't have that need, but humans do."

Aranimas did not take offense at Derec's tone. "I have observed that humans are even less efficient than Narwe. You would make very poor workers, wasting one third of your time in rest." He turned his back on Derec and went to where the robot stood. "But then perhaps that is why you have invented such machines, which labor in your service tirelessly. How is it done?"

"What do you mean?" Derec asked, coming to his feet.

"What is the source of energy?" Aranimas asked, tracing a line down the robot's torso with his long fingers.

Derec knew that being evasive or pretending ignorance would only anger the alien. "A microfusion powerpack," he said. "There's one on the bench there, just to the left of the scanner."

Aranimas picked up the damaged powerpack and studied it. "So small. How days' service does it contain?"

"It depends on how hard the robot is working. The fuel capsule is good for several hundred days of light duty, like domestic service. A laborer would obviously need refueling more often."

"Remarkable," Aranimas said, returning the powerpack to the bench. One of his eyes seemed to focus briefly on the transplanted arm, then swung back toward Derec. "You are making progress?"

"I am."

"How long until you are ready to activate it?"

"I'll be ready to start testing its systems tomorrow or the next day. How soon it'll be ready will depend on how much is wrong."

Aranimas seemed to accept that. "The first job of this robot will be to help you make more robots."

Frowning, Derec stepped forward. "How many more?"

"We will begin with fifty."

Derec wondered if that figure represented the number of Narwe on board. He briefly enjoyed the thought of Aranimas replacing his browbeaten crew with an array of obedient robots, only to discover that, at a word from Derec, he couldn't command them at all. But he could not kid himself or allow Aranimas to entertain unreasonable expectations.

"I don't think you understand the complexity of these machines," Derec said. "They're not something you put together as a hobby, no matter how good a materials lab you have. And frankly, this isn't a very good one. I'll probably be able to get this robot put together and keep it repaired. But if you want fifty robots, you're going to have to look somewhere else for them. I'm not magician enough to pull positronic brains or microfusion cells out of a hat."

"If you had not destroyed your robot colony—," Aranimas said, his voice rising.

"I told you before, the robots did that on their own," Derec insisted. "But that doesn't mean you're stuck. You take this ship to any Spacer world and you'll find millions of robots. And you won't have to steal them, either. Robots are a major trade item between the worlds. Any one of them would be happy for a new customer."

That was not entirely true, of course. It was highly doubtful the Spacers would willingly turn over examples of their most advanced technology to an alien race, and even if they were willing, there was the problem of what Aranimas could offer as payment. But if Derec could make Aranimas believe it was the truth, coax him to take the ship to a human world, he would at least have succeeded in alerting them to the aliens' existence, and possibly have laid the groundwork for his own release.

"If commerce is so welcome, why did your robots destroy themselves?"

"Because you came in firing your weapons and declared yourself an enemy," Derec said. "If you'd come in as a friend, it would have been different. Take me to your navigator. I'll help him set a course for the nearest Spacer world." And find out where we are in the process, he added silently.

"I will evaluate the options," Aranimas said, moving toward the corridor. "In the meantime, you will continue your work. I will return tomorrow to see my robot activated."

The reprogramming could not be postponed any longer, Derec decided, He did not think Aranimas would return soon. He would have to hope that Wolruf would not, either.

Unfortunately, Derec did not have the equipment to alter the robot's programming directly, which would have been risky anyway. Since it was intimately bound up in the Laws of Robotics, the robot's definition of what a human was comprised some of the most crucial and most deeply engraved patterns within its brain. What needed doing would have to be done more indirectly.

"Alpha," he said. "Did you scan the organism that was just here?"

"Yes, Derec."

"And earlier today, did you scan another type of organism visiting the lab?"

"Yes, Derec."

"What'd you think of them?"

"I have no previous knowledge of humans of this type—"

That was the kind of response Derec had been fearing. "Stop. They're not humans."

"Sir, I am aware that my data library is not complete. However, I am unable to categorize them in any other fashion unless you can provide me with evidence for your assertion."

"Compare their appearance with mine."

"Sir, I acknowledge that there are numerous anomalous differences. However, those differences fall in areas where the definition of a human has a wide latitude, such as skin color and covering, dimensions, and vocal timbre. The similarities are in more fundamental areas such as bilateral symmetry, bipedal locomotion, oxygen respiration—"

"They are humanoid, as you are. But they are not human."

"I note your assertion, sir, but I am unable to confirm it."

Derec understood that he was not being called a liar.

When it had no independent knowledge, a robot would ordinarily accept the word of a human as gospel. But a robot was under no obligation to accept a human's claim that it was raining when its own sensors told it otherwise.

This was not that clear-cut an issue, but the robot was biased toward a generous definition of what a human was. Otherwise there was the danger of a robot's being used as an assassin by the simple step of persuading it that its target was not a human. Derec understood, but even so was annoyed. "I suppose that if they had twelve arms and belched fire when they talked, you might believe me."

"Sir, in the matter at hand the morphological considerations are not primary in my analysis."

"Explain. What are the discriminators?"

"Sir, I base my conclusion on the observation that the organisms called Aranimas and Wolruf are intelligent beings capable of independent reasoned thought."

"How do you know?"

"Sir, you carried on a dialogue with each of them. Although humans on occasion talk to nonanimate objects and may give the appearance of carrying on a dialogue with certain animals, I perceived your discussions as having a qualitatively different character."

"Are you saying that because I treated them as human, you have to think of them that way?"

"Where there is uncertainty, as thee may be when a human wears a costume or disguise, I am obliged to use such cues as are available. Your behavior created a strong presumption that Aranimas and Wolruf are human."

"I talk to you the same way I talked to them. Does that make you a human?"

"No, Derec. I am a robot, a technological artifact. To the degree that I may seem to be human, it is only because I have been designed to do so in order to more easily interact with humans."

Derec was growing frustrated. "Tell me this, then. How do you tell the difference between a robot and a human at a distance?"

"Sir, just as I have an operational definition of that class of organisms called humans, I also have one of that class of objects called robots. It is ordinarily possible to distinguish between the two based on the characteristics they do not have in common. It is not a perfect system, however, and may be fooled, as by a humaniform robot of the type developed by Dr. Han Fastolfe."

Derec had to concede the point to the robot. *If only I could show it skin scrapings from the three of us—but if Aranimas or Wolruf happened to have a cellular structure, I'd be no better off. It might even decide its right arm is human—*

"Robot, are Spacers, Settlers, and Earthpeople all human?" he asked suddenly.

"Yes."

"Have you personally observed every member of those groups?"

"No, Derec. There are approximately eight billion Earthpeople, five billion Spacers, and—"

"If you have not observed them individually, how is it you are able to classify them all as human?"

"Spacers and Settlers are descendants of the original human community on Earth," the robot replied. "Therefore, any individual correctly identified as a Settler or Spacer cannot be other than human."

"Why is that?" Derec asked, though he knew the answer.

"They share a phylogenetic relationship. The offspring of a human must be human."

"In other words, what really counts is biology—the genes and DNA humans carry in their cells."

"Yes."

"And the guidelines that are built into your definition of a human are simply shortcuts to make it unnecessary for you to subject everyone you encounter to a biological assay. The final criterion is DNA."

"That is correct, Derec."

"But you have no way of examining a person's DNA directly."

"No, sir."

"Fine. You said that each of the anomalies in Aranimas's appearance fell within the acceptable parameters for natural variation and mutation."

"Yes, sir."

"I ask you to calculate the probability that all of Aranimas's anomalies would appear in a single organism."

The robot scarcely hesitated. "The probability is extremely small."

"And for Wolruf?"

"The probability is somewhat higher, but still on the order of one chance in ten to the fifteenth power."

"In other words, there is less than a one in ten thousand chance that a mutation this extreme would have arisen once in all of human history. And here there are two of them, not only alive at the same time but in the same place, and both as different from each other as they are from me."

"It is quite remarkable. No doubt further study of these individuals would be of great benefit."

Derec sighed exasperatedly. "Listen, my thick-headed

robot friend. Stop thinking one step at a time. Isn't the probability that an independently evolved lifeform might be bipedal, bilateral, and oxygen-breathing greater than the probability that these creatures are mutant humans? Can't Aranimas and Wolruf be intelligent without being human?"

"Yes, that is possible." The robot paused, a sign of great activity in its positronic pathways. "However, since no independently evolved intelligent lifeforms are known, it is difficult to assign a probability to a specific form."

"I challenge your premise," Derec pounced. "Why are most robots humanoid?"

"Higher robots are humanoid because it is a successful generalized design and because—"

"The other reasons don't matter," Derec said. "Apply that standard to the question of Aranimas and Wolruf."

Again the robot paused before answering. "My positromotive potentials are extremely high on both sides of the question," it said at last. "I believe this state may be similar to that which a human describes as confusion."

"Get to the point. What's the verdict?"

"It is my tentative conclusion that Aranimas and Wolruf are not human."

"You are not obliged by the First Law to protect them or the Second Law to obey them?"

"No, Derec."

"Good," he said with relief. "You can live. Now listen closely. I have some important instructions for you concerning our alien hosts—"

CHAPTER 11

TAMPERING

Within the greater world of the raider ship, Derec had been confined to one small island. As he prepared to begin his nocturnal wanderings, that island consisted of the route from the lab (in what he thought of as Hull L) to the dispensary and Personal (in Hull D). Linking the ends of the trail were two sections of storage corridor forming a short transfer tunnel between the hulls. And that was all Derec knew.

He did not know where the lab was in relation to Aranimas's command center, though he felt certain that it was some distance away. For that matter, he did not know the way to any of the other places he had been—the hull where he had seen the star-creatures, the corridor in which he had awoken, the hold from which the salvage team had operated, the section of lockers where the robot parts had been stored. He did not know where Wolruf slept, or where the fifty Narwe were most likely to be found.

The corridor to the dispensary was also the only part of the ship which he had explicit permission to be in. Aranimas had not forbidden him to roam farther afield, but neither had he invited it. It seemed to Derec as though it might be some kind of test. The problem was, he didn't know whether he would fail through action or inaction: by exploring, or by staying close to home.

In the end, Derec set aside his uncertainties with the thought that it was always better to know more than to know less. If Aranimas found out and objected, Derec could always offer the excuse that he was scouting for places and tasks to test the robot.

The ranks of closed lockers in the transfer tunnel had been gnawing at his curiosity for nearly two days, and he started by opening all that were within his reach. He did not know exactly what he had expected to find, but the fact that more than half the lockers were empty came as a surprise.

Those that were full contained some recognizable objects, such as bolts of the cloth from which the Narwe clothing was made, replacement electrodes for the microwelder in the lab, and vacuum-sealed food stores. A few of the lockers were either jammed or locked—Derec could not determine which.

Just as he was finishing in the section closest to the dispensary, one of the false-horned Narwe entered through the single side door. Startled, Derec jumped guiltily, then froze. Without making any sign of acknowledgment Derec could recognize, the alien turned its back and left by the lab-end door, saying nothing.

Alone again, Derec felt foolish, for he had every right to be there and the alien had seen nothing incriminating. But his heart raced as though he had been caught by Aranimas himself. He was not worried about the Narwe trying to stop him, since he was confident that he could be at least as intimidating as Wolruf.

But there was always the chance a Narwe, perhaps hoping to curry favor, would carry a tale to Aranimas and bring him investigating. Since Derec did not want to give Aranimas reasons to mistrust him, he decided he would have to forego rummaging through the lockers, at least as long as there were still Narwe afoot. It was the one activity his excuse would not cover.

Derec next took up a fuller exploration of the two hulls he had ready access to. Three doors down from the Personal in Hull D, he found a compartment containing five deep-cushioned chairs arrayed in a circle and facing inward. At the center of the circle was a pale white globe mounted on a black cylindrical base. The globe was so large that Derec's arms could reach barely halfway around.

But finding did not mean understanding. For all he could divine, the globe could as easily be a religious totem as a communications device, and the compartment as easily a sanctuary as a bridge.

And there was no point in risking his position just to multiply his ignorance. So for the second time in half an hour, Derec altered his strategy. All that mattered was rediscovering the route back to Hull A—Aranimas's quarters—and to Hull T, where the transfer bay and perhaps his augment could be found. Nothing else was of any consequence whatsoever.

There were five exits from the deck of Hull D, two from Hull L, and two from the transfer tunnel. He considered simply taking one and following it wherever it led, but he did not trust himself to find his way back.

Instead, he worked at expanding the boundaries of his

known world slowly. Each time he opened a new door and started off on an unfamiliar corridor, he would turn left and then left again as soon as possible in the hopes of returning in a loop to some part of the world he knew. Only when he had memorized each of those additions would he take a branch off a branch.

The first time, his strategy worked. The side door in the transfer tunnel led him, three turns later, to Hull L, one deck down from the lab. Despite the fact that he sighted two Narwe along the way, the success gave him a rush of confidence.

But then it began to get messy. The other exit from the lab level of Hull L went on through seven sections with no side branches. Possibly it went on still farther, but Derec would never know, since he grew timid and turned back.

One of the exits from Hull D led down a sloping ramp into a weapons turret occupied by one of Aranimas's kin and a Narwe—another hasty retreat. Another, farther aft, led to one of the hexagonal junction points. He chose a door at random and found himself in another junction.

There was just no way around it. The ship was an impenetrable maze, its key elements linked in a hopelessly inefficient and disorderly manner. Derec could think of only two explanations for it. One had to do with defense. The arrangement probably served to disguise the crucial targets, and was certain to frustrate intruders.

The other explanation was that the ship was just what it appeared to be—a jury-rigged mishmash of ships that had never been intended to be joined together.

Whichever was the case, Derec was on the verge of concluding that the ship was too complex for him ever to hold its plan in his head, when he felt a queer momentary sensation of being turned inside out. The moment he felt it, he started back toward the laboratory, his jaw set in a grim expression. He wanted to believe it was only a moment of dizziness, a sign of creeping fatigue, but he could not.

For the feeling was nothing new to Derec. It was a Jump, that oddly incomprehensible, almost mystical, momentary transition through hyperspace that transferred a ship and all it contained from one point in space to another, light-years away. Wherever they had been, they were somewhere else now. Far away from the asteroid base—far away from any ship that might have been en route there to rescue him.

He should have guessed that the raiders had Jump technology, for the design of the ship would never have stood up to any sort of conventional propulsion. But he had not, and the discovery jolted him, bringing back full force the feeling of powerlessness that he had felt in the robots' custody.

No one's going to find me now, he thought despairingly. *Not if I live to be a thousand—*

The lab was empty except for the robot when Derec reached it.

"Alpha."

"Yes, Derec."

"Did you monitor a Jump a short time ago?"

"No, Derec. Since the reflexes of my positronic brain are so much faster than yours, robots do not experience the disorientation common among humans."

"Then you can't tell me anything about it—how far we might have Jumped."

"Without knowing the power curve of the vessel's drive, I would not have been able to interpolate from the duration of the Jump in any case," the robot said. "However, that does not rule out secondhand evidence concerning our destination."

"What secondhand evidence? Where did you get it?"

"Sir, Aranimas and Wolruf held a discussion about this in my presence."

"When?"

"This evening, less than one decad ago. It was my impression that they had come here to find you, but in your absence lingered to examine me. Wolruf described the work she had observed you doing, told how my position varied each time she visited, and pointed out to Aranimas several of my access ports and described what lay under them."

"I thought she was spying on me," Derec fumed. "What else happened?"

"Aranimas seemed disturbed that you were absent without supervision, and ordered Wolruf to watch you more closely in the future—"

"Get to the point. Where are we? Where are we going?"

"I was forced to make certain inferences from what I heard, but I believe we are making an inbound approach to a site where Aranimas expects to obtain a large quantity of additional robots."

"Repeat the relevant part of the conversation."

"Yes, Derec."

The voices were so faithfully duplicated that if Derec closed his eyes he would have sworn Aranimas and Wolruf were in the room with him.

"We'ave been away from Mrassdf a long time," said Wolruf. "The Narwe arr restless for their 'ome 'erds. Even I grow weary from time to time. Iss it truly necessary to go to another 'uman nest?"

"I will not go back empty-handed," Aranimas said.

" 'U have the jewel, this robot, and more besides. 'U have exceeded 'ur promises to Wiwera. Surely enough glory will flow from those accomplishments—"

"It is not for discussion," Aranimas said curtly. "I will have robots to serve me. The human Derec said that there would be robots at any human world, that they would trade with us if we come in peace. We will allow them to think we come in peace and then take what we need. Then, and only then, will we set course for Mrassdf."

Wolruf's voice took on a pleading, whining tone. "The Narwe are truly worthless ones, there can be no doubt. But if we were to lose the jewel in hand while reaching for a bit of glass—"

The robot interrupted himself. "At this point, Aranimas produced a weapon I cannot identify and pointed it at Wolruf. It seemed to cause Wolruf great distress."

Then it continued in Aranimas's voice. "You disappoint me, Wolruf. I thought you had more vision than that. Without the robots, I will have to surrender that jewel to Wiwera when we return—which I have no intention of doing. Better that you and I are turned to atoms here than to give up the key to such as Wiwera."

The robot fell silent, and Derec found himself with nothing to say. One more stop, and the raiders were going home with their treasure. Where that stop was, there was no guessing. There were hundreds of Spacer facilities scattered over hundreds of light-years. It could be a Customs station lying between Settler and Spacer territory, a mining or processing center, or even one of the research complexes. It might be staffed with humans, humans and robots, or robots alone.

It didn't matter. He would never see it.

Aranimas would use him—his knowledge, his voice, perhaps even his image—to gain entry to the installation. And when the alien's business there was done, the ship would leave for Mrassdf, where Derec was destined to be nothing better than a slave, and perhaps nothing more than a curiosity.

The realization of his impotence shattered Derec. He had taken the lone road and done everything he could by himself. He had schemed and blustered and fought and finagled his way past each succeeding challenge.

But the challenge now facing him seemed insurmountable. Sometime within the next few days, he had to escape—from a ship in which he could not yet even find his way around, from a jailer whose capabilities he had not yet fully gauged, to a refuge whose promise of safety was more hopeful than real.

The fight drained out of him as he confronted the bleak possibilities. Aranimas had all the advantages. He would have Derec watched constantly while they were docked at the installation—if they docked at all. And Derec could not move sooner, for he could never hold the ship. He was outnumbered eighty to one by the crew.

All Derec had was the robot, and that was not enough. I can't do it, he thought despairingly. But I can't just give up—

The conflicting thoughts chased each other through his mind, neither gaining the advantage. Weary and confused, he retreated to the far side of the room and huddled there against the base of the wall.

I've got to have help, he realized at last. I've got to stop trying to do it all myself—got to trust someone. It's that or resign myself to living the rest of my life on an alien world—

And then it came to him that there was someone else

on board who was just as alone, just as helpless, who might take not only comfort but courage from a companion. Someone, in fact, who had already proclaimed herself Derec's friend.

If she'll help, Derec thought, we just might do it, at that—

An hour of waiting had slipped by. Reinvigorated by hope, Derec's attention had wandered from watching the doorway to playing with the pieces of the puzzle.

" 'Ur back," a gruff voice intruded.

Derec raised his head and looked toward Wolruf. "I went walking. You've been looking for me, haven't you?"

"Aranimas was looking for 'u," Wolruf corrected. " 'U stay 'ere now, okay?"

"Is he coming back?"

"Boss iss resting now. 'E'll come to see 'u in the morning. Best 'u be 'ere," Wolruf said, turning away.

"You got in trouble with Aranimas because I was gone, didn't you?" Derec called after her.

The caninoid stopped, looked back, and shrugged.

"I'm sorry," Derec said. "I put you in a bad position."

"Iss nothing new. I put myself therr enough."

Derec smiled. "Tell me something, Wolruf. What are you doing here? Why are you working for someone like Aranimas?"

"Too long a story to explain."

"You're not on board by choice, are you."

"Too complicated to explain."

"I've got the time—and I really want to know."

Wolruf hesitated, then advanced a few steps into the room. "Should go sleep," she said gruffly.

"Why not do what you want to instead of what you ought to?"

Crouching an arm's length away, Wolruf grinned. "That the secret of 'ur success?"

It took longer than it should have to sort out the story. Wolruf had never had to talk about her home and life to someone who did not know the thousand and one things that a person living within a culture knows without thinking. Again and again, Derec had to ask her to go back and fill in some clarifying detail.

Beyond that, there were language problems, as some of what Wolruf was trying to convey ran up against the limits of her Standard vocabulary. At other times she seemed to be talking around some fact or idea that she did not feel comfortable disclosing.

Piecing together what he heard and filling in a few of the blanks on his own, Derec gained a reasonably coherent answer to his question. Despite Wolruf's boast of two hundred inhabited worlds, the crew of the ship was from a single solar system. Aranimas's kind—the Erani—and the Narwe lived on the second planet, Mrassdf, which by Wolruf's description was a hot, windswept, unpleasant world. Wolruf's kind—the name was just as unpronounceable as Wolruf's own—and the elusive star-creatures were from the temperate fourth planet.

The relationship between the Narwe and the Erani was like that between sheep and their shepherds, except that the Narwe were more intelligent and physically adept than sheep. But the comparison was still apt. The Narwe vastly outnumbered the Erani, but the Erani—aggressive, inventive, acquisitive—were completely dominant.

The relationship between the two worlds was rather

more complex, and Derec did not completely understand it. Neither planet seemed to have a unified government. That might have been the only thing that kept them from going to war, for there clearly was a basic antipathy between them. Despite that, there was active commerce between the worlds. At the center of it were trading companies operated by several factions of Erani and goods produced by several families of Wolruf's people.

Wolruf would not talk much about Aranimas in particular, but he seemed to be a younger member of one of the more powerful Erani factions. Derec gleaned that somehow Wolruf's family had run afoul of Aranimas's trading company.

"My service on this mission lifts the *dhierggra* from my family," she explained.

The *dhierggra*, Derec determined after much questioning, was equivalent to a blacklist—while it was in effect, no Erani would deal with the family. That made Wolruf, in essence, an indentured servant—a slave, working off her family's debt.

"Why were you chosen?"

"I am youngest, least valuable to my family."

Derec did not want to rush to judge an entire culture on one story from one member, but he found himself getting angry over the injustice. "Is that why Aranimas treats you the way he does? Is that part of the deal, that he gets to push you around?"

"That iss the Erani way. They treat everyone so."

"Not each other," Derec said. "That's what makes it wrong."

It was then that Derec realized that somewhere in the course of the conversation, something unexpected had happened. He had drawn Wolruf out selfishly, calculating. It was just another angle to exploit. But as he had listened to her, his false sympathy for her plight became real empathy for her pain. She was a victim, just as he was.

But she seemed uncomfortable with his concern. "Not 'ur trouble."

"Wolruf—you said you were my friend. Let me be yours."

"What do 'u mean?"

"Aranimas is working you like a slave and abusing you like an animal. It doesn't have to be that way. We can put a stop to it, together."

"How?"

"I have a tool," he said, nodding toward the robot. "And I have some ideas. But I need you to tell me some things—about Aranimas, and about how this ship is controlled."

Wolruf looked uncomfortable, and Derec was afraid that he had gone too fast and frightened her. "You want the jewel back," she said.

Honesty was an imperative. "I do."

" 'U will take it and leave me to face Aranimas."

Derec shook his head emphatically. "I do have to get away. I can't let Aranimas take me back to Mrassdf. But if I can't leave you in a better situation than you're in now, I'll take you with me. Wolruf—we're the only ones who can help each other. If we don't try, then we deserve what happens to us."

The caninoid met Derec's questioning gaze unblinkingly. "That iss true. Okay—friend. Less try."

There seemed to be something in the biology of Wolruf's kind which sharpened the imperative for sleep and rejuvenation. It was almost as though there was within them a metabolic switch which, once tripped, told them in no uncertain terms that the primary energy fund had been exhausted and it was time to withdraw.

A half-hour after they began talking, with only some of Derec's questions answered and their plan barely sketched out, Wolruf's alarm went off. Her eyes narrowed to slits, her breath took on a sour tang, and her fur lay flat and seemed to lose luster.

Though he still had many urgent questions, Derec did not even get a chance to try to coax her to stay. With no more explanation than a muttered "must sleep," she rose and was gone.

Wolruf's departure made Derec suddenly aware of his own weary limbs. But there was one further task he had to see to before he could think about curling up on the thin mattress.

The robot was waiting where it had settled after completing Derec's last order several hours ago, but that was no surprise. There had been an unnatural passiveness to the robot's behavior ever since Derec had activated it, a passiveness above and beyond the wait-states he had prescribed. A normal robot had a variety of duties it attended to without external direction, following the default orders built into it for its primary function: domestic, laborer, engineer, and the like.

The robot's initiative had apparently fallen victim to the burned-out memory cubes and the cold powerdown. But it still had the Second Law, and so it sat and waited patiently for the words from Derec that would give it something to do.

Derec's first act was to pull the Mathematics cube and replace it with the Personal Defense cube. The additional pathways in the PD cube would enhance the robot's sense of impending harm and its anxiety to act to prevent it. But they would also suppress the robot's normal inclination to protect him from immediate, concrete risks without regard to the consequences of doing so. The First Law did not have any exceptions built into it for taking well-intentioned gambles; the PD cube provided them.

"Alpha," Derec said when he was done. "My previous instructions for you to go into a wait-state when one of the aliens approaches are now cancelled. But where possible, you are still to avoid revealing the unique capabilities of your right arm."

"I understand, Derec."

"I am now going to give you a block of instructions which will not become operative until you hear the initiate code. The initiate code, which must come from me, is the question, 'Who is your master?' The disable code is the word 'Aurora.'"

"I understand, Derec."

"Begin instruction block. You will answer the initiate code with the reply 'Aranimas.' You'll go with Aranimas wherever he wishes you to go. You are to follow his orders except where they conflict with the First, Second, or Third Laws or this instruction block. You will not follow orders given by Wolruf or any other nonhuman member of the crew. You will not accept any additional orders from me unless preceded by the disable code. You will respond to informational inquiries from Wolruf or myself. However, you will not relate, replay, or in any way communicate to Aranimas this conversation or any other conversation with me which he did not witness."

"Clarification. You wish for Aranimas to believe that I am completely in his service?"

"Suspend. I do," Derec said. "If he's going to get any

use out of you, he's going to have to teach you about the ship. Anything you learn will help us escape."

"I understand the necessity for intelligence, sir," the robot said. "But if I am to protect you I must remain at your side."

Derec had expected the objection—PD circuits made robots more argumentative. "Since Arnaimas is in command of this ship, he is the real threat to me. Only his actions or his orders can harm me. By remaining close to him, you will be best able to protect me."

"I understand, sir."

"All right. Resume. There are two things that we particularly need to know. A valuable object came aboard with me, a metallic rectangle, silver color, about five by ten centimeters. I think it's the same object Aranimas called the key, and Wolruf the jewel. It's apparently valuable and powerful. We need to know where it is."

"Yes, Derec. I will be particularly alert for clues to this object's whereabouts."

"The other thing we need to know is what Spacer facility we're heading for and when we're going to get there. If we wait too long to move, Aranimas will have us locked up somewhere to keep us out of his hair while he's stealing robots."

"That would be a prudent precaution."

"Which means that Aranimas will probably think of it," Derec said. "If you learn where the key is located, you are to wait one decad and then simulate a Code 804 malfunction. If you learn where we are headed or when we are to arrive, you are to wait fifteen centads and then simulate a Code 3033 malfunction. End instruction block."

Though he knew what he hoped would happen from that point onward, Derec stopped there. Verbal instruction-in-advance was a tricky enough matter, requiring the skills of a semanticist with the foresight of a seer. He did not wish to saddle the robot with excessively specific and possibly useless orders.

Much work and intelligence had gone into designing the PD library cube. Derec would have to trust that, when the time came, Alpha would grasp the situation and do what was required.

CHAPTER 12

MUTINY

Despite how little of the night was left when Derec was done, he slept well and awoke rested, with his head clear and his spirits up. He began clearing one end of the room as though to make a stage, determined to put on a good show. Presently, Aranimas arrived with Wolruf in tow.

Derec did not have a Handbook of Robotics with its extensive diagnostic interrogatory, but he knew the main lines of questioning used to test the various positronic functions.

"If the daughter of a woman with red hair owns two dogs and the father of a boy with a broken leg is unemployed, what day does the barber give shaves?"

Wolruf hooted at that one, and Aranimas looked puzzled. But the robot calmly answered, "It is not possible to determine the answer from the information given."

"What is the value of hex 144C times 16F2?"

"Hex 1D1B7D8."

"Touch your right index finger to the middle of your forehead."

The robot complied.

"State the Rayleigh law of magnetic permeability—"

For fifteen minutes, Derec peppered the robot with commands and questions, less to impress Aranimas with the robot's abilities than to underscore his own competence. He did not want Aranimas thinking that with the robot operational, he, Derec, was now expendable.

Then, before Aranimas could grow impatient, Derec asked the final question. "Alpha, who is your master?"

"Aranimas," the robot replied.

Derec turned to Aranimas. "The robot's yours now," he said. "You will have to teach it what you want it to do, but you won't have to show it more than once."

Aranimas rose. "Order it to attack Wolruf," the alien said.

"What?"

"I will not share control of this servant. Order it to attack Wolruf."

Derec's hesitation was calculated. He turned to the robot and said, "Pick up that brace and strike Wolruf in the head."

Wolruf whimpered, but the robot did not move. "I may not comply, sir."

Then Aranimas repeated the command. "Servant. Pick up the brace and strike Wolruf."

Derec held his breath. If there was going to be a First Law conflict over treatment of the aliens, now was when it would surface.

"Yes, master," the robot said, turning and reaching for the metal rod.

Wolruf crabbed nervously toward the door. Derec released a small sigh of relief.

"Stop, servant," Aranimas ordered. To Derec he said, "You have done as you promised. It seems that you are worth keeping alive after all. Wolruf will find other duties for you."

That was a wild card Derec had not expected, and he could not let it be played unchallenged. "No," Derec said boldly. "I'm a roboticist, not a laborer. Not a Narwe. If you want to keep your new servant in good order, you're going to keep me working here."

"Doing what?"

"First, disassembling the other body for spare parts. Some of the patches I did on this robot are temporary. I can work on better fixes. Some of the damaged components may be repairable if I can get certain supplies."

Derec plunged on, gathering a head of steam. "Out in the real world, there are repair technician robots which do nothing but maintain other robots. You only have one robot at the moment, so I'm your technician. You've seen what I can do. How long did you have those parts? How much time did you spend looking at them and figuring out nothing? Why do you want to start treating me like a particularly ugly Narwe?"

Aranimas stared, then made a hissing sound which might have been laughter. "Come, servant. We will leave the master roboticist to his work."

It was difficult for Derec to watch Alpha walk away with Aranimas. It was even more difficult to wait patiently for some sign whether the fragile plan he and Wolruf had concocted would even pass the first threshold.

He was still isolated in his little corner of the ship. There was no way for him to know what Aranimas was doing with the robot. He did not know from one minute to the next whether his instructions to the robot were still intact. Perhaps Aranimas had only pretended to be ignorant about robots. Perhaps he had already undone all of Derec's careful conditioning.

Even if the instructions were still intact, they could well be irrelevant. Derec had assumed that Aranimas would be so fond of his new toy that he would keep it close at hand. Everything depended on that being true. But if he was wrong, if Aranimas had simply dispatched Alpha to some far corner of the ship to perform some menial function, then his plan was foredoomed to failure. Derec would have given up the robot and gotten nothing in return for it.

Derec had work to do, some to maintain the fiction he was Aranimas's faithful employee, some for his own purposes. He tried to make the hours pass more quickly by immersing himself in it. But work could not dull the edge of his impatience or his anxiety. Even with no clock to watch, time crawled by.

Wolruf was in and out several times the rest of that day, and even when she was gone she was never far away. He welcomed the interruptions, but he worried that Aranimas might detect the change in her working patterns and wonder why. And without Alpha to alert him to Aranimas's approach, Derec was reluctant to talk about their evolving plot against the alien commander.

But it was not entirely avoidable. The call could come at any time, and a key problem remained unsolved. Derec knew, or thought he did, how they could disarm Aranimas. The unanswered question was how to disable him.

With surprising vehemence, Wolruf ruled out killing the Erani. Derec did not much regret it. He could not picture himself walking up to Aranimas with a club and battering him to death. But at the same time, as long as Aranimas was alive he was dangerous.

Derec first proposed a stunner, made from a recharged

microcell and a few bits of wire. But there was no way to be sure that Aranimas was vulnerable to electric shocks, or to assure that the high-voltage current wouldn't kill him.

"The chamber with the star-creatures," Derec said abruptly. "When we passed through it, Aranimas's eyes started to water. Do you know why? Those things are from your world. Is there something in the air there that's not in the rest of the ship?"

"Yes," Wolruf said. "The yellow-gas. That iss the only part of the ship wherr it iss used. The star-creatures release yellow-gas when they move."

That would account for it, Derec thought. A digestive by-product, or some sort of chemical communication—"So the air in there is like the atmosphere of your world?"

"Yes."

"Which means that the Erani probably can't spend any time on your world without getting sick," Derec concluded.

"We arr protected from the Erani temper," Wolruf agreed.

Derec paused and considered. "You said the star-creatures were part of an experiment. Could Aranimas be trying to find a way to neutralize the gas, so that the Erani can invade?"

"It iss possible."

"Are there samples, bottled up?"

"There is a liquid that turns to yellow-gas when freed."

"Perfect. Get me some."

When Derec turned in that night, he was a bundle of restless energy, and sleep did not come easily. When it finally did come, it seemed as though he closed his eyes one moment and the next someone was shaking him. He looked up to see Wolruf standing over him.

"Aranimas wants 'u," Wolruf said.

"Is it the robot?"

"New servant won't listen to the boss anymore," Wolruf said. "It just sits there."

"This could be it, then," Derec said, scrambling to his feet. "I'll get my tools."

As Derec followed Wolruf through the passageways, his anticipation and anxiety both spiraled upward. When they reached the hex junction, he stopped and caught the caninoid's arm. "Does he expect you to come in?"

"No. Only to deliver 'u. But I could come in and see if he sends me away—"

"No," Derec said. "Don't do anything out of the ordinary. I can handle the first part myself. Just wait here."

Inside Hull A, Derec spotted Aranimas across the main compartment and picked his way around the mesh bulkheads to where the alien waited.

"The robot has malfunctioned," Aranimas said, gesturing, "Repair it."

The robot sat on the edge of a low counter, motionless except for his left hand, rotating slowly and aimlessly at the wrist joint. Code 3033—our location! Derec thought.

"What did you do to it?" Derec demanded, moving within arm's reach of the robot.

"I did nothing. The mechanism ceased to obey me."

"You must have done something." Derec bent at the waist to peer directly into the glowing eyes. "Alpha. Acknowledge."

"Yess, ssir," the robot said, its words slurred and distorted.

Code 804! The key! But he had to be sure. "Alpha. Default 1-A-1-B. Execute."

The robot sat inert.

"Alpha. Default 2-C-2-D. Execute."

Still there was no response.

"What's wrong with my servant?" Aranimas demanded.

Stalling for time, Derec opened his small tool clutch and then the robot's left shoulder access plate. As he peered inside, he thought the next step through. The reworking he had done on the robot's instinct to protect intelligent life was a delicate business. It had already been stressed unexpectedly when Aranimas took possession of the robot.

If he were to release the robot from its instruction block and order it to move against Aranimas, that would create a Second Law obligation to break the First Law. His careful adjustments might come apart under the stress, and the robot would freeze up in a way Derec would not be able to repair.

He did not want to take that risk. It was much more straightforward for the robot to act in obedience to the First Law than in defiance of it. But that meant it was necessary to provoke Aranimas into an attack.

"It looks like a failure of the volitional initiator," Derec double talked. "If two contradictory impulses reach it on the same pulse, it can set up a standing wave in the oscillator. It's almost always the owner's fault. What did you ask it to do?"

"I did nothing wrong, I was explaining the functions of the equipment in this section when its hand began to twirl foolishly that way."

"Don't lie to me," Derec said. "I should have known that a race as backward as yours couldn't cope with sophisticated machinery—"

"You are worse than the Narwe," Aranimas snarled. "You do not have the good sense to know when you are in the service of a true superior." As he spoke, his hand moved toward the gap in his robelike blouse.

"Aurora!" Derec shouted.

But the robot had begun to move even before Derec uttered the word, the First Law overcoming the strictures of the instruction block. The race between Aranimas's reflexes and the robot's was no contest. Before the stylus had even cleared the folds of Aranimas's robe, the robot had grabbed the alien's wrist with its right hand and plucked the stylus from his grasp with its left.

"Release me!" Aranimas squalled shrilly. He squirmed and fought, but could not free himself from the grip of the single mechanical hand.

"I cannot allow you to harm Derec," the robot said.

"You are my servant. Obey my orders! Release me!"

"No, Aranimas," Derec said, stepping forward. "Alpha is my servant, and always was." Then he called back over his shoulder, "Wolruf! You can come in now!"

Retrieving the stylus from the floor, Derec turned it over in his hand. There were no obvious switches or controls on it. Holding it the way Aranimas had, Derec pointed it at the alien. Aranimas remained unaffected.

"My own weapons cannot be used against me," Aranimas said with stiff pride.

"A very clever management technique," Derec said. He reached into the tool clutch and retrieved the little toy he had made earlier that day. Attached to a small pressure bottle halffull of mustard-yellow liquid was a miniature pump salvaged from the disabled robot. "But I have my own weapon."

As Wolruf joined him, Derec pointed the pump's outlet valve at Aranimas and pressed the switch. A fine mist blasted from the tiny opening and caught the alien in the face.

A human would have gasped in surprise. Aranimas lunged for the aerosol with his free hand and nearly got it, his arm span being almost equal to the makeshift device's range.

But a moment later, a reddish liquid began streaming from Aranimas's eyes, and the skin of his face seemed to pucker. He went rigid and reached high in the air with his free hand, the fingers curling as though grasping for something, the ropelike muscles of his arm and shoulder visible under the skin for the first time. As the aerosol began to sputter, the alien's eyes closed, and his arm dropped limply to his side.

"Release him," Derec said, thumbing the switch. The robot's hand opened, and the alien crumpled to the deck and lay there motionless.

"I—detect—no respiration," the robot said haltingly.

The robot's speech impediment was a warning sign to Derec. I should have warned it what was going to happen, he realized belatedly. "He's not dead," Derec said. "His system has received a poison shock, but he will recover."

"I—will try—to integrate—"

"Alpha—analyze the situation. This is Aranimas's ship. He had all the advantages. He could have done a hundred things to stop us and we'd never have known until it was too late. He had to be neutralized."

"I understand—and accept."

"Are you all right?"

"I detect a moderate disturbance—in my brain potentials which I attribute—to witnessing violence against an intelligent-being-not-a-human," the robot said, its speech gradually returning to normal. "The disturbance is abating and I do not believe that it will affect my functioning."

"Good," Derec said, dropping the spent aerosol on top of the tools. "What did you find out?"

"We are approaching an independent free-flying space station."

"Frost," Derec said emphatically. "I was hoping he'd take us right in to one of the Spacer worlds. How much time do we have?"

"I am unable to accurately estimate our arrival time. However, I did determine that the ship's crew is presently at the lowest level of alert."

"So we probably have more than a few hours," Derec said. "Has Aranimas been in contact with the station?"

"Not that I am aware of, sir. This vessel does not appear to have hyperwave communications—only simple carrier-wave radio."

That agreed with Derec's experience on the asteroid, but it raised a puzzle. How had the aliens found the asteroid? Derec had assumed along with Monitor 5 that they had intercepted the distress message sent on his behalf. But without a hyperwave viewer, that was clearly impossible.

Perhaps Wolruf could shed some light—but it would have to wait. "Okay. What about the key? Do you know where it is?"

"Within limits. I believe it is concealed beneath one of the deck tiles of the command center."

The last time he had been in the command center, Derec had been in too much pain to pay attention to his surroundings. "Let's go see," Derec said, starting off. "How did you find it?" he called back over his shoulder.

"Aranimas showed the key to me and questioned me about it," the robot said. "When he left with it, I was not able to see precisely what disposition he made of it. However, the time he was gone limited the radius of concealment to this deck, and the sounds I heard were consistent with the removal and replacement of a floor tile."

They reached the command center then, and Derec saw that the deck was a mosaic of several hundred hexagonal metal tiles the size of a dinner plate. The surface of each tile had a pattern of small holes, but there was no obvious fingerlift—in fact, no obvious way to lift an individual tile. All six edges were flush with the adjoining tiles.

"Any idea where I should start?"

"The strategy of concealment would argue against obvious positions such as the center and corners. Beyond that, I cannot say."

"You can't detect it under the deck? It's not giving off some kind of radio signal, or generating a magnetic field?"

"Not that I am able to detect."

That, too, was consistent with what had happened on the asteroid. If the key had declared its presence in any measurable way, the robots' scans would have turned it up long before the raider ship arrived.

"All right," Derec said slowly. He turned to Wolruf, who had been a silent spectator since joining them. "We need a place to lock up Aranimas."

Wolruf glanced nervously back toward where they had left the Erani. "Therr arr some lockers outside, on the side passage, which would be large enough—"

Derec nodded. "Alpha—pick up Aranimas and go with Wolruf. She will show you where to put him. Wolruf, make sure it's something Aranimas can't open from the inside. Then both of you come back here." He caught the look of apprehension in Wolruf's eyes and added. "I know—you don't like the robot."

"Maybe 'u surprise Wolruf like 'u surprise Aranimas."

"I promise you, it'll be all right," Derec said, patting the caninoid's arm. "No surprises. I'll be waiting for you here."

When the robot was gone, Derec lowered himself to his hands and knees to examine the holes in the tiles. They proved to be tapered pits barely a half-centimeter deep. There seemed to be no way of hooking anything into one to lift the tile. Derec wondered if he would have to build some sort of vacuum clamp before he could locate the key.

Then he realized that the openings were about the diameter of the tip of Aranimas's stylus. Of course, Derec thought as he fumbled for the instrument. Let's hope this feature doesn't work only for Aranimas, too—

He touched the conical tip to one of the openings, and the tile seemed to seize hold of the stylus and stand it straight up. Gripping the stylus with one and then both hands, Derec tried to lift the tile straight up. The tile did not budge. But when he used the stylus as a lever, he was easily able to tip the tile back, like peeling the lid off a can. Underneath was a small hexagonal compartment—empty.

No beginner's luck, eh? he thought. When he replaced the tile, the stylus came free. Very nice, he thought, touching the stylus to the adjacent tile. The trick wasn't done with magnetics; the stylus seemed to actually bond to the tile. Perhaps a metallic affinity, followed by a little shot of current to jostle the atoms and break the bonds. Cute trick—

There was a humming sound behind him, and Derec whirled. Half a dozen meters down the central corridor, a circular platform was descending from the ceiling, suspended on four slender wires. And standing on the platform was a woman—a young human female, no more than a year or two older than Derec but a good eight centimeters taller.

The broad-shouldered sash blazer she was wearing was cut in an aristocratic style, but showed many days of wear.

Her expression was one of surprise, even shock. Her mouth worked as though trying to form a word. "You?" she said disbelievingly as the platform reached floor level. "Here?"

Wild thoughts filled Derec's head, and reason had to fight for control. That would sure help explain Aranimas's success—if he had had a human consort all along to guide him—

"You'd better tell me real fast who you are and what you're doing here," he said, slowly coming to his feet. "I don't have a lot of time to decide what to do about you."

"What to do about me?" she echoed angrily. "I don't know why I owe *you* any answers, not after what you did."

The meaning of the condition of the girl's clothes finally impressed itself on Derec. She was a prisoner, just as he. But Derec realized that to her, he might be the one who seemed to have thrown in with the raiders.

"I only helped Aranimas to buy time and save my neck. The robot's mine now, and Aranimas can't hurt you," Derec said. "We're going to get of here."

The hostility faded from her face, leaving behind bewilderment. "But what are you doing here? How long have you been on board?"

Derec took a step toward her. "It doesn't take long to tell. Five days ago I woke up in a survival pod on the surface of an asteroid. I was found by a colony of robots mining the asteroid. Aranimas raided the colony and took me prisoner." That's enough. No sense muddying the waters with details even I don't understand yet, he thought.

She was looking at him curiously. "So you weren't looking for me."

"I didn't know anyone else was on the ship," he said, throwing his hands in the air. "Wolruf told me that they had captured a couple of human ships, but she left the impression the crews were all—gone."

"I think Aranimas kept me alive because he was interested in my robots," she said. "Are you the one that repaired Capek?"

"Was that its old name? It answers to Alpha now. Yes, I'm the one who fixed it."

"You did a rotten job," she said with a hint of childish petulance. "It doesn't remember me. The new arm is ugly, too."

"I'm sorry."

"And you don't remember me, either."

Derec swallowed. "I had the feeling you thought I should—"

"I thought you were just being cruel," she said slowly. "I didn't want to give you the satisfaction. But you don't know who I am, do you?"

"I don't even know who I am," Derec answered with a weak smile. "When I woke up on the asteroid, I was wearing a safesuit with the name Derec on the chest, so I've been calling myself that. But I can't remember anything that happened before I woke up on the asteroid."

"Nothing at all?"

"Nothing personal. I remember a lot of facts—things I learned sometime, I guess. But I don't know where I'm from or where I was going." Derec was badly confused. "So you know me?"

"I thought I did," she said.

"Then for mercy's sake, tell me—"

A chirping sound came from the huge control console at that moment.

"Someone's paging Aranimas," the girl said, a flash of nervousness crossing her face. "You said we were going to get out of here. Maybe we should worry about that first. What were you doing when I surprised you? What were you looking for?"

"Some of my property—that Aranimas took when I came aboard."

"The key? Was that yours?"

"You know about it?"

"Aranimas showed it to me. Is that where it's hidden?"

"According to Alpha."

"Is it important?"

"I think so."

"Then let's get it and get out of here," she said anxiously.

Wondering what was keeping Alpha and Wolruf, Derec slowly turned back to the floor grid. He checked the second tile, stole a glance back over his shoulder at her, then moved crabwise to the right to try a third.

"I can look for the key and listen at the same time," he said, attaching the stylus to the next tile. "Can't you tell me what you know about me?"

If she gave an answer, Derec never heard it. One moment he was starting to lift the tile, and the next there was a flash, a roaring sound, and a tremendous wash of heat. Something heavy struck Derec across the back and he toppled forward, catching the hard edge of the tile across his chest and driving the air from his lungs. His mind had time to think one word—*booby trap*—before it retreated from the fury to a dark, quiet recess where it would not be disturbed.

CHAPTER 13

ROCKLIFFE STATION

Soft-edged images drifted through a dreamlike haze. A sea of light surrounded Derec, buoying him up. He was as transparent as glass, as inconsequential as the wind. His consciousness resided on a mote of dust, floating on gentle currents of time.

Faceless figures floated there with him. Some drew near as though aware of him, only to turn away again and withdraw. The only sounds were the fragrance-songs of flowers and the color-songs of sunsets, and those played in his head without understanding.

None of it seemed to make sense, and yet he did not care. He only thought that after everything that had happened, all that he had survived, it would be a terrible disappointment to be dead.

After a time, his body returned to him. He was still floating, still adrift, but his consciousness again inhabited its familiar place, filled its familiar space. But his thoughts were as sluggish as his limbs, as though the burdens of once again managing his body's functions had overwhelmed the simple processes of his mind.

Presently he became aware that the dreamlike world of light and shadow which he was inhabiting existed entirely within himself. If he chose to, he could open his eyes to the larger world beyond, to survey it, to enter it. He was certain that when he saw that world he would know his place in it, would know then who and what he was. But he would pay a price in peace and silence, and that was too high a price to pay.

No, Derec thought firmly. *There are limits. I don't want to see it*, he told himself. *I don't want to know.*

Time passed, and the enveloping womb of solitude slowly became a prison. Silence became deafness. Stillness became death. Whether because he was healed or haunted, what he had was not enough.

The larger world outside himself still beckoned. It was not a friendly world, he knew. At best it was indifferent to him. Unlike the gentle currents that had borne him as he healed, the larger world was filled with forces that could bear him along like driftwood in the spume of a breaking wave.

But he was not without power himself. Perhaps he could not turn back the wave, but he could ride it, and set his own course.

It was that realization which freed him. He saw that he was not a prisoner, and never had been. There were five doors through which he could free himself—the five doors of his senses. All were unlocked, waiting only his touch to swing open and let the world in and himself out.

And he would open them, he knew. But not yet. Not

until he had floated with the gentle currents awhile longer. For if he could leave whenever he chose to, then the womb of solitude was not such an unpleasant place to be after all—

The first door Derec tried to open was hearing. At first he wondered if he had succeeded, for the silence without was as complete as the silence within. Then he became aware of the faint rhythmic sound of his own breathing. It was a small step, but it was the first information to come from outside his cocoon in what felt like a very long time.

Experimentally, Derec opened his eyes a crack, and immediately closed them again. The world outside was disturbingly familiar. He was floating enveloped in light—light that was somehow bright without being harsh. A faceless shadow, tall and slender, moved gracefully through the haze which seemed to surround him.

Reality had been inverted. The dream had become reality, or the dream world and the real world were one and the same. It seemed like some sort of perverse trick, one in spirit with a "present" which turns out to be a series of ever-smaller empty boxes. Would every doorway lead to the same place? Would each step he took only hold him more firmly where he was?

"Good morning."

Derec was puzzled at the sound of another voice. If he was alone, then he had to be the one who had spoken. But he had not spoken, and so he was not alone. But if he was not alone, then he could not still be inside his dream world, and what he had seen when he had opened his eyes must be real.

But if it was real, then he was alive. He tried to remember the last incontrovertibly real thing he had known. It was a difficult business, remembering. There had been sunsets and flower-songs, but they had not been real. Before that ... before that ...

Before that there had been a terrible moment, a moment so full of surprise and pain that even in fleeing it, he had brought it inside his cocoon. He had transformed the eruption into the blossoming of a flower, the flame into the colors of a spectacular sunset. Then he had replayed the moment endlessly to render it harmless.

Yes! The last real thing he had known had been the explosion.

Derec opened his eyes once more to the light. A shadow loomed over him, faceless and nearly formless, as before. He tried to reach out and touch it, but his limbs would not obey.

"Turn off the sterilization field," the voice said, and the haze of light vanished. The shadow became the copper-colored head and clothed torso of a robot. The robot was gazing solicitously down at him. "Good morning," it repeated. "Please don't try to move."

Derec's mind was slowly working its way backward from the explosion. He understood that he was no longer in the command center. The robot hovering over him was not Alpha. Which meant—

"Aranimas got his robots," Derec croaked.

"Excuse me, sir?"

"He won," Derec whispered. "I didn't get away."

"Sir?"

"Tell Aranimas I won't stop trying—"

"Sir, I would be happy to deliver the message for you. However, the person you named is unknown to me. Where may this individual be found?"

"Aranimas is the ship's boss—"

"This individual was a member of the ship's company?"

"Yes—" The robot's responses were beginning to puzzle Derec.

"Sir, I regret to inform you that no person of that name was found when the paramedics boarded—"

"I'm not on the ship?"

"You are resting on a therapeutic diamagnetic force field, more commonly known as an airbed. The airbed is in the Intensive Care Ward of the hospital at Rockliffe Station."

The wave of relief that swept through Derec on hearing those words seemed to take all his energy with it. He closed his eyes and allowed himself to float on the gentle currents of sleep once more. Distantly, he heard voices, but could not rouse himself to think about what they were saying.

"He is fatigued," the robot said.

"We need his assistance," a new voice answered.

"Our needs are less pressing than his own," the robot said. "We will wait."

The next time Derec awoke, the copper-skinned robot was again nearby.

"Good evening," it said, coming to his side. "How are you feeling?"

Derec managed an anemic smile. "I was just lying here thinking about all the times in the last week that I closed my eyes one place and opened them somewhere else. Every time it happened I found myself in worse surroundings and deeper trouble—until the first time I woke up here."

The robot nodded gravely. "I promise that you will receive the best of care."

"I know I will," Derec said. "Do you have a name?"

"My assigned designation is Human Diagnostic Medicine Specialist 4. However, the supervisor of medicine for this district refers to me as Dr. Galen."

"Why?"

"He has never explained this to me. However, I have determined that Galen was the name of a Greek physician of the classical age who wrote on the subject of the 'vital forces' inhabiting the body. I believe that my supervisor found it amusing to call an advanced diagnostic technician by the name of a primitive medical mystic. Since this question concerns humor, I cannot offer an authoritative conclusion."

"I think you're probably right," Derec said. "You won't be offended if I call you Dr. Galen? It's a good bit handier than your other name."

"Why should I be offended, sir?"

"No reason," Derec said. At least not when I say it, he added silently. But that supervisor is definitely expressing some hostility. Probably has a secret fantasy of being a family practice doctor on a Settler world instead of tender-to-robots. "Where is your supervisor?"

"On Nexon."

Derec knew the name: it was one of the larger Spacer worlds, and the second-farthest from Earth. "You said this is Rockliffe Station?"

"That is correct, sir."

"Where is your local supervisor? The hospital director?"

"Sir, I am hospital director at present."

Derec frowned. "Maybe you'd better tell me some more about Rockliffe Station, then."

"Certainly, sir. What would you like to know?"

Rockliffe Station, Dr. Galen explained, was a centuries-old Spacer facility, a way station dating from the days when a long interstellar journey could only be managed through a series of shorter Jumps. Dozens of way stations had been built while the Earth emigrants who would become the Spacers were colonizing the fifty worlds that would become their homes.

With the coming of more powerful drives capable of spanning known space in one or two Jumps, most of the way stations had long since been abandoned. A few, of which this was one, had been fortunately enough placed that they outlived their original function.

Rockliffe Station lay in the middle of one of the largest "open" regions along the fringes of Spacer territory, looking out toward the quarantine zone beyond which lay the Settler worlds. There were no livable worlds in the nearest star system, but there was one planet with a crust rich enough in iridium to justify a small mining and processing center.

So Rockliffe had survived on the strength of its usefulness as a listening post on the frontier, as a transshipment point for processed iridium, and a military outpost should relations with the Settlers deteriorate. But those were not reason enough to keep it active at the peak level of the early days—not enough even to maintain a human presence there.

According to Dr. Galen, less than ten percent of the station was occupied, and that entirely by robots. The human supervision they required was provided by means of hypervision and the ships that called every two months.

Only because of the chance that those visiting crews might need its services had the hospital been kept staffed. But the managers on Nexon were realists. Dr. Galen was hospital administrator because his caseload was usually zero, while the only other medical robot on station, a nurse-orderly, had a full schedule of cleaning and maintenance.

No wonder the supervisor makes jokes at Dr. Galen's expense, Derec thought.

"You seem disturbed by this information," Dr. Galen said. "Is there a problem?"

Derec thought about the question for a moment. He *had* grown progressively unhappier as Dr. Galen's explanation had proceeded. But did it matter so much that he apparently was still alone? At least Rockliffe Station was more or less familiar territory, unlike the asteroid colony or the raider ship. He should be able to have his own way more easily here.

"No. No problem," Derec said. "Except I'd like to know a little more about what happened. How did I get here? You said something about paramedics—"

"I do not know all the details. The dispatcher or dock supervisor would be better sources of information."

"Tell me what you know."

"Apparently your ship was disabled following its Jump. Exactly what happened next is not clear. The dispatcher will no doubt want to inquire about the circumstances. However, it appeared as though your ship discarded or released a smaller vessel, a shuttle or lifeboat, before changing course and heading into the Q-zone."

"They must have cut us loose after the explosion—" Derec said thoughtfully.

"The smaller vessel apparently was following an unacceptable approach vector and did not respond to the dispatcher's commands. On the assumption that it was a derelict, a tug was dispatched to intercept it and bring it in. When the derelict was boarded you were found and brought here."

"Did they bring the ship—our ship—in, then?"

"That is my understanding. Of course, my concern since that time has been with your care."

"Of course," Derec echoed. If Aranimas's ship is here, maybe I didn't lose the artifact after all, he thought joyously. "Listen, Dr. Galen, what would you say to my getting up and doing a little walking? Airbeds are as comfortable as beds get, but I'm tired of just lying here. Maybe I could go see what kind of shape the ship is in, answer any questions the dispatcher has."

"I'm sorry, sir," Dr. Galen said. "Your injuries are not yet sufficiently healed to permit that."

"What are my injuries?"

"You suffered flash burns over fifteen percent of your body, primarily over your arms, face, and neck. Three of your ribs were cracked—"

"I must have fallen on the tile I was lifting."

"—one puncturing your right lung and causing it to collapse. Your right eardrum was perforated and had to be replaced."

"Frost! How long have I been here?"

"The ship on which you were found was boarded six weeks ago."

"Six weeks! Was I in a coma or something?"

"Burns are extremely painful, as is reconstructive epidermal surgery," Dr. Galen said. "I kept you under chemical narcosis during treatment and the initial phase of recovery."

"I guess I should be grateful. But six weeks—" Belatedly Derec remembered that he had not been alone on the raider ship. "Where're the others? Wolruf—Alpha—the girl. What've they been doing while I was narc'd?"

"I am sorry. The only persons found were yourself and a female human."

Feeling a sudden tightness in his chest, Derec looked

away. It did not mean that Wolruf was dead and Alpha destroyed—there was a chance, perhaps even a good one, that they were on the larger portion of the ship still in space. But it did mean that while Derec had escaped and survived, he had not lived up to his promises to the caninoid. "I'm sorry, Wolruf," he whispered.

"Excuse me, sir?"

"Nevermind," Derec said. "Tell me about the girl."

"She was found near you inside the ship—"

"That's not what I mean. Tell me how she is."

"Patient Katherine's physical—"

"Katherine—is that her name?"

"Is there some error?"

"No—no, that's her," Derec said. "Where is she?"

Dr. Galen turned away to the right and gestured with his hand. "Orderly, draw the curtain back."

Derec turned his head to the right. What appeared to be the wall of his room suddenly become transparent, allowing him to see a slight human figure floating in a halo of light. She was naked, and he looked away, faintly embarrassed. When he did, he realized that he was naked, too. It was very straightforward and practical for them to be naked in a hospital, but something of a surprise all the same.

"How is she?"

"Her integumentary injuries were more extensive than your own, but she is healing well. Of course, her chronic condition remains unchanged."

"What condition is that?"

"I'm sorry." The robot paused. "I see that I have made an error. Since you were traveling together, I did not think that I was betraying any secrets by discussing Katherine's chart. I will have to report myself for this indiscretion."

"I don't care about that," Derec said impatiently. "Has she been awake?"

"No. Nor would we have allowed you to awaken if we did not need your assistance." Dr. Galen gestured with his right hand. "Close the curtain."

"Assistance with what?" Derec asked as the wall became opaque again.

"Sir, in the course of your care certain services have been rendered on account. It has not only been our obligation but our pleasure to be able to help you. However, as hospital administrator I am obliged to determine whether this account is collectable or is to be charged against regular station operations."

"You woke me up to ask me for my insurance card?"

"There is also the question of medical history. We can determine genetic endowment directly, but it is not always possible to determine all the synergistic outcomes of a particular gene complex. Without direct evidence, I have been obliged to follow more conservative parameters in your care, which in turn has had the effect of prolonging your recovery somewhat."

"I don't understand. What about her?" Derec demanded. "You said she was hurt more badly than I was. Wouldn't it be even more important to find out who she is and get her medical history? Why me and not her?"

"Sir, while you were unconscious, we attempted to identify you by means of all the standard systems. We were not successful."

"Standard systems—"

"Fingerprint, retinagraph, absolute blood protein typing, and twenty-third chromosome codon map. We were not able to establish a match."

"Of course you weren't. I'm not from here."

"Sir, by hyperwave we have direct access to the records of all fifty Spacer worlds."

"Did you check the records for Aurora?"

"Yes. We were not able to establish a match."

"But I'm from there—I know I am."

"I'm afraid that's not possible. Aurora keeps scrupulous records on their citizens as part of their population-control program. If you were an Auroran, this conversation would not have been necessary."

"But you found out who she is," he said.

"That is correct. Katherine's full records were made available to me."

With sudden fury, Derec demanded, "Are you telling me that you searched the citizenship records of fifty planets and can't find out who I am?"

"No," Dr. Galen said. "We have searched the records of fifty-five worlds, including Earth and the four nearest Settler planets. We do have a right of request with most Settler worlds for access to their records. Unfortunately those records are not as complete as we are accustomed to dealing with, and in some cases are not even centralized. Also, certain worlds charge exorbitant fees to respond to data requests from Spacers and then are exceedingly slow to respond. For all these reasons, it seemed to us that a more straightforward inquiry was in order.

"Therefore, could you please tell us who you are?"

The empty feeling had returned full force. "I wish I could," Derec said hoarsely. "Stars, how I wish I could."

CHAPTER 14

KATE

"How interesting!" Dr. Galen exclaimed. "Do you mean to say that you have no personal memories whatsoever?"

Derec repeated the now familiar litany of events which began with his waking in the survival capsule. Partly because he was growing weary of the tale himself and partly to minimize questions, he glossed over some of the details, including the fact that the raider had been screwed by aliens.

"I will have to amend your chart to reflect this state of retrograde amnesia," Dr. Galen said when Derec was through. "This is a much more fascinating problem than your other injuries. As a matter of fact, amnesia is a hobby of mine."

"What do you mean, a hobby?"

"Perhaps I should say specialty, but that does not convey the deep intellectual satisfaction it gives me."

"How many cases have you treated?"

"You will be my first," Dr, Galen said. "I am tremendously pleased by the opportunity."

"Your first?" Derec said, incredulous. "How can you call yourself a specialist, then? And what do you mean saying that you're 'fascinated' or 'pleased'? You're not programmed to experience emotion."

"Strictly speaking, that is correct," Dr. Galen agreed. "But the concept of losing one's sense of identity has always created the kind of positive positronic state which I associate with the term *fascination*. You see, due to the memory structure of the positronic brain, it is quite impossible for a robot to forget anything, least of all its own identity. Amnesia represents a state for which robot experience offers no analogue."

"The lure of the unknown."

"Diagnostic robots such as myself are constructed with a reinforced curiosity integral," Dr. Galen said. "Perhaps that is a contributing factor."

Derec felt as though he were being lectured in his own specialty. "But positronic brains go south all the time," he protested. "They're vulnerable to hard radiation, to glitches in the power supply—lots of things can go wrong."

"That is correct, Derec. But those conditions you describe would result in mental shutdown, and in some instances the complete destruction of the positronic brain. However, humans are frequently able to continue to function with such a major system failure. That is what I find fascinating. Beyond that, I believe that robots have much to contribute to the investigation of human brain function, including memory defects."

"Why is that?"

"I note that many human philosophers have recognized that the search for self-knowledge is the hardest search of all. It is extremely difficult for the human brain to contemplate and analyze the human brain. Its limitations make it impossible to see its limitations."

Derec found himself in agreement with the robot. "The only thing a camera can't see is itself. The only thing a ruler can't measure is itself."

"Quite. Questions of human brain functions have therefore been the slowest to yield to investigation by human researchers. Many aspects of human behavior are still puzzles despite centuries of neurological and biochemical studies."

"So what do you think *you* can do?"

Dr. Galen spread his hands wide. "Positronic brains were not developed by copying how human brains function. They were developed by copying how human beings behave. Therefore, though the positronic brain is the product of the human brain, it represents a distinct form of intelligence and a different perspective."

"Are you saying that positronic brains are more capable than human brains?"

"The key is that a robot does what it does differently than a human brain," Dr. Galen said diplomatically. "I am convinced that it is an invention of the human brain which will eventually unlock the secrets of the human brain. So I am pleased to have the opportunity to do more than study and speculate."

Derec shook his head. "Forget it. I don't want to be a lab animal."

"Forgive me," Dr. Galen said. "In my enthusiasm I neglected to make clear that my primary interest is to help you. There are tests which I can perform to determine the cause of your condition. Depending on the cause, there may be measures which can be taken to reverse your condition."

"Do you mean you can bring my memory back?"

"I will not know the likelihood of that until I have examined you."

Derec regarded the promise of a magic cure with skepticism. "Look, I'm not going to be here very long," he said. "Let's not start something we won't have time to finish."

"I do not understand."

"You said that ships call here every two months. If I've been here six weeks, my ride out of here should show up in two weeks—probably less."

"No, Derec," Dr. Galen corrected. "*Fariis* came and went while you were recovering. The next vessel, the *Heritage*, is due in six weeks, three days."

Derec stared. "A ship's already been here? Then why am I still here?" he demanded.

"This station's medical facilities are superior to those on board *Fariis*. It was not possible to release you to them in your condition."

Derec closed his eyes and sighed. "All right. Probe away." His eyes opened and he struggled to a seated position. "But I want to know what you're doing before you do it, do you hear?"

"Thank you, Derec," Dr. Galen said politely. "What do you know of amnesia?"

"Just what I see on the hypervision."

"That is unfortunate," Dr. Galen said.

"It's just a saying. Actually, I don't even remember that."

"That is just as well," Dr. Galen replied. "Amnesia has been used as a convenient device in fiction for centuries, usually in defiance of known facts. A common plot is for a victim to suffer a blow to the head, forget everything and everyone and begin leading a new life, then be restored in the closing scene by another blow."

"That does sound sort of familiar. Maybe I have seen one or two like that," Derec admitted.

"Please do your best to forget them," Dr. Galen said disapprovingly. "They will only hinder understanding."

Over the next three days, Derec learned a great deal about amnesia. He had had no idea how many kinds of amnesia there were and how many different causes had been identified. Under other circumstances, it would have been more than he wanted to know. But since he was personally affected, he avidly absorbed everything Dr. Galen told him.

Amnesia could affect the past (retrograde) or the present (anterograde). It could have physical causes (organic) or emotional ones (psychogenic). Some amnesiacs were unable to remember anything for more than a few seconds, while others would forget everything for only a few seconds at a time. Some victims knew that they were having difficulty, while others passionately denied it.

Nine out of every ten cases of amnesia, Derec learned, had some specific physical cause. Those causes were as different as inflammation of the whorled and folded outer layer of the brain, hardening of the cerebral arteries, electric shock, and deficiency of B vitamins. (Also on the list, but nowhere near the top, was a blow to the head.)

"In more primitive times, many cases of true organic amnesia were wrongly diagnosed as psychogenic," Dr. Galen said as though outraged by the fact. "Patients who needed drugs or surgery were offered hypnosis and psychotherapy."

"Maybe all amnesias have some physical cause," Derec suggested. "Maybe the ten percent we still think are psychogenic are the ones we just haven't found the organic cause for."

But Dr. Galen dissented. "The distinction between mind and brain has not been completely erased by medical science. The mind is more than the sum of the brain's parts. There are things that happen at that level of synergy which cannot be traced to specific physical events."

Even so, the testing focused first on the possible physical causes. Dr. Galen subjected him to cortical analysis, an endorphin response test, three different nondestructive scans of his brain, and even a biopsy and culture for encephalitis.

"Your own awareness of your loss of memory is a clue, as your apparently unimpaired intelligence," Dr. Galen told Derec. "You retain your sense of time and of the connectedness of events. All of these things are meaningful."

But the unhappy truth was that all the clues added up to naught, and all the tests revealed nothing. Derec learned several new words to describe his condition—"fractionated retrograde hypnosis-resistant psychogenic amnesia"—but he learned nothing about himself.

"I can find no physical cause," Dr. Galen concluded reluctantly at the end of a week. "Your cortex, thalamus, mammillary bodies, and fornix bundle are all normal. And yet you have not responded to any psychogenic therapy I am aware of. I am sorry, Derec, I have failed you."

"Don't take it so hard," Derec said, sighing. "I'm beginning to get used to life in the dark."

In the course of the testing, Dr. Galen had gradually allowed Derec more and more freedom of movement until he had the run of the small hospital complex. Physically, he was nearly completely restored. His new skin was no longer painful to the touch and was gradually becoming less sensitive to variations in temperature. His ribs had knitted while he was kept unconscious, and the only sign they had even been broken was an occasional stitch of dull pain when he drew a deep breath or stretched the wrong way.

Despite that progress, Dr. Galen resisted releasing Derec from his care. The furthest he would go was to allow Derec to move from the ICU to a private room with more traditional accommodations. But the robot's recalcitrance was not entirely a surprise. With their special First Law responsibility as healers, robot doctors were notorious for their caution.

But Derec suspected that it was not the injuries to his body that concerned Dr. Galen, but the injury to Derec's mind. The real reason for keeping Derec nearby was to keep him under observation while he treated Katherine. Since Dr. Galen could not be in two places at once, he was keeping his two patients in one place.

Derec could not order Dr. Galen to stop worrying about him, so he resigned himself to living within the robot's restrictions. In some ways, Derec welcomed the vacation from responsibility. His body had had time to heal, but his mind still vividly remembered the erupting surface of the asteroid, the electric blue pain from Aranimas's stylus, the sudden flash of the booby trap exploding in his face. He had a right to a few days of peace.

Or so Derec thought. But one day of idleness was enough to satisfy that need. The next morning he did not wait for Dr. Galen's ritual visit and examination, but went looking for the robot himself. He found him standing at the biomedical monitor at the foot of Katherine's bed in the ICU.

"Good morning, Derec," the robot said. "I am sorry that I was delayed. How are you feeling today?"

"Restless," Derec said. "I'm ready to get back to a normal life."

"But you are in the fugue state of an amnesiac episode," Dr. Galen said. "A normal life is not possible for you now."

"I'll settle for the substitute at hand," Derec said. "I can't just sit around here hoping my memory will come back."

"What is it you wish to do?"

"I guess I won't know until I find out what's already been done for me," Derec said. "Outside of the robots on the station, who knows that I'm here? Is anybody trying to find out who I am?"

"I cannot say," Dr. Galen said. "I am certain that the station manager reported your arrival to the district supervisor at Nexon, as I did to the medical supervisor. That information may have been passed to any number of interested parties in the interval since. Why, is there someone you would like to contact?"

Derec pointed across the room at the sleeping Katherine. "Her. How much longer till you bring her out?"

"I concluded some days ago that she might hold the key to unlocking your loss of memory, and decided to allow her to wake at the earliest opportunity when her own health and comfort would not be at risk," said Dr. Galen. "She was taken off the sleep-inducing drug at midnight. According to her brain waves, she is dreaming now. I expect her to wake sometime this morning."

Derec glanced around the ward. There was nowhere to sit except the floor.

"There is no need for you to conduct a vigil," Dr. Galen said as though reading his thoughts.

"I want to be here when she wakes up."

Dr. Galen nodded understandingly. "I promise, I will call you."

Derec whiled away one hour, then another, with a book-film titled "The Architects of the Machine." He hoped to find among its profiles of notable designers and engineers a clue as to who the "minimalist" behind the asteroid colony might have been. With all the more tangible evidence lost or destroyed, it was one of the few unexplored leads left to him. Genius of that sort had to have left a trail.

But only three of the biographies were of contemporary designers, and the choices were entirely predictable. The roboticist Fastolfe. March, the Havalean wizard of microm-agnetics. The human ecologist Rutan, whose services were so much in demand by the wealthy on a dozen Spacer worlds.

All three had become celebrities, acclaimed by those who knew nothing about what it took to do what they did. But the engineering community had its own celebrities, based on its own standards. Every exclusive group did—those persons who had won the respect and admiration of their peers but were completely unknown outside the circle. Fastolfe ranked here, too, but March was regarded as a toy-maker and Rutan as a joke.

Yes, he needed an insider's perspective. Someone would know Derec's mysterious genius—

"Master Derec, if I may interrupt."

Derec's head jerked up. It was the medical orderly. Like Dr. Galen, the orderly had fallen victim to the supervisor's perverse sense of humor. "Yes, Florence."

"Dr. Galen said that you should come right away."

Pushing back the viewer, Derec jumped to his feet. "Coming."

When he reached the ICU, the sterilization lights were already off and Katherine was beginning to stir. She now wore an ankle-to-neck beige gown, etiquette having changed along with Dr. Galen's changing perception of their relationship. Derec hung back as Dr. Galen bent over Katherine and spoke softly to her.

"Good morning," he said. "Don't try to move."

But she lifted her head a few centimeters all the same and surveyed the room. "Hospital?" she asked hoarsely.

"Yes, Katherine. I am Dr. Galen."

"On what station?"

"Rockliffe Station."

She nodded and looked past Dr. Galen to Derec. "Some rescue," she said.

Despite her hoarseness, there was a laughing note to her voice that Derec did not like. Taking a step closer, he said stiffly, "We're both alive, aren't we?"

"Which just goes to show that there's no justice in the Galaxy," she answered, closing her eyes. "I thought you'd have been smart enough to disable Aranimas's security system before you started to poke around in his hidey-hole."

"Look, I'm sorry it didn't go more smoothly," Derec said, coming to the side of the bed. "But we did get away. And there was something we were going to talk about once we did—"

Her eyes fluttered open and searched past Derec for the robot's face. "Dr. Galen, the headaches are back," she said. "Would you ask Derec to leave, please? I just don't think I can deal with company now."

"How long could it take to tell me my surname, my homeworld—"

But Dr. Galen intervened, gently pushing Derec back toward the door. "I understand your impatience, Derec. But I must consider Katherine's health, too. Please leave. I will find out what I can. When she is stronger you can talk with her again, if she consents."

Derec took his frustration for a walk, leaving the hospital by the main entrance. He was sure that Dr. Galen would report him or send a robot after him to bring him back, but he did not care. He simply could not calmly stay there and wait. To be so close to answers, to the promise of being whole again, was too great a test for his patience.

The section of the station where the hospital was located was a tomb. He walked dimly lit streets past ranks of closed stores and sealed residential blocks. Only the main through-way was even lit. The side streets and courtyards were black pits.

No robot pursued him. He walked and walked until the edge was off his jumbled emotions, and then he turned back. He stalked through the reception area and into Dr. Galen's office.

"Did she tell you anything?"

"She was not able to offer any insight into your affliction."

"You discussed my condition with her? But you wouldn't tell me—"

"Correction. She was already aware of your condition."

"What did she do, ask your advice on how to deal with me?"

"Derec, I promised Katherine that I would not discuss our conversation with you."

Crossing his arms over his chest, Derec blew a sigh ceiling-ward. "I don't understand why she's being so secretive. If she knows something about me, she should just tell me." He cast a raised-eyebrow glance in Dr. Galen's direction. "Isn't that right?"

"The advisability of that would vary from case to case, depending on the individual, the cause of the dysfunction, and the particular personal data concerned," was Dr. Galen's measured answer.

"You won't even give me a hint, will you?" Derec said ruefully.

"I regret that I may not."

Derec frowned. "Can I see her, at least?"

The robot turned to one of the two active displays on the wall behind him. "She is awake and her algesia has moderated. But she is the final arbiter."

"Then I'm going to go see what she has to say."

They found Katherine sitting up in her bed. "I was hoping someone would come to see me," she said with a smile.

"You left me with some good reasons to," Derec said, scanning the room fruitlessly for a chair to move beside the bed.

Her face clouded over. "Da—Derec," she said, stumbling over his name as though she had forgotten it. "I'm afraid you're going to be angry with me. We have a lot of ground to make up together—all the things that happened on the ship. I don't think we should start with the little I know about you."

The look that Derec shot at Dr. Galen was black and poisonous. "What is this? What did you tell her? I thought you were trying to help me—"

"I cannot do otherwise," the robot said calmly.

The truth of that slowed Derec's rush to anger. He turned back to Katherine and said, "So you're going to keep secrets from me."

She shook her head. "Derec—let's say that you were President of New Liberty—"

"New Liberty has a council-manager government," Derec interrupted.

"It doesn't matter. Let's say you were President of New Liberty and lost your memory. If I tell you that you're the President, does that make you the President? Can you start acting like the person you used to be just because you know that?"

Derec avoided her eyes. "I suppose not. But hearing it could make me remember—"

"It is far more likely to cause you severe anxiety," Dr. Galen began. "Most often—"

Derec opened his mouth to answer, but Katherine was faster. "Dr. Galen, go away," she snapped. "Go back to your office and leave us alone. Don't monitor me and don't listen in. We'll call you if we need you."

The robot stared a moment, then lowered its head and exited.

"You didn't have to get so personal," Derec said, surprised at her forcefulness. "I'll bet you put a kink in poor Dr. Galen's self-worth integral that he'll be an hour working out."

"Oh, I don't care," Katherine said peevishly, staring at the empty doorway. "Medical robots are such busybodies. They've got ten thousand opinions but they don't really know anything. And they can't really understand what someone's feeling when they're sick, now, can they? Because they're machines and they never get sick, or die."

Is that what's the matter with you? Derec wondered,

looking at her face. Are you dying from something the doctors can't cure? Is that what Dr. Galen wouldn't talk about?

Before he could find the courage to ask her aloud, she looked toward him and patted the bed beside her. "Are you going to stand all the way over there? The field can hold both of us."

After a moment's hesitation, Derec settled on the edge of the bed by Katherine's feet.

"There, that's better," she said. "Now I don't feel so much like a prisoner being questioned."

"I'm not sure what we have left to talk about."

"Well—I'm sure there's more to what happened on the asteroid than you told me on the ship. Then there's the ship and what we went through there. And there's me."

"Let's start there. Your name, for starters. The robot called you Katherine—"

"I am Katherine Ariel Burgess to my mother and the computers. Everyone else calls me Kate," she said. "My father says that calling me Katherine is false advertising—that it doesn't give people any warning what they're in for. Katherine is please and thank you and dresses that cover you to the neck. Kate is—"

"Sharp-tongued and strong-willed and I-can-take-care-of-my-self-thank-you," Derec supplied.

Katherine brightened as though she had been complimented. "Something like that. My father says that I have spice."

"I think I'll stick to Katherine. What were you doing on Aranimas's ship?"

"Why, I was a prisoner just like you were. My robots and I were kidnapped off a courier ship." She snapped her fingers. "I just remembered. Where's the key? You didn't let the robots have it, did you?"

"I don't know where it is," he said. "I don't even know that it was ever where I thought it was."

"Is the ship here? Have you been back in it?"

"Frost, I don't know. I hadn't even been out of the hospital until this morning," Derec said, annoyed. "Will you tell me this—why is that key so important? What is it? What's it the key *to?*"

"I don't know," Katherine said soberly. "I only know that Aranimas thought it was worth anything to get. Wait—I thought you said the key was your property. Don't *you* know why it's important?"

"It is my property," Derec asserted. "Space salvage. Or a gift. Either way, I have the best claim to it."

"But you don't know what it is?"

"No."

She seemed disappointed. "Maybe you do know—but it's one of the things you've forgotten."

"I guess that's possible," Derec acceded. "Did Aranimas come to the asteroid specifically looking for the key? Not because I was there?"

"I don't think so—"

"You don't think so what?"

"I think he went to the asteroid on purpose. I don't think he knew the key was there. I'm almost positive he didn't know you were there," she said. "I think you were just lucky—or would it be unlucky?"

Derec considered. "Lucky, the way it fell out. I'd sure rather be here on Rockliffe Station than back on that asteroid."

"Lucky, then." She paused. "Look, if it is yours, maybe getting it back in your hands would help you remember something. And even if it doesn't, we need to find out what happened to the key. Aranimas had to have some reason for wanting it."

"Wolruf called it 'the jewel' when she talked to Aranimas," Derec said thoughtfully. "But I don't think she meant it literally."

"Either way, it's something valuable. Are we going to try to find it, or not?"

"We?" For a brief moment, Derec bristled defensively. Then he reminded himself what it had been like to be a loner on the raider ship. He felt at home here—but Katherine clearly didn't. She was hurting, and she was alone, and she wanted to be his friend. And beyond that, she knew something about who he was—and wanted to help him remember.

"Sure," he said. "Of course we are."

CHAPTER 15

OH SEVEN B

Despite all the good intentions, the partnership almost fell apart before it began. Derec had somehow visualized the arrangement with himself making all the decisions and Katherine gratefully following his lead. But he found out very quickly that it was Kate, not Katherine, with whom he'd made his pact.

Derec was eager to get started looking for the artifact. Since Dr. Galen had raised no protest about Derec's excursion out of the hospital, he felt he had won the right to roam where he wanted. At the very least, it would be several days before Kate was accorded the same freedom.

But when Derec proposed that he go scouting alone and then report back to Katherine on his discoveries, she balked. "We go together or all promises are off," she said firmly. "If we're going to be a team, we have to work as a team."

"Being a team doesn't mean we have to be handcuffed together," Derec argued. "Everybody should do what they do best, and right now what I can do best is be our eyes and ears."

"What are you going to do?"

Derec shrugged. "Talk to the dock supervisor and the station manager. Start finding out what's happened while we were here."

"They're robots," she said. "Let them come here."

It was a perfectly reasonable idea, and the fact that it had not occurred to Derec jarred him for a moment. He had been thinking of talking to the station staff ever since he had regained consciousness, but always in terms of going to see them. He realized that he had made an unspoken assumption: *they're busy—they don't have time to come down here to talk to me.*

He had never once thought of ordering them to leave their work. Katherine had thought of it immediately. Derec knew somehow that the difference said something important about the two of them—something about their background, the subculture which had shaped their attitudes about robots.

It was as though he respected the importance of the robots' work and saw them more or less as equals, while she thought of them only as servants. But whether it meant he had more experience with robots than she or less, he could not say.

All the same, it was another tiny piece in his puzzle. He was not like Katherine. They came from different worlds—culturally if not geographically. It made him wonder how it was she knew him.

All these thoughts cascaded through Derec's mind in a fraction of a second, allowing him to carry on the conversation with only the faintest hesitation. "Look, I'm willing to share the decision-making. Maybe we could get the robots to come here," he said. "There's still the ship. I should go have a look at it."

"That's something we should do together."

"Why? What's hidden there that you don't want me to find?"

Katherine crossed her arms and sighed. "If you're going to be suspicious of me all the time, this isn't going to work."

"I'm not suspicious of you!" Derec exclaimed, throwing his hands in the air. "I just don't understand why you don't seem to want to let me out of your sight."

"And I don't understand your hurry," Katherine said stiffly. "You say that we're a team, but you want to go run off and do everything yourself."

"The hurry is because we want to get there first," Derec said impatiently. "We don't want anyone else taking it."

She looked at him quizzically. "We've been here six weeks. Do you really think that they pulled us out and then locked the ship up somewhere until we could claim it? Think! That's an alien starship. How long do you think it took them to realize they'd never seen one like it before—not just the design, but the whole technology? This is a frontier base. Do you think they just take it in stride when an unregistered ship shows up with two injured humans aboard?"

Belatedly, Derec understood. "So they've been all over it. Photographed it, X-rayed it, the whole works. They might have even torn it down, sent pieces of it out on *Fariis* to the district offices. They're probably wondering about us, too."

"Of course they are. That's why I sent Dr. Galen away."

"Do you think he's been spying on us?"

"All robots are spies for their masters," she said bitterly.

"What?" Derec asked, surprised by her intensity.

"Nevermind," she said. "I just think we ought to play

innocents abroad for a while, do all the things they expect us to—until we understand what kind of game we're in."

"Be helpless and worried. Play dumb."

"Just so," Katherine said. "Sometimes it's the smartest thing you can do."

At their request, Dr. Galen had a multicom brought to the ICU and tied into the station net. Very quickly, they learned that the Rockliffe Station welcome mat was a bit threadbare.

The station manager was fully scheduled until the following morning and thought that they really wanted to talk to the dock supervisor anyway. The dock supervisor was conducting an overhaul of the dock pressurization system, a priority task which had to be completed in the shortest possible time, and had they tried the dispatcher?

The dispatcher couldn't answer their questions without clearance from the security chief, who deferred to the associate manager for station operations. The AMSOP was one step down the ladder from the station manager and probably the robot to which they should have been recommended in the first place.

The AMSOP was busy at the moment but would be free in an hour if they wanted to make an appointment. It seemed to be the best they could do, so they took it.

"So what do we do while we're waiting?" Derec said as he turned off the viewer.

"We could spend the time getting to know each other better—"

"Should I entertain you with stories about my family?"

She laughed—a nice laugh. "Maybe not."

"*You* could tell me stories about my family."

"No, I couldn't."

"Katherine—the only person who knows anything about me is you," Derec said pleadingly. "Why don't you tell me some of it now?"

"Not yet."

"Still following Dr. Galen's advice?"

"This really is the best way," she said, touching his hand.

"It doesn't feel like it to me," he said gruffly. "All right. Tell me about you, then."

"It's boring," she warned.

He cocked an eyebrow. "Being hijacked by an alien spacecraft was boring?"

"My life is boring. That's the first exciting thing that ever happened." She added, "Except it wasn't exactly a hijacking."

"Tell me about it. What was the name of your courier ship?"

"*Golden Eagle*, out of Viking. We were carrying a diplomatic pouch to Frier's Planet—"

At least in a first reading, the story had the ring of truth.

According to Katherine, she and her robots had been outbound from Viking on the courier ship *Golden Eagle*, along with a pilot and two diplomats. Just before they were about to make their Jump at the fringe of the Viking system, the pilot spotted Aranimas's ship, apparently adrift.

Taking it for an uncharted wreck—in part because of its appearance and in part because they could not raise it on any channel—they abandoned their exit trajectory and went to investigate. Suddenly they were fired upon, and their ship disabled. Katherine and the robots were taken off the courier by the Narwe, and then the courier was set adrift. A short time later the courier exploded, probably, Katherine said, because of a bomb that had been placed aboard.

There were no screaming contradictions in the story, but there were several little points that nagged at Derec. Katherine was vague about just why she was on the courier. At first she seemed to want him to think that she was part of the diplomatic mission. But even though she wanted him to think that she was old enough for such duty, she clearly was not.

When he questioned her on it, she hastily explained that she had been a passenger, using the courier instead of a commercial carrier because she wanted privacy. He wondered aloud at a courier taking on passengers. She responded by hinting that she was important enough to justify any exception that might have been required.

But the biggest sticking point, and the one on which he kept his own counsel, was the behavior of the courier pilot. Couriers carried important people, emergency supplies, engineering prototypes, irreplaceable documents. It didn't make sense that a courier pilot would endanger his cargo by poking around a wreck. It seemed far more likely that the pilot would report the sighting to the Patrol post on Viking, then make his Jump on schedule.

Derec recalled that the first time her capture had come up, Katherine had quickly changed the subject. He wondered now if that was because she didn't have her story ready. Perhaps he was being fed half-truths as some sort of test— Dr. Galen's prescription for crippled minds. If so, he resented it.

But the arrival at last of the Assistant Manager for Station Operations pushed those thoughts to the back of Derec's mind.

"I am called Hajime," the AMSOP said, "Dr. Galen tells

me that both of you are recovering from your injuries. That is good news."

"Especially to us," Derec said under his breath.

"I understand that you have questions about your presence here. I hope that I will be able to answer them."

Derec opened his mouth to answer, but before he could speak Katherine jumped in. "Begin with when the station first detected our ship and tell us what you observed," she ordered.

"Yes, madam. The station's sensors detected an unidentified ship immediately after it emerged from its Jump—as you may know, the termination of a Jump is accompanied by a minor spacetime disturbance comparable to the atmospheric disturbance caused by a discharge of lightning—"

"We know all that," Derec said. "Get on with it."

"Forgive me, sir," the robot said with a slight bow. "I only wanted to be certain that you understood how we were able to detect your ship at such a great distance."

"Why? How far out were we?"

"Eighty-three astronomical units. At such a distance, the station's sensors were only able to determine the position and velocity of the vessel. Since there was no direct identification through a transponder or indirect identification through sensor data, this vessel was designated UPH-07."

"UPH?" Katherine asked.

"Forgive me. Unidentified, Potentially Hostile," Hajime supplied.

"Go on, Hajime."

"Thank you, sir. We tracked Oh Seven inbound for two days. We were just beginning to acquire some preliminary data on its mass and profile when an anomalous event took place. UPH-07 divided into two independent bodies, UPH-

07A and UPH-07B. The larger vessel, Oh Seven A, made a course correction which carried it out of the station's zone of control—"

"They cut us loose and then turned around and went away," Katherine said.

"Looks like it," Derec said. "Did the big ship Jump?"

"Not while it was within range of our sensors, sir," Hajime answered. "It is not possible to say what happened once contact was lost."

Derec and Katherine exchanged glances that said, So they could still be out there somewhere, waiting.

"And the other vessel, Oh Seven B, it continued inbound?" Katherine asked. "That's where you found us?"

"Yes, madam. A scout with a rescue and retrieval team aboard was dispatched immediately."

"Can you show us a navigational plot of all this?" Derec asked.

"Certainly, sir." The robot went to the hyperviewer and entered a code on the keyboard, and a moment later the far wall dissolved into the black of space.

It was all there as the robot had described it. A blue trace from the top of the plot traced the raider's approach to the station, represented by a golden hexagon at the bottom. One-third of the way there, the blue trace split. A thick green trace angled off the plot to the upper right, while a thin red one continued curling inbound on the original trajectory. Two-thirds of the way down the plot, the red trace intersected a golden trace climbing up out of the station: the rescue ship.

"Can we have a copy of that?" Derec said.

"I will file it in a directory under your name," Hajime said, his touch on the controls turning the far wall into a wall once more.

"Was the boarding recorded?" Katherine asked.

"Yes, madam."

"I'd like to see the recording," Katherine said, beckoning Derec to come sit on the edge of the bed beside her. When he did, she took his hand and gripped it tightly, as though seeking reassurance. The skin contact surprised and unsettled Derec.

"The recording was made by means of a witness robot," Hajime said. "The multicom will not be able to display the full bandwidth—"

"What's a witness robot?" Katherine whispered to Derec.

"I'll explain later," Derec whispered back. Witness robots were odd-looking, with their bullet heads and 360-degree scanning slit instead of eye sensors, but invaluable for such operations. Their sole responsibility was to position themselves so that their scanners and recorders captured unfolding events clearly. Many a bungled operation had been reconstructed from the data supplied by witness robots before they were destroyed.

"—so if you wish to move the window left or right at any point please tell me so."

From the outside, Aranimas's ship looked like a fat arrowhead trailing bits of the twine which had held it to the shaft. The arrowhead was in fact an atmosphere-piercing lifting body, and the twine the tattered remnants of several transfer corridors which had been attached to the hexagonal junction between the engine exhaust bells at the stern.

Together Derec and Katherine watched as the rescue robots fit a self-cutting emergency hatch to the upper hull. When the hatch's contact ring had burned through the hull and fused itself in place, the robots entered—one at a time, the witness first.

"This is where Aranimas had me living," she whispered as the hypervision panned the atticlike upper deck.

"How long were you there?"

"Two months. Believe me, it seemed longer."

When the witness robot led the way down to the main deck, the first thing they saw was a robot standing in the central corridor.

"Alpha," Derec cried.

"Capek," Katherine said at the same instant. "Where's my robot?"

Hajime suspended the recording. "This robot was removed and taken away for diagnostic examination and repair."

"I want him back, just the way he was," Derec said. "You've got no right to tinker with him without a work order."

"The robot resisted our efforts to rescue you. It was judged to be operating in a substandard and hazardous manner and was deactivated. Standard procedure in such cases is to perform a full examination so that the anomaly may be reported to the manufacturer."

Katherine was nodding in reluctant agreement, and Derec took his cue from her. "All right," he said. "Go on."

When the recording continued, they saw themselves for the first time. They were lying head to foot along one wall in the central walkway of the main deck. Katherine winced and turned away at the sight of her own burn-blistered face and bloody clothing. Derec gritted his teeth and tried not to feel the pain all over again that was reflected in his burned skin.

"I thought so," Derec whispered under his breath. "I thought so."

"What?" Katherine demanded. "What are you talking about?"

"Alpha. He kept us alive."

"You heard Hajime—the robot was abnormal. He wouldn't let them rescue us."

"That was just the PD cube being careful. Look," Derec said, gesturing. "Those aren't positions that you fall into naturally after an accident like that, or even crawl into. We were moved. And more: we were at least five days out when I tripped the booby trap. It took the rescue ship two and a half days to reach us. There's no quarreling with the fact that we were badly injured—"

"No," she said with a little shiver.

"I was wondering how we survived until the paramedics got to us. We should have died right there on the ship. All they should have found were corpses. Alpha is the reason they didn't." Derec looked toward the robot. "Hajime, could you pause the recording and give us privacy, please?"

"Of course, Derec." The image and the robot both froze.

"What? What's going on?"

"I just want to point out that someone else might have been on the ship, too."

"What are you thinking about?"

"I had wondered why Wolruf and the robot were taking so long to get back from their errand. What if Aranimas regained consciousness? They might still have been trying to lock him up when the bomb went off. Alpha would have come running back. He wouldn't worry about Aranimas. He probably wouldn't even worry about what Aranimas might do to Wolruf. Aranimas and Alpha could both have gotten back into Hull A before it was cut loose."

"And Alpha would have protected us from him, just as it tried to protect us from the rescue crew."

"That might even explain *why* Alpha gave the robots trouble."

"He could have hidden," Katherine said thoughtfully. "It was his ship. He would have known where he'd be safe. Until the ship was brought in—"

"Just what I was thinking. If he doesn't have the key, he's looking for it—or us. If he's got it, he still may be looking for us. Either way, the key's not safe, and neither are we. And we can't just sit around and tell ourselves there's no rush. We have to start doing something right now."

Katherine cast her gaze downward into her lap. "All right," she said at last.

"Hajime," Derec said. "You can rejoin us."

The robot stirred again. "Thank you, sir. Shall I continue with the recording?"

"No. Terminate the replay. We've seen enough," Katherine said.

"Very well, madam," the robot said, complying. "Do you have other questions?"

"Yes. Where is Oh Seven B now?"

"I do not know, madam."

The answer brought Derec up off the bed, his face reddening. "What do you mean, you don't know?" he demanded. "You're the second highest ranking staffer on the station."

"That is correct, sir."

"And you don't know where our ship is?"

"I only know that Oh Seven B is no longer in the berth at which it was moored when first towed into the station."

"Was it stolen?" Derec pressed. "Are you trying to tell me it's gone?"

"It was not stolen. It was moved under the authorization of the station manager."

"Why didn't you say so from the start?" Katherine snapped.

"Derec asked if I knew where Oh Seven B was berthed. I do not, and so informed him."

"Then find out where our ship is. I want you to take us to it."

"I am sorry," Hajime said. "I am not permitted to do that."

"Then find us a robot who is permitted," Derec snapped.

"I have been instructed to refer all inquiries of this sort to the station manager."

Derec sighed. "All right. You can go."

"Thank you, sir." The robot paused. "May I make an inquiry, sir?"

"What about?"

"Do you continue to refer to Oh Seven B as 'our ship' out of habit or as a matter of affection?"

"What do you mean?"

"I have been informed that the vessel known as Oh Seven B is no longer your property."

CHAPTER 16

INTO THE DARKNESS

The station manager, a robot named Anazon, would not come to see them, but agreed to a brief vidcall.

"Is the care you are receiving satisfactory?" Anazon asked politely. "I hope that Hajime is seeing to your other needs—"

Derec did not waste any time on pleasantries. "Where is our ship? Where is Oh Seven B?" he demanded.

"I regret, sir, that I am not permitted to tell you," the robot said without a hint of regret in his voice.

"Who gave that order?"

"I regret, sir, that I am not permitted to tell you that, either."

Derec was determined not to be thwarted. "Who is your supervisor? What's his name?"

"My supervisor's name is Aram Jacobson."

"Get him on this channel."

"Mr. Jacobson may not be available at this time—"

"Do it. Use whatever priority you have to to get him to

answer. And keep the line open. I want to hear what you say."

The robot reached forward for the hyperviewer controls. "This is Anazon, Manager of Rockliffe Station, requesting a conference with Mr. Jacobson."

A voice said "One moment," and there was a pause.

"Yes, Anazon," a new voice said. The words were muddied by the faint electronic echo which was the telltale sign of a scrambler somewhere in the link. "What is it?"

"Anazon called you on my behalf," Derec cut in. "Your robots have appropriated my ship. I expect you to order them to return it."

"And our robot," Katherine added. "We want Capek back, too."

The hypervision image of Anazon faded and was replaced an instant later by one of a round-faced man with narrow eyes and shiny black hair. In sharp contrast to the robot's slender physique, Jacobson's stout body was perched precariously on his executive chair like an egg on a teaspoon.

"Excuse me, by whom do I have the pleasure of being ordered about?" he asked with exaggerated politeness.

"My name is Derec. This is—"

"Just Derec? No last name, like a robot?"

"Don't be cute. You know all about me. I'm sure there's a file on me in your library."

"I have many files in my library," Jacobson said. "I'm responsible for facilities which employ twenty-six hundred humans and nearly eight thousand robots. Believe me when I tell you that neither your name nor your face are familiar to me." His gaze flicked toward Katherine. "And you, miss?"

"Katherine Burgess. And don't call me miss."

"My apologies if I insulted you," Jacobson said, bowing

his head slightly. "Now if I could ask you to restate your complaint—this is most irregular, to have someone barge in on a private call. I'm afraid it rather distracted me."

Derec was too furious for words, but Katherine took over smoothly. "We were found on a damaged spacecraft and brought here to Rockliffe Station. Now the station manager refuses to allow us access to our ship."

"Refuses you access?" Jacobson asked, wrinkling his forehead. "Whatever for?"

"It won't tell us," Derec said. "It says it's been ordered not to tell us—my guess is by you."

"I assure you not," Jacobson said, reaching for his computer. "If you'll just allow me a moment to check the records—" He turned his back to them briefly. "Oh yes, of course," he said to himself as he studied the screen.

"Of course what?"

Jacobson turned back to face them. "I do recall hearing about you after all, Derec. You're the amnesia case Dr. Galen is studying. That explains a great deal."

"Not to me."

"But it does all the same. You see, the care you've been receiving is quite costly—"

"Dr. Galen said my bill would be charged against a station account."

"I'm afraid Dr. Galen made an error," Jacobson said. "That would be the case if you were indigent and unable to pay, or if the costs of your care exceeded the guarantee made by your homeworld on behalf of its citizens."

"But my case is different—"

"Indeed. Your citizenship is unknown. Your financial assets are unknown. Indeed, there is even some question about your majority under Spacer law," said Jacobson.

"I'm old enough."

"We have decided to presume so," he said. "But in any case, since you have not been able to supply us with identification, we have no choice but to seize your tangible personal assets in payment of your account."

"My tangible assets—"

"Your ship and its contents have been appraised generously, I assure you," Jacobson said, glancing back at his computer. "Even so, I'm afraid there's not much left after subtracting the salvage fee and the expenses of the rescue operation. Still, there's more than enough to cover passage to Nexon on the next shuttle and keep you fed in the meantime."

Derec gaped disbelievingly. "You can't do that. You can't just take everything a man owns."

"It's the judgment of the minister of finance that anyone who has assets enough to own such a ship in the first place can quite afford to pay his bills," Jacobson said, sitting back in his chair. "If we were to let you get away with this, I'd be overwhelmed by freeloaders, all claiming to have forgotten where their funds are held."

"Are you accusing me of making this up? Ask Dr. Galen—"

"Dr. Galen does not set policy for the station. I do."

"At least you finally admit that this is your doing," Derec retorted. "I can't believe you have the nerve to charge me for rescuing me. You'd have gone out to intercept that ship whether we'd been on it or not."

"From our point of view, that ship wouldn't have been there endangering our facility *unless* you were in it," Jacobson said lightly.

"Just a moment," Katherine said. "That ship is half mine. Maybe you can grab his half for payment, but you can't touch mine. You know who I am. I authorized a draft on my account at the Auroran Exchange."

"So you did," Jacobson said. "Tell me, what sort of account was it?"

"A Living Share—a family trust—" Katherine's face was beginning to go gray.

"Which is a revocable trust, is it not?"

"I—I guess."

"I regret to inform you that on May 26, your account was closed and all funds withdrawn. Have you other assets of which we may not be aware?"

"No," Katherine said, her expression acutely pained. "That was my Living Share. How could they take it back? How could they do such a thing?"

"I cannot say. The fact remains, they did. You are legally an adult and responsible for your own debts. Therefore we have been obliged to exercise our rights to your portion of the property as well."

"You won't get away with this," Derec threatened feebly.

"It is not a question of 'getting away with' anything," Jacobson replied. "We are well within our rights. You should be grateful that you're alive, instead of fussing over a ship which I understand is not in flyable condition in any case. Since you couldn't have paid for its repair, you would have had to try to sell it anyway, and I doubt very much you could have gotten anything near the price you were paid by us."

"You—" Derec sputtered.

"Now, if you'll excuse me, I have other business to attend to."

The link dissolved before Derec could reply. "Do you

believe that performance?" he exclaimed, turning to Katherine. He was shocked to see how empty of spirit her eyes were.

"Performance?" she asked mechanically.

"This isn't what it looks like. This is just a way of separating us from the ship. To pay us for it they'd have to have proof that we own it—more than our word and the fact that they found us in it. Do you know why they're not asking us for that proof? They don't want to know. Just like they don't want to know whether I'm too young to be responsible for my own debts."

"It doesn't matter," she said. "None of it matters."

Derec stared at her. "What's bothering you?"

"My money. My family took my money—"

"Is that any great surprise? The Patrol probably reported you missing when they went out and picked over what was left of the *Golden Eagle*."

"They didn't even give me a chance to explain—" she said despairingly.

"Explain to who?" he asked gently.

But his question seemed to awaken her to her loss of control. The line of her jaw stiffened and her eyes hardened. "Frost them. Frost them all," she said tersely. "It's ancient history. What do we do now?"

"What are you game for?"

"I'll tell you what I'm *not* going to do. I'm not going to wait around quietly until the next freighter comes and then meekly traipse off to Nexon," she declared. "And I'm not about to let a bunch of robots keep me away from my property, even if they are following the orders of that milkface."

"Sounds like I'm going to need to start calling you Kate."

Surprised, she smiled. "Maybe you'd better."

"Good. Because I think we're going to need her," Derec said. "This isn't going to be easy."

"I know. But there's a limit to how many places you can hide a ship of that size, even in a station this large. If it's still here, we'll find it."

"Probably so," Derec agreed. "Chances are they moved it from the active dock to one of the deactivated ones—in the military wing, would be my guess. Even if the station directory won't tell us where the other dock facilities are, we can figure it out. But that won't help us much."

"Why not?"

"Because the key is what matters, not the ship. Jacobson is right. We don't have any use for the ship."

"We find the ship, we find the key."

Derec shook his head unhappily. "The key won't be there. The robots have it."

"Jacobson didn't say anything about it."

"Why should he take the chance of being the first to call our attention to it?" Derec asked rhetorically. "I just know that the whole time we talked to him, he was sitting there waiting for us to ask about our personal effects or give some sign we know about the key—waiting to pounce if we did. It was a test. We passed, so they're going to let us go. If we hadn't—"

"Why should they take any special notice of the key? It doesn't look like anything special. They don't know what Aranimas went through to get it. I do, and I still don't' know why it's so important."

"So you say."

"Do you think I'm lying?"

Yes, he thought. Or at least not telling the whole truth. I'm starting to believe that everybody knows what this thing is but me—that you're pretending that you're just as ignorant as I am, while all the time you know exactly what it is and why it's important.

But he said none of that. "I don't know what to think," Derec said, frustration thick in his voice.

"I think the key's still hidden wherever Aranimas kept it. Jacobson didn't mention the key because he doesn't know anything about it. He's just worried about the ship in general."

"He knows. I'm sure of it," Derec said stubbornly.

"Look, if Jacobson knows about the key and the robots found it, then it went out on *Fariis*. Which means he has it by now. End of story."

"Not necessarily," Derec said, shaking his head. "The packets are contract haulers, not Nexonian nationals. Do you think he'd trust them with something that's probably ten times more valuable than their whole fleet contract? For that matter, do you think he'd put it on an unarmed vessel with the raiders still sitting out there somewhere trying to figure out how to get it back?"

"What, then?"

"Put yourself in their shoes. First you protect your find from being disturbed, and then you get together a team to go retrieve and investigate it. As long as you've done the first one right, you can take your time doing the second. They'll be here when they've assembled the people and the hardware they need. At the very least they'll need to scare up a bulk freighter to carry the spacecraft back and a warship to give the raiders second thoughts."

Katherine sighed. "What a mess. Maybe we ought to just let them have it."

"The hell with that," Derec spat. "As long as Aranimas doesn't have the key, and the raiders don't attack, and Jacobson is still on Nexon—we've got a chance."

"But it's a race."

"Yes. It's a race. And we can't wait around for you to get a clean bill of health from Dr. Galen before we start," Derec said pointedly, bracing for an argument.

The argument never came. "You're right," she said simply, swinging her legs over the side of the bed and feeling for the floor. "Where to?"

Before that question could be considered, there was Dr. Galen to deal with. The robot came bursting into the room before Katherine's bare feet even had a chance to pick up a chill from the floor.

"Please return to the bed, patient Katherine," Dr. Galen requested. "Florence can see to whatever needs you might have."

Derec was girding himself for another protracted argument, but Katherine surprised him. "I'll go where I want when I want," she snapped. "And if you start trying to act like a warden instead of a doctor I'll have your brain reprogrammed for basket-weaving."

"I must protest strongly—"

"Am I in danger of dying?"

"No, patient Katherine. But your recovery—"

"Then save your protest for your medical log: 'Patient Katherine Burgess disregarded recommended rehabilitation program.' Isn't that the phraseology? Derec and I are going for a walk. If you don't want me catching pneumonia you'd better get me some normal clothes. And something for my feet."

Any human addressed in that tone would have been clenching his fists and strongly considering using them. But Dr. Galen only nodded slightly. "I will have clothing brought."

"If it's not here in five minutes I'm going out like this,"

she warned him. "And don't get any ideas about following us around. If I have any problems, Derec will be there to bring me back."

When the robot left, Derec stared at Katherine in amazement. "How'd you learn how to do that?"

She shrugged. "Medical robots are as bossy as they come, but they can't make it stick unless you're really in some danger. I'm not."

"All the same, it would have taken me twenty minutes to get to the same point, if I'd ever gotten there at all."

"That's because you always let yourself get suckered into arguing with the robots. I just give them orders. Much more efficient."

"I guess it is, sometimes," Derec said. "But you ought to know, in about four hours your dermal analgesic is going to wear off and your skin is going to start feeling like someone's scraping it off with a spatula."

As Derec spoke, Florence entered, wordlessly laid a sleeveless jump suit and a pair of foot pillows on the end of the bed, and then left.

"Thanks for the warning. Let's make a point of being back in three and a half," Katherine said. "Now get out of here while I change."

By the time Katherine emerged from the ward, Derec had decided to go along with her proposal that they look for Aranimas's ship first. He had several reasons for surrendering—that the ship was the last known location of the key, that even if the key had been found and removed it might logically be kept nearby. But the most important reason was that if he didn't show her early that she was wrong, she'd soon be trying to order him around as she did the robots.

The electronic map on the wall of the lobby offered little

help, Rockliffe Station was built out of three connected spheres. The central sphere, called C Section, contained some forty levels from top to bottom. Two satellite spheres barely half as large were anchored to it by cylindrical pylons only a few levels in diameter.

Large areas within the station's outline were colored black and labeled "Inactive." No amount of coaxing could persuade the map's controller to reveal what facilities were in those areas or even show the traffic grid.

Less than fifteen percent of C Section was drawn in with the pale blue color, labels, and identifying symbols of the active zone. Most of E Section, which contained the known dock facilities, was blue. But W Section, together with its connecting pylon, was completely black.

"There," Katherine said, pointing to W Section. "They probably had an east terminal and a west terminal."

"Symmetrical design," Derec agreed. "Makes sense."

"It's a good place to start, anyway."

"Let's hope that those sections are just closed down, not closed off."

The hospital was located near the center of C Section, three levels down from the main thoroughfare. Together, Katherine and Derec climbed up to the main level and headed west. There were no physical barriers, though the four-lane express slidewalk was not operating, obliging them to walk.

But past the boundary of subsection 42, the corridor lights were out and the directional "lightworms" were off. Based on what he had seen during his earlier excursion, Derec had thought that might be the case. He had hoped for either a local control option or a presence sensor, but in vain. With eighteen subsections of blackness ahead of them, they were forced to turn back.

They recruited the first robot they encountered to show them where hand lanterns were kept, and soon returned to the subsection 42 threshold. The beams of the powerful portable lights stabbed deep into the cavelike corridor and created a cozy island of light around them. But they were very aware of the darkness beyond, the way their footsteps echoed hollowly, the chill of the unused spaces they were entering.

Ten minutes of walking brought them to the great triple pressure seal doors at the outer boundary of C Section. The doors were resting retracted in their grooves, apparently de-activated. Past the interlock, the throughway narrowed to a single-lane slidewalk in each direction with far fewer jump-offs and side passages than before.

Derec expected to find robots guarding the entry to W Section, and told Katherine so. But when they reached the far end of the slidewalk, they were still alone. The west docks were there, just as they had guessed. But the main public entrance to the complex was not even locked.

"No guards, no locks," Derec said as they stood on the threshold. "This looks very bad. Maybe they had one of the tugs take the ship and stand off a hundred klicks from the base."

"Let's find out," Katherine said, starting ahead.

If the west docks were being held for possible military use as Dr. Galen had implied, it was merely as a line item on some logistics officer's list of resources. There was no sign that the complex had even been or ever would be anything other than a general purpose cargo and passenger transfer node. All the familiar facilities were there: Import Registry, Customs, the travelers' Personals.

Katherine led Derec past the unstaffed security stations and up the loading ramp to the upper concourse. Along the

length of the high-ceilinged room were six check-in stations, six glassed-in waiting areas, and six two-story viewports each of which looked out onto an enormous docking
slip and space beyond. All six slips were empty and dark.
Nothing could be seen through the viewports except a few
dim and distant stars.

"Downstairs?" Derec asked.

Her lips pressed into a tight line, Katherine answered by
leading the way back down the ramp. The lower concourse
seemed like a mirror image of the upper. All six bays on
the lower concourse were dark—but one was not empty.

"Bingo," Derec said, sprinting through the check-in station and up the boarding tunnel.

"I don't understand," she said, dogging his heels.
"Where are the guards? There ought to be guards."

"Maybe they're inside," Derec said, pulling up short. The
boarding tunnel was connected to the emergency hatch they
had seen being installed, and across the lock-side seam there
was a security seal. It was a token seal, however, meant only
to give notice that the hatch had been opened. It could not
stop them from going aboard.

Nothing inside had been disturbed, it seemed, since they
had been found and removed. For that matter, except for
cracks in three of the screens above the great command
console, it did not even seem as though there had been an
explosion on the main deck. Yet there were a dozen black-
ened fist-sized pits in the walls and ceiling to mark where
the charges had been.

"You don't blow up your house because a burglar
breaks in," Katherine observed. "Aranimas's security would
have been tailored to his own species. Whatever you want
to call what we tripped—"

"Radiation bomb, maybe."

"—must have been designed to kill or disable an Erani without doing serious damage to the ship."

"It did a good enough job on us."

Though they could not find Aranimas's stylus, whatever locked the deck plates in place had apparently been disabled when the ship was powered down. Twenty minutes later, they had torn up the whole floor, but found nothing.

"Shall we put it back?" Katherine asked, gesturing at the mess they had created.

"No point. The robots are going to know we were here anyway."

"They have the key, don't they?"

"Almost certainly. If they don't, Jacobson does."

Katherine sighed. "How are we ever going to find it? The size of this station—even if it were just lying in open view in a corridor somewhere, it'd take us weeks to find it. And you know that they've hidden it better than that."

"There's a lot of places they could put it that you can be sure they didn't," Derec said, looking around the main cabin one last time. "They won't leave it unattended, you can count on that. Not like they left this ship."

"Do you have any idea why they let us in here?"

Derec nodded slowly. "I think so. To send us a message. To tell us just how harmless they think we are. That there's nothing we can do to them." He sighed. "And they may just be right. Let's get out of here, huh?"

CHAPTER 17

PARTNERS IN CRIME

Squeak.

Brush.

Squeak.

Brush.

The sounds were soft and distant, but they were there, all right. If either he or Katherine had been talking, as they had been the first third of the way back, there would have been no way he would have heard them. But ever since they had fallen silent in individual introspection, the sounds had played at the threshold of Derec's hearing.

At first he had thought them echoes of their own footsteps, or merely the product of paranoia. But as they were passing into subsection 51, Derec decided that they were real and not imagined. Something was following them.

"Don't say anything and don't turn around," Derec whispered. "You hold both lamps. Keep walking."

"What?"

"Ssssh. Keep walking. Keep the beams angled down so

you won't be silhouetted. Try to make it look like you're two people."

"What's this about?" she demanded. But she contained her curiosity to a whisper, and kept walking as he had asked.

Handing the torch to her at arm's length, Derec slipped away into the darkness and squeezed back against the wall. As he waited, he wondered who he was waiting for. One of Dr. Galen's robots? One of Jacobson's? Or Aranimas? He wished he still had the gas aerosol, or had kept his torch to use as a club.

Have to do it on your own, he told himself, dropping to his knees and huddling against the base of the wall.

The shadow was past Derec before he even saw it. Only when he looked back toward Katherine and caught a glimpse of it silhouetted against the glow of her torch did he move. Gathering himself up, he took three running steps and launched himself at the figure's legs. He struck cloth and bone, not syntheskin and metal, and the stranger came down in a heap on top of Derec, squealing protest.

They wrestled furiously in the darkness, each with different objectives. Derec was trying to get a firm grip on an arm, leg, or neck and pin the other to the floor. His adversary was trying only to break Derec's grip and escape.

Derec was much the more skilled. He had no difficulty getting what he thought were solid holds on the other. The difficulty was in maintaining them for more than a few seconds. Had they been wrestling in competition, he would have been getting the takedowns, his opponent the escape points. Part of the reason was the other's compact strength, and part the slippery fabric its clothes were made of.

But in the dark, luck counted for more than skill or strength, and neutralized both. The two combatants rolled from one side of the passageway to the other, neither able to gain a lasting advantage. Then, with a sudden twist and a lucky grab, Derec found himself on top, straddling the other's waist and with each of his hands locked in an iron grip on one of his opponent's wrists.

Just then Katherine shone one of the lamps full on the shadow's face. His adversary squinted up at him out of eyes nearly hidden by mottled gold and brown fur, and its mouth twisted into a familiar grimace.

"Wolruf!" Derec exclaimed.

" 'Ur stronger than 'u look, Derec," Wolruf said, still grinning. "But I 'ope 'u know I let 'u win."

Derec grinned back. "As ugly as you are, I'm awfully glad to see you. I was afraid we'd lost you when we were cut loose."

"Why are you treating it like some long-lost friend?" Katherine demanded. "It's Aranimas's fetch-boy."

"Girl," he corrected. "Besides, you don't understand," he added, helping Wolruf to her feet. "She's my friend."

"Partners," Wolruf said proudly.

"Oh? Then why was it skulking along behind us like that?"

"Following," Wolruf said.

"What were you planning to do?"

"I never 'urt 'u—"

"You were waiting for us to find the key, weren't you? And then you were going to steal it—"

"Katherine—she's sick," Derec said suddenly.

"What?"

"Look at her," he urged. "Look at me," he added, re-claiming his torch and turning its beam on himself. His clothing was covered with long gold and brown hairs. In the light of Katherine's torch, the alien's fur was so thin in patches that Derec could see the pale leathery skin beneath.

And there was something about Wolruf's eyes that tele-graphed the distress she had been enduring.

"What's wrong with you?" Katherine asked, a faint note of suspicion tainting her concern.

" 'Ungry," she said simply.

"Of course," Derec said. "She's starving. There isn't even any food she could steal here."

Katherine squinted at the alien through narrow-slitted eyes. "Is that why you were following us? Not to get the key, but to find out where we were getting our food?"

"I don' care about the jewel," Wolruf said. "Juss 'ungry. I 'ide, follow the robots, look for food. I follow them every-wherr and never smell food."

"You don't like the robots, do you? It isn't just Alpha," Derec said.

"Brood-captain tell me a 'undred times, never trust strange animal until 'u've seen its meal table," she said weakly.

It sounded like an attempt at a joke. "And robots never eat," Derec completed. "Well, we'll get you something. I hope we can get you something. Can you eat what we eat?"

"Just hold on," Katherine interrupted. "You were on the ship with us the whole time? And you've been hiding out ever since?"

"I wass coming through interlock—Alpha, too—when heard the bomb go off," Wolruf said. "Noise bring other Erani. Controls dead an' 'u not much better. So I cut us loose. When robots come I 'ide, when ship dock I slip out. Been 'iding ever since."

"Where's Aranimas?"

"Don't know. Left behind." Wolruf was noticeably un-steady on her feet.

"We can sort the rest of this out later," Derec said sharply. "We've got to get her something, quickly."

"Not so quickly," Katherine said, stepping closer. "Where have you been hiding? Here, in the dark sections?"

"Mostly. No robots here. I like the dark better than I like robots."

"How much of the dark sections have you been through, looking for food?"

"Lots," Wolruf said. "But the jewel's not there, if thass what 'u're wondering."

"How do you know?" Katherine demanded. "Because you put it somewhere else?"

"I don' want the jewel. Juss trouble for everyone," Wolruf said. "But I know wherr it iss."

Derec impulsively grabbed the alien by both cheeks and planted a kiss on her forehead. "All right!" he declared. "We're in business!"

Katherine held her enthusiasm in check. "How do you know?" she repeated.

"I follow when they took it from the ship. I think they take it to 'umans, 'umans 'ave food. Wrong. Robots took it wherr therr are lots of robots, no 'umans, no food. I almoss got caught."

"Do you remember exactly where? Can you take us there?" Katherine asked.

"Thought robots 'ur servants," Wolruf said, wrinkling her face in puzzlement. "Why not juss ask them to bring it to 'u?"

"Nevermind about that," Derec said gently. "Answer Katherine's questions. Do you remember the way? Can you take us there?"

"I remember, always, so I can take 'u. Don' want to.

Don' want key, don' want to see robots or robots to see me. But 'u be my friend and feed me and I be 'ur friend and show 'u. Okay?"

Derec looked to Katherine. "I'm taking her to find some food," he said. "If you don't like it, you're welcome to go solo from here on."

"Oh, no, you don't," she said quickly. "You can't get rid of me that easily."

"Come on, then," he said as he started brushing futilely at the fur clinging to his clothing. He looked back to Wolruf and smiled. "Let's see if we find you some food before I choke to death on your dander."

They ended up returning to the hospital, both because it was relatively close and because it was one of the few facilities they knew anything about. Katherine entered first, demanding care and attention as she swept through toward the ICU and making sure to gather up both Dr. Galen and Florence along the way. A minute later, Derec and Wolruf slipped inside and headed in the other direction, toward the kitchens.

"Meat, breads, vegetables—what's best for you?" Derec said, scanning the menu of the autogalley.

"Plants," Wolruf said, crouching. "Something to work my teeth on."

"Everything's synthetic, I'm afraid—the farm is one of the things they closed down. Let's see—I think they make the apple wedges with a lot of fiber."

"Do 'u know what 'ur going to do with the key when 'u find it?" Wolruf asked from behind.

"No." Derec turned around and presented the alien with a white tray filled with pale yellow puply slices of apple. With surprising patience, Wolruf selected a wedge, sniffed it experimentally, then balanced it on her narrow tongue and delicately took it into her mouth. As far as Derec could tell, she did not chew it, but swallowed it whole.

That created a minor paradox—though Wolruf did not appear to be eating quickly, the plate rapidly emptied. She ate as though she were trying to make up for all seven weeks of deprivation at one sitting, and yet was scrupulously neat and almost completely silent. There were none of the wet crunching noises that any human trying to keep pace would have made.

I wouldn't be surprised if she finds our eating habits repulsive, he thought as he watched her.

When the tray was empty, Wolruf offered it up to Derec with a hopeful look. "I guess 'u can trust me now, right?" she said.

"Except I'm not the one you have to win over," he said, taking the tray and turning back to the autogalley for a refill. "Katherine is. Which reminds me—why didn't you tell me she was on board?"

Wolruf shrugged. "No chance to. Always something 'appening, somebody 'terrupting."

"That's true enough," Derec said, surrendering the replenished tray. "There's questions I've been wanting to ask you since that first night and I haven't gotten a chance to."

"Ask," Wolruf said, then rolled out her tongue for another bite.

Derec considered a moment. "This one isn't important to anyone but me. You didn't know I was on the asteroid, did you?"

"Not until gunners spot you. Then thought you were robot."

"Which is why you didn't fire at me—"

"Aranimas's orders—not perfectly followed."

"You meant the robot that was with me? That was a self-destruct."

"Fine distinctions escape Aranimas. Ask gunner who hit him."

Derec smiled. "Did you know the key was on the asteroid?"

"No twice."

"That's what I thought. But then why were you there? Was it just the dumbest luck that you showed up?"

"Purpose, not luck. Aranimas build very fine starglass. Saw ast'roid being made and became very curious."

"Say that again? I didn't catch your meaning."

She cupped her hands and made motions like forming a snowball. "With starglass, Aranimas watched the ast'roid-making. Boss very curious. Not something Erani ever do. 'U do it often?"

"No," Derec said, still blinking in surprise. An artificial world—it was remotely possible. Use a small fleet of haulers to bring in the raw material—maybe just smaller planetoids brought in from the nearest dirty system. Drive the pieces together at just the right speed and fuse them into a larger body—but why?

The answer came to him almost immediately. To hide the key. To bury it away where no one would ever find it, as though it were as dangerous as a cask of plutonium waste. Buried cleverly, not at the heart of the asteroid where the first shaft sunk would uncover it, but tucked invisibly under the surface.

Except that someone saw or found out, and sent the robots to retrieve it.

"Are you sure about this?" Derec demanded.

"Sure. Aranimas saw it all. Very good starglass." She offered up the empty tray hopefully.

Then we're in over our heads, Derec thought as he turned back to the autogalley. Way over—

Wolruf was finishing her third helping when Katherine joined them. She had drawn on station supply for a long-sleeved blouse to wear over the jump suit, and traded the foot pillows for soft-soled shoes.

"I sent Florence on an errand and gave Dr. Galen a task that should keep him out of the lobby for at least half an hour," she said. "And I made Dr. Galen fit me with a loaded medipump just in case it's not convenient to come back. Though my skin really doesn't feel too bad. Are you two almost ready?"

Wolruf made the last two wedges disappear. "I am."

"Then it's time to pay the bill for the meal," Katherine said, reclaiming the empty plate. "Let's go look at the map."

They stood elbow to elbow in the deserted lobby, Wolruf in the middle.

"Here's where we are," Katherine said, pointing. "And here's about the spot you and Derec went to the mat. All you have to do now is tell us where the key is, and we'll go get it. You can go back to the dark and never have to see another robot."

But Wolruf was unable to understand the map in any of its modes or projections, even though both Derec and Katherine made labored efforts to try to explain it. "I know it in my feet and my nose," Wolruf said. "I go with 'u and show 'u."

Katherine frowned and looked to Derec. "How are we going to smuggle her through the halls? It was risky enough bringing her here. And she said she almost got caught the first time."

"I was thinking while we were walking that a place this

large probably used to have some kind of personal trans-port."

"Jitneys," she said.

"That's the word." An image of a three-wheeled utility vehicle snapped into focus in his mind. In automatic mode, they were essentially wheeled robots. In semi-auto, they served as smart taxis for visitors to the station. But in man-ual mode, they should offer freedom from Central Services control and privacy from Security curiosity. "The robots don't need them, but I'll bet they're all lined up somewhere ready to roll."

"Won't the robots think it's unusual, seeing one out in the streets?"

"I don't think so," Derec said. "When a ship's in port the crew probably uses them. And seeing one of the carts won't strike them as any more strange than our presence alone would. Robots *notice* people. It's the way they're made. But we don't need to be invisible—we just need to be left alone. What do you say?"

Katherine pursed her lips and considered. "I think if we don't find any jitneys, it doesn't matter what I think."

CHAPTER 18

THEATER

Happily, the jitney accumulator areas were clearly marked on the station map. It took less than five minutes for Derec to walk to the nearest one and return with one of the nimble little electric carts. The version he had chosen had a single driver's seat in back over the solo wheel, and an open passenger cab slung between the other wheels in front.

Wolruf curled up on the floor of the passenger cab under a white hospital robe. Katherine sat in one of the two seats, her legs further helping to conceal the alien, and Derec took the controls.

For Wolruf to find her place in her scent map, they were forced to backtrack into the dark sections. From there it was relatively simple: up three levels, north two subsections, up another level, and then west five blocks into a large plaza.

When Wolruf warned them they were nearing their destination, Derec slowed the vehicle to a moderate walking pace. A moment later the alien stole a peek over the edge of the cab, then jabbed a fat finger in the direction of the circular building at the center of the plaza.

"In there? Are you sure?" Derec hissed.

"Yes, Derec. Thass wherr the jewel iss."

The lightworm sign outside the main entrance said "Station Operations Center—Restricted," and robots were everywhere. The center itself was a single room twenty meters in diameter and encircled with windows looking out on the plaza.

"Great. Just great," Derec grumbled, driving slowly across the plaza at an oblique angel. "How are we going to get in there? We can't sneak up."

"How about the front door?" Katherine said, twisting around to look at him. "Maybe they'll let you in."

Derec regarded her dubiously.

"Go ahead—it's worth a try."

"I still don't understand," Wolruf chimed in. "Aren't robots 'ur servants?"

Before answering, Derec drove the jitney a short distance down a connecting corridor, then pulled to one side and stopped. "I don't know about this," he said to Katherine. "Maybe they're just setting up, like with Aranimas's ship. If we try to get in there, if we show any interest in the thing at all, maybe that's just going to bring them down on our necks like a tonne of slag."

"You want to just leave it with them? After all we've gone through because of it?"

"When we were prisoners on the ship, I thought it was important to get the thing away from the aliens and back in human hands. Well, that's where it is. Jacobson made it clear they're willing to let us walk away and leave this mess to them. Maybe that's what we ought to do."

"Don't you have any curiosity?" she demanded. "Don't you want to know what this has all been about?"

"Sure, I've got curiosity. I've also got problems of my

own to sort out. I don't see where that thing is going to help any."

"What's happened to your nerve?" she said. "Look, these are the same people that stole our spacecraft, spirited away my robot, and then tried to tell us we should be grateful that they're sending us away as paupers instead of criminals. I'm not about to let them get away with it."

"Don't you understand?" Derec shouted angrily. "You think we're going to be able to just walk in there, put it under our arm, and say 'Thanks for looking after it'? This thing came off a heavily armed alien ship—"

"They don't know that," Katherine pointed out. "They never saw Aranimas, or even Wolruf."

"All right," Derec said tiredly. "Maybe you're right. If they did think it was an alien ship, they probably wouldn't let us go. But these people aren't playing. They wanted the ship, and they took it. They wanted the robot, and they took it. They want the jewel, and they have it. We're not going to be able to take it back. We won't even get in the door."

"Maybe their orders weren't that specific."

"I'd have made them so."

"You didn't give them. Go on—try."

"What's the point? Wolruf's right—the key is just trouble for everybody."

Katherine sighed. "If you want something done—" And before Derec could stop her, she climbed out of the jitney and headed back to the plaza on foot.

In less than ten minutes Katherine was clambering back into her seat. "They let me in, even gave me a little tour," she said breezily. "Very accommodating."

"I figured that out when you weren't back in two minutes. What about the key?"

"It's there all right, sitting out in plain sight. What id-iots!"

Derec eased the jitney into motion down the corridor, mulling over Katherine's news. "Not really. Describe what you saw."

"It's a big semicircular room, with glass all around except for the offices at the back. There're five robots at work stations, including Amazon. Then there're two more near the center of the room doing nothing but sitting facing each other with the artifact on a table between them. There was some sort of funny emblem on the shoulder of those robots, a blue *F* in a double gold circle—"

Derec groaned. "Falke X-50s."

"Does that mean something?"

"It means trouble. They have superfast reflexes. If a bomb went off five meters in the opposite direction, they might be distracted long enough for you to get your hands on the key, but you'd never get out of the room with it. If we're going to get it back, we're going to have to have some way to neutralize seven robots at once—and I don't know any."

"Can you explain to me why it's out in plain sight? Could it be a copy, a fake? Maybe you're right about the trap."

"No," Derec said with a shake of his head. "I'd guess the robots were probably ordered to watch it constantly, in principle if not in so many words."

"If you put it in a vault and nobody opens the vault, it isn't going to vanish into the ozone."

"No," Derec agreed, "but that understanding requires a fairly advanced and rather subtle mental function called object permanence. Robots are strongly biased toward the concrete and away from the inferred. If they lock something away out of sight, they don't really know it's there except when they check on it."

"That's illogical. No human would think that way."

"Some would," Derec dissented. "But you're right, it's not logical."

"So why do the roboticists let that happen?"

"No engineered system is perfect," Derec said with a shrug. "This is just one of those little things that doesn't always behave the way you wish it would. A robot's uncertainty about whether it's satisfactorily fulfilling its orders can drive it into an anxiety state—specifically, they develop an elevated K-integral in the W-14 level. So they begin checking on the thing they're guarding more and more often at shorter and shorter intervals."

"And eventually it ends up sitting on the table next to them," Katherine said.

"Right." Derec fell into a thoughtful silence, then suddenly caught himself. "Damn it all, you've got me trying to figure out how to get to it."

"See, I knew you didn't want to let them have it," Katherine said with a bemused smile. "Any ideas?"

"Not yet." A moment later he added, "Except that no matter how carefully worded and strongly impressed their orders to protect the key are, they're only covered by the Second Law."

Katherine was mute for a time, as Derec drove aimlessly through the streets bounding the Operations bloc.

"Following orders is Second Law," she said finally.

"That's what I just said."

"What if Wolruf and I gave them a First Law reason to disregard them?"

Wolruf peeked out from under the robe at the mention of her name and looked hopefully at Derec.

"That's the way to go, obviously," Derec said. "But how?"

"I've got some ideas. A little—robot theater, shall we say."

"Do you think you can be convincing?" Derec asked skeptically.

"I'd rather try than not," she said. "Let's not stop ourselves. Let's make them stop us."

"Wolruf?" he asked. "Do you want to try?"

"Whatever 'u want, Derec."

The burden was back on him, whether he wanted it or not. "All right, then," Derec said slowly. "Let's go somewhere more private and talk it through."

Peering down the corridor into the plaza, Derec shook his head. "This will never work," he whispered.

"It's worked so far, hasn't it?"

Derec had to admit that it had. The first problem had been to eliminate most of the robot traffic in the plaza. They had considered half a dozen ideas for accomplishing that, from setting up hallblocks with robot monitors to trying to draw them away with invented errands elsewhere in the station.

In the end, they settled for a whisper campaign, a simple variation on the unkind children's game—"Billy is a cootie; pass it on." Derec had stopped a robot at random just outside the Operations bloc and spoken briefly to it:

"Robot. Management has ordered that there be a test of station emergency communications in this subsection. Your instructions are as follows. First, you are not to discuss the test or your part in it over the command link. Second, you are not to enter or remain in subsector 100 at any time between 1200 hours and 1400 hours today. Third, you are to relay these orders to the next robot that you see."

The instructions were innocuous enough that the robot did not challenge them. Like a runaway infection, the whisper had raced through the body of the station staff. Within half an hour, the traffic in the plaza had thinned dramatically. Within the hour, the plaza was deserted, and several robots had even left the Operations Center.

Three robots remained. From where he was crouching beside the jitney, Derec could see them inside the Operations Center—the two X-50s guarding the artifact, and Anazon, darting from one work station to the next trying to oversee critical operations. Their particular responsibilities were too strongly impressed on them for Derec's little trick to pull them away.

"It'll work," Katherine prodded. "Go on. We'll do our part. You just make sure you do yours."

Swallowing hard, Derec nodded and started off down the corridor. He crossed the empty plaza and climbed the single step up into the Operations Center. None of the robots took any notice of him.

"Anazon."

"Yes, Derec."

"I've decided not to wait for the Nexon shuttle. I want to charter a ship to come and get me and take me to Aurora. Tell me the procedure I should follow."

Without ever turning away from the console, the robot began to answer. "There are seven ships of Nexonian registry licensed for Auroran space and available for hire. You may contact any of their owners by hyperwave—"

Suddenly the peace of the plaza was broken by the roaring sound of a jitney in high gear. A moment later the vehicle burst out of one of the connecting corridors, Katherine at the controls. Pursuing close behind was Wolruf, running with an easy loping gait that used all four of her limbs.

Halfway across the plaza, Wolruf got close enough to reach out and catch Katherine by the arm from behind. The jitney veered suddenly, breaking the alien's grip. But the veer turned into a skid that ended with the jitney sliding sideways with a jolt into the rockform base of a tree planter. In a moment, Wolruf caught up and pounced on Katherine. The air was filled with her convincingly terrified cries of "It's killing me!" and the alien's ominous growls.

When the jitney veered, Anazon had started toward the exit and one of the X-50s began to rise. But when the guard robot saw Anazon responding, it sat back down again. Derec knew immediately that meant the guards' instructions were so strongly worded that the expectation that Anazon would handle the First Law situation relieved them of responsibility. Only if Anazon failed would they act.

The moment was slipping away quickly. "Robots—help that woman," Derec said sharply, stepping forward. "She is being harmed. She may be killed."

One of the X-50s stirred slightly. "Anazon will protect her—"

"The creature attacking her is strong and fast. Anazon will not be able to protect her from injury. Go! Help her! Now!"

First one, then the other guard rose and took a halting step or two toward the exit. Then they hesitated, the conflicting positronic potentials having reached a new equilibrium. Anazon would reach Katherine and Wolruf in a few more strides and the stunt would be over, a failure.

Just then, Katherine loosed a blood-chilling cry that even Derec thought real, and the guard robots started forward again. Derec waited no longer. Snatching the artifact up from the table, he turned and ran the other way, vaulting over a console and out through the window.

His heart pounding, Derec fled the plaza and down an empty corridor. He heard the jitney's motors whine, but he did not look back. He could not afford to worry about Katherine and Wolruf. He thought he heard the metronomelike running strides of a robot, but he did not look back. Even if he was being chased, knowing it could not make his legs pump faster.

All he wanted was to reach the dark sections unmolested. All he could think of were the escape route and the rendezvous he had chosen. He ran until his chest ached and his legs were iron, until each breath was pain, until darkness swallowed him and hid him from those who wanted to find him.

CHAPTER 19

THE KEY TO PERIHELION

Derec huddled in pitch blackness in the corner of the room and waited. He could not say how long he had been alone there, except that it seemed an eternity. He held the artifact tightly in both hands and sat, rigid and silent.

Then without warning, he was not alone. Since the corridor outside was as dark as the room inside, Derec could not see when the door opened. But he heard it slide back, and rustling steps as someone entered. His heart began to beat faster and his nerves jangled.

"Derec?"

He sighed, and the tension flowed out of him. It was Katherine's voice. "Here," he said. "In the corner."

She thumbed her torch on and swung it in his direction, and the polished surface of the object he held in his hands sent an answering beam of light back at her and Wolruf. "You did it!" she exulted. "Let me see."

Derec crossed his arms protectively over the artifact. "No. Don't come near me."

"What's going on? What's happening to you?" Katherine demanded. "We did it. We've got it."

"So we do. It's confessions time, that's all," Derec said, sliding up the wall to a standing position. "I've had some time to sit here and think about things. It's amazing how being scared will focus your thoughts."

"What are you talking about?" Katherine demanded.

He waggled the key above his head. "It's real simple. Which one of you is going to stop playing dumb and tell me just what it is we've got?"

Katherine stared at him. "If you're trying to say that I've been holding out on you—"

"Haven't you been?" Derec interrupted. "You and Wolruf both. I'm tired of being the one in the dark, the one who's always one step behind. I want to know everything you know. I'd rather give it back to the robots than have it and not know what it is."

"Derec, I don't know anything more than I already told you," Katherine said pleadingly, taking a step forward.

Derec stiffened and gripped the artifact even more tightly. "Don't try it. Talk to me."

Katherine retreated a step. "Derec, I don't want to fight you. But this is crazy. We're all part of a team. I'm not keeping any secrets from you. I never saw or heard of that thing before Aranimas asked me about it. I couldn't tell him anything and he didn't tell me anything."

She turned and looked into the half-shadow where Wolruf stood. "But Wolruf *was* Aranimas's top aide. And when the robots took the key from the spacecraft, she thought it was worth the risk to follow and find out where it was taken. How about it, Wolruf?"

"I was 'ungry. I thought there would be food."

"Really? How hungry? Not six weeks' worth. Three days, that's all. Is that hungry enough to send you out where the robots were and take the chance of being caught by them? Especially considering how you feel about robots."

"If anyone's keeping secrets, p'rhaps iss 'u, Derec," Wolruf said challengingly. "The key was found on the asteroid 'u claim 'u were shipwrecked on. Why did 'u go to that spot when 'u were escaping? Because 'u knew that it was therr? Maybe because 'u'd put it therr and wanted to get it back?"

Without warning, the lights in the room suddenly flared to life. The only one who did not jump was Derec; he had been expecting it. "The robots are looking for us," he said. "They've reactivated this section, maybe the whole station. They can use the environmental systems to find out where lights are being used, where the oxygen demand is up."

"We can't stay here," Katherine said simply. "We've got to move. We've got to get the key hidden again before they find us."

Derec shook his head. "Wrong. Unless one of you starts talking, I'm going to wait right here until the robots show up and then hand it to them," he said with quiet calm. "It's up to you."

"If you let them have it back, we'll never be able to get it again," Katherine said angrily.

"I think you can count on that," Derec said, undisturbed.

She turned on Wolruf. "If you do know something, you'd better tell him straight and tell him fast, or the key's lost," she ordered. "If you wait any longer we'll never get away."

A wild look in her eyes, Wolruf backed away a step. " 'U'll take it and leave me and I'll never get 'ome," she said desperately.

"That won't happen," Katherine said. "We won't abandon you."

"I already promised you that," Derec said. "I meant it."

"Tell him," Katherine prodded. "Tell us."

Wolruf's darting eyes fixed first on Katherine's face, then on Derec's. "Iss one of the Keys to Perihelion," she said finally.

"Perihelion? What's that?" Katherine said.

"Iss said to be the place nearest to every other place in the universe," Wolruf said. " 'U 'old the key to the room which is the center of all. With the key, through Perihelion, 'u should be able to travel anywherr."

Derec shook his head in disbelief. "Some kind of matter transporter?"

"No," Wolruf said. "It is a key that opens the door to Perihelion."

Her anger forgotten for the moment, Katherine looked to Derec. "Could it be something that uses the same principle as the Jump?"

"In a package this size?" he asked skeptically. To Wolruf he added, "You said one of the keys. How many are there?"

"By the stories Aranimas 'eard, seven."

"What stories? Where did he hear them?"

"Therr werr three ships before this one came aboard," Wolruf said, gesturing toward Katherine. "Aranimas learned much from the 'umans aboard before he 'urt them so much they died. Learn 'ur language. 'ear many stories."

Katherine looked at Derec. "I've never heard any stories about a Key to Perihelion. They must have been Settler ships."

"That fits—otherwise Aranimas would have run into robots sooner." Derec turned to Wolruf. "Where did the keys come from?"

Wolruf twitched her cheeks, a gesture equivalent to a shrug. "Aranimas could not even learn wherr the tales came from."

Derec looked back to the key and turned it over in his hands. "How does it work? Where are the controls?"

"There iss only one control that Aranimas could find," Wolruf said. "Push each corner in turn. A button will appear."

"Press the corners clockwise or counterclockwise? Starting where? And which side?"

"It does not matter," Wolruf said. "Turn it any way 'u choose. The button always appears in the last corner 'u touch and always on the side facing 'u. If 'u do nothing, the button disappears again."

"And if you push the button you go to Perihelion?" asked Katherine.

"No," Wolruf said sadly. "That is what should 'appen, I think. But it does not. The key does not function."

"You tried it? With Aranimas?"

"Many times."

Derec looked down at the glittering metal bar resting in his hands. Its finish was mirror-smooth and seamless. There was no sign of a concealed switch. When he squeezed the upper right corner between thumb and forefinger, there was no give, no sign he had done anything at all.

But when Derec pressed the fourth corner, it pressed back against his thumb. A three-centimeter square section on the corner sprang smoothly upward, looking just like a button waiting to be pushed. At the same time, it seemed to be an immovable part of the rest of the artifact, as though the silver covering was some sort of metallic membrane.

Katherine looked back to Wolruf. "If it doesn't work, why were you so eager to get it back?"

"Maybe Wolruf can fix," was her forlorn reply. "Only way to go 'ome now."

Just then, they heard a voice calling them from the corridor outside. "Derec—Katherine—come out," it said. "Derec—Katherine—you do not have to hide."

Wolruf dropped to her crouch and loosed a barrage of guttural moaning sounds. "Shut up!" Katherine hissed at the alien, then turned to Derec. "Do something," she urged.

"What?" Derec snapped back. "This room has only one exit."

At that moment the door slid open, drawing Derec's attention away from Katherine. He glimpsed a golden robot filling the doorway and advancing across the threshold. Then suddenly Katherine was blocking his view. She had moved closer and was reaching for the key, a determined expression on her face.

Derec's immediate thought was that she was going to grab the key and try to run. He did not have enough time to snatch the gleaming artifact out of her reach. There was time only to tighten his grip.

Too late he realized Katherine had never meant to take the key. Her hands closed firmly over his, locking them in place. Her thumb drove the small square button back down into the body of the key.

"No!" cried Wolruf.

"Wait—" Derec started to say.

But there was nothing anyone could do to stop it—not Derec, not the robot, not even Katherine. There was a soundless burst of color that stabbed deep into Derec's eyes, driving out the sight of all else. And when the light faded to gray and his sight was restored, Wolruf, the robot, and the room had all vanished.

• • •

They found themselves standing as they had been standing, both gripping the key, at the center of a tiny place within a great space. There was nothing to prevent them from seeing vast distances, except that there was nothing to see.

All around them was a soft gray light that was to the eye what a hum is to the ear. The air had the fuggy, dusty odor of a house that has been closed up for the summer. There was no sound except their own tight, frightened breathing.

They clung to each other and to the key and tried to understand and accept their sudden displacement to this unreal reality. It was a place which could be nowhere in space. They were somewhere outside, thrown there by the staggering power of the little silver bar. It was a place without time, without life.

"Perihelion," Katherine whispered.

"Wolruf said that it was the nearest place to everywhere," Derec said. "It feels more like the farthest place from anywhere."

Katherine twisted her head around, looking. "Where is she?"

"Back on Rockliffe Station, I guess. Left behind."

"Why didn't the key bring her with us?"

"Maybe for the same reason it wouldn't work for her," Derec said. "Maybe because she was too far away from us. Maybe you have to be touching it, or touching someone who's touching it. I don't know. But we have to go back and get her."

"But the robots—"

Derec shook his head. "It was Alpha. You didn't even look. It was Alpha."

"I didn't know," Katherine whispered. "Press it again. Let's go back."

"How do we know we will?"

"I was thinking about escape when I pushed it. Think about going back."

Wordlessly Derec complied. The button appeared as before. There was another flash of color, and another few seconds of adjustment. Then their returning vision told them something that should not be, could not be. They were not at Perihelion, but neither were they back in Rockliffe Station.

They were standing in open sunlight atop a great pyramidal tower, looking down at a still greater city spread out before them. The tower they were on was taller by half than any other building in sight. It was like standing on top of the world, like looking down from an eagle's eyrie.

"What is this?" Katherine hissed. "Where did you send us?"

Derec stared unbelievingly at the towers, cubes, and spires stretching from the base of the pyramid to the horizon. "I don't know," he said hoarsely. "I had Rockliffe Station in my mind."

She released her grip on the key and grabbed tight to his arm. "Are we on Earth?" She asked it as though the prospect frightened her.

Derec looked west at the low-hanging disc of the sun. "No," he said. "The star is too white and too small." But he knew why she had asked. No Spacer world had a city this vast. Only on Earth had city-building ever been practiced on this scale, and they were not cities but Cities, enclosed and largely underground. "You don't recognize it?"

"I've never seen such a thing before," she whispered. "Is it Wolruf's homeworld? Or Aranimas's?"

"I don't know," Derec said. "We can find the answer easily enough, though."

"How?"

"By going down there." He gestured toward the city spread out below them.

"No," she said with a shudder. "Send us back."

Derec realized that he was still gripping the key in his unfeeling hands. "I don't know if I can," he said.

"Try," she urged. "Or let me try."

"We'll try," he agreed.

Holding an image of the gray emptiness of Perihelion in his mind, Derec called up the control button and pressed it. This time, nothing happened. "What it did has to take a lot of power. Maybe it has to recharge—or be recharged," he said. "Either way, it looks like we're here for a while at least."

"I don't want to go down there," Katherine said. "It'll be night soon. Let's stay here until morning and then try the key again."

The sun had indeed slipped a fraction of a degree toward the horizon, lengthening the already long shadow of the tower on the city below. "Aren't you afraid of going over the side in your sleep?" he asked. There was no railing or footwall enclosing the table-flat top of the pyramid.

"I don't expect to be able to sleep," she said soberly.

As the sun descended toward the horizon, a breeze kicked up, teasing at their hair and clothing. It carried with it no scent Derec knew. In fact, for a world so obviously teeming with life, it carried remarkably little scent at all.

Below them, the city was becoming alive with light—light cascading down the sides of buildings, light puddling in the streets. In those streets, hundreds of other lights were in restless motion, reminding Derec of the bustle within a colony of bees or ants.

Too emotionally numbed even to be afraid, they avoided talk. Katherine withdrew into herself, sitting in the lotus position near the center of the tile-covered plaza. Derec wandered near the edges, looking out and trying to abstract the pattern on which the city had been built.

When the stars came out, he studied them, hoping against hope to recognize their patterns. There was a red star as bright as a planet that might have been Betelgeuse, and a fierce white one that might have been Sirius.

But each could just as easily be any of a thousand other stars named or merely numbered. There was no way to tell without a spectrometer to take the optical fingerprint of each suspect and a general astrographical catalog in which to search for matches.

"Do you remember what the stars look like from Aurora?" he called across to Katherine, sitting huddled against herself on the other side of the plaza.

"I never knew," she admitted. "I wasn't interested."

Giving up, he went and sat facing her. She was idly rubbing her right bicep through the sleeve of her Lindbergh blouse.

"Having trouble with the pump?"

"That's not what hurts," she said, tugging the sleeve up and showing him a purple crescent bruise.

"Nice."

"My most convincing scream," she said with a rueful smile.

"Wolruf?"

"She got carried away and bit me. She's not as harmless as she wanted us to think."

"Anything living knows how to defend itself," he said, then added wistfully, "I wonder what's happened to her."

"I don't understand why you liked her."

"She's a victim—a prisoner—just like us."

"I have trouble thinking of her that way."

Derec sighed. "Doesn't matter now, I guess. I've abandoned her again."

Conversation lapsed after that. "I don't understand why it was Alpha that came after us," Katherine said finally. "It can't have been roaming free like Wolruf since we came to the station, can it? Looking for us?"

"Just another one of Jacobson's tricks," Derec said. "He knew we wanted the robot back. What better bait to draw us out?"

They were silent together for a while, sitting close but not touching. "Your first name is David," she said unexpectedly.

Hearing the name brought no sudden revelations, and caution born out of experience kept him from feeling any gratitude. "Why tell me now?"

"So I can stop the mental gymnastics every time I start to talk to you. Because I thought you'd want to know."

"And because we don't know what's going to happen to us?"

"I won't think like that," she said. "I don't believe in it."

"I should have known better," Derec said with a faint smile. "Are you going to drop more than one crumb? How is it you know me? Where did we meet?"

She turned her head to look at him. "You were the engineer's mate on a Settler merchantman—the *Daniel O'Neill*, I think it was called," she said. "Does it sound familiar?"

"No," he said unhappily. "What else can you tell me?"

She hesitated. "I'm afraid I don't know you as well as I let you think. We crossed paths in the spaceport."

"If I'm a Settler drudge and you're a Spacer topcrust—"

"Your captain was having trouble with Customs coming in and we were delayed going out by mechanical problems. We ended up in the same waiting area. We talked for a while." She hesitated, then added, "You were funny. You made me laugh."

"Did I talk about my family—my home—"

"You don't remember any of it, do you? Meeting me— the *O'Neill*—"

"No."

"I'm sorry." She hesitated. "Even so, I thought you'd be happier, knowing."

"I'd be happier remembering," he said, and was silent for a moment. "Anyway, it doesn't seem to matter as much at the moment. I don't know a thing about this David. At least I know a little about Derec. I think I'll just stay Derec for the time being."

"I didn't tell you everything," she said. "I didn't tell you about—"

"Don't," he said. "If my name didn't bring it back, nothing will. Save the rest. You'll be able to tell me whether I'm remembering or inventing."

"I know your memory will come back. It has to."

He nodded absently, acknowledging her words without accepting them. "If you want to try to sleep, I'll watch to make sure you don't get restless and try to air-walk."

Shaking her head, she said, "I can't sleep without a pillow."

Derec stretched out on his back and tapped his left shoulder with his right hand. "I have an unoccupied pillow available, no charge."

He expected her to refuse the offer. But she crawled

wordlessly to where he lay and snuggled against his left side, her head resting on his arm. Closing her eyes, she seemed to fall asleep almost at once.

They fit together easily, and, innocent though the embrace was, there was something pleasing about her closeness. Probably it's just that she's not talking, Derec told himself. He lay there looking up at the stars and listening to her slow, peaceful breathing until his own eyelids were too heavy to keep open.

David Derec, he thought just before sleep took him. It *would* be nice to have two names again—

CHAPTER 20

MORNING ON THE MOUNT

They woke thoroughly chilled from their night on the exposed promontory, and the early rays of the rising sun did little to warm them. Despite the cold, Katherine quickly separated herself from him as though embarrassed by the contact.

"Let's try the key," she said nervously as she stood up.

Derec pulled himself up to a sitting position. "No hello? No good morning?" he said with a half-grin. But he reached for the key, lying an arm's length away on the tile.

"Come on," she said impatiently. "I had a bad dream that I'd like to rule out as quickly as possible."

"What happened?"

"I was stuck here with you."

Smiling, he stood and held it out toward her. "Do the honors?"

She quickly went through the activation sequence, then glanced up and met Derec's eyes. "Ready?" she asked.

"What do we think of? Perihelion or the Station?"

"Perihelion first. I think we have to."

He inclined his head in agreement. "Ready if you are."

Her thumb went hard against the button, as though the vehemence with which she pushed it would speed their return. Light exploded against their retinas, the sunlight vanished, and they found themselves in the gray world of Perihelion once more.

"Now the Station?" Derec asked.

"How about Aurora?" she asked, her eyes glowing with excitement. "Wolruf said we could go anywhere with it. Why should we take ourselves back to trouble?"

"No," Derec said. "First we go back to get Wolruf. I owe her."

"I don't want to go back there," Katherine said anxiously. "We won't be able to use the key again to get away, not for hours. They'll have us locked up and it locked up by then, and we won't have done anything for Wolruf. You could get help on Aurora—get a ship and go back for her."

"How?"

"I have friends on Aurora—"

"The same ones that closed your account?"

She winced at the reminder, but was adamant. "More friends than we have on Rockliffe Station."

"You'll have to do the steering. I don't have a clear enough image of Aurora in my head."

"Happy to do it. Hold tight," she said, and triggered the key once more.

Perihelion vanished on cue, but it was not the pastoral landscape of Aurora which replaced it. It took only an instant for Derec to realize that they had returned to the top of the tower that looked out on the great mystery city.

A heartbeat later, the same understanding impressed itself on Katherine. "Frost!" she declared, throwing her hands in the air and rushing to the edge with a vigor that alarmed Derec. "What went wrong?"

Derec looked past her to the nearer structures of the city. "Hard to say, since we don't really know what happens when it goes right," he said. "Obviously there's more to controlling the key than just thinking about where you want to go."

"But why here, then, a place that neither one of us knows?"

"I don't know," Derec said. "But it could be worse."

"I'd like to know how," she said, turning to face him and planting her fists on her hips.

"Well, just consider," he said, stepping closer. "Whatever we are, we're a long way from Rockliffe Station, and the way we left we're not easily going to be followed. That means in one fell swoop we got away from Jacobson, Anazon's robots, and the raiders. And as a little bonus we got away with the key."

"Which we don't know how to make work right. We've lost Alpha, we don't know where we are, we have no ship, no money, no food, nothing but the clothes we're wearing and that useless key." It could not have been more of a tantrum of self-pity if she had ended it by stamping her foot.

"I didn't say it was all good. I just said it could be worse." Squatting on his heels, he stared at the key as he passed it from right hand to left and back again restlessly. "I can hardly believe what this thing does. For a machine this size to be able to transport matter ten feet, much less ten light-years, is the most fantastic feat of engineering— damn near magic. I can't tell you how much I'd love to take it apart and see how it works. And finally I understand why everybody wants it. What I don't understand is why someone tried to hide it."

"What do you mean?"

He looked up. "Something Wolruf told me. The asteroid that I woke up on—it was artificial. Somebody meant it to be the final hiding place for this."

Katherine was quick to pick up the implication. "As though it were dangerous, not just powerful."

"Exactly."

"Well—just think what a terrorist or assassin could do with it. Or an army where every soldier had one. Especially an alien army."

"It'd be impossible to protect yourself against them," Derec said, staring at the key again. "A lot of responsibility goes along with ownership of this thing. Maybe more responsibility than I want."

"The monkey getting heavy already?"

Derec nodded. "On top of everything else, I still don't know what I'm doing mixed up in the middle of this." He looked up at her. "I suppose you think the pod was from the *Daniel O'Neill*, that I ejected in some emergency."

"It's the straightest line between two points."

"I guess it is. But you know, there's something that doesn't fit in. Why did Monitor 5 think it was so important to give the key to me? Me, who'd been nothing but a nuisance to the robots up till then? It said something like 'I found the key, Derec. You have to take it.' How do you explain that?"

She gestured helplessly. "I don't."

Derec stood and walked to where she stood, at the edge of the plaza. "And this place," he said, spreading his hands wide to take in the city surrounding them. "Just look at it.

It's glorious. Doesn't just seeing it make you feel exhilarated? Can't you sense the unifying vision, the way it all fits together as one seamless whole? Look at the turrets with mansard roofs—beautiful! Look at the way the five Pythagorean perfect solids are used as structural shapes to focus—"

As he looked to the north, he stopped short. "That's funny," he said, puzzled. "I would have sworn that last night there was a grouping of three icosahedrons right there along that boulevard."

"Icosahedrons?"

"The most complex perfect solid—twenty triangular faces." He shook his head. "I must have been mistaken about the grouping. Maybe I was dreaming about this place last night. Anyway, I'm almost looking forward to going down there. If we'd managed to get back to Rockliffe Station last night or on to Aurora this morning, I'd have felt cheated by not having my chance to explore."

"Have you bothered to notice that this city isn't just a collection of buildings?" she asked petulantly.

"What do you mean?"

She pointed down over the edge at the small figures moving in the streets. "You go down there and you're going to have to deal with the creatures that built this city. Is it as much fun thinking about having a hundred thousand monsters like Aranimas after you? We're trespassers, you know. We weren't invited."

Derec folded his arms over his chest and scanned the city outward to the horizon. "I'd say more like a million or more inhabitants in a city this size. But they won't be like Aranimas—or like Wolruf, for that matter."

"What makes you so sure?"

"First, because Wolruf told me about his world and the Erani world, and this doesn't fit the description—"

"She could have lied."

"True. But you say you didn't pick this destination, and I know I didn't. That means it was the key that decided to bring us here."

"So?"

"So, the key wasn't made by Aranimas's people, and it wasn't made by Wolruf's. If it was, they'd have known how to make the key work. They could probably even have made one with a lot less trouble than they seem to have gone through to find this one," Derec said. "So why should it take us to either of their worlds?"

"Maybe they did learn how to set the destination," she pointed out.

"Maybe. Or maybe the key was built to return to a certain place when it's activated without guidance—as a way of reclaiming them when they fall into the wrong hands."

"Then the creatures down there—"

"Might be not only the builders of this city, but the builders of the key," Derec completed. "Which means that maybe we were invited."

She squinted in his direction. "You're going to go down there whether I do or not, aren't you."

"Yes. I'll leave the key with you, if you want."

"I thought we were a team."

"Are we still?" he said, raising an eyebrow questioningly.

"Don't you want to be?"

"I don't know if we want the same things," he said slowly. "You want to get back to Aurora. I want to do something to help Wolruf—and then look into this business of the *Daniel O'Neill*."

"Both of which require getting off this planet," she pointed out. "Our interests overlap at least that far."

"They do, indeed," Derec admitted. "All right, then. We're still a team."

"At least until we beg, borrow, or steal a spaceship."

"Or learn how to control the Key to Perihelion, which-ever comes first," he amended.

"Or Aranimas shows up with fire in his eye and uses us for thrust mass," Katherine said with a grin. She peeked over the side again. "Or we kill ourselves trying to get down from here. Maybe we can make them come to us?"

Katherine's concern was justified. The only way down from the promontory seemed to be to climb down one of the sloping faces of the pyramid. Those faces were steep, much more nearly vertical than the faces of the Incan and Mayan temples of ancient Earth which the tower otherwise resembled. But unlike those temples, there were no wide ceremonial staircases cut into any of the four faces.

Instead, there was a regular pattern of holes down the center of each plasticrete face, a pattern that seemed to extend all the way to the ground. Each hole was wider than his handspan and twenty centimeters deep, and they were spaced in such a way that they would make convenient handholds and footholds.

It was possible they had been placed there purely for decorative reasons. "The fact is, I can't see why anyone would want to climb up here—there's nothing up here except a good view," he told Katherine. "And if the view was important to them, they could have run a lift up through the center of the tower."

Even so, the holes were in some ways better than a staircase. Hugging the face of the tower, with both hands and feet to provide good purchase and their backs to the view out and down that could inspire vertigo, they might just make it.

"You're going to be hurting by the time we get to the bottom," he told Katherine.

"I've got an eighty percent charge in my medipump and I feel fine. Besides, didn't anyone ever tell you that women have more endurance than men?" she teased. "Let's stop talking and get going."

The worst part was going over the edge and feeling for that first foothold. Derec led the way, being careful not to dislodge the key from its spot tucked into his waistband. A moment later Katherine was beside him, clinging more tightly than she needed to the lip of the holes she was using as handholds.

"I almost hate to bring this up, but I wonder what sort of creatures might have decided these holes would make great nests," Katherine said breathlessly.

"Flying snakes," Derec said straight-faced. "A meter long with three rows of sharp teeth. Nothing to worry about."

"You're so considerate," she said crossly, starting down.

"No charge," he said with a smile, and followed after her.

If he had ever thought that Katherine would be the kind to pick her way timidly down the wall, letting him lead the way and guide her steps, the first few minutes would have banished that notion. Katherine—Kate—was agile and aggressive and, most of all, fast. In ten minutes they were a fourth of the way down the tower's face. Since he had to be wary of moving too quickly and dislodging the key, Derec had trouble keeping pace.

"Hey, partner," he called down to her. "Time-out for a conference."

"I thought you were already taking a time-out, as slow as you move," she shot back. But she stopped and waited for him all the same. "What's up?" she asked as he joined her.

"A thought about the key. Do we really want to take it down there, not knowing what we're walking into?"

She frowned. "That would be taking a risk, wouldn't it? If we knew how to control it, I'd say keep it with us. We could always use it to escape from a tight spot—"

"If we knew how to control it, we wouldn't have to do this," Derec said.

"You want to leave it here, in one of these holes?"

"That's what I was thinking. The key is heavy enough and the holes deep enough that nothing's going to dislodge it."

"I don't much like the idea of being separated from it," Katherine said, her eyes clouded by concern. "It's one of our two chances to get out of here, maybe the better one, for all we know."

"I like the idea of being separated from it by force even less," Derec said. "What do you say?"

She nodded reluctantly. "You're right. Let's hide it."

At Katherine's insistence, they left the key right there where they were, in the leftmost hole of the pattern.

"It's going to be a harder climb up than it is down," Derec warned as they started down again.

"For them, too," she said.

Freed from his burden, Derec could more readily keep pace, and the rest of the descent turned into an undeclared race. But the race ended prematurely when, sneaking a peek over her shoulder to see how much farther they had to go, Katherine saw something that made her want to start climbing upward again.

"Reception committee," she hissed, reaching out and seizing Derec by the sleeve.

Letting go with his right hand, Derec twisted at the waist and looked down. At ground level, a hundred meters below their feet, a dozen figures stood in a half-circle. All twelve faces were tipped upward, looking back at him.

A happy grin spread slowly across Derec's face. "But look who's on the committee," he exulted. "They're robots!"

Katherine stole another glance down. "Considering recent history, I don't know why that's such good news," she said.

"It means that this has to be a Spacer world—"

"Rockliffe was a Spacer station," she said.

"—which means that our biggest problem from here on out is going to be bureaucratic red tape."

"Optimist."

"You'll see," he said, starting down.

The only response came from one of the robots waiting below. "Please move slowly and exercise all possible care," it called up to them. "Climbing the Compass Tower is a dangerous activity."

CHAPTER 21

ROBOT CITY

Eager to hasten the meeting, Derec skipped the last few steps, swinging out and jumping down to the ground. As Katherine clambered down behind him, he turned to face the robots.

Several were already leaving. Derec presumed that they were medical specialists who had been there in case of a fall, plus perhaps a few riggers who could have climbed up the wall to help them. Their skills no longer needed, they were efficiently moving on to other tasks.

The robots that remained were similar in appearance to each other, but not identical—variations on a theme. One had a seemingly purposeless swatch of blue enamel above the right ear, a second brilliant green optical scanner, still another sensor mesh wrapped around its skull like a headband.

"What's your name?" Derec asked, singling one of them out.

The robot took a step forward. "I am M-3323."

"Very well. M-3323, take me—us—to the city manager."

"The city as presently constituted does not have a manager," the robot replied. "What is your name, please?"

"Derec," he said. "David Derec. But—"

"And I'm Katherine Burgess," she said, stepping forward. "Look, we don't need to talk to the person on top, no matter what you call them—city manager, king, president, god. We need a place to see to our hygienic needs—something with a shower and a Personal. While we're busy with that, you can arrange a meeting for us with someone who can help us with our other problems. Is there any problem with that?"

"No, Katherine," M-3323 said. "Arrangements are now being made. If you will follow me, I will lead you to the appropriate facilities."

Mercifully, the house they were taken to was less than a minute's walk away. It was nestled between two great six-sided towers like a child hiding amongst its mother's skirts. The interior was startlingly new and pristine, as though the house had not only never been occupied, but never entered.

But the house contained everything they needed, including two Personals that opened off a room containing a futonlike sleeping platform. The three robots which had accompanied them inside waited downstairs, which afforded them an extra measure of privacy.

"There," Katherine said, emerging from her Personal after twenty minutes. "More presentable?"

Derec rose from where he had been seated on the edge of the platform. "You're very easy on the eyes."

"A quaint expression," she said, obviously pleased. "Do you have any idea where we are?"

"None whatsoever," Derec confessed.

"But we're on our way out of this," she said with some

anxiety. "I'm going to get to go home. You're going to get to go find home."

He held up crossed fingers.

"You promised me there'd be nothing more than red tape," she said warningly.

"That was a prediction, not a promise."

"Still stand behind your forecast?"

"Sure," Derec said. "Let's go start hacking through the tangle."

M-3323 led them out of the house and guided them back the way they had come, up the street toward the great central tower. It was a strange little procession—a pair of robots in the lead, matching stride for stride—M-3323 walking between Derec and Katherine like a vigilant chaperone—another pair of robots trailing a few steps behind.

Were the extra robots an honor guard, bodyguards, or prison guards? The pair following silently behind bothered Derec the most. Before they had gone half a block, he glanced back over his shoulder to check on what they were doing. What he saw behind the robots—or, more to the point, what he did not see—made him do a double-take. The house they had just left was gone. The gap between the two towers which had flanked it had closed.

He shook his head and chided himself for foolishness. It must be the angle, he told himself. The house is set farther back than you realized. It's there, between the towers. You just can't see it. Then he remembered the grouping of icosahedrons he had seen, and then not seen, from the high plaza.

"Excuse me," he said to Katherine and M-3323. "I'll be right back."

He ran back down the street until he had gone far enough that he should have been able to see the house, and then slowed to a walk. He could scarcely believe his eyes. The house *was* gone. The two towers now flanked an open courtyard.

He looked around wildly, wanting to believe that he had taken a wrong turn, that he was the victim of some sort of illusion. The house had been just what Katherine had asked for, and so conveniently located. Could they possibly have built it just for us, and then torn it down again?

It was an insane thought, and he did not want to deal with it just then. Demand-driven architecture—a modular structure that swapped whole buildings around like toy blocks or fabricated them from elemental forms—what kind of society was this? How could people live in a city like this?

With an effort, he tore himself away from the sight of the empty courtyard and found two of the escort robots standing two steps away behind him.

"Are you finished here, sir?" one asked politely.

He grunted. "Yeah, I'm finished."

There was no keeping the troubled expression off his face as he rejoined the others.

"Is there a problem, David Derec?" asked M-3323.

"You bet there's a problem. What happened to the house we were just in?"

"My apologies. Did you have other needs that you did not previously identify? Or do you have additional personal needs?"

"I *need* a straight answer. Where's the house?"

"That facility has been released to the general inventory."

"So I'm not just imagining that it's gone—you brought it there for us and then cleaned up when we were done."

"Yes, David Derec."

"Do you do that all the time around here?"

"All physical resources are managed for maximum efficiency."

"I'll take that as yes. Crazy," Derec shook his head.

"But it doesn't matter to us," Katherine said.

"No," Derec agreed. "So forget it and let's get on with this."

They walked on until they came to a great plaza at the convergence of several main streets. In the center of the plaza was a great white tetrahedron perhaps fifteen stories tall. Their guides directed them toward an entrance on the right.

"M-3323—"

"Yes, David Derec?"

"Is this part of the city exclusively used by robots? I didn't see any people along the way here."

"Yes, Derec."

"I thought so. Where *are* all the people?"

"I do not know, sir," M-3323 said. "This way, please." It led them through a lobby area which was itself a tetrahedron and down a corridor. At the third door, the robot turned and paused. "In here, please."

"Who are we meeting?" Katherine asked, pausing in the open doorway.

"Rydberg and Euler," M-3323 said. "They are waiting for you in the inner office."

*Rydberg—Euler—*The names gnawed familiarly at Derec's memory as he followed Katherine first through one doorway, then through another. *Where have I heard them be-fore—*

Preoccupied, he entered the inner office with his eyes lowered. When he looked up, he received a jolt. The spartan compartment contained three straight-backed chairs, a quarter-circle work station with a sophisticated hypervision computer terminal, and two blue-skinned robots with silver slits for optical sensors.

*This can't be—*A chill went through Derec as he stared at robots that were clones of the supervisors on the asteroid. *It's all connected. I don't understand—*"Kate—" he started.

Just then the robot on the left stepped forward. "I am Rydberg."

"I am Euler," the other robot said.

"I'm afraid there's some mistake," Katherine said. "We want to talk to people."

"There is no error. We are the representatives assigned to your case," Euler said.

"Kate, this is wrong," Derec said hoarsely.

Pursing her lips, Katherine decided, "If they want to do it this way, I don't care." She addressed Euler. "We need to see about transportation to Aurora and Nexon—that is where you're going to go, isn't it, Derec?—and temporary accommodations."

"I am afraid that that is not possible," Euler said, shaking his head gravely.

"What?" exclaimed Katherine. "Why not?"

"Friend Euler's statement was imprecise," Rydberg said. "It is possible to leave. But there is a problem. A human being has been killed—"

"Why does that involve us?" Derec asked.

"It would be an unthinkable violation of the Laws of Robotics for a robot to harm a human being," Rydberg said.

"I am unable even to form the thought without experiencing distress."

"Of course it wasn't a robot," Derec said impatiently. "Another human being did it, obviously."

Euler said, "Disregarding yourselves, there are no other humans here."

"Our guide said something about that," Derec said. "But just because they have no business here doesn't mean that they didn't come over from some other sector anyway. Someone who'd murder wouldn't worry too long about proper travel passes or whatever it is you use here."

"I will clarify," Rydberg interjected. "Friend Euler meant to say that there are no other human beings in this city."

"Then from one of the other cities—," Katherine began.

"There are no other cities on this planet."

"What are you saying? Where are we?" she demanded.

"I regret that I may not identify this planet or its star," Rydberg said. "But we who live here call this place Robot City."

"There's nothing but robots here?" Derec said slowly, an uncomfortable idea pricking at him.

"Discounting yourselves, that is correct," Euler said.

Katherine gaped. "No one in this whole city—it must be fifty hectares—"

"Two hundred five," Euler corrected.

Derec interrupted. "Where are the inhabitants? The builders? Where did they go?"

Rydberg cocked his head slightly. "We are the inhabitants, and the builders, Friend Derec," he said matter-of-factly.

It was the answer he had been expecting, but he still resisted its implications. "Where are your owners?" Derec persisted. "Where are the people you report to?"

"Your question is based on an erroneous assumption," Euler replied. "Robot City is a free and autonomous community."

"That can't be," he protested. "Maybe there are no humans here now. Maybe you're not presently in contact with any. But they must have brought you here, or sent you here. You must still be following their directives."

"No, Friend Derec. We are self-directed," Euler said. "But we are not unaware of human beings. We have a vast library of book-films by and about human beings. And we have accepted our responsibility to see that humans do not come to harm."

"I hope you understand, Friend Derec, why we are obliged to delay your departure," Rydberg said. "This is our first experience with death. We need your help in understanding how it happened, and in understanding how the experience of death should be integrated into our study of the Laws of Humanics."

"The Laws of Humanics? What are they?" Katherine asked, puzzled.

"The human counterparts of the Laws of Robotics—those guiding principles which govern human behavior."

Euler continued, "At present the Laws of Humanics are a theoretical construct. We are attempting to determine if Laws of Humanics exist, and if they do, what they are. This incident has placed the research project in crisis. You must help us. I assure you that you will be afforded every possible comfort."

As Euler was speaking, Katherine had slowly edged closer and closer to Derec, and now was standing at his elbow. "This is crazy," she said under her breath. "A city of robots, with no one to guide them? Doing research on human beings, like we were some curiosity?"

And in that moment, Derec stopped fighting the truth and embraced it: *The community on the asteroid and the great city surrounding him were products of the same mind, the same plan. He hadn't escaped at all.*

But at least he at last understood why—why he was given the key, and why it had brought them there. For the last to touch it had been Monitor 5, an advanced robot desperate to fulfill its First Law obligation to save him. Knowing what it was and what it was capable of, the robot could do nothing other than give it to him—programmed for what it knew would be a safe destination, a sister colony of robots light-years away.

"Sssh," he said to Katherine, then looked to the robots. "Could you excuse us for a moment? We need to talk."

"Certainly, Friend Derec," Euler replied, "We will—"

"You stay. We'll leave," Derec said, taking Katherine's hand and leading her out the door.

"Where are we going?" she asked breathlessly as he guided her a dozen meters down the corridor. "They're going to follow us."

He stopped short and released her hand. "We're not going anywhere. At least I'm not. I really did want to talk privately."

"What do you mean, you're not going anywhere?"

"I'm going to stay," he said. "I won't tell them that, though. I'll offer to stay and cooperate on the condition they arrange transportation for you. They don't need both of us."

"No!" she said emphatically. "You don't have to do that. They've got no right to hold us. They have to let us both go. They're robots, aren't they? They have to help us."

"They're robots, yes. But not like any you're used to. I don't think they'd agree with your definition of their obligations," Derec said, shaking his head. "But that's not the point. I'm not going to stay just to appease them, or to get them to let you go. I'm staying because I want to."

"Want to! Why?"

Derec flashed a tight-lipped smile. "I started thinking about how I'd feel if they did what we asked and put us on a ship to Aurora, or wherever. How I'd feel if I never found out any more about the key—"

"We could take it with us."

"—never found out where this planet is or why the robots are here—never went back for Wolruf or found out what happened to her. I thought about it and realized I couldn't just walk away. It's true that I don't know who I am. Even so, I know that's not the kind of person I want to be."

There was a studied silence, which Derec finally broke. "Part friends?"

Her eyes flicked upward and her gaze met his. "No," she said, shaking her head. "Because if you're staying, I'm staying, too."

It was his turn to protest. "You don't have to do that. They're my causes, not yours. This is a safe world. I'll be fine alone."

"You don't like my company?"

He shrugged. "We get on all right."

"Then are you trying to tell me that this is something a girl can't handle or shouldn't worry her head about?"

"Of course not."

"Then it's okay if I stay just because I want to?"

Derec surrendered. "Sure."

"Then let's go tell Euler and Rydberg."

"After you," he said, bowing with a flourish of his hand.

Wearing a contented smile, Katherine led the way back to the office. As the door opened, she turned and whispered back over her shoulder. "Just tell me this—when do our lives turn normal again?"

Derec laughed aloud, startling the robots. "Maybe never, Katherine," he said. "Why are you complaining? You said your life was dull, didn't you?"

"Dull isn't so bad," she said wistfully. "Dull has its good points."

Chuckling to himself, Derec picked out a chair and settled in it as though planning to stay for a while. "We'll do what we can to help," he said to Rydberg. "Tell us the story. Who're the suspects?"

But the robot's dispassionate answer erased the smiles from both their faces so thoroughly it was as though they had never been there. Like a bitter aftertaste to a sweet drink, it stole all the pleasure that had come before.

"Yes, David Derec," Rydberg said. "There are two suspects. Yourself—and Katherine Burgess. We are most curious to learn which of you committed the act, and why."

THE LAWS OF HUMANICS

by ISAAC ASIMOV

I am pleased by the way in which the Robot City books pick up the various themes and references in my robot stories and carry on with them.

For instance, my first three robot novels were, essentially, murder mysteries, with Elijah Baley as the detective. Of these first three, the second novel, *The Naked Sun*, was a locked-room mystery, in the sense that the murdered person was found with no weapon on the site and yet no weapon could have been removed either.

I managed to produce a satisfactory solution but I did not do that sort of thing again, and I am delighted that Mike McQuay has tried his hand at it here.

The fourth robot novel, *Robots and Empire*, was not primarily a murder mystery. Elijah Baley had died a natural death at a good, old age, the book veered toward the Foundation universe so that it was clear that both my notable series, the Robot series and the Foundation series, were going to be fused into a broader whole. (No, I didn't do this for some arbitrary reason. The necessities arising out of writing sequels in the 1980s to tales originally written in the 1940s and 1950s forced my hand.)

In *Robots and Empire*, my robot character, Giskard, of

whom I was very fond, began to concern himself with "the Laws of Humanics," which, I indicated, might eventually serve as the basis for the science of psychohistory, which plays such a large role in the Foundation series.

Strictly speaking, the Laws of Humanics should be a description, in concise form, of how human beings actually behave. No such description exists, of course. Even psychologists, who study the matter scientifically (at least, I hope they do) cannot present any "laws" but can only make lengthy and diffuse descriptions of what people seem to do. And none of them are prescriptive. When a psychologist says that people respond in this way to a stimulus of that sort, he merely means that some do at some times. Others may do it at other times, or may not do it at all.

If we have to wait for actual laws prescribing human behavior in order to establish psychohistory (and surely we must) then I suppose we will have to wait a long time.

Well, then, what are we going to do about the Laws of Humanics? I suppose what we can do is to start in a very small way, and then later slowly build it up, if we can.

Thus, in *Robots and Empire*, it is a robot, Giskard, who raises the question of the Laws of Humanics. Being a robot, he must view everything from the standpoint of the Three Laws of Robotics—these robotic laws being truly prescriptive, since robots are forced to obey them and cannot disobey them.

The Three Laws of Robotics are:

1—A robot may not injure a human being, or, through inaction, allow a human being to come to harm.

2—A robot must obey the orders given it by human beings except where such orders would conflict with the First Law.

3—A robot must protect its own existence as long as

such protection does not conflict with the First or Second Law.

Well, then, it seems to me that a robot could not help but think that human beings ought to behave in such a way as to make it easier for robots to obey those laws.

In fact, it seems to me that ethical human beings should be as anxious to make life easier for robots as the robots themselves would. I took up this matter in my story "The Bicentennial Man," which was published in 1976. In it, I had a human character say in part:

"If a man has the right to give a robot any order that does not involve harm to a human being, he should have the decency never to give a robot any order that involves harm to a robot, unless human safety absolutely requires it. With great power goes great responsibility, and if the robots have Three Laws to protect men, is it too much to ask that men have a law or two to protect robots?"

For instance, the First Law is in two parts. The first part, "A robot may not injure a human being," is absolute and nothing need be done about that. The second part, "or, through inaction, allow a human being to come to harm," leaves things open a bit. A human being might be about to come to harm because of some event involving an inanimate object. A heavy weight might be likely to fall upon him, or he may slip and be about to fall into a lake, or any one of uncountable other misadventures of the sort may be involved. Here the robot simply must try to rescue the human being; pull him from under, steady him on his feet and so on. Or a human being might be threatened by some form of life other than human—a lion, for instance—and the robot must come to his defense.

But what if harm to a human being is threatened by the action of another human being? There a robot must decide what to do. Can he save one human being without harming the other? Or if there must be harm, what course of action must he pursue to make it minimal?

It would be a lot easier for the robot, if human beings were as concerned about the welfare of human beings, as robots are expected to be. And, indeed, any reasonable human code of ethics would instruct human beings to care for each other and to do no harm to each other. Which is, after all, the mandate that humans gave robots. Therefore the First Law of Humanics from the robots' standpoint is:

1—A human being may not injure another human being, or, through inaction, allow a human being to come to harm.

If this law is carried through, the robot will be left guarding the human being from misadventures with inanimate objects and with non-human life, something which poses no ethical dilemmas for it. Of course, the robot must still guard against harm done a human being *unwittingly* by another human being. It must also stand ready to come to the aid of a threatened human being, if another human being on the scene simply cannot get to the scene of action quickly enough. But then, even a robot may *unwittingly* harm a human being, and even a robot may not be fast enough to get to the scene of action in time or skilled enough to take the necessary action. Nothing is perfect.

That brings us to the Second Law of Robotics, which compels a robot to obey all orders given it by human beings except where such orders would conflict with the First Law. This means that human beings can give robots any order without limitation as long as it does not involve harm to a human being.

But then a human being might order a robot to do something impossible, or give it an order that might involve a robot in a dilemma that would do damage to its brain.

Thus, in my short story "Liar!," published in 1940, I had a human being deliberately put a robot into a dilemma where its brain burnt out and ceased to function.

We might even imagine that as a robot becomes more intelligent and self-aware, its brain might become sensitive enough to undergo harm if it were forced to do something needlessly embarrassing or undignified. Consequently, the Second Law of Humanics would be:

2—A human being must give orders to a robot that preserve robotic existence, unless such orders cause harm or discomfort to human beings.

The Third Law of Robotics is designed to protect the robot, but from the robotic view it can be seen that it does not go far enough. The robot must sacrifice its existence if the First or Second Law makes that necessary. Where the First Law is concerned, there can be no argument. A robot must give up its existence if that is the only way it can avoid doing harm to a human being or can prevent harm from coming to a human being. If we admit the innate superiority of any human being to any robot (which is something I am a little reluctant to admit, actually), then this is inevitable.

On the other hand, must a robot give up its existence merely in obedience to an order that might be trivial, or even malicious? In "The Bicentennial Man," I have some hoodlums deliberately order a robot to take itself apart for the fun of watching that happen. The Third Law of Humanics must therefore be:

3—A human being must not harm a robot, or, through inaction, allow a robot to come to harm, unless such harm is needed to keep a human being from harm or to allow a vital order to be carried out.

Of course, we cannot enforce these laws as we can the

Robotic Laws. We cannot design human brains as we design robot brains. It is, however, a beginning, and I honestly think that if we are to have power over intelligent robots, we must feel a corresponding responsibility for them, as the human character in my story "The Bicentennial Man" said.

Certainly in Robot City, these are the sorts of rules that robots might suggest for the only human beings on the planet, as you may soon learn.

BOOK TWO

SUSPICION

MIKE McQUAY

CHAPTER 1

PARADES

It was sunset in the city of robots, and it was snowing paper.

The sun was a yellow one and the atmosphere, mostly nitrogen/oxygen blue, was flush with the veins of iron oxides that traced through it, making the whole twilight sky glow bright orange like a forest fire.

The one who called himself Derec marveled at the sunset from the back of the huge earthmover as it slowly made its way through the city streets, crowds of robots lining the avenue to watch him and his companions make this tour of the city. The tiny shards of paper floated down from the upper stories of the crystal-like buildings, thrown (for reasons that escaped Derec) by the robots that crowded the windows to watch him.

Derec took it all in, sure that it must have significance or the robots wouldn't do it. And that was the only thing he was sure of—for Derec was a person without memory, without notion of who he was. Worse still, he had come to this impossible world, unpopulated by humans, by means that still astounded him; and he had no idea, *no idea*, of where in the universe he was.

He was young, the cape of manhood still new on his shoulders, and he only knew that by observing himself in a mirror. Even his name—Derec—wasn't really his. It was a borrowed name, a convenient thing to call himself because not having a name was like not existing. And he desperately wanted to exist, to know who, to know *what* he was.

And why.

Beside him sat a young woman called Katherine Burgess, who had said she'd known him, briefly, when he'd had a name. But he wasn't sure of her, of her truth or her motivations. She had told him his real name was David and that he'd crewed on a Settler ship, but neither the name nor the classification seemed to fit as well as the identity he'd already been building for himself; so he continued to call himself by his chosen name, Derec, until he had solid proof of his other existence.

Flanking the humans on either side were two robots of advanced sophistication (Derec knew that, but didn't know how he knew it). One was named Euler, the other Rydberg, and they couldn't, or wouldn't, tell him any more than he already knew—nothing. The robots wanted information from him, however. They wanted to know why he was a murderer.

The First Law of Robotics made it impossible for robots to harm human beings, so when the only other human inhabitant of Robot City turned up dead, Derec and Katherine were the only suspects. Derec's brief past had not included killing, but convincing Euler and Rydberg of that was not an easy task. They were being held, but treated with respect—innocent, perhaps, until proven guilty.

Both robots had shiny silver heads molded roughly to

human equivalent. Both had glowing photocells where eyes would be. But where Euler had a round mesh screen in place of a human mouth, Rydberg had a small loudspeaker mounted atop his dome.

"Do you enjoy this, Friend Derec?" Euler asked him, indicating the falling paper and the seemingly endless stream of robots that lined the route of their drive.

Derec had no idea of what he was supposed to enjoy about this demonstration, but he didn't want to offend his hosts, who were being very polite despite their accusations. "It's really . . . very nice," he replied, brushing a piece of paper off his lips.

"Nice?" Katherine said from beside him, angry. "Nice?" She ran fingers through her long black hair. "I'll be a week getting all this junk out of my hair."

"Surely it won't take you that length of time," Rydberg said, the speaker on his head crackling. "Perhaps there's something I don't understand, but it seems from a cursory examination that it shouldn't take you any longer than . . ."

"All right," Katherine said. "All right."

". . . one or two hours. Unless of course you're speaking microscopically, in which case . . ."

"Please," she said. "No more. I was mistaken about the time."

"Our studies of human culture," Euler told Derec, "indicate that the parade is indigenous to all human civilizations. We very much want to make you feel at home here, our differences notwithstanding."

Derec looked out on both sides of the huge, open-air, V-shaped mover. The robots lining the streets stood quite still, their variegated bodies giving no hint of curiosity, though Derec felt it quite possible that he and Katherine were the first humans many of them had ever seen. Knowing nothing, Derec knew nothing of parades, but it seemed to be a friendly enough ritual, except for the paper, and it made him feel good that they should want him to feel at home.

"Is it not customary to wave?" Euler asked.

"What?" Derec replied.

"To wave your arm to the crowd," Euler explained. "Is it no customary?"

"Of course," Derec said, and waved on both sides of the machine that clanked steadily down the wide street, the robots returning the gesture with more nonreadable silence.

"Don't you feel like a proper fool?" Katherine asked, scrunching up her nose at his antics.

"They're just trying to be hospitable," Derec replied. "With the trouble we're in here, I don't think it hurts to return a friendly gesture."

"Is there some problem, Friend Katherine?" Euler asked.

"Only with her mouth," Derec replied.

Rydberg leaned forward to stare intently at Katherine's face. "Is there something we can do?"

"Yeah," the girl answered. "Get me something to eat. I'm starving."

Rydberg swiveled his head toward Euler. "Another untruth," he said. "This is very discouraging."

"What do you mean?" Derec asked.

"Our hypotheses concerning the philosophical nature of humanics," Rydberg said, "must have their foundation in truth among species. Twice Katherine has said things that aren't true . . ."

"I *am* starving!" Katherine complained.

". . . and how can any postulate be universally self-evident if the postulators do not adhere to the same truths? Perhaps this is the mark of a murderer."

"Now wait a minute," Derec said. "All humans make . . . creative use of the language. It's no proof of anything."

Rydberg examined Katherine's face closely. Then he pressed a pincer to her bare arm, the place turning white for a second before resuming its natural color. "You say you are starving, but your color is good, your pulse rate strong and even, and you have no signs of physical deterioration. I must conclude, reluctantly, that you are not starving."

"We are hungry, though," Derec said. "Please take us where we might eat."

Katherine fixed him with a sidelong glance. "And do it quickly."

"Of course," Euler said. "You will find that we are fully equipped to deal with any human emergency here. This is to be the perfect human world."

"But there are no humans here," Derec said.

"No."

"Are you expecting any?"

"We have no expectations."

"Oh."

Euler directed the spider-like robot guiding the mover, and the machine turned dutifully at the next corner, taking them down a double-width street that was bisected by a large aqueduct, whose waters had turned dark under the ever-deepening twilight.

Derec sat back and stole a glance at Katherine, but she was busily pulling bits of paper from her hair and didn't notice him. He had a million questions, but they seemed better left for later. As it was, he had conflicting emotions to analyze and react to within himself.

He was a nonperson whose life had begun scant weeks before, when he'd awakened without past or memory to find himself in a life-support pod, stranded upon an asteriod that was being mined by robots. They had been searching for something, something he had accidentally stumbled upon— the Key to Perihelion, at least one of the seven Keys to Perihelion. It had seemed of incredible import to the robots on the asteroid. Unfortunately, he had had no idea of what the Keys to Perihelion were or what to do with them.

After that was the bad time. The asteroid was destroyed by Aranimas, an alien space raider, who captured Derec and tortured him for information about the Key, information that Derec could not supply. There he had met Katherine, just before the destruction of Aranimas's vessel and their dubious salvation at the hands of the Spacers' robots.

The Spacers also wanted the Key, though their means of attaining it seemed slightly more civilized and bureau- cratic than Aranimas's. Katherine and Derec were polite prisoners of bureaucracy for a time on Rockliffe Station, their personalities clashing until they were forced to form an alliance with Wolruf, another alien from Aranimas's ship, to escape their gentle captivity with the Key.

They found that if they pressed the corners of the silver slab and thought themselves away from the Spacer station, they were whisked bodily to a dark gray void that they assumed to be Perihelion. Pressing the corners again, an- other thought brought them to Robot City. And then their thinking took them no farther, stranding them in a world populated by nothing but robots.

And that was it, the sum total of Derec's conscious life. He had reached several conclusions, though, scant as his reserve of information was: First, he had an innate knowl- edge of robots and their workings, though he had no idea from where his knowledge emanated; next, Katherine knew more about him than she was willing to tell; finally, he couldn't escape the feeling that he was here for a purpose, that this was all some elaborate test designed especially for him.

But why? Why?

It was worlds that were being turned here, physical and spatial laws that were being forced upside down—all for him? Nothing made sense.

And then there was the Key, the object that everyone wanted, the object that was safely hidden by the person who couldn't control it. The robots here didn't know he had it. Were they looking for it, too? He'd have to find out. The Key seemed to be the one strain that held everything else together.

Keeping that in mind, he determined to move slowly, to try always to get more in the way of information than he gave. He'd been at a disadvantage for the entire length of his memory. From this point, he wanted to keep the upper hand as far as possible.

But there was, of course, the murder.

Derec stood on the balcony of the apartment given to him and Katherine by the robots, looking out over the night city. A stiff, cold wind had come up, the starfield totally obscured by dark, angry clouds that seemed to boil up out of nowhere. Lightning flashed in the distance, electrons seeking partner protons on the surface. It was a beautiful sight, and frightening. Derec watched the distant buildings light to near daytime before plunging once more into darkness.

"There," he said, pointing to a distant tower. "It wasn't there a centad ago."

Katherine walked up beside him, leaning against the balcony rail. "Where was it?" she asked, mocking.

"It wasn't anywhere," he replied, turning to take her by the shoulders. "It didn't exist."

"That's impossible," she replied, then turned and walked back into the large, airy apartment that sat at the top of another tower like the one Derec said had sprung from nowhere. "I wish they'd get here with our food."

"They're probably fixing us something extra special," Derec said, joining her in the living room. "And impossible seems to be the way of our lives right now, doesn't it? I'm telling you, Katherine, that along with everything else that doesn't make sense, this . . . city is growing, changing right before our eyes."

"How can that be?" she asked, and looked around uneasily. "I mean . . . cities are built, aren't they? They don't just grow."

Derec stared a circle around the room. It was hexagonal, like standing on the inside of a crystal, with no visible line of demarcation for the ceilings and floor. The furniture seemed to flow from the walls, as the table seemed to flow upward from the floor. Light concentrated from the ceiling and lit the room comfortably, but it seemed the ceiling itself that was alight, with no external apparatus to make it happen.

"Look around you," Derec said. "Everything's connected to everything else, and connected seamlessly. And it all seems to be made from the same material." He walked to a sofa that flowed out of the wall and sat on the cushion that formed its base. "Comfortable," he said, "but I think it's made from the same material as the harder stuff—some kind of steel and plastic alloy—just in different measure."

Katherine had walked to the table and was staring at it. "If you look closely," she said, "you can see a pattern to the material."

Derec stood and walked up beside her, leaning down on the table to get a close look. The pattern was faint, but readable. The table was made up of a collection of trapezoidal shapes, interwoven and repeated over and over.

"Interesting," Derec said.

"How so?"

"Is the shape familiar to you?"

She narrowed her brows in concentration for a moment, then looked at him with wide eyes. "The same shape as the Key," she said.

He nodded.

Katherine left him standing there and hurried back out to the balcony.

"It's almost like individual pieces stuck together," he called to her. "I wonder how they connect . . ."

"It's gone!" she shrieked, and Derec hurried onto the balcony. "Your tower from before, it's gone!"

"No it's not," he said, pointing farther to the east.

"It's moved?"

He shook his head. "I don't think so." He pointed to the huge, pyramidal structure that dominated the landscape to the west. It was at the top of that place where they were first brought by the Key. "That's the only building I think doesn't change. And we couldn't see it from the balcony a moment ago."

"You mean, *we've* changed?"

"Something like that."

She put a hand to her head. "I didn't see . . . feel, I . . ."

"It's kind of like watching clouds," he said. "If you stare at them from moment to moment, they seem to be solid and stationary, but once you turn away and then look back, they've changed. It's almost like some sort of evolutionary growth . . ."

"In a building?"

"If you stay out there much longer, you will probably get wet," came a voice from behind them. They turned to see Euler's glowing eyes staring at them in the darkness.

"We've gotten wet before," Katherine returned, looking past Euler to the food being set out on their table. "Ah, a last meal for the condemned."

"The rain here is particularly cool," the robot said, and watched as Katherine shoved past him and ran into the dining area, "perhaps uncomfortably cool for the human body temperature."

Thunder rumbled loudly in the distance, a brilliant shaft of lightning striking the top of the towering pyramid. Derec turned from the spectacle and moved toward the doorway, Euler stepping aside to let him pass.

He walked to the table, sitting across from Katherine, who was already piling food from a large golden bowl onto her plate, also gold-colored. The food seemed to be of a uniform, paste-like consistency, its color drifting somewhere between blue and gray. Golden cups filled with water sat beside the plates.

"Are these utensils made of gold?" Derec asked, clanging a spoon melodiously against his plate.

"Correct," Rydberg said. "It's a relatively useless soft metal that is a by-product of our mining operations. Its one major virtue besides its use as a conductor is the fact that it doesn't tarnish, making it ideal for human eating utensils. We made these things for David's visit."

Derec watched the serving spoon slip from Katherine's grasp to clang loudly against her plate. And for just a second her face turned white.

"That's what you told me *my* name was," Derec said, finding the coincidence a little too close for his comfort.

She fixed him with unfocused eyes, then shrugged, looking normal again. "It's a common enough name on Spacer worlds," she said, returning her attention to her plate.

She picked up the spoon and went back to the job at hand. Derec looked up at the robots who stood beside the table and the small servo Type-I:5 robot waiting patiently near the door for the return of the utensils.

"Would you care to sit with us while we eat?" Derec asked, and felt Katherine kick him under the table.

"Delighted," Euler said without hesitation, and the two robots sat at table attentively, apparently enjoying in their way the human familiarity.

Derec took the serving spoon and began filling his own plate. "I take it that David was the other human who came here?" he asked.

"That is correct," Rydberg said.

"Then he came in a ship?" Derec pressed.

"No," Euler said. "He simply walked into the city one day."

"From where?"

"I don't know."

"Aaaahhh!" Katherine yelled, spitting out food and grabbing for the glass of water, drinking furiously. The robots swiveled their heads to watch, then exchanged glances. "Are you trying to feed us or kill us?" she demanded.

"Our programming would never allow us to kill you," Rydberg said. "That would be quite impossible."

Derec tentatively dipped his spoon into the porridge-like mixture, taking a small bite. Not sour, not sweet, it simply had a strange, *alien* taste accompanied by a slight noxious odor, one he was also uncomfortable with.

"This stuff stinks!" Katherine said loudly, the robots looking at her, then turning expectantly toward Derec.

"She's right," Derec replied. "What is this?"

"A perfect, nontoxic mixture of local plant matter, high in protein and balanced carbohydrates," Rydberg said. "It's good for you."

"The other human ate this?" Derec asked.

"Quite enthusiastically," Euler said.

"No wonder he's dead," Katherine muttered. "This is simply unacceptable. You're going to have to find us something else, something that tastes good."

Derec took another bite, this time holding his nose. Disassociating the smell from the food helped some, but not too much. The gruel left an unpleasant aftertaste. How could the other man have eaten it and not complained? Less made sense all the time.

"How long before you can get us something else?" Derec asked.

"Tomorrow?" Rydberg suggested. "Although they were proud of this in food services. Finding something of equal nutritional value will be difficult."

"Forget nutritional value to a degree," Derec said. "Study other human foods and see how well those can be duplicated exactly with the know-how you have here." He looked at Katherine. "We should probably try and choke some of this down to keep our strength."

She nodded grimly. "I'd already figured that," she said, and looked at Rydberg. "Bring me lots of water."

The robot hurried to comply, fetching a gold pitcher from the servo-cart and refilling her cup.

"When did he die, this David?" Derec asked, holding his nose and taking another bite.

"Seven days ago," Rydberg said, sitting again and carefully positioning the pitcher within everyone's easy reach on the table.

"Well, that rules us out as suspect then," Derec said happily. "We didn't arrive here until last night."

"You'll have to excuse me," Rydberg said politely, "but Katherine has already exhibited a penchant for speaking less than honestly—"

"What's that supposed to mean?" Katherine said angrily.

"No disrespect intended," Rydberg said. "It is simply the case that your veracity must be in question in light of our conversations of this afternoon. At this point, we don't know if we can trust anything either of you says."

"We don't even know where this place is," Derec said.

"Then how did you get here?" Euler asked, swiveling his head to stare directly at Derec.

"I . . ." Derec began, then stopped himself. He wasn't ready to admit any knowledge of the Key. It was their only weapon, their only potential salvation; he couldn't give it over so early in the game. "I don't know."

Rydberg stared for several seconds before saying, "To believe you means that you either materialized out of the ether or were somehow brought here totally without your knowledge or consent."

Derec responded by taking the conversation away from the robot's control. "You say this David also seemed to appear out of nowhere. Did you ever question him about his origins?"

"Yes," Euler said simply.

"And you know nothing about his background," Derec said, trying to keep his mind off the food by concentrating on the investigation. Across from him, Katherine was swallowing her food whole and washing it down with large gulps of water. "How was he dressed?"

"He was naked," Euler said. "And he stayed naked."

The two humans shared a look. Nudity was common and casual on many Spacer worlds, but the climate here would hardly recommend it. "When can we see the body?" Derec asked.

"That's not possible," Euler told her.

"Why?"

"I cannot tell you why."

"Cannot or will not?" Derec asked, exasperated.

"Cannot and will not," Euler replied.

"Then how do you expect us to investigate the cause of death?" Kate asked.

"If either or both of you are the murderers," Euler said, "you already know the cause of death."

"You've already decided our guilt," Derec said, pointing. "That's not fair or just."

"There are no other possibilities," Rydberg said.

"When the possible has been exhausted," Derec replied, "it is time to examine the impossible. We are innocent, and you can't prove that we aren't. It only follows that the death was caused by something else."

"Humans can murder," Euler said, as thunder crashed loudly outside. "Humans can lie. You are the only humans here, and murder has been done."

"We came out of nowhere," Derec returned. "So did David. Others could also have come out of nowhere, others you haven't discovered yet. Why, had we committed a murder, would we stay around for you to catch?"

The robots looked at one another again. "You raised

logical questions that must be answered," Euler said. "We certainly sanction your investigation."

"How can we investigate without full access?"

"With all the other resources at your command," Rydberg said, then stood. "Are you finished eating?"

"For now," Derec said. "We'll want real food tomorrow, though."

"We will do our best," Euler said, and he, also, stood. "Until then, you will stay here."

"I thought I might go out," Derec said.

"The rains will come. It's too dangerous. For your own safety, you will stay here tonight. We have found that we cannot be certain if what you tell us is correct, so we're leaving a robot at the door to make certain you stay in."

"You don't know that we've done anything wrong. You can't treat us like prisoners," Katherine said.

"And we shall not," Rydberg said, moving toward the door; the servo whirred up to the table, its metal talons pulling the bowls and plates into its innards.

"There are many things we need to talk with you about," Derec said.

"Tomorrow will be the time," Euler said. "We will have a long interview at a prescribed time, where many issues will be discussed. Until then, we cannot fit it into our schedule. We are currently quite busy." The robots turned to go.

"A couple of questions first," Derec said, hurrying to put himself between the door and the robots. "You say we aren't prisoners, yet you have locked us up. How long do we have to stay in this place?"

"Until it is safe," Rydberg said.

"Then if you do let us out," Derec persisted, "how can you be sure we won't try to escape?"

"We will have to keep a very close watch on you," Euler replied.

With that, the robot firmly, but gently, pushed Derec aside and moved out the door, the servo following quickly behind. Derec tried to follow them out, but a squared-off utility robot blocked his path, its body streaked with random bands of different colored paints like the colors on an artist's pallet.

"Stand aside," Derec told the machine.

"It is dangerous for you outside. I am to keep you inside where it is safe, and have no more conversation with you lest you try and deceive me."

"Me?" Derec said. "Deceive?"

The robot pushed the door stud and the unit slid closed. Derec turned to Katherine. "What do you make of it?"

She moved to sit on the sofa, then stretched out, looking tired. "We're being held prisoner by a bunch of robots with no one in charge," she said, sighing deeply. "The dead man was an exhibitionist who could, apparently, eat anything. They want us to prove our innocence, but refuse to let us see the body or investigate." She sat up abruptly, eyes narrowing. "Derec, we've got to get out of here."

"They won't do anything to us without proof of our guilt," Derec replied. "It's not in their nature. We'll stay around and get this straightened out. Then they'll be happy to send us on our way. Besides, this place has got me really curious. How does it work . . . *why* does it work?"

She lay down again, staring at the ceiling. "I'm not so sure they'd really let us leave," she said, voice distant. "I think we've stumbled into something completely crazy. A robot world without humans could take any sort of bizarre turn."

"But not a . . . what did you say . . . completely crazy

turn," he replied. "They can't be crazy; there's no logic to crazy. Besides, what makes you think we've stumbled into anything? We were brought here, plain and simple, for a reason that hasn't been made clear yet. Maybe a little time here will help us ferret it out."

"You ferret it out," she said. "I'm tired."

"Well, I'm not." He moved to the balcony, feeling the stiff wind on his face as the light show continued to rage outside. "I'm going out tonight and do a little poking around."

She was up from the couch, moving toward him. "They said it was dangerous," she said quietly, a hand going to his forearm. "Go out tomorrow."

"Under their watchful eye?" he said, then shook his head. "We need to get around on our own, and this is the time. Besides, a little rain can't hurt me."

"Stay," she said. "I'm afraid."

"You?" He laughed. "Afraid?"

She pulled her hand away. "All right," she said. "Go out and get yourself killed. I'm tired of looking out for you anyway."

"You're angry."

"And you're an idiot." She turned from him and stared out across the magnificent city, realizing that its beauty was for them alone to appreciate. There was something unutterably sad about that. "How will you get past the door guard?"

"We'll take his advice and deceive him," Derec said.

"*We?*"

"Will you help me?"

She turned and walked back into the apartment. "Anything to get you out of my hair," she said over her shoulder.

Derec's plan was simple enough, but it was one he could

use only once. The robots learned quickly enough of human duplicity, arming themselves with the knowledge as a protection. But just this once, it might work.

He crouched beside the sofa, knotting into a tight ball. Just as soon as he was well out of sight of the door, Kate took a deep breath and tried to open it—locked.

She shrugged once in Derec's direction, then began screaming in terror. A second later the door slid open, the utility robot blocking the entry.

"What's wrong?"

"It's Derec!" she cried, pointing. "He fell from the balcony!"

Without hesitation, the robot rolled into the room, ready to check her story for lies and deceit. He quickly moved toward the balcony, leaning way over the edge to get a look into the night.

Derec jumped up from behind the couch and hurried quietly out the door and into the elevator that took him all the way to the ground and his first positive step in uncovering the mystery of Robot City. He was free, but what that meant here he could only guess.

CHAPTER 2

THE SLUICE

Derec exited onto the wide street, hurrying across it to the shadows of buildings a half a block away. From there he took a few minutes to turn back and study the surroundings he had just left behind, trying to memorize the positions and shapes of the buildings near his tower. If his feelings were correct and the city was evolving outward, finding his way back could be a difficult, if not impossible, task. He didn't worry too much about it, though. He felt completely safe in this world of robots and figured that if he got lost, he'd simply turn himself in to the nearest robot of decent sophistication and be sent back.

That dwelt upon, he turned his attention completely to exploring the new world that an unseen fate had guided him to. In his current pristine state of innocence and aware-ness, it was difficult for Derec not to see the hand of destiny in his wanderings. It was as if his amnesia was an emotional and intellectual purging of sorts, set in motion to prepare him for a journey of which Robot City could be only a part. Since that was the only feeling or need he had to work with, he plunged himself into it with relish, enthusiasm, and as much good humor as he could muster. Katherine would never understand his feelings in this matter, but then Katherine had a life to go back to and memories to sustain her. For Derec, this was it, his whole world, and he wanted to know as much about it as he possibly could.

The city stretched all around him like some magnificent clockwork. The shapes of the buildings, from towering spires to squat storage warehouses, were all precise and multifaceted, like growing crystals. And the shapes seemed to be designed as much for aesthetic pleasure as pragmatic necessity. This concept formed the core of a theory within Derec's mind, and one that he would want to explore in greater detail when he had time for reflection. For nothing exists in a vacuum. Robots were not motivated independently by unreasoning emotion. They had to have reasons for their actions, and by what Derec had seen, their actions were all directed absolutely, despite Rydberg's claims of autonomy.

The cold winds sliced through him like a knife through water, and the sky rumbled and quaked, yet all around him he watched a furious activity that kept the mechanism of Robot City moving to its own internal rhythm and purpose. Hundreds of robots filled the streets around him, all moving and directed. All ignored his presence.

Streets were cleaned, even as spray painting was conducted on dull-sheened buildings, the sprayers held close to the target in the stiff wind—which probably explained the bands of paint on the utility robot that guarded the humans. Converted mining cars sped by, filled with broken equipment and scrap metal, their beamed headlights illuminating the streets before them like roving mechanical fireflies. Once he took to the shadows as a whole squad of drones, accompanied by a supervisor robot he hadn't seen before, drove past in an open-bed equipment mover and passed his position without a look before disappearing around a distant corner. He thought about following them, but decided that he would continue exploring slowly at first, getting a feel for his world and its parameters.

The questions in his mind seemed endless, and their answers only led to more questions. Who began Robot City, and why did the robots not know of their own origin? Why this place, this particular planet? Why a city of human proportions for a world of the nonhuman? Euler had called Robot City the perfect place for humans—why? The murder, to Derec, was nothing but a small nuisance with large complications. What really interested him was the motivation behind the city itself.

The lousy food raised a great many further questions in his mind. Spacer robots were designed solely as mechanical helpmates to human masters. Spacer robots *knew* how human beings reacted to food. The robots here had basic human knowledge and the Laws of Robotics as their core, yet remained ignorant of specific, conditioned reactions to humans. It was almost as if their design had geared them toward an equal human partnership, rather than a master/servant relationship, and they were feeling out their relationship with the animal called *human*. It was a dizzying concept to Derec, one that he'd also have to think out in greater detail.

And, finally, the dead man. Where did he fit into the picture . . . and why? Derec's mind, being a blank slate, soaked up everything around him like a sponge, unhampered by the intrusion of past thoughts and feelings that muddied observation. His eye for detail missed nothing, especially the reaction of Katherine to hearing Euler say the man's name—David.

What could it mean? He had literally stumbled upon Katherine, yet she seemed an indispensable part of the puzzle. What role did she play? Again, destiny seemed to rule the day—a place for everything, everything in its place. He was a blind man with a jigsaw puzzle, feeling his way through, groping sightlessly for the connections. He liked the girl, couldn't help it, and felt a strong physical attraction for her that he wouldn't even try to wish away; yet he couldn't shake the feeling that she was deeply involved in covering up his real identity and purpose. And again, his eternal question—why?

He continued moving down the street. Though the buildings were beautiful, they were nondescript, without markings of any kind. He recognized warehouses because parts were being moved in and out of them, but everything else seemed devoid of purpose. If he could find an official building, he could try to hook up to a terminal and make his own inquiries. The pyramid where he and Katherine had materialized, the place the robots called the Compass Tower, had seemed solid to him. Even though it appeared to be the point upon which all else hinged, he wasn't ready to go back to it yet.

The robots on the street ignored him as he moved through their midst. There seemed to be a sense of urgency to them that he couldn't understand. He stopped a utility robot like the one he had snuck past at the apartment, except this one had huge scoops for hands.

"Can you talk?" he asked.

"Yes, most assuredly," the robot answered.

"I need to find the administration building."

"I don't believe we have one here."

"Where would I find the closest computer terminal?"

"I regret that I cannot say."

Derec sighed. The runaround. Again. "Why can't you say?"

"If I told you that, you'd know everything."

"Know everything about what?"

"About the thing that I cannot talk about. If you'd like, you can stay here and I'll report to a supervisor and have him come out and find you."

"No, thanks," Derec replied, and the robot turned to walk away. "Hey, what's your hurry?"

"The rain," the utility said, pointing toward the sky. "The rain is coming. You had better get to shelter." The robot turned and hurried off, his box-like body weaving from side to side as he rolled along.

"What about the rain!?" Derec yelled, but his words were lost in a sudden gust of wind.

He watched the figure of the robot for a moment, realizing that the street he had come down looked different than it had a moment before. The whole block, street and all, had seemed to shift positions, bowing out to curve what had once been straight. A tall, tetrahedral structure, which he had used as a reference point, had disappeared completely. Ten minutes on the street and he was totally lost.

He pressed on, the wind colder now, more intense. If this was such a perfect world for humans, then why did the weather seem so bad?

He reached an unmarked corner and found himself on the street he had ridden down earlier, during the parade. It was extra wide, a large aqueduct bisecting it.

He moved to the edge of the aqueduct and stared down at the dark, rushing waters that filled it no more than a quarter full. Where had the waters come from? Where were they going? Had Robot City been built here for the water, or was the water somehow a consequence of the building?

The water rushed past, dark and inscrutable, much like the problem of Derec's past and, perhaps, his future. Yet he could know about the water. He could trace it to its source; he could follow it to its destination. He could *know*. The thought heartened him, for he could do the same with his life. Accepting that destiny and not chance had brought him to this impossible place, it then followed that the sources of that destiny could be traced through the city itself.

If he pursued it properly, he could trace the origins of the city and, hence, find his own origins. It seemed eminently logical, for he couldn't escape the concept that he and Robot City were inextricably linked, physically, emotionally, and, perhaps, metaphysically.

If his searching came to naught, at least he'd be keeping himself, keeping his blank mind, occupied. He'd begin with the water—trace it through source and destination, find out the why of it. He'd work on the robots, finding out what they knew, what they didn't know, what they'd be willing to tell him, and what he could find out from them unwillingly. And there was Katherine. He'd have to treat her like a friendly adversary and use whatever limited wiles he had at his disposal to find out her place in all this.

The water plopped below him, as if a large stone had been tossed in. He looked around but saw nothing save the gently glowing buildings and the distant robots hurrying about their secret business.

The water plopped again, farther down the aqueduct, then again, near the last place. He turned to stare in that direction when his shoulder was splashed by a drop of icy water.

A drop hardly described it. What hit him was more like a glassful. His jumpsuit sleeve was soaked, his shoulder cold. Water splashed on the street beside him, a drop bigger than a clenched fist, leaving a wet ring.

Derec had about a second to appreciate what was happening, for his mind to begin to realize what a major storm could mean, when the deluge struck.

With a force that nearly doubled him over, the rain fell upon Derec in opaque sheets that immediately cut off his field of vision. He was cold, freezing; the rain lashing him unmercifully, its sound a hollow roar in his ears.

He used his arms to cover and protect his head as the freezing downpour numbed his shoulders and back. He had to get to shelter quickly, but he had already lost his bearings in the curtain of water that surrounded him three-sixty.

He tentatively put out a foot, hoping he was moving in the direction of the buildings across from the aqueduct. Were he to move in the wrong direction, he'd fall into the aqueduct and be lost in its flowing waters.

Movement was slow as he felt his way, still doubled over, toward the buildings and safety. It seemed as if he should have reached them three times over—they couldn't have been more than ten meters distant—yet he hadn't gotten there yet. Could he have gotten turned the wrong way and simply be moving down the center of the street?

Keeping his balance was getting more difficult. Water on the street was up to his ankles, moving rapidly against his direction. He lost his footing and went to his knee, but managed to rise again. His clothes were now soaked through, and hung like icicles from his body. Every step was a labor.

"The perfect world," he muttered, a thin smile stretching his lips despite his predicament.

Just as he was about to give up on his present direction and pick another one at random, the hulk of a building began to define itself in his vision. A few more treacherous steps and he was suddenly out of the rain, standing beneath a short awning that overhung the building front.

He used a hand to wipe the water from his face, then hugged himself, shivering, against the damp cold, taking stock of his position. The overhang protected the building front only for about a meter, and it extended for perhaps three meters in either direction from where he stood.

Beyond the awning, he could see nothing. The roaring water was impenetrable. The building front was no better. It was totally blank, no doors or windows. Yet, oddly enough, when he touched it, it felt warm, resisting the chill of the air. He was stuck in a world one meter wide by five meters long. The ground water had risen from his ankles to his calves, its current always pulling at him.

He stood there for several minutes, cold, teeth chattering, cursing the fate that would bring him to this hellhole. His numbness and melancholy soon, inevitably, turned to anger.

"Damn you!" he screamed, to whom, to what, he didn't know. "Why me?"

In frustration, he turned to the wall behind him. Hands balled into fists, he pounded viciously at the wall and—his hands sank right into it!

"Aaaahh!"

He screamed in surprise, instinctively jumping backward.

The water cascading from the awning caught him on the face, and as he tried to duck away from it, the ground current took him down.

He went under, then came up gasping for breath. But his control was gone and he was caught in the current. It pulled him back across the street; even the street itself seemed tilted at an angle toward the aqueduct. At this point, trying to regain his footing was out of the question. Keeping his head above water was the only priority. Staying alive was everything.

He felt himself go over the lip of the aqueduct and plunge into its raging waters. He bobbed down, at no point touching bottom, then rose again, totally numb and choking as the swift current carried him away, pulling at him, sucking him ever down.

He had wanted to see the terminal point of the waters. He would now see it quickly—if he could stay alive long enough.

Katherine stood with Euler by the opening to the balcony, staring out at a completely opaque wall of water that made her think that Robot City didn't really exist at all, but was simply an image conjured by an overactive brain exposed to too much cosmic radiation. The rain came down in never-ending torrents, rain such as she'd never seen or even thought could exist. It frightened her, a fright that almost overcame her anger at their predicament. Almost.

"Why did he go out?" Euler asked.

"I've already told you," she replied, turning away from the incredible downpour and moving back into the apartment. "He wanted to see the city."

"But we told him it was dangerous."

Katherine sat on the couch, folding her arms across her chest. A black hole could swallow Derec *and* his robots for all she cared. "Her either didn't believe you or didn't care," she said. "Why are you standing here asking me the same thing over and over when you could be out there looking for him?"

Rydberg came in from the bedroom, where he had apparently been searching in case Katherine had been lying. "Everything that can be done is being done," he said. "We appreciate your concern. Ours is every bit as great as yours."

"I'm not concerned," she said. "I couldn't care less."

The robots exchanged glances. "You don't care about the possible loss of a human life?" Euler asked.

Katherine jumped up from the couch. "You mean he could possibly be . . . be . . . ?"

"Dead?" Rydberg helped. "Of course. We warned you that it was dangerous."

For the fiftieth time since Derec's leaving, she hurried back to the balcony doorway and stared into the blank wall of water. He'd had been gone for several hours, far longer than he should have been. If anything had happened to him—

"Why did he go out?" Euler asked from beside her.

"Again!" she said loudly. "That same question. Why do you keep asking me that?"

"Because we don't understand," Rydberg said, moving up to join them. "You must know that robots don't lie."

"Yes," she replied.

"Then, when we said it was dangerous, why did he risk his life?" Euler asked.

"To begin with, his definition of danger might be different from yours," she said. "But beyond that, he wanted to know about this crazy city of yours more than he was afraid of the danger."

"You mean," Euler said, "that he could have purposely risked his life just for the sake of curiosity?"

"Something like that."

"Astounding."

"Let me ask you a question," she said, poking Euler in his chest sensors with an index finger. "If you want people to live here so much, why did you pick a place with such dangerous weather?"

Rydberg seemed to hesitate, as if he were weighing the answer he was about to give by some sort of internal scale. "The weather here is not naturally like this," he said at last.

"Naturally," she repeated, zeroing in on the key word. "Does this mean that something has affected the weather adversely?"

"Yes," Euler said.

"What?" she asked.

"We cannot tell you that," Rydberg said, and walked over to peer beneath the couch.

"Will it stop soon?" Kate asked.

"Probably within the next hour," Euler said. "At which time we can conduct an extensive search for Friend Derec."

A thought struck Katherine. She wanted to suppress it, but couldn't. "Is this how the other man . . . David, died?"

"He may have caused the rains," Euler said. "but he didn't die from them."

"I don't understand."

"It is quite late for humans," Rydberg said, moving toward the door. "You must sleep now or risk damaging your health."

With that, the two supervisor robots moved silently into the hallway, the door sliding shut behind them.

Katherine was alone, except for the robot standing guard in the hallway outside. She moved to the couch and curled into a tight ball. "Oh, David," she cried into the sleeve of her jumper. "Why did this have to happen?"

CHAPTER 3

THE EXTRUDER

Derec rode the aqueduct like a log in a sluice, his body numb, his senses and his fate out of control. The waters raged in his ears as his entire existence turned on the simple act of trying to keep his head above water. Nothing else mattered; life had reduced itself to its essence. There was no fear, no time for it, and any yearnings to have his life pass before his eyes went unsatisfied, since he had no life to reflect upon. There was only the water and the numbing cold—and the ubiquitous companionship of Death

His ride could have lasted a minute or an eternity—he was beyond calculating time—but when he felt himself free-falling in midair, his brain snapped to the new reality and questioned.

He was falling, surrounded by a hot, moist wind. A bare glow of light seemed to envelope him, but before he had a chance to appreciate it, he splashed into hot water.

He had gulped down water with his quickly sucked breath, and when he bobbed to the surface like a cork, he was choking and coughing, his head pounding with a heartbeat throb. He panicked, then forced himself into control when he realized the water he was in wasn't flowing, but pooling.

As he treaded water, he found himself grateful to his former life for giving him the lifesaving advantage of swimming lessons. He leaned back and floated on his back, small currents pulling him this way and that. His body ached horribly from the battering he had taken in the aqueduct; every bit of strength had drained from him.

There was a ceiling of some sort above him, tiny lights making it dimly visible. The roar of waterfalls filled the hollow cavern completely, and he turned his head to the side to get a glimpse of his surroundings.

He was a hundred meters from the edge of a large square pool that stretched perhaps a thousand meters across. Red lights set at regular intervals bathed the entire area in an eerie glow. In the middle of each side of the pool were aqueduct runoffs, four in all, their cascades shimmering like fading pulsars in the red haze. These four runoffs provided the incredible noise that churned inside his head, all of it echoing within the confined space.

Where was he? A collection point of some kind, perhaps a reservoir. Any city needed a water supply. This was probably connected to a water treatment plant meant to sustain the human population that didn't live there. This only strengthened Derec's earlier speculation that this was not a city simply meant for robots. What was going on here was serious colonization.

Another realization occurred to him, too. The reservoir had saved his life. He had been showing the beginning signs of hypothermia during his wild ride down the aqueduct, but the hot water of the reservoir was thawing him out.

Why hot water? The water was definitely warmer than human body temperature, perhaps as much as fifteen degrees, and incredibly hot winds were raging through the chamber, competing with the charging runoff waters in loudness. In fact, the soothing heat and the rest were already beginning to lull his senses, and he realized that if he wasn't careful, he could end up at the other end of the physical spectrum with hyperthermia. Whether hypo or hyper, though, the results were still the same. He was going to have to get out of the water or risk overburdening his heart.

Still on his back, he churned his legs lightly while propelling himself with his arms. There seemed to be robotic movement at the far end of the reservoir, but he didn't have the strength to swim that far. Having no idea of which way to go, he simply moved toward the closest shoreline. The process was time-consuming, though, for the runoffs created their own currents.

He swam with leisure, but determination, taking the time to check out his body. He had taken a beating in his wild ride down the aqueduct, but besides general bruises, nothing major seemed to be wrong.

As he neared the edge of the pool, he could see that the runoff streams had slowed considerably, leading him to speculate that the rain had stopped outside. Fuzzy light was also beginning to seep in around the dark edges of the covered pool, and he realized that day had broken.

He finally reached the edge of the pool, its surface made from the same material as the rest of the city. Metal ladders were set at regular intervals around the edge, and he floated to the nearest one to begin his climb out.

The water was barely three meters from the top of the pool, and fortunately so, because as soon as Derec began his climb he knew he wasn't doing well. His body, so light in the water, felt like it weighed a ton. The combination of emotional stress, the ordeal of the aqueduct, and the overheated water of the pool had all had an effect on his body. He dragged himself slowly up the ladder, then rolled, gasping, onto the edge of the pool and lay there.

He closed his eyes, just for a minute, and he was gone. He didn't know how long he had slept, but when he awoke, it was with a start. A loud rumble assailed his hearing. He sat up quickly, darting his head around, and saw a large vehicle moving around the pool toward him, its engine noises amplified to a roar in the cavern-like surroundings.

Standing was a problem, since Derec still felt weak. But he got up on shaky legs and moved toward the areas of light beyond the reservoir. While he was still out and on the loose, he wanted to see as much as he could. For, this time, the robots wouldn't be so quick to let him out of their sight.

As he moved toward the light, he passed open caverns that were filled with conduits for moving water. The huge pipes were twisted like knotted rope and seemed to be moving, writhing, like a snake pit—almost as if they were alive. He was taken over these areas by railed walkways that simply extended from the edges of the pit at his approach, growing—like crystals—before his eyes.

After the pits, he passed several squat buildings where he surmised the actual water treatment was performed. Drone robots moved in and out of the facilities rapidly, mostly moving machinery in both directions. Derec briefly considered going into one of the structures to search for a terminal, but the still-approaching vehicle made him change his mind.

"HUMAN!" came a loudspeakered voice. "YOU WILL HALT YOUR PROGRESS WHERE YOU ARE. IT IS UNLAWFUL FOR YOU TO PROCEED."

He turned to the sound. It was coming from the robot-controlled vehicle that was rapidly closing the distance on him. It was time to move!

He ran past the building toward glowing walls of light just beyond.

"HUMAN!" the loudspeaker called again.

He raced to the wall, his legs heavy. The entire wall seemed lit and wrapped a circle around the reservoir area. It was translucent, like a shower curtain, and he realized that it was simply so thin that outside light passed right through. He pushed on it, but it felt solid. He pushed harder, and it gave under his hand, just like the wall last night.

Just then, he saw a drone approach the wall twenty meters distant and move right through it. He hurried there, with the robots in the vehicle closing rapidly on him. He stood at the spot, seeing no entry, but when he raised his hands to push against it, the wall irised open and he stepped through into the daylight.

It was morning, bright and calm, with no sign of the deluge that had taken place the previous night. The sun was still low in the sky, but Robot City was alive and active.

He was in the very heart of it here, the hub upon which the wheel of the city turned. He could see the aqueduct that had brought him cutting through the city like a spoke, and he could see other aqueducts, other spokes, slicing through the wheel of the city. And he began to think of the areas between the spokes as quadrants.

Robots in large numbers hurried quickly through the streets, always going somewhere, always busy with predetermined tasks. Many of them were disappearing into the treatment plant.

He moved a small distance from his exit point, then looked back at the reservoir, shocked to find a forest there! Then he realized that the forest had been planted above the reservoir, the land area serving double duty. But why a forest? Not for robots, certainly.

Out of the corner of his eye, he noticed the large, wheeled vehicle that had been tracking him within the reservoir moving through the exit point to the outside. He looked back at the city, then up at the forest. He would find escape in its random chaos.

Angling himself away from his pursuers, he ran back toward the huge reservoir building, preparing to climb one of the struts that helped support the outside edge of the forest. But as soon as he reached the place and put his hands on the arched strut, it seemed to melt away, changing into a gently sloping stairway.

He hurried up the stairs without a question and entered the forest. The ground was moist and spongy, muddying his already-soaked shoes. The trees were small, in many cases smaller than the underbrush that grew thick around them. A haze seemed to fill the entire forest, and the farther he plunged into it, the hazier it became.

Derec was no expert in vegetation, but he assumed the trees were all offspring, many generations removed, of trees that had once grown on Earth. Spacers, though hating to mention any connection to the planet of their ancestry, nevertheless made it a point to bring Earth vegetation and animal life to whatever planet they colonized. Where he' gotten such information, he had no idea; the small glimpses of his own mind were maddening in their incompleteness.

He wandered the forest, pushing through the haze and the dense undergrowth, feeling jittery in untamed surroundings. And he knew that these were also the feelings of a Spacer pushing through his mind. He didn't much like the forest; he longed for the order of the city. But for a human being, this had its place. Untamed but finite, aesthetically pleasing without being uncontrollable. This place existed for the aesthetics—for human aesthetics.

His foot hit something hard and uncompromising, and he tripped, going hard to soft ground, getting mud all over himself. He turned to the object that had caused his fall and found a small section of pipe sticking out of the ground. A fog-like haze was pumping from the pipe, the same haze that filled the entire area, and Derec began to see a master plan at work here.

He stood, then ducked when he saw a shadow moving through the haze not five meters from him. It was one of the robots. He listened and could hear them thrashing through the brush all around. They were slowly cordoning off the entire area, boxing him in.

He took a deep breath, then scrunched up into a ball and lay on the ground, listening as they moved near him. The forest was built over the reservoir so that condensing water could feed up to the trees from beneath and nourish the roots directly. Further, the haze was probably carbon dioxide vapor feeding the forest to promote health and growth. Where did the CO_2 come from? Perhaps a bleed-off from their industrial processes, which could also explain the heat in the reservoir area. The set-up was sophisticated and civilized, a city built around its ecological needs. Was it all of robot design?

A metal foot clanked down just an arm's reach away from his position. He stifled the urge to rise up for a breath of normal air. Within seconds, the robot moved on.

As he heard the search party sweep past, he jumped to his feet and charged back in the direction he had come. The robots were much faster and stronger than he was, so he was going to have to make things happen quickly at this point.

He reached the edge of the forest in minutes, and rushed to the place where he had climbed up. The strut was already solid again, the steps nowhere to be seen. He looked over the edge of the forest. It was ten meters to the ground; jumping was out of the question.

"You, Derec!" came a robot voice behind. "Stop now! Stop!"

He sat on the ground and dangled his legs over the edge of the strut. Steps miraculously formed again. He ran down just as several robots reached the edge of the forest, calling for him to stop.

Amidst the confusion near the water treatment facility, he saw a large flatbed vehicle, filled with what looked like broken computers, ready to pull out. He took the last steps in leaps and charged the machine, the robots behind already reaching the bottom of the stairs.

The truck pulled out before he reached it, but with a burst of speed, he caught it and jumped into the back. A small, round drone the size of his head squeaked at him from among the broken computers.

Katherine stood at the wash basin, watching the lukewarm water flow from the tap, and wondered how plumbing could possibly be accomplished in a city that didn't stand still. She splashed her face with water, then stared into the small mirror that was inset above the basin. Her eyes were puffy and dark, showing the results of no sleep, but her face remained calm, remarkably calm considering the terror that had been flashing through her for most of the long night.

He was gone, perhaps dead, and she was alone on this crazy world. Though David/Derec, whatever he wanted to call himself, had never looked on this place as anything but an adventure, to her it had been nothing but a prison. A first priority for anyone marooned in a Spacer port would be access to radio communications to inform search parties and anxious waiters; yet the robots seemed reluctant—no, evasive—when it came to the topic of communications. That frightened her more than anything else that was going on.

"Did you sleep well?"

She jumped to the sound, turning quickly to see Rydberg standing in the doorway, a light static issuing from his loudspeaker.

"I didn't invite you in here!" she said in anger and frustration. "Get out! Now!"

The robot turned without a word and moved from the door, Katherine following him out into a small hallway.

"What do you want?" she asked. "Has there been any . . . news about Derec?"

Rydberg turned back to her. "I did not mean to intrude upon your privacy," he said. "Please accept my apologies. I've brought you food."

"I'm not hungry."

Rydberg just stared at her.

"Has there been any word about Derec?" she asked again, softly this time.

"Yes," the robot replied. "He was seen not three decads ago, but ran away when another of our supervisors called to him."

She clapped her hands together loudly. "So, he's alive!"

"Apparently so. Why would he run away? Is this a sign of guilt?"

"It's a sign that he wants to check out this crazy place without a gaggle of robots hanging all over him." She moved past him toward the living room. "Now, where's that food? I'm so hungry I could eat a . . ." She stopped herself, then looked at the robot. "I'm hungry."

"But you just said . . ."

"Forget what I just said. Correction!" She caught herself before the robot could explain its memory. "I mean never mind. Where's the food?"

He led her back down the hall to the living room, where the food sat at the same table she had eaten at the night before. Strangely enough, the room was different, squatter, wider than it had been the previous night, the table closer to the wall.

She moved quickly to the table. There was a variety of what appeared to be fruits and cooked vegetables there. She sat down and tentatively ate a small piece of greenish fruit. It was delicious. Rydberg stood nearby as she greedily sampled everything on the table, all of it good. She didn't invite the robot to sit with her as Derec had done. The machines were servants and needed to be treated as such. She'd never understand his insistence on treating them as anything other than the machines they were.

"When do we get to make outside radio contact?" she asked once the initial hunger pangs had died down.

"We will all meet later and discuss those questions."

"Are you going to put us on trial," she asked, "for the murder of this other human? We are entitled to a trial, you know."

"Derec has told us that he will try to solve this mystery," Rydberg said.

Katherine stopped eating and stared at him. "And what if he doesn't? What if we don't *ever* discover what really happened? You have no right to hold us here as it is. We can't go on indefinitely like this."

"If he cannot find out the truth of the matter," Rydberg said, "then we will assume our original supposition to be correct."

"I don't believe you," she said. "You have no right to determine my guilt or innocence without proper evidence. I'm not Derec, and I hold no romantic visions of a robot-controlled world. You cannot be allowed to have any power over the way I live my life. If you want to hold me for murder, you must put me on trial and prove it. If you put me on trial, I must be allowed to defend myself. I therefore demand immediate access to a radio so that I may provide myself with proper defense representation. I want a certified legal rep, and I want one now!"

"We will discuss the situation later today," the robot said, "after Friend Derec has been returned to us. Meanwhile, your food is getting cold and will lose its appeal."

"It already has," Katherine returned, pushing the plate away from herself. She didn't like the way this was turning. The radio seemed to get more and more distant to her, and with it, any hopes of ever leaving this place. Her arguments to Rydberg were based solely on laws and customs common to Auroran society. But all law, all freedom, was merely a rationalization away where a robot civilization was concerned.

The final result to her was quite simple: the machines were in charge and they could do anything they wanted.

Derec knew nothing with which to compare the size of Robot City, but as he drove its breadth, he couldn't help but feel its vastness.

As the parts truck moved quickly through the city streets, the round drone bounced from one machine to another, squeaking loudly, its silver body lighting up in dozens of places, then winking out again as it performed automatic (but definitely sub-robotic) pre-troubleshooting functions on the broken machinery. Finally, it came to rest on Derec's lap, all of its lights blinking madly, its squeaks turning into a high-pitched whine.

"So, where are we going?" he asked the troubleshooter while idly stroking its dome.

The machine whirred and bounced, but never answered. All at once, its whine turned to a loud, siren-like wail.

"Stop it!" Derec ordered, turning to the front of the truck to make sure he wasn't attracting attention. He bent double over the thing, trying to muffle its sound without success.

"You're going to have to stop," he told the thing. "I can't just..."

It sent a jolt of electricity through its body, shocking Derec, moving him off.

"All right," he said, pointing a shaking finger at the silver ball. "I don't have to take that from you."

The thing started bouncing up and down, higher and higher. Derec looked both ways over the truck back, then calmly brought up a foot and shoved the thing right off the truck, where it hit the street angrily, its wail louder as it bounced around like a rubber ball.

Within a few blocks, the vehicle slowed its pace, then got in line behind several other trucks, all filled with equipment. Derec got on his knees and looked over the piles of computers.

The trucks were pulled up to a gate, where a whole line of robots were moving up to the truck back, each taking a single piece of equipment and returning with it to a blockhouse that wasn't much larger than a single doorway. Beside the blockhouse was the most amazing thing Derec had ever seen in his short memory.

A huge, gray machine rumbled softly, yet with undeniable strength and power. From it issued what could only be described as a ribbon of city. In five-meter-square slabs, the city appeared to be simply extruding from underground through the medium of the gray machine.

It pushed itself along, the slabs gradually forming and reforming as they moved, following some incredible pre-programming that actually let them *build* themselves. And as the slabs formed walls and floors and corners and stories and windows, they spun off in every direction in a slow, graceful dance that pushed against the already existing buildings, the mechanism that triggered the entire magnificent clockwork of Robot City.

It was as if the entire city were one mammoth, living organism always growing outward, always changing and replicating like the cells in a body, moving in imprinted patterns toward a complete, fully formed being.

It was a plan of monumental scale, an atmosphere of total, logical control for a given end. As he watched a skyscraper literally build itself from the ground up, each story pushing up the story above it and self-welding according to some unseen plan, he experienced the grandeur of an idea so vast that his limited knowledge was humbled by its power. This civilization was the product of a mind that refused to believe in limited options, a mind that accepted that what the imagination could conceive, the hands could make.

To such a mind, anything was possible. Even, perhaps, Perihelion.

The truck lurched, nearly knocking him from his knees. It had pulled up to the gate. The line of robots was now reaching into *his* bed for their equipment.

If all the action was happening below ground, that's where Derec wanted to be. Hurrying out of the truck, he grabbed a small terminal that looked as if it had been shorted out by water, and took his place behind a robot heading toward that doorway into the ground.

He reached the doorway, cradling the computer like a baby. Warm air greeted him as he stepped through into barely lit darkness. He was confronted by a short flight of stairs leading down, and followed the robot that walked down before him.

The stairs terminated in a large holding area, brightly lit, frenetic with activity. Automated carts carried robots and mining equipment at breakneck pace. The cars zipped around one another in seemingly rehearsed fashion, their movements perfected over time, since it seemed impossible to Derec that they could move so quickly without hitting one another.

On the far wall sat a bank of elevators, perhaps twenty in all, some of them remarkably large. The robots that moved down the stairs headed toward these elevators, apparently going from here to a lower level where repair or scrap work was being done.

Having no idea of where to go, Derec chose an elevator at random and moved toward it with his burden. A large elevator nearby slid open, and a group of minerbots, covered with mud and soot, moved out bearing the non-operating carcass of one of their own above their shoulders.

Derec reached the elevator. It had no formal controls, but opened for him as soon as he stepped near.

A voice boomed behind him. "Nothing awaits you below, but death!"

He turned to see a huge supervisor robot, twice the size of a man, glaring down at him with red photocells. The robot's body was burnished a bright, shimmering black.

"I've come to inspect your operation," Derec said, feigning authority. He turned back to the elevator and began to step in.

The robot's arm flashed out, his mammoth pincers clanging loudly around Derec's forearm, squeezing tightly but not painfully.

"You are caught," the machine said, and Derec's computer crashed loudly at his feet.

CHAPTER 4

THE COMPASS TOWER

As the door to the apartment slid open, Derec tucked under the arm of the big robot, watched Katherine's facial expression change from horror, to relief, to unbridled amusement— all in the space of three seconds.

"Let me guess," she said, putting a finger to her lips, "you're a ditty bag."

"Cute," Derec returned as the robot set him gently on the ground. He looked up at the huge, black machine. "Thanks for the ride, Avernus."

"My pleasure, Friend Derec," the robot replied, bending slightly so that the hallway could accommodate his height. "But I must ask you to stay away from the underground. It is no place for a human."

"I appreciate your concern," Derec said noncommittally. He walked into the apartment, then turned back to Avernus. "Will we see you at the meeting?"

"Most assuredly," he returned. "All of us look forward to it with great expectation."

"You can go now," Katherine told Avernus coldly, the

robot nodding slightly and moving off, the utility robot guard sliding quickly to fill the door space with his squat body.

Katherine punched the door stud, the panel sliding closed. "You missed breakfast *and* lunch," she said, moving to sit listlessly on the couch.

"Avernus got me something before he brought me back," Derec said. "He got my wounds cleaned up, and even let me sleep for a while." Finally, he couldn't ignore her mood any longer. "What's wrong?"

"You," she said, "this place . . . everything. I don't know which way is up anymore. Did you find out anything?"

Derec spotted the CRT screen set up on the table and walked to stand before it. "It's a place designed for humans," he said, "and the building is going on at a furious pace, as if they're in some kind of hurry to get finished. I think the buildings may be . . . I don't know, alive, I guess is the best way to put it." He pointed to the screen. "Where did this come from?"

"Rydberg brought it," she answered, "But it only receives. What do you mean, the city's alive?"

"Watch this," Derec said, and ran full speed across the room, banging into the far wall. The wall gave with him, caving inward, then gently pushed itself back to a solid position.

"I laid awake all night worrying about you, while you were discovering the walls are made of rubber?" she asked loudly.

He turned to her, smiling. "Did you *really* worry about me?"

"No," she replied. "What else?"

He walked over and sat on the couch with her, his tones hushed. "I saw the city building itself, literally extruding itself from the ground. I tried to go down there, but Avernus caught me. I think he's in charge down there. The only thing I can figure is that there are immense mining operations underway below ground and that the buildings are positronic, some kind of cellular robots that make up a complete whole. It's fascinating!"

Katherine was unimpressed. "Did you find a way out of here?"

He shook his head. "Not yet," he answered, "but I don't really think that's going to be a problem."

"That's because you're so eaten up with your robot friends you *can't* think of anything else!" She suddenly jerked her head toward the wall. "If the walls are robots, I wonder if they can hear us now?"

Just then the screen on the table came to life, Rydberg's face filling it. "So, you are back, Derec," he said. "Good. Prepare yourselves. An honor guard is coming right now to bring you to your preliminary trial."

"Trial?" Derec said.

"Uh oh," Katherine said, putting a hand to her mouth. "That may be my fault. I all but dared them to put us on trial."

"But we haven't had a chance to investigate yet."

She shrugged. "I was trying to find if we could have access to outside communications." She snapped her fingers. "Maybe this means we're going to get it."

"Yeah ... maybe," Derec said, but he was skeptical. Robot City was too precious a gem to be hanging out in the ether for anyone to pluck. At this point, he wasn't even sure if he *wanted* to communicate with the outside.

He looked at the screen. It had already gone blank. "Whatever the reason," he said, "I believe we're going to get some answers at this point."

"Let's hope they're answers we can live with," she sighed. "I don't want to spend the rest of my life here."

Within minutes, the utility robot was knocking on the door. Derec hurried to open it. Euler greeted him, accompanied by a supervisor robot he'd not seen before. This one was the robot most closely molded to a human that Derec had seen, with chiseled, though blank, mannequin-like features.

"Friend Derec," Euler said, "Friend Katherine Burgess, may I present Arion, who will be in attendance at our meeting."

"Pleased to meet you," Derec said.

"Rydberg called it a trial," Katherine said.

"This is a great moment for us here," Arion said. "I trust that your stay so far has been satisfactory. I am doing my best with what little time I have to try and prepare some entertainment for you. We know that humans enjoy mind diversions."

"We'd appreciate anything you could do," Derec said.

"Sure," Katherine said. "How about conjuring up a radio for us to call the outside for help?"

"Oh, that's quite impossible," Arion said.

"That's what I thought," Katherine answered.

"I have a present for each of you," Euler said, extending his right arm. "Then we must be off to the meeting."

Derec moved to the robot. His pincers held two large watches, dangling on gold chains. "You may know the time here now," Euler said. "It is of importance to humans, and so, to us. We will do more to make you feel comfortable in this regard."

Derec took the watches, giving one of them to Katherine. They had square faces encased in gold. On both of them, the LCD faces read 3:35. "They run on a twenty-four hour day," said Euler. "We thought it would be more comfortable for you if we adjusted the length of our hour than if you had to adjust to a twenty-and-one-half hour day. Our hours, decads, and centads are approximately eighty-five percent of standard." Derec walked out onto the veranda and looked into the sky. The sun had already passed its apex and was slowly crawling toward the eventual shadows of evening.

"Right on the money," he said, returning to the apartment.

"You doubted it?" Arion asked, looking at Euler.

"Do you understand now?" Euler said to him.

"Interesting," Arion said, cocking his head in an almost human fashion.

"We must go," Euler said and hurried out of the apartment, the others following.

They rode the elevator to street level and boarded a multi-car tram that had no apparent driver. It started off immediately when they were seated. Euler turned to Derec, who sat, with Katherine, behind him and Arion. "You put yourself in extreme danger last night," the robot said. "Why?"

"I've a better question," Derec returned. "If this is such a perfect human world, why was it so dangerous?"

"Spacer worlds conquered weather problems eons ago," Katherine interjected. "For you to have them in such an advanced culture makes no sense."

Arion turned to her and bowed his head. "Thank you for calling our culture advanced."

"The weather," Euler said, "is quite honestly part of our overall problem right now. It is under our control, but also not under our control. Unfortunately, for security reasons, we cannot discuss it in detail."

"Great," Katherine said. "Everybody can do something about the weather, but nobody talks about it."

"To answer your original question," Derec told Euler, as he watched them move in a direct line toward the tower where they had initially materialized, "I have no memory and no past. My curiosity, my search for answers about myself, leads me to do things not necessarily in my best interest."

"Amnesia?" Euler asked. "Or something else?"

Derec looked at him in surprise. "What else?"

The robot answered his question with another question, an old one. "How, then, did you come to our planet?"

Derec realized that the robot was playing word games with him that tied directly to the word games Derec had initiated the night before. He decided to keep playing. "What did the dead man, David, say when you asked him that question?"

"He said he didn't know," Euler replied, and turned back around in his seat. Over his shoulder, he said, "He claimed he'd had amnesia."

The tram came to a halt beside the mammoth pyramid that dominated the landscape of Robot City, the place the inhabitants called the Compass Tower. Katherine put a hand on Derec's arm, squeezing, and he knew she had the same fear that he'd felt. Here, about halfway up the tower, was where they had hidden the Key to Perihelion that had brought them to the city. Had the robots found it? Were they confronting them with the evidence, or, worse yet, taking it away?

But Euler said nothing of the Key. Instead, he simply climbed from the tram and led them directly to the base of the tower, a tower that Derec had surmised was solid.

He'd never been more wrong.

At the robot's approach, an entire block of the solid matter that formed the base simply melted away, leaving a gently sloping runway leading into the structure, another example of Derec's theory about the intelligence of the building materials themselves.

They moved into the pyramid through a short, dark hallway that emptied into a maze of criss-crossing aisles and stairs that, in turn, led off in all directions within the structure.

"Try and memorize our path," Derec whispered to Katherine. "Just in case."

"In case of what?" she asked. "In case you haven't figured it out, we're not going anywhere."

"This is the most important building in our city," Euler said, as he took them up a series of stairs and escalators that zig-zagged at every landing and culminated in a long, well-lit hallway. "This is where decisions are made, where . . . understanding takes place."

They walked the hall, Arion hurrying ahead and disappearing down some stairs. The surrounding walls glowed lightly, with connecting hallways intersecting every ten feet.

They followed Arion's path, changing direction several times before finding themselves standing in a large, well-lit room whose four walls angled in toward a ceiling, fifteen meters above, that poured in sunshine like a skylight.

The floor of the room was tiled in the form of a large compass, its four points forming the cornerstones of Robot City. In the center of the compass, under the direct rays of the sun, stood six robots in a circle, arms outstretched, their pincers grasping those of their neighbors on either side with space left for one more—Euler.

"This is the place where we seek perfection," Euler said, and joined the circle, closing it.

"It's almost religious," Derec whispered to Katherine.

"Yeah," she replied. "It give me the creeps."

Derec looked around the room. There were no chairs or tables, nothing upon which a human being could rest. The walls were inset with CRTs jammed side to side around the entire perimeter. Each screen showed its own view of Robot City. Many showed excavation sites, the large movers pushing and leveling soil. Other pictures were of the extrusion plant he had visited, and he was led to conjecture that there might be more than one. There were pictures of the reservoir he had splashed into, and strange, underground pictures taken through the eyes of roving cambots that showed mining tunnels, kilometer after kilometer of deserted tunnel. And finally, many of the screens simply showed the pink-tinged blue of the sky.

"You have come to this place," Euler said loudly, "to help us in our search for correctness, for perfection, for completeness. We are the keys—human and robot—to the synergy of spirit. Synnoetics is our goal. I will introduce the rest of us and we will begin."

"Synnoetics?" Katherine whispered.

"Man and machine," Derec replied, "the whole greater than the sum of the parts."

"It *is* religious!" she rasped. "And how did you know that?"

Derec shrugged. "This all feels so ... comfortable to me."

"You know Rydberg," Euler said, "and Avernus and Arion." The robots nodded as their names were called. "The rest of us ... Waldeyer ..."

"Good day," said a squat, roundish robot with wheels.

"Dante ..."

"I welcome you," Dante said, his telescopic eyes sticking out several inches from his dome.

"And Wohler."

A magnificent golden machine bowed formally without removing his pincers from his neighbors'. "We are honored," Wohler said.

"We will answer what questions we can from you," Euler said, "and hope that you will do the same."

"If, as you say," Derec told them, "we are all looking for truth and perfection, then our meeting will be fruitful. I would like to begin by asking you why there are certain areas of life here that you will not discuss with us."

Rydberg spoke. "We are in a standby security mode that renders certain information classified by our programming."

"Did our arrival prompt the institution of the security mode?" Katherine asked.

"No," Euler said. "It was in effect when you arrived. If, in fact, you arrived when you said you did. We must ask you again how you came to be here."

Derec decided to try a little truth. It couldn't hurt as long as no mention was made of the Key. Perhaps a dose of the truth might get them to open up about the Key's existence. "We materialized out of thin air atop this very building."

"And where were you before that?" Wohler, the gold one, asked.

Derec walked slowly around the circle, studying his questioners. "A Spacer way station named Rockliffe near Nexon, right on the edge of the Settlement Worlds quarantine zone."

Arion, the mannequin, asked, "What means, then, did you use to get from one place to the other?"

"No means," Derec said. "We were simply transported here."

There was silence for a moment. "This does not coordinate with any information extant in memory," Avernus said, his large dome following Derec's progress around the circle.

"You've found no ship that could have brought us," Derec said, "and I'm sure you've searched."

"That is correct," Euler said, "and our radar picked up no activity that could have been construed to be a vessel in our atmosphere."

"I can't explain it beyond that," Derec said. "Now, you answer a question for me. Where did you come from?"

"Who are you addressing?" Euler asked.

"All of you," Derec said.

Avernus answered. "All of them except for me were constructed here, on Robot City," he said. "I was . . . awakened here, but believe I was constructed elsewhere."

"Where?"

"I do not know," the large robot replied. "My first i/o memories are of this place. Nothing in my pre-programming suggested anything of an origin."

"Are you trying to say," Katherine broke in, "that all of you know nothing but the company of other robots? That your entire existence is here?"

"Correct," Rydberg said. "Our master programming is well aware of human beings and their societies, but no formal relationship exists between our species."

"Then how did you come to build this place?" Derec asked. "How then, did it become important to you to make a world for humans?"

"We are incomplete without human beings," Waldeyer said, his squat dome swiveling to Derec and then Katherine.

"The very laws that govern our existence revolve around human interaction. We exist to serve independent thought, the higher realms of creativity that we are incapable of alone. We discovered this very quickly, without being told. Alone, we simply exist to no end, no purpose. Even artificial intelligence must have a reason to utilize itself. This world is the first utilization of that intelligence. We've been building it for humans, in order to make the perfect atmosphere in which human creativity can flourish to the greater completeness of us all. Without this world we are nothing. With it, we are vital contributing factors to the ongoing evolution of the universe."

"Why would that matter to you?" Katherine asked.

"I have a theory about that," Dante said, his elongated eyes glowing bright yellow. "We are the product, the child if you will, of higher realms of creative thought. It seems impossible that the drives of that creative thought *wouldn't* permeate every aspect of our programming. We want for nothing. We desire nothing. Yet, the incompleteness of our inactivity makes us . . . feel, for lack of a better word, useless and extraneous. Given the total freedom of our own world, we were driven to function in service."

Derec suddenly felt a terrible sadness well up in him for these unhappy creatures of man's intelligence. "You've done all this, even though you never knew if any people would come here?"

"That is correct," Euler said. "Then David came, and we thought that all would be right. Then came his death, then the calamities, then you . . . suspects to murder. We never meant for anything to be this way."

"When you say calamities," Derec said, "are you speaking of the problems with the storms?"

"Yes," Rydberg said. "The rains threaten our civilization

itself, and it's all our own fault. We are breaking apart from the inside out, with nothing to be done about it."

"I don't understand," Derec said.

"We don't expect you to, nor can we tell you why it must be this way," Euler said.

Derec thought about the hot air pumping through the reservoir. "Is the city's rapid growth rate normal?" he asked.

"No," Euler said. "It coincides with David's death."

"Is it because of David's death?"

"We do not know the answer to that," Euler said.

"Wait a moment," Katherine said, walking away from the circle to sit on the floor, her back up against the north wall. "I want to talk to you about our connection with all this . . . and why Rydberg called this a preliminary trial."

"You were the one who first mentioned the concept of trial," the robot replied, leaning out of the circle to stare at her. "I only used that term to make you feel comfortable."

"Okay," she said. "I'll play. You say this is a civilization of robots that have never had human interaction, yet obviously someone gave you your initial programming and ability to perform the work on this city."

"Someone . . . yes," Euler said.

"Someone who's in charge," she said.

"No," Euler said. "We are now in group communication with our master programming unit, but it simply provides us with information from which logical decisions are made. Our overall philosophy is service; our means are logical. Other than that, our society has no direction."

"Then why put us on trial at all?" she asked.

"Respect for human life is our First Law," Rydberg said. "When we envisioned our perfect human/robot world, we saw a world in which all shared respect for the First Law.

We envisioned a system of humanics that would guide human behavior, just as the Laws of Robotics guide our behavior, just as the Laws of Robotics guide our behavior. Of course, we have been working entirely from theory, but we have made a preliminary list of three laws that would provide the basis for an understanding of humans."

"Cute," Katherine said. "Now they want us to follow the Laws of Robotics."

Derec interrupted her complaint. "Wait. Let's see what they've come up with."

"Thank you, Friend Derec. Our provisional First Law of Humanics is: A human being may not injure another human being, or, through inaction, allow a human being to come to harm."

"Admirable," conceded Derec, "even if it isn't always obeyed. What is your Second Law?"

Rydberg's hesitation before answering gave Derec the clear impression that the robot wanted to ask a question of its own, but his took precedence under the Second Law of Robotics.

"The Second Law of Humanics is: A human being must give only reasonable orders to a robot and require nothing of it that would needlessly put it into the kind of dilemma that might cause it harm or discomfort."

"Still admirable, but still too altruistic to be always obeyed. And the third?"

"The Third Law of Humanics is: A human being must not harm a robot, or through inaction, allow a robot to come to harm, unless such harm is needed to keep a human being from harm or to allow a vital order to be carried out."

"Not only is your experience with humans limited, so is your programming," Derec said, shaking his head. "These 'laws' might describe a utopian society of humans and robots, but they certainly don't describe the way humans really behave."

"We have become aware of that," said Rydberg. "Obviously, we are going to have to reconsider our conclusions. Since your arrival we have been subjected to human lies and deceit, concepts beyond our limited understanding."

"But the First Law must stand!" Avernus said loudly, his red photocells glowing brightly. "Human or robot, all are subject to respect for life."

"We certainly aren't arguing that point," Derec said.

"No!" Katherine said, standing angrily and walking back to the circle. "What we're talking about is the lack of respect with which *we're* being treated here!"

"Kath . . ." Derec began.

"Shut up," Katherine said. "I've been listening to you having wonderful little philosophical conversations with your robot buddies, and I'm getting a little tired of it. Listen, folks. First thing, I demand that you give us access to communications with the outside and that you let us leave. You have no authority to hold us here."

"This is our world," Euler said. "We mean no offense, but all societies are governed by laws, and we fear you have broken our greatest law."

"And what if we have?" she asked. "What happens then?"

"Well," Euler said. "We would do nothing more than keep you from the society of other humans who you could harm."

"Great. So, how do you prove we did anything in order to hold us?"

"Process of elimination," Waldeyer said. "Friend Derec has previously suggested some other possible avenues of explanation, but we feel it is incumbent upon both of you to explore them—not because we are trying to make it difficult for you, but because we respect your creative intelligence more than we respect our own deductive intelligence in an area like this."

Derec watched as Katherine ran hands through her long black hair and took several deep breaths as she tried to get herself together and in a position to work with this. "All right," she said, more calmly. "You said before that you won't let us see the body."

"No," Euler said. "We said that we *can't* let you see the body."

"Why?"

There was silence. Finally Rydberg spoke. "We don't know where it is," he said. "The city began replicating too quickly and we20lost it."

"Lost it?" Derec said.

Derec knew it was impossible for a robot to be or look embarrassed, but that was exactly the feeling he was getting from the entire group.

"We really have no idea of where it is," Euler said.

Derec saw an opening and quickly took it. "In order to do this investigation and prove that we're innocent of any First Law transgressions, we *must* have freedom of movement around your city."

"We exist to protect your lives," Euler said. "You've been caught in the rains; you know how dangerous they are. We can't let you out under those conditions."

"Is there advance warning of the rain?" he asked.

"Yes," Rydberg said. "The clouds build in the late afternoon, and the rain comes at night."

"Suppose we promise to not go out when the conditions are unfavorable?" Derec asked.

Wohler, the golden robot, said, "What are human promises worth?"

Katherine pushed her way beneath the hands of the robots to stand in the center of the circle. "What are our lives worth without freedom?"

"Freedom," Wohler echoed.

A dark cloud passed above the skylight, plunging the room into a gray, melancholy halflight, illumination provided by a score of CRT screens, many of them now showing pictures of madly roiling clouds.

The circle broke immediately, the robots, agitated, hurrying toward the door.

"Come," Euler said, motioning to the humans. "The rains are approaching. We must get you back to shelter. There is so much to do."

"What about my suggestion?" Derec called loudly to them.

"Hurry," Euler called, waving his arm as Derec and Katherine walked toward him. "We will think about it and let you know tomorrow."

"And if we can investigate and prove our innocence," Katherine said, "will you then let us contact the outside?"

Euler stood still and fixed her with his photocells. "Let me put it this way," he said. "If you don't prove your innocence, you'll *never* be allowed to contact the outside."

CHAPTER 5

A WITNESS

Derec sat before the CRT screen on the apartment table and watched the "entertainment" that Arion was providing him in the form, at this moment, of sentences and their grammatic diagrams. Before that it had been a compendium of various failed angle trisection theorems, and before that, an incredibly long list of the powers of ten and the various words that had been invented to describe the astronomical numbers those powers represented. It was an insomniac's nightmare.

It was a dark, gray morning, the air heavy with the chill of the night and the rain that had pounded Robot City for many hours. The sky was slate as the remnants of the night's devastation drifted slowly away on the wings of the morning.

He felt like a caged animal, his nerves jangling madly with the notion that he couldn't leave the apartment if he wanted to. They had been dropped off in the early evening after the meeting at the Compass Tower and hadn't seen a supervisor robot since. The CRT had no keyboard and only received whatever data they chose to show him from moment to moment. At this particular time, they apparently felt the need to amuse him; but the time filler of the viewscreen only increased his frustration.

He hadn't slept well. The apartment only had one bed and Katherine was using it. Derec slept on the couch. It had been too short for him, and that didn't make sleeping any easier. But that wasn't the real reason he'd been awake.

It was the rain.

He couldn't get out of his head the fact that the reservoir had been nearly filled when he'd been flung into it the night before. How, then, could it possibly hold the immense amounts of water that continued to pour into it with each successive rainfall? He'd worried over that point: the more rain, the greater the worry. The fact that the supervisors hadn't contacted him since before the storm seemed ominous. All of their efforts seemed to revolve around the weather problems.

How did the weather tie in with the rapid growth rate of the city? Were the two linked?

"You're up early," came Katherine's voice behind him.

He turned to see her, face soft from sleep, framed by the diffused light. She looked good, a night's sleep bringing out her natural beauty. She was wrapped in the pale green cover from her bed. He wondered idly what she was wearing beneath it, then turned unconsciously to his awakening, after the explosion in Aranimas's ship, in the medical wing of the Rockliffe Station to find her naked on the bed beside. Embarrassed, he pushed that thought aside, but its residue left another thought from that time, something he had completely forgotten about.

"Can I ask you a question?" he said.

Her face darkened and he watched her tighten up. "What is it?" she asked.

"When we were at Rockliffe, Dr. Galen mentioned you had a chronic condition," he said. "Later, when he began to talk about it, you shut him up."

She walked up to look at the screen, refusing to meet his gaze. "You're mistaken," she said. "I'm fine . . . the picture of health."

She turned slightly from him, and there seemed to be a small catch in her voice. When she turned back, her face was set firm, quite unlike the vulnerable morning creature he'd seen a moment ago. "What's happening on the screen?" she asked.

He looked. A pleasant, always changing pattern of computer generated images was juicing through the CRT, accompanied by a random melody bleeped out of the machine's tiny speaker.

"You make it very hard for me to believe you," he said, ignoring the screen. "Why, when we need total honesty and trust between us, do I feel that you're holding back vital information from me?"

"You're just paranoid," she said, and he could tell he was going to get nothing from her. "And if you don't change the subject quickly, I'm going to find myself getting angry, and that's no way to start the day."

He reluctantly agreed. "I'm worried about the rains," he said. "They were worse last night than the night before."

She sat at the table with him. "Well, if this place is getting ready to have major problems, I hope we're out of here before they happen. We've got to get something going with the murder investigation."

"Do you know what makes rain?" he asked, ignoring the issue of the murder.

"What has that got to do with our investigation?" she asked, on edge.

"Nothing," he said. "I'm just wondering about these rains, I . . ."

"Don't say it," she replied holding up a hand. "You're worried about your robot friends. Well, let me tell you something, your friends are in the process of keeping us locked up for the rest of our lives . . ."

"Not locked up, surely," he interrupted.

"This is serious!" she said, angry now. "We have a very good chance of being kept prisoner here for life. You know, once they make a decision like that, I see no reason that they would ever change it. Don't you understand the gravity of the situation?"

He looked at her calmly, placing a hand over hers on the table. She drew it away, and he felt his own anger rise, then rapidly subside. "I understand the problem," he explained, "but I fear the problem with the city is more pressing, more . . . immediate."

"But it's not *our* problem. The murder is."

"Indulge me," he said. "Let's talk about weather for just a minute."

She sighed, shaking her head. "Let's see what I remember," she said. "Molecules respond to heat, separating, moving more quickly. Water molecules are no exception. On a hot day, they rise into the atmosphere and cling to dust particles in the air. When they rise into the cooler atmosphere, they turn into clouds. When the clouds get too heavy, too full of water, they return to the ground in the form of rain."

"Okay," he said. "And wind is simply the interplay of heat and cold in the atmosphere."

She shrugged. "The cold, heavier air pushes down and forces the warm air to move—wind."

"I think I'm beginning to see a connection," he said, excited. "Look. Robot City is building at a furious pace, sending a great deal of dust into the atmosphere." He thought about the reservoir. "Meanwhile, they are somehow liberating a great deal of water from the mining processes that are needed to build the city. Along with the mining processes comes a tremendous amount of kinetic energy, heat, which they are venting into the atmosphere near the water, forcing the heated molecules to rise as water vapor and cling to the dust particles that are thick in the atmosphere right now. At night, the temperature cools down a great deal..."

"That could be an uncompensated ozone layer," she said.

He pointed to her. "Ozone. That's what seals in our atmosphere. As goes the ozone layer, so go our temperature inversions. So, it cools at night, the rain clouds forming, the cool air bringing on the big winds, and the rain falls."

"So," Katherine said, "if they slowed down the building pace, it could slow down the weather."

"It seems logical to me," he replied.

"So why don't they do it?"

"That's the mystery, isn't it?"

The door slid open and Wohler, the golden robot, moved into the room, flanked on either side by smaller robots.

"Good morning," Wohler said. "I trust your sleep-time was beneficial."

"You're going to have to learn to knock before you come barging in here," Katherine said. "Now go out and do it again."

Derec watched the robot dutifully march outside the door and slide it closed. He knew that Katherine was simply venting frustration. On Spacer worlds, robots were considered simply part of the furniture and their presence was not thought about in terms of privacy.

There was a gentle tapping on the door, the nature of the material muffling the sound somewhat.

"Come in," Katherine said with satisfaction, and the door slid open, the robots reentering.

"Is this the preferred method of treatment in future?" Wohler asked.

"It is," she replied.

"Very well," the robot said, then noticed Derec's sleeping covers on the sofa. "Should these be returned to the bedroom?"

"You only provided us with one bed," Derec replied. "I slept out here."

Wohler moved farther into the room, coming up near the table. "Did we err? Was the sleeping space too small . . ."

"Katherine and I would simply like . . . separate places to sleep," Derec said.

"Privacy?" Wohler asked. "As with the knocking on the door?"

"Yes," Katherine said, and he could tell she was unwilling to delve into the social aspects of human sleeping arrangements, so he left it alone, too.

"On-line time is a matter of priorities right now," the robot said, "but we will see if we can arrange something for you that is more private."

"Thanks," Derec said. "And if it takes another day to arrange it, that's all right with me. It's Katherine's turn to sleep on the couch tonight."

"What?" she said loudly. Derec grinned broadly at her. She wasn't amused.

He quickly changed the subject. "What brings you here this morning, Wohler?" he asked. "Have you reached a decision about our requests of yesterday?"

"Yes," the robot replied. "And it is our sincerest wish that the decision be one that all of us can accept. First, in addressing the issue of your investigation and freedom of movement. We conferred at as great a length as time would permit under the present circumstances, and decided that, despite your flaws, you *are* human, and that fact in and of itself demands that we give you the benefit of the doubt in this situation. Many of our number were concerned about your veracity, or lack of it, but I reminded them that a great *human* philosopher once said, 'Isn't it better to have men being ungrateful than to miss a chance to do good?' And so my fellows voted to do good in this regard."

"Excellent," Derec said.

"But . . ." Katherine helped.

"Indeed," Wohler returned. "It is my place to philosophize in any given situation, and I need remind you now that one must always be prepared to take bad along with good."

"Just get on with it," Katherine said.

Wohler nodded. "On the matter of your safety, and your . . . unpredictability, it was decided that each of you would have a robot companion to . . . help you in your investigations."

"You mean to guard us," Katherine said.

"Merely a matter of semantics," Wohler countered, and Derec could tell that the robot had been geared for diplomacy. "Actually, in this case, I believe you may find these robots more useful as assistants than as protection. In fact, one of them was present during the death of David and the subsequent confusion."

Katherine perked up. "Really? Which one?"

The robot to Wohler's left came forward. Its body was tubular, its dome a series of bristling sensors and photocells. Without arms, it seemed useless in almost any sense.

"What are you called?" Katherine asked the machine.

The machine's tones were clipped and precise. "I am Event Recorder B-23, Model 13 Alpha 4."

"I'll call you Eve, if that's all right," Katherine said, standing and wrapping her blanket a little tighter around herself. She looked at Derec. "I want this one."

"Fine," Derec said, then to the other, "come here."

The robot moved up close to him. "You'll answer to Rec."

"Rec," the robot repeated.

"We call these robots witnesses," Wohler said. "Their only function is to witness events precisely for later report-ing."

"That's why they have no arms," Derec said.

"Correct," Wohler replied. "They are unequipped to do anything but witness. Once involvement begins on any level, the witness function falters in any creature. These ro-bots only witness and report. They will know the how of almost everything, but never the why. They will answer all of your questions to the best of their ability, but again, they are unable to make any second-level connections by putting events together to form reasons."

"I'm going to go get dressed," Katherine said, the hap-piest Derec had seen her in days. She hurried out of the room, disappearing down the hall to the bedroom.

"Where will we be denied access?" Derec asked. "Or is the entire planet open to us?"

"Alas, no," Wohler said. "You will be denied access to certain parts of the city and certain operations. Your witness, however, will tell you when you've stepped into dangerous water, as it were."

"What are the chances of me getting around a terminal," Derec asked, "and talking to the central core?"

"The central core has sealed itself off because of our present state of emergency," Wohler said. "It will not accept input from any sources save the supervisors, and we are unable to help you in this regard."

"How do the day-to-day operations survive?" he asked.

"Essential information can be gathered through any terminal," the robot answered. "But input is limited."

"You don't mind if I try?"

"That is between you and the central core. We all have our jobs to do. All that we insist upon is that you honor your commitment to come back here when the rains approach. We must put your safety above all else. Having failed in this regard with your predecessor, we perhaps err on the side of caution. But all privileges will be denied should this directive be overlooked or ignored."

"I understand," Derec replied, "and will respect your wishes."

"Your words, unfortunately, mean very little right now," the robot said, turning to the door, his head swiveling back to Derec. "By your deeds we will judge you in future. As an Earth philosopher once said, 'The quality of a life is determined by its activities.' Now, I must go."

With that, Wohler moved quickly through the opening and departed hurriedly down the elevator. The activity bothered Derec; it said to him that things were not going well in Robot City. He had intended to ask Wohler about the effects of last night's rain, but then decided a first-hand look might be better and determined that Rec would take him where he wanted to go.

"There," Katherine said, coming down the hall to bustle around the room. She wore a blue one-piece that the dinner servo-robot had brought with it the night before. "Finally, we can start moving in a positive direction. Where do you want to start?"

"I thought I'd go down to the reservoir," he replied, "and see how much rain fell last night."

She stopped walking and stared, unbelieving, at him. "Don't you realize that every moment is precious right now? We need to find that body and see what happened. It could be . . . decomposing or something at this very minute."

"I've got to see if there was any damage," he said. "I'll try and join you later."

"Never mind," she said angrily, and walked quickly to the door. "Satisfy your stupid urges. I don't *want* you with me. You'll just get in the way anyhow. Come on, Eve. We've got a *corpus delecti* to find."

She walked out of the apartment without a backward glance and was gone, Derec frowning after her. He couldn't help the way his feelings ran on this. He felt that so much of his own life, his own reasons for being, hinged upon the future of Robot City that its troubles seemed to be his own.

"I want to go to the reservoir," he told Rec. "Can you take me there?"

"Yes, Friend Derec," the robot answered, and they left together.

When they arrived at street level, Derec was disappointed to find that the supervisors hadn't left any transportation for him to use. A great deal of time would be wasted walking from place to place. Perhaps he could talk to Euler about it later, though he feared that the reasons had much to do with keeping him from going very far from home.

"Do you want to go the most direct route?" the witness asked him.

"Yes, of course," Derec said as they set out walking. "Let me ask you a question. Is the rain a result of the work being done on the city?"

"For the most part," Rec answered through a speaker located on Derec's side of his dome. "It is also the rainy season here."

"If they slowed down the building, would it slow down the rain?"

"I do not know."

Derec was going about this wrong, asking the wrong questions of a witness. "How does the city make rain?" he asked.

The robot began talking, recalling information in an encyclopedic fashion. "Olivine is mined below ground and crushed in vacuum, releasing carbon, hydrogen, oxygen, and nitrogen, from which water vapor, carbon dioxide, methane gas, and traces of other chemicals are liberated. Iron ore is also being mined for building materials, along with petroleum products for plastics . . ."

"Plastics?" Derec asked.

"Plastics are used as alloys in making the material from which the city is constructed. Do you wish me to go on with my previous line of witnessing?"

"Let me tell you," Derec said, "and you tell me if I'm right. Water vapor, along with the heat energy from the mining process, is pumped into the air, heat also being pumped into the reservoir. The CO_2 is bled into the forest to help growth. The reason that the weather is so rainy now is that the city is growing too fast, giving off too much heat, dust, and water."

"I do not know why the weather is *so* rainy right now," Rec said. "I do not even understand what *so* rainy means. The other statements you made are juxtapositional with statements I heard Supervisor Avernus make, which I assume to be correct."

"Fine," Derec said. "Is there a problem with the ozone layer?"

"Problem?" the robot asked.

Derec rephrased. "Is any work being done on the ozone layer?"

"I do not know," Rec said, "although I did hear Supervisor Avernus say on one occasion that the 'ozone layer needs to be increased photochemically to ten parts per million.' "

"Good," Derec said. "Very good."

"You are pleased with my witnessing?" Rec asked.

"Yes," Derec replied. "Will the supervisors be asking you to witness later what we've discussed?"

"That is my function, Friend Derec."

They walked for nearly an hour by Derec's watch, the city still subtly changing around them. It sometimes took a while to get information out of the witness, but if questions were phrased properly, Derec found Rec an endless source of information, and he wondered how Katherine was faring with her witness.

Derec knew they were nearing the reservoir long before they arrived there. A long stream of robots was moving toward and away from the site, followed by large vehicles bearing slabs of city building material.

They walked into an area sonorous with activity, echoes raising the pitch enough that Derec covered his ears against the din. Within the confines of the reservoir area, his worst fears were realized. The water had reached the top of the pool and was splashing over slightly in various areas.

For their part, the robots were doing their best to stop it. Large machines, obviously converted from mining work, had been modified to lift huge slabs of the building material to the top of the pool, where utility robots with laser torches were welding the higher sections together, trying for more room, bathing the area in various sections in showers of yellow sparks.

It was a massive job, the reservoir covering many acres, as the robots worked frantically to finish before the next rain. And to Derec's mind, this could be no more than a stopgap measure, for unless the rain was halted, it would overflow even the extra section in a day or two.

"What happens if the water overflows?" he asked Rec.

"I am unable to speculate on such matters, Friend Derec," the robot said. "It is not overflowing. When it does, I will witness."

"Right," Derec said, and moved forward, closing on the workers.

"Do not get too close," Rec called. "It is dangerous for you."

Derec ignored him and moved closer, recognizing Euler, who was helping with the movement of a slab. He was directing a large, heavy-based machine with a telescoping arm that held a six-by-six-meter slab in magnetic grips. He was holding his pincers at the approximate distance the arm had yet to travel so that it would be flush with the edge of the pool and the slab next to it. Utility robots physically guided the slabs to the ground and held them so the welders could set to work immediately.

"Euler!" Derec called, the robot jerking to the sound of his name.

"It is too dangerous for you here!" Euler called back, waving him away. "We have no safety controls over this area!"

"I'll only stay a centad," Derec said, moving up close to him. He could look past the end of the last slab and see the dark waters churning the top of the pool. In the distance, all around the reservoir, he could see the same operation being repeated by other crews.

"What are you doing here?" Euler asked him.

"I had to see for myself," Derec answered. "I knew the levels were rising. Why don't you stop the building pace and let these waters recede?"

"I can't tell you why," Euler said.

"But what happens when this overflows?"

"We lose the treatment plant," Euler said, holding his pincers up to signify to the arm to stop moving the slab. Then he motioned toward the ground, the arm bringing the slab down very slowly. "We lose much of our mining operations. We lose a great many miners. We will have failed."

"Then stop the building!"

"We can't!"

Just then, a utility robot working the slab was bumped slightly by the moving metal and lost its footing on the wet floor. Soundlessly and without drama, it slipped from the edge of the pool and fell into the dark waters, disappearing immediately.

Everything stopped.

Euler pushed past Derec to hurry to the water's edge, where he stood, head down, watching. The rest of the crew did the same, lining up quietly beside the water. Derec moved to join Euler.

"I'm sorry," he said.

Euler slowly turned his head to look at the boy, not saying anything for a long time. "I should have paid more attention," he said.

"How deep is the water?" Derec asked.

"Very deep," Euler replied. "I was talking with you and didn't give the job my complete attention."

"Can it be saved?"

"Had there been more time," Euler said, "the job would have been studied for safety and feasibility and this wouldn't have happened. Had I known better, I wouldn't have allowed you to come so close. A robot is lost, and the supervisor is to blame."

"There was nothing you could have done," Derec said.

"A robot is dead today," Euler told him. "I will not answer any more of your questions right now."

CHAPTER 6

THE TUNNELS

"If the city keeps moving," Katherine asked, "how can you take me to the location of the murder?"

"Triangulation," Eve, the witness, said. "Using the Compass Tower as one point and the exact position of the sun at a given time as another point, my sensors are able to triangulate the position where I first witnessed the body. The time is the only real factor at this point. We must gauge the sun in exactly 13.24 decads to get the position right."

They were walking through the city, Katherine feeling a mixture of fear and exuberance at her first solo trip outside. They were walking high up, above many of the buildings, bridges between structures seemingly growing for her to walk across, then melting away after her passage. Eve apparently needed the height in order to take the precise measurements.

Katherine was angry at Derec for his lack of interest in their predicament, but she knew him well enough to know how stubborn he could be. She, in fact, knew him far better than he knew himself, and that was maddening. They were caught in a web of intrigue that existed on a massive level, and as long as she was trapped there, she had to play the situation with as much control as she could muster. And that included not telling Derec any more about his life than he could figure out for himself. Her own existence was at stake, and until she could escape the maze that had locked up their activities, she desperately feared saying anything more.

She *had* to get away from Robot City. The pain had increased since her arrival here, and, for the first time in her life, death was a topic she found herself dwelling upon.

And her only crime was love.

She felt the tears begin to well up and fought them back with an iron will. They wouldn't help her here. Nothing would, except her own tenacity and intelligence.

"Tell me about your involvement in David's death," she asked Eve, who was busy calibrating against the sun.

"In approximately two decads," the robot said, "it will have happened exactly nine days ago. We go down from here."

Eve moved directly to the corner of the six-story structure they were standing upon, and railed stairs formed for them to walk down. As they descended, the robot continued talking.

"I was called upon to witness the attempts to free Friend David from an enclosed room."

"An enclosed room?" Katherine said. "I've never heard about this. How could he get trapped like that in this place?"

"The room grew around him." Eve said. They reached street level and the robot headed west, away from the Compass Tower. "It sealed him in and wouldn't let him leave."

"Why?"

"I do not know."

"Does anyone know?"

"I do not know."

"All right," Katherine said, watching a team of robots carry what looked to be gymnasium equipment into one of the buildings. "Just report what you saw."

"Gladly. I was called upon to witness the attempt to free Friend David from the sealed room. When I arrived, Supervisor Dante was already on the scene..."The robot stopped moving and for several seconds stared up into the sun. "Precisely here." Eve pointed to a section of the street. "Friend David was caught inside the structure and we could hear him shouting to be let out."

"Who?"

"Myself, Supervisor Dante, a utility robot with a torch, and another household utility robot who first discovered Friend David's problem."

"What happened then?"

"Then Supervisor Dante asked Utility Robot #237-5 if the laser torch was safe to use in such close proximity to a human being, and Utility Robot #237-5 assured him that it was. At that point, Supervisor Dante tried to reason with the room to release Friend David, and failing that, he requested that the room be cut into with the torch."

"And that request was complied with?"

"Yes. Supervisor Dante, in fact, asked Utility Robot #237-5 to complete the project quickly."

"Why?"

"I do not know."

Katherine thought about the nature of the witness and asked another question. "Were there any other events that coincided with this event?"

"Yes," Eve said. "Food Services complained that Friend David could not be served lunch on time and inquired if that would be dangerous to his health; several of the supervisors were meeting in the Compass Tower to discuss ways in which Friend David might have come to the city without their knowledge; and the city itself was put on general security alert."

"Does a general security alert alter the way in which functions are performed?" she asked.

"Yes. We were all called to other emergency duties, and were here only because of the danger to Friend David and the need to release him."

"Which you did."

"Not me," Eve said. "I only witnessed. But Friend David was freed from the enclosed room."

"Did you notice anything odd at that point?"

"Odd? Friend Katherine, I can only . . ."

"I know," she interrupted, a touch frustrated. "You only witness. Then tell me exactly what happened."

"Supervisor Dante asked Friend David to return to his apartment because a security alert had been called. Friend David said that he was not ready to return to his apartment, that he had business to do. Then he complained of a headache. Then he started laughing and walked away. Utility Robot #237-5 then asked Supervisor Dante if Friend David should be apprehended, and Supervisor Dante said he had weighed the priorities and had decided that the security alert took precedence and ordered us to proceed to our emergency duties, which, in my case, involved witnessing something that I am not at liberty to discuss with you."

"Then what?" Katherine asked, anxious.

"Then I performed the security duty that I had been assigned."

"No, no," Katherine said. "What happened then in regard to David?"

"Approximately nine decades later, I was again called upon." Eve began moving quickly down the street, Katherine right behind, having to run to keep up. "I am taking you to the approximate place of the second incident," the robot called from a speaker set in the back of its dome. "I was called here, along with Supervisor Euler this time, by Utility Robot #716-14, who had discovered several waste control robots trying to take the body of Friend David away."

Eve moved quickly around a corner, then stopped abruptly, Katherine nearly running into the robot.

"Here," Eve said, "is the approximate place where the body was alleged to have fallen."

"Alleged?"

"It was no longer here upon my arrival."

"What story did the utility robot tell?"

"Utility Robot #716-14 said that he sent the waste control robots away, then examined Friend David for signs of life without success. During the course of the examination another room began to grow around the body and enclose it, at which point Utility Robot #716-14 removed himself before becoming trapped, and put in an emergency call to us. We returned to the scene together, but the body was gone. That is the last time anyone has seen Friend David."

"Were there signs of violence on the body?"

"Utility Robot #716-14 reported that the body appeared perfectly normal except for a small cut on the left foot. Since I can only report hearsay in this regard, I am unable to render this as an accurate examination."

Katherine leaned against the wall of a one-story parts depot, the wall giving slightly under her pressure. It seemed more than coincidence that David's plight in the sealed room and the alert conditions of the city happened concurrently—but how were they connected?

"Do you feel, then, that the body moved simply because the city moved it?" she asked.

"I cannot speculate on such a theory," the witness said, "but I heard Supervisor Euler make a pronouncement similar to yours—hearsay again."

"Given the growth rate of the city," Katherine said, "calculate how far and in what direction the body of David could have traveled if, indeed, the movement of the city took him from this place."

"Approximately ten and one-half blocks," Eve said without hesitation, "in *any* direction. The city works according to a plan that is not known to me."

"Ten and a half blocks," Katherine said low. "Well, it'll sure give me something to do to fill in the time." She looked at Eve's bristling dome. "Let's take a walk."

"That is your decision," the robot replied, as Katherine picked a direction at random and began walking, looking for what, she didn't know.

ACCESS DENIED was written in bold letters across the CRT, and it was a phrase Derec had run into over a dozen times in as many minutes.

He stood at a small counter set beside a large, open window. Through the billowing clouds of iron-red dust floating into the sky, he could see the long line of earth-movers inching their way along the rocky ground, the teeth of their heavy front diggers easily chewing up the ground to a depth of 70 centimeters, then laying out the mulch in a flat, even plain behind, holes filling, rises falling, the ground absolutely uniform behind. A series of heavy rollers completed the unique vehicles, packing the ground hard for the slab base of the city to push its way into that section as it was completed.

After leaving the reservoir and its tragedy behind, he had asked Rec to take him to the edge of the city. He had wanted to see for himself the creation of the cloud dust and also to try and find access to a terminal far out of the reach of the supervisors. The robot had been hesitant at first, but after Derec had assured him that he'd go no farther than city's edge, Rec had readily agreed.

But now that he was here, Derec resented the time it had taken to come this far out. The terminal had been a complete bust. He'd found himself able to access any amount of information when it came to this part of the city operation: troubleshooting info, repair info, time references, equipment specs, personnel delineation, and SOPs of all kinds; but beyond that, access was impossible.

He had tried various methods of obtaining passwords, but it seemed he was stymied before he got started. He came away with the impression that once the city was on alert, terminals became place-oriented, only able to pick up specific data as it related to their possible function in a given location. He found this difficult to believe, for if the robots were in total charge of access and passwords it belied the nature of their "perfect human world." It struck him that access would have to be humanly possible for very basic philosophical reasons.

But not here; not at this terminal.

So, where did that leave him? The rains still came, with or without his presence; the central core was still denied to him, and with it any answers it might possess; he was still a prisoner (a fact he *did* take seriously, despite Katherine's feelings); and he still knew nothing about his origins or reasons for being in Robot City.

That thought returned him to the basics. When he had visited the Compass Tower, Avernus had been pointed out as the first supervisor robot, the one that had initiated the construction of the other supervisors. Derec had been successful in determining the origin and destination of the water; now he would work on the origin of the city itself. The only place to start was with Avernus and the underground. The mining was needed to produce the raw materials to build the city. Everything else sprang from that foundation. He would go to the source—to Avernus.

He shut down the useless terminal and walked out of the otherwise bare room to find Rec intently studying the rising dust clouds, taking readings. It was his obsession.

"I want to go into the mines and speak with Avernus," he told the robot. "Is that acceptable?"

"I will take you to the mines, Friend Derec," Rec answered, "but from that point on, the decision will belong to Avernus."

"Fair enough," Derec said, and prepared for another long walk. Then he spotted one of the trams parked near the excavation and walked toward it. "Let's ride this time."

"We were not given this machine," Rec said. "It is not ours to take."

"Were you told *not* to let me take the machine?" Derec countered.

"No, but . . ."

"Then let's go."

Derec jumped in the front, but saw no controls with which to drive it. He knew that this was probably the means by which the robots working the movers got here, but the witness was unable to make that speculation and consequently folded up. "How does it work?"

"You speak your destination into the microphone," Rec said.

"The underground," Derec said, then shrugged at Rec.

Within seconds, the car lurched forward and moved speedily away from the digs.

They traveled quickly, moving through an entire section full of nothing but robot production facilities that were running full tilt, furiously trying to keep up with the record-setting building pace. As the number of buildings increased, so, too, did the number of robots to service those buildings and the people who didn't live in them. They passed vehicle after vehicle jammed full of new, functionally designed robots who stared all around, seeing their world for the first time.

They also passed other small forests and what seemed to be large sections of hydroponic greenhouses, for when large-scale food production became a reality. Then they whizzed past a large, open area that seemed to serve no function.

"What's that?" Derec asked.

"Nothing," Rec answered.

"I don't mean now," Derec said. "What's it going to be?"

"I do not often deal in potential," the robot replied, several red lights on his dome blinking madly, "but I recall Supervisor Euler once referring to this place as a future spaceport."

Derec was a bit taken aback. Robot City was absolutely unable to deal with incoming or outgoing ships in any form. It led him down another avenue.

"If the spaceport hasn't been constructed yet," he said, "where do you keep your hyperwave transmitters?"

He asked the question casually, knowing full well that Rec would undoubtedly tell him the information was classified; but he was totally unprepared for the answer he received.

"I do not know what a hyperwave transmitter is," the robot replied.

"A device designed for communication over long distances in space," Derec said. "Perhaps you call it something else."

"I have witnessed nothing designed to communicate beyond our atmosphere," Rec answered.

"You don't send and receive information from off-planet?"

"I know of no such instance," Rec replied. "We are self-contained here."

The tram jerked to a stop, jerking Derec's thoughts along with it. Somehow, it had never occurred to him that they really were trapped on this planet. The Key and its proper use suddenly became of paramount importance to him.

"We have arrived, Friend Derec," Rec said.

"So we have," Derec replied, getting slowly out of the car. What was going on here? Who created this place? And why? It was a pristine civilization removed from contact with anything beyond itself, yet its Spacer roots were obvious. Could David, the dead man, have been the creator?

He walked past the lines of robots carrying their damaged equipment, past the huge extruder and its never-ending ribbon of city, and stood at the entrance to the underground. He turned to see Rec standing beside him.

"Find Avernus," he said. "Tell him I want to speak with him. I don't want to break protocol by going somewhere off-limits to humans."

"Yes, Friend Derec," the robot answered and moved aside to commune with its net of radio communications.

Derec sat on the ground beside the doorway and watched the robots walking back and forth past him. He was beginning to feel like a useless appendage with nothing to do. He felt guilty even ordering the robots around; they had more important things to do.

He glanced at his watch. It was two in the afternoon, and soon they'd be approaching another night of rain, another useless night of speculation as the water level rose higher and higher. "We will have failed," Euler had said, and in that sentence the robot had spoken volumes. Like Derec, the supervisor knew that Robot City was a test, a test designed for all of then. If Euler and the others were unable to solve the problem of the rain, they would have failed in their attempt to build a workable world. He also knew that the salvation of this world would take a creative form of thought that most people felt robots incapable of. Perhaps that's where Derec fit in. Synnoetics, they had called it, the whole greater than the sum of the parts. For that to take place, Derec would have to begin by convincing the robots they had to confide in him despite their security measures.

"I'm extremely busy, Friend Derec," the voice said loudly. "What do you want of me?"

Derec looked up to see Avernus's massive form bending to fit in the door space.

"We need to speak of saving this place," Derec said. "We need to approach one another as equals, and not adversaries."

"You may have done murder, Derec," Avernus said. "I am not the equal of that."

"Neither is Euler," Derec replied, "but his inattention caused a robot to die today."

"You were also present."

Derec looked at the ground. "Y-yes," he said. "I had no right to bring that up."

"Tell me what you want of me."

"Answers," Derec said. "Understanding. I want to help with the city . . . the rains. I want someone to know and appreciate that."

The robot looked at him for a long moment, then motioned him inside. They walked down the stairs together and into the holding area, Rec following behind at a respectable distance. Avernus then took him aside, away from the activity, and made a seat for him by piling up a number of broken machines of various kinds.

Derec climbed atop the junk pile and sat, Avernus standing nearby. "We are in an emergency situation, and my programming limits my communication with you."

"I understand that," Derec replied. "I also know that many situations require judgment calls that you must sift through your logic circuits. I ask only that you think synnoetically."

"If you ask that of me," the robot said, "I must tell you something. The concept of death holds more weight with me than with the others. My logic circuits are different because of my work."

"I don't understand."

"The robot's stock-in-trade is efficiency," Avernus answered, "and in jobs requiring labor, cost efficiency. But in the mines cost efficiency isn't necessarily cost efficient."

"Now I'm really confused."

"The most cost-effective way to approach mine work may be the most dangerous way to approach it, but the most dangerous way to approach it may result in the loss of a great many workers because of the nature of the mines. So, the most effective way to work the mines may not be the most cost-efficient in the long run. Consequently, I am programmed to have a respect for life—even robotic life—that far and away exceeds what one could consider normal. The lives of my workers are of prime importance to me beyond any concept of efficiency."

"What has that got to do with me?" Derec asked.

"If you have killed, Derec, you will be anathema to me. The fact that you are accused and could be capable of such an action is almost more than I can bear. I voted against your freedom when we met on this issue."

"I swear to you that I am innocent," Derec said.

"Humans lie," the robot answered. "Now, do you still wish me to be the one to 'appreciate' your position?"

"Yes," Derec answered firmly. "I ask only that I be given the opportunity to show you that I have the best interests of Robot City at heart. I am innocent, and the truth will free me."

"Well said. What do you want to know."

"You are the first supervisor," Derec said. "What are your first recollections?"

"I was awakened by a utility robot we call 1-1," Avernus said, his red photocells fixed on Derec. "1-1 had already awakened fifty other utility machines. I awakened with a full knowledge of who and what I was: a semi-autonomous robot whose function was to supervise the mines for city building, and to supervise the building of other supervisors to fulfill various tasks."

"Were you programmed to serve humans?"

"No," Avernus said quickly. "We were programmed with human information, both within us and within the core unit, which was also operational when I was awakened. Our decision to service was one we arrived at independently."

"Could that be the reason that the robots here have been less than enthusiastic about Katherine and me?" Derec asked. "Not knowing human reality, you accepted an ideal that was impossible for us to live up to."

"That is, perhaps, true," Avernus agreed.

"How long ago did your awakening take place?"

"A year ago, give or take."

"And did you see any human beings, or have knowledge of any, at that time?"

"No. Our first action was the construction of the Compass Tower. After that, we began our philosophical deliberations as to our purpose in the universe."

"How about 1-1? Did he have any contact with humans?"

"It never occurred to us to ask," Avernus said.

"Where is 1-1 now?" Derec asked, feeling himself working toward something.

"In the tunnels," Avernus said, gesturing toward the elevators. "1-1 works the mines."

Derec jumped off the makeshift seat. "Take me there," he said.

"Security . . ." the robot began.

"I'm a human being," Derec said. "This world was designed for me and my kind. I'm sorry, Avernus, but if you exist to serve, it's time you started to act like it. If you respect your own philosophies, you must accept the fact that your security measures were not designed to keep you secure from human beings. If they were, there is something desperately wrong with your basic philosophy."

"It is dangerous in the mines," Avernus replied.

"You can protect me."

The robot stood looking between Derec and the elevator doors. "I must deny you the central core," he said at length. "I must deny you knowledge of our emergency measures. But you are a human being, and this is your world to share with us. I will take you to 1-1 and protect you. If, at some point, protecting you means sending you back to the surface, I will do that."

"Fair enough," Derec said, looking at his watch. "We must go."

They moved toward the elevators, Rec joining them within the large car. In deference to the supervisor, the other robots let them have the car to themselves. Avernus pushed a stud in the wall and the door closed. The car started downward.

It went down a long way.

"The trick to movement in the mines is deliberation," Avernus said, as the car shuddered to a stop.

"Deliberation," Derec repeated.

The door slid open to delirious activity. Thousands of utility robots moved through a huge cavern that stretched as far as Derec could see in either direction. A continuous line of train cars rolled past on movable tracks, delivering raw ore to the giant smelters that refined it to more workable stages where it was heated and alloyed with other materials. The ceiling was thirty-five meters high and cut from the raw earth. Clean rooms filled the space at regular intervals.

"Iron!" Avernus said, stretching his arms wide. "The foundation upon which the ferrous metals are based, from which the modern world is made possible. We mine it in huge quantities, using it in its raw state to make our equipment, and alloyed with special plastics to form our city. There!"

He pointed to a machine through which layers of iron were belt-feeding, together with imprinted patterns of micro-circuits. The congealed mass issued from the top of the machine and proceeded through the ceiling in a continuous ribbon, the building material that Derec had seen extruded on the surface.

"That is the stuff of Robot City," Avernus said. "Iron and plastic alloy, cut with large amounts of carbon, and using carbon monoxide as a reducing agent. The 'skin' is then im-printed with millions of micro-circuits per square meter. In centimeter, independent sections, the 'skin' is alive with ro-botic intelligence, geared to human needs and protection. The whole is pre-programmed to build and behave in a prescribed fashion, and to react to human needs as they arise."

"That's why the walls give when I push on them," Derec said, moving gingerly out of the elevator and staying close to Avernus.

"Exactly. Now remember, deliberation. Stay close."

Avernus moved out into the middle of the furious ac-tivity, machines and robots and train cars rushing quickly all around them. As Avernus stepped into the path of on-rushing vehicles, Derec froze, wanting to pull back. But the expected accidents never took place, the robots and their machines gauging all the actions around them and reacting perfectly to them.

That's when the concept of deliberation became clear to Derec. Movement needed to be deliberate, with constant for-ward momentum. All judgment was based on the idea that movement would be steady and could be avoided once gauged. It was the erratic movement that was dangerous—the abrupt stop, the jump back; down here, such movements would be fatal.

Once he understood the concept, it became easier to walk into the path of on-rushing vehicles. And as they moved through the center of the great hall, Derec began to feel more comfortable.

"Let me ask you a question," he said to the big robot. "Did you invent the 'skin' of Robot City?"

"No," Avernus replied. "Its program was already within the central core."

"So its activities are all pre-programmed?"

"Correct. All we did was use it once we decided to be of service to humanity."

They reached an edge of the hall, dozens of smaller tunnels branching off from it.

"We ride now," Avernus said, climbing into a cart that was far too small for his immense bulk. Derec and Rec climbed in with him, and Avernus started off right away, taking them down a barely lit tunnel.

"This one looks deserted," Derec said, and they hurried along at a fast clip.

"It was, until two days ago," Avernus said. "It is now, perhaps, going to save us."

"How?"

"You will see."

They rode for several more minutes through the dark, going deeper into the earth. Then Derec heard activity ahead.

"We are approaching," Avernus said.

"Approaching what?" Derec asked.

Avernus turned a corner and they were suddenly confronted by a widening of the tunnel, several hundred robots working furiously within an ever-growing space, scooping out dirt into any available container or skid, anything that would move earth. They then would take the earth and move quickly with it down adjoining tunnels, refilling that which had been excavated sometime previously. Like an ant farm, they moved in graceful cooperation and determination, and standing atop a cart, looming above them, was Rydberg, silently pointing as he transmitted his orders by radio to the toiling robots.

Avernus turned and looked at Derec. "Somewhere in there," he said, "you will find l-l."

CHAPTER 7

ONE-ONE

Katherine's first thought had been that it was a monument, but then she realized there were no monuments on Robot City. It was set on a narrow pedestal about one hundred feet in the air. Located in the middle of a block, the city had simply built itself around the object in a semicircle, leaving it set apart from all other structures by a gap of fifty feet. She had spent several hours walking the changing topography of Robot City without success, but she stopped the moment she came upon this place. If she wanted to compare the workings of the living city to a human body, this room atop the pedestal was like a wound, sealing itself off with scar tissue to protect it from the vital workings of the rest of the body.

It was no more than a room. Katherine stood at ground level staring up at the thing. A box, perhaps five meters square, totally enclosed. The robots took the workings of their city for granted and simply accepted this anomaly. To the creative eye, it stuck out like a solar eclipse on a bright afternoon.

Katherine continued to stare up at it because she didn't want to lose it. Even now, the city continued to move, to grow before her eyes, and as the buildings turned in their slow waltz of life, she turned with them, always keeping the room within her vision. Eve, meanwhile, was trying to round up a supervisor who could effect a means of getting inside the structure and checking it out.

During the course of this excursion, Katherine had begun to develop a grudging respect for the workings of the city. Obviously, things were not going well right now, but in the long run such a system could be quite beneficial to the humans and robots who inhabited it. The safety factor alone made the system worthwhile. Derec's harrowing ride down through the aqueduct resulted in nothing more than fatigue and a few bruises, all because the system itself was trying to protect him. To Katherine's mind, such a journey on Aurora would have caused Derec's death. She smiled at the thought of a Derec-proof city.

She'd also had time, while waiting for Eve to reach a supervisor, to notice the changes taking place around her. She felt as if she were visiting a resort at the tail end of the off season, all the seasonal workers arriving and getting the place shipshape for the influx of visitors. Clocks were being installed in various parts of the city, and street signs were beginning to go up. The largest change taking place, however, was the increased production and distribution of chairs. Robots had no need for sitting or reclining, and chairs were at a premium; but as they tried to make their city as welcome as possible for humans, they worked diligently to do things just right, despite the fact that the city's emergency measures were forcing many of them into extra duty. She wondered if she'd be this gracious if it were her city. The thought humbled her a bit.

Despite the differences, despite the bind the robots had put them in, they really were trying to make this world as perfect as they could for the travelers, travelers whom they suspected of murder. She had never before considered just how symbiotic the binding of humans to robots really was and, at least for the robots, how essential. She hoped that they would, eventually, have their civilization, complete with humans to order them around stupidly. She found herself smiling again. Her mother had a phrase that could apply to the robots' longing for human companionship—a glutton for punishment.

She heard a noise behind her and turned, expecting to see a supervisor arriving. Instead she saw two utility robots moving toward her, carrying between them what looked for all the world like a park bench. Without a word, they moved right up to her and placed the bench just behind. She sat, and they hurried off.

She sat for barely a decad before Arion came clanking around a corner, along with a utility robot with a bulky laser torch strapped on his back. It took her back for a second, a seeming replay of the scene Eve had described to her when David had first become trapped in the sealed room.

"Good afternoon, Friend Katherine," Arion said as he moved up to her. "I see you are taking advantage of one of our chairs to rest your body. Very good."

"What's that on your wrist," Katherine asked, "a watch?"

The supervisor held up his arm, displaying the timepiece. "A show of solidarity," he said.

"You're in charge of human-creative functions on Robot City, aren't you?" she asked.

"Human-creative is a redundant term," Arion replied.

"Creativity is the human stock-in-trade. I hope you've found satisfactory the entertainments I've provided for you."

"We'll talk about that later," she answered.

"Of course."

"I thank you for coming so promptly," Katherine said.

"This is a priority matter," the robot said, gazing up at the sealed room. "You believe this to be the location of the body?"

"I'm certain of it."

"Very good. Let's take a closer look."

Katherine stood and walked to the base of the tower with Arion. The pedestal was approximately the size of a large tree trunk, just large enough that she could almost reach around it if she tired. Arion reached out and touched the smooth, blue skin, and magically a spiral staircase with railing jutted from the surface and wound around the exterior of the tower.

"After you," the robot said politely.

Katherine started up, the design of the staircase keeping her from any sense of vertigo. As she climbed, she could feel that the air was cooling down, the presage to another night of destructive rain. Behind her, Arion, the utility robot, and the witness followed dutifully, and she realized that she was in the lead because it was the natural position for her in regard to this inquiry. This was her notion, her case—the robots at this point were merely her willing cohorts. Finally, she could give orders again and have them carried out!

She reached the top quickly. The flat disc of the pedestal top curled up and inward all around to make it impossible for her to fall off. That left the room itself. Uncolored, it was a natural gray-red and perfectly square. She walked completely around it looking for entry, but her first assessment had been correct: it was locked up tight.

"What do you propose at this point?" Arion asked her, as he followed her around the perimeter of the room.

"We're going to have to get inside," she said, "and see what there is to see. I suppose there's no other way to get in except by using the torch?"

"Normally, this situation would never arise," Arion told her. "There are no other buildings in the city that behave like this. There is no reason to seal up a room."

"You mean you don't know why or how the rooms have sealed themselves up?"

"The city program was given to us intact through the central core, and only the central core contains the program information. Other than through observation, we don't know exactly how the city operates."

Katherine was taken aback. "So, the city is actually a highly advanced autonomous robot in its own right, operating outside of your control."

"Your statement is basically inaccurate, but containing the germ of truth," Arion said. "To begin with, it is not highly advanced, at least not in the same sense that a ... supervisor robot, for example, is highly advanced."

"Do I detect a shade of rivalry here?" she asked.

"Certainly not," Arion said. "We are not capable of such feelings as competitiveness. I was simply stating a known fact. Furthermore, the city's autonomy is tied directly to the central core. Although it does, in fact, operate outside of supervisor control."

"Can you affect the city program, then?"

"Not directly," Arion said, running his pincers up and down the contours of the building as if checking for openings. "The central core controls the city program, and the supervisors do not make policy by direct programming."

"I think I'm beginning to truly understand," Katherine

said, motioning for the robot with the torch to come closer. "The data contained in the central core is the well from which your entire city springs. All of your activities here are merely an extension of the programming contained therein, for good or ill."

"We are robots, Friend Katherine," Arion said. "It could not be otherwise. Robots are not forces of change, but merely extensions of extant thought. That is why we so desperately need the companionship of humans."

"Cut here," Katherine said pointing to the wall, and the utility robot waited until she had backed away to a safer distance before charging the power packs and moving close with the nozzle-like hose that was the business end of the laser torch. She turned to Arion. "Does cutting through the wall like this break contact with the main program?"

"No," the robot answered as the torch came on with a whine, its beam invisible as a small section of the wall glowed bright red, smoking slightly. "The synapses simply reroute themselves and make connection elsewhere."

There was a sound of suction as the torch broke through to the other side of the wall, a sound that any Spacer knew well, the rushing of air into a vacuum. The room had sealed totally and airlessly. The torch moved more quickly now, cutting a circular hole just large enough for a human being to get through without working at it.

The edges tore jaggedly, the walls that seemed so fluid under program fighting tenaciously to hold together otherwise. Despite Arion's claims, Katherine was still impressed with the city-robot.

The welder was halfway done, pulling down the jagged slab of city as he cut. Katherine had to fight down the urge to run up and peer through the opening already made, but her fear of the torch ultimately won out over her impatience.

"Are you capable of doing autopsies here?" she asked Arion as an afterthought.

"The medical programming is in existence, and at this very moment several medically trained robots are being turned out of our production facilities, along with diagnostic tables and a number of machines. Synthesized drugs and instruments are coming at a slower rate. So much of the city is geared toward building right now, and these considerations never became a problem for us until David's death."

"Done," the utility robot said, the cut section falling to clang on the base disc.

"Witness!" Arion called, as Katherine hurried to the place and climbed through the hole.

The naked body lay, face down, in the middle of the floor. Katherine walked boldly toward it, then stopped, a hand going to her chest. She had been so intent upon fulfilling her mission that she had failed to consider that it was death—real death—she'd be dealing with. It horrified her. She began shaking, her heart rate increasing.

"Is something wrong?" Eve asked from the cut-out.

"N-no," she replied, her eyes glued to the body, unable either to move forward or pull back.

"If there's a problem," she heard Arion say, "come out now. Don't jeopardize yourself."

Come on, old girl. Get yourself together. "I'm fine," she said. *You've got to do this. Don't stop now.*

She took a deep breath, then another, and continued her walk to the body. Bending, she touched it gingerly. The surface was cool, the muscles tight.

"Is everything all right?" Arion asked.

"Yes," she said. *Won't they leave me alone?*

There was no sign of decomposition, and she realized

that it was because the room had been airless. At least that was something.

She examined the body from the back, her heart rate still up, her breath coming fast. Looking at the foot, she could see a small cut on the left instep and realized immediately what had caused it. Something stupid. Something she had done herself before. A misstep, perhaps a broken fall, and the bare feet came together, a too-long toenail on the other foot scraping the instep. It was nothing. There was some dried blood on the side and bottom of the foot, but that was it. She was going to have to roll the body over.

She moved to the side of the body, reaching out to try and turn it over, finding her hands shaking wildly. *Will this be me soon—fifty kilos of dead meat?* She tried to push the body onto its back, but there was no strength in her arms.

"Could you help me with this?" she called over her shoulder. Arion came through the cut-out to bend down beside her. She looked up at the nearly human-looking machine. "I want to roll it over."

"Surely," Arion said, reaching out with his pincers to push gently against the side of the body. It rolled over easily, dead eyes staring straight at Katherine.

She heard herself screaming from far away as the shock of recognition hit her. It was Derec! Derec!

The room began spinning as she felt it in her stomach and in her head. Then she felt the floor reach up and pull her down; everything else was lost in the numbing bliss of unconsciousness.

"Don't try to leave without me to lead you!" Avernus called to Derec as the boy waded into the churning sea of robots. "You could become hopelessly lost in these tunnels."

"Don't worry!" Derec called back, thinking more about the danger of the main chamber than the labyrinthine caves.

He moved slowly through the throng, walking toward Rydberg. It was damp, musty in there, plus a bit claustrophobic, but Derec was so fascinated by the spectacle of the eleventh-hour plans that he never allowed his mind to dwell on the all-too-human problems of the location.

Rydberg saw him approaching, and turned to stare as Derec closed on him. He climbed atop the cart and joined the supervisor.

"What are you doing here?" Rydberg asked, the words crackling through the speaker atop his dome. "It is too dangerous underground for you."

"I talked Avernus into bringing me down and protecting me," Derec replied. "What's going on here?"

"We're trying to tunnel up to the reservoir," Rydberg said. "We are trying to work out a way to drain off some of the reservoir into the deserted tunnels below to keep it from flooding."

Derec felt an electric charge run through him. "That's wonderful!" he yelled. "You've made a third-level connection—a creative leap!"

"It was only logical. Since the water was going to come into the mines anyway, it only made sense that we should try to direct it to parts of the mines that would cause the least amount of damage. Unfortunately, our estimates show such a move could only hold off the inevitable for a day or two longer. It may all be in vain."

"Why are you digging by hand?" Derec asked. "Where are the machines?"

"They are tied up in the mining process," Rydberg said. "The current rate of city-building must take precedence over all other activities." The robot turned his dome to watch the excavations.

Derec put his hands on the robot's arm. "But the city-building is what's killing you!"

"It must be done."

"Why?"

"I cannot answer that."

Derec looked all around him, at the frantic rush of momentum, at a civilization trying to survive. No, they weren't human, but it didn't mean their lives weren't worthwhile. What was the gauge? There was intelligence, and a concerted effort toward perfection of spirit. There was more worth, more human value here in the mines than in anything he had seen in his brief glimpse of humanity. And then it struck him, the reason for all of this and the reason for the state of emergency and security.

"It's defensive, isn't it?" he said. "The city-building is a way for the city to defend itself against alien invasion?"

Rydberg just stared at him.

He grabbed the robot's arm again, tighter. "That *is* it, isn't it?"

"I cannot answer that question."

"Then tell me I am wrong!"

"I cannot answer that question."

"I knew it," he said, convinced now. "And if it coincided with David's appearance in the city, then it is somehow tied to him. For once, Katherine's in the right place.

"This whole thing is a central core program," Derec said, "and obviously the program is in error. There must be some way you can circumvent it."

"Robots do not make programs, Derec," Rydberg said.

"Then let me into it!"

"I cannot," Rydberg replied, then added softly. "I'm sorry."

Derec just stared at him, wanting to argue him into compliance, and fearing that the argument would simply present the robot with a contradiction so vast it would freeze his mental facilities and lock him up beyond hope. He didn't know where to go from here. He'd had a tantalizing glimpse of the problem, yet, like a holographic image, it still eluded his grasp.

"You still have not told me why you came down into the mines," Rydberg said. "Humans have such a poor sense of personal danger that I fail to see how your species has survived to this point. If you cannot present me a compelling reason for your presence, I fear I must send you away now."

"If humans have a poor sense of personal danger," Derec said, angry at Robot City's inability even to try to save itself, "then it has been justly inherited in *your* programming. I've come down to visit 1-1 on a matter not of your concern. Would you please point him out to me?"

"Our first citizen?" Rydberg said, and Derec could tell the robot wanted to say more. Instead, he turned up his volume. "WILL ROBOT 1-1 PLEASE COME FORWARD."

Within a minute, a small, rather innocuous utility robot with large, powerful looking pincer grips moved up to the cart. "I am here, Supervisor Rydberg," the robot said.

"Friend Derec wishes to speak with you on a personal matter," the supervisor said. "Do as he asks, but do not take an excessive amount of time."

Derec jumped off the cart. "I hear you were the first robot awakened on this planet," he said.

"That is correct," the robot said.

"Come with me," Derec said. "Let's get out of the confusion."

They moved through the rapidly widening chamber to the place where Avernus had first dropped him. "I am searching through the origins of Robot City," Derec said, "and that search has led me to you. You were the first."

"Yes. Logical. I was the first."

"I want you to tell me exactly what your first visual input was and what followed subsequently."

"My first visual input was of a human arm connecting my power supply," the robot said. "Then the human turned and walked away from me."

"Did you see the human face?"

"No."

"What happened then?"

"The human walked a distance from me, then disappeared behind some machinery meant to help in our early mining. I was to wait for one hour, then turn on the other inoperative robots in the area. Then we were to begin work, which we did."

"Of what did that original work consist?"

"There were fifty utility, plus Supervisor Avernus. Twenty-five of us built the Compass Tower from materials left for us, while Supervisor Avernus and the other twenty-five began the design and construction of the underground facilities and commenced the mining operations."

Derec was puzzled. "Avernus didn't supervise the construction of the Compass Tower?"

"No. It was meant as a separate entity from the rest of the city. It was fully planned, fully materialized. There was no need for Supervisor Avernus to take an interest in it."

Derec heard an engine noise and saw lights, far in the tunnel distance, gradually closing on his position. "What do you mean when you say it was 'meant as a separate entity?' " Derec asked.

"The Compass Tower is unique in several respects, Friend Derec," l-l said. "It is not part of the overall city plan in any respect; it has the off limits homing platform atop it; and it contains a fully furnished, human administration office."

"What!" Derec said loudly, as he watched the mine tram rushing closer toward him in the tunnel. "An office for whom?"

"I do not know. Perhaps the person who awakened me."

"You've never spoken of this with the supervisors?"

"No one has ever inquired before now."

"Why did you call it the administration office?"

"The construction plans are locked within my data banks," l-l answered. "That is what it was called on the plans."

The tram car screeched to a halt right beside Darren, the huge bulk of Avernus stuffed in its front seat. "We must go," the supervisor said.

"Just a minute," Derec said. "Why did you call it a homing platform?"

"We must go now," Avernus said.

"It was designed as a landing point of some kind," l-l said. "Nothing is ever allowed on its surface, or within twenty meters of its airspace."

Avernus took hold of Derec's arm and gently, but firmly, turned him face to face. "We must go," Avernus said. "Something has happened to Friend Katherine."

Derec reeled as if he'd been hit. "What? What happened? Is she all right?"

"She is unconscious," Avernus said. "Beyond that, we do not know."

CHAPTER 8

IDENTITY CRISIS

Derec hurried into the apartment to buzzing activity. Arion was there, and Euler, plus Eve and several utility robots. There was also a rather frail-looking machine with multiple appendages that Derec surmised to be a med-bot.

The living room seemed different, much squatter, but he really wasn't paying attention.

"Friend Derec..." Euler began, hurrying to intercept Derec as he crossed the living room floor.

"Where is she?" he asked, still moving.

"The bedroom," Euler said. "She has regained consciousness and is resting. I do not think you should try and see her just yet."

"Nonsense," Derec said, hurrying past him. "I've *got* to see her."

"But you don't underst..."

"Later," Derec said, moving down the hallway. There were now two bedroom doors. He opened one to an empty room, then turned to the other, pushing the stud. It slid open. Katherine was sitting up in bed, her face drained of all color, her eyes red.

"Are you all right?" he asked.

Her eyes focused on him, then grew wide in horror.

"Noooo!" she screamed, hands going to her straining face.

Derec ran to her and took her by the shoulders. She kept screaming, loudly, hysterically, her body vibrating madly on the bed.

"You're dead!" she yelled. "Dead! Dead!"

"No!" he yelled. "I'm here. It's all right. It's all . . ."

Euler was pulling him away from her, robots filling the room. "What are you doing?" he yelled. "Let go, I . . ."

"You must leave now," Euler said, lifting him bodily in the air and carrying him, Katherine's screams still filling the apartment.

"Katherine!" he called to her as Euler carried him out the door. "Katherine!"

Euler carried him all the way to the living room, then simply held him there, the med-bot slipping into her bed-room and sliding the door closed, muffling the screams somewhat.

"Put me down!" Derec yelled. "Would you put me down?"

"You must not go in there," Euler said. "It is dangerous for Katherine if you go in there."

He felt the anger draining out of him. "What's going on?" he asked sheepishly. "What's happened to her?"

"She's suffered some sort of emotional trauma," the su-pervisor said. "May I put you down?"

"Believe me," Derec said, "at this point, I don't want to go back in."

Euler set him gently on the floor. Derec rubbed his arms to get the circulation back into them.

"I am sorry if I caused you any discomfort," Euler said. "Truly."

"It's all right," Derec replied. "Tell me what happened."

Thunder crashed loudly outside, both Derec and Euler turning to look at the building thunderheads through the open patio door. They were in for another bad one. From the bedroom, the sounds of screaming had died to occasional whimpers.

"Katherine found the body of David," Euler said, "and had a utility robot cut into the sealed room that contained it." The robot swiveled its head to take in the rest of the room. "Perhaps it is better to have Arion witness the story. He was present for it." He motioned for the human-like machine to join the discussion.

"Friend Derec," Arion said as he moved up close. "I had no idea that seeing the body would have this kind of effect on Friend Katherine. I would never have allowed her to come close to it had I known."

"I understand," Derec said. "Just tell me what happened."

"She was examining the deceased," Arion said, "when she called me in to help her roll the body over. I, of course, complied. She screamed when she saw the face, then lapsed into a state of unconsciousness."

"She's been disconsolate ever since," Euler said. "Most peculiar. She persisted in the belief that the dead man was you."

"Why would she do that?" he asked, moving to sit at the table. Arion's CRT was busily finding the cube roots of tendigit numbers.

"I don't know," Euler said. "Perhaps because the body looked like yours."

Derec sat up straight, staring hard. "You mean . . . just like me?"

The robots looked at one another. "Perfectly," Arion said.

"Doesn't that strike you as odd?" Derec said, dumbfounded, still not believing the information.

"No," Euler said.

"I don't understand," Derec said. "When you first saw me, didn't you take note of the similarity of our appearances?"

"Yes," Euler said, "but it didn't mean anything to us."

"Why not?"

Arion spoke up. "Why should it? We've only seen three human beings. Robots certainly can look exactly alike, why not humans? We knew you and Katherine were different, but that didn't mean that you and David couldn't be the same. Besides, we *knew* that David was dead; so, consequently, we *knew* that you couldn't be David. Simple."

The med-bot came gliding down the hall, moving quickly up to Derec. "She's calm now," the robot said. "She's lightly sedated with her own pituitary endorphins, and wants to see you."

Derec stood, uneasy after the last time. "It'll be all right?" he asked the med-bot.

"I believe she understands the situation now," the med-bot responded in a gentle, fatherly voice.

"I'd like to see her alone," he told the others.

Euler nodded. "We'll wait out here."

He moved down the hall, unsure of his feelings. It had hurt him to see her in such pain, hurt him emotionally. She could get on his nerves so badly, yet seemed such an integral part of him.

He knocked lightly on her door, then opened it. She sat up in bed, her face still sad. She held her arms out to him. "Oh, Derec ..."

He hurried to the bed, sitting next to her, holding her. She began to sob gently into his shoulder. "I was so afraid," she said. "I thought ... thought ..."

"I know," he said, stroking her hair. "Arion told me. I'm so sorry."

"I don't know what I'd do without you," she said, then pulled away from him. "Oh, Derec. I know we've walls between us ... but please believe me, I have no idea what this place is and what's going on here."

"I believe you," he said, reaching up to wipe tears from her eyes. He smiled. "Don't worry about that now. How are you doing?"

"Better," she said. "The med-bot stuck me a couple of times, but it really helped. All I've got is a headache."

Thunder rolled again outside. "Good," he said. "It looks like we're locked in for the night anyway. What do you say we send the robots away, get some dinner sent up, and compare notes. I've got a lot to tell you."

"Me, too," she said. "It sounds good."

They had a vegetable soup for dinner that was the best thing Derec had eaten for quite some time. The rains pounded frenetically outside, but Derec didn't worry so much since he figured the precautions taken by Euler and Rydberg would, at least, get them through the night. And the best he could do now was to live day to day. Even Arion's entertainment was beginning to diversify. The CRT was exhibiting an animated game of tennis played by computer-generated stick figures on a slippery surface. It was actually quite amusing.

After the servo had cleared the dishes away and left, they made themselves comfortable on the couch and recounted the details of the day. Derec, for reasons he wasn't quite sure of, left out the fact that there were no hyperwave transmission stations on the planet. Counting on Katherine's experiences to help him, he listened alertly to her account of the discovery of the body.

"The fact that he looked just like you," she asked when she'd finished, "what does it mean?"

"To begin with," he said, "it finally knocks the idea of our trip to Robot City being an accident right out the air lock. We were brought here; why, I don't know. The dead man is either the one who brought us or was brought himself. We'll have to continue to ferret that out. What interests me more is the fact that the city-robot works independently. I believe that the city is somehow replicating itself as a defensive measure. If it operates independently, the supervisors may not be *able* to stop it."

"What does that mean?"

He looked at her. "It means that I've got to."

"That brings us back to our same old argument," she said, darkening a bit. "The city or the murder investigation."

"Not necessarily," he said, standing. "This should make you happy." He walked back to the patio door and idly watched the downpour, feeling now that it could, eventually, be beaten. He turned back to her. "I believe that David and the city alert and replication are inexorably linked."

She jumped up, excited, and ran to him, throwing her arms around him. "You're going to help me solve the murder, aren't you?"

"Yes," he laughed, returning the embrace. "Tomorrow

we go back to the body and pick up where you left off." He moved away from her and intertwined his fingers. "It's all like this, all connected. If we can put a few of the pieces together, I'll bet the rest fall into place. Whatever, or who-ever, killed David, is the reason for the alert."

"First thing in the morning, we'll have Eve take us back there."

"Not first thing," he said. "First thing, I've set up a brief meeting with the supervisors at the Compass Tower."

"Why?"

"Two reasons. First, I want to ask them some questions about their underground operations; and second, I want to be able to poke around the building for a bit."

"Looking for the office?"

He nodded. "l-l said it was fully furnished. I bet we'll find answers there."

Her face got suddenly serious. "I hope you find the kind of answers you're looking for," she said.

CHAPTER 9

THE OFFICE

A table had been set up in the meeting room. It was long and narrow and included seats for nine. Derec sat at the head of the table, with Katherine at his right. The supervisors took up the rest of the seats, still holding hands, with the two at the end of the line holding hands over the table-top.

"Why do human beings lie, Friend Derec?" Supervisor Dante asked, his elongated, magnifying eyes staring all the way down the table. "The most difficulty we've had with you is your penchant for lies and exaggeration. It is what keeps us from trusting you completely."

Derec licked dry lips and watched them all expectantly watching him. He knew he'd have to get beyond this hurdle if he were to work with them in solving the city's problems.

"Robots receive their input in two ways," he said, hoping his explanation would be adequate. He'd gotten up early to think it out and prepare it. "Through direct programming, and through input garnered through the sensors that is then tested in analog against existing programming. Your sensors record events accurately, with mathematic precision, and classify them through the scientific validity of several thousand years of empirical thought. You are then able, through your positronics, to reason deductively by weighing, again through analog, incoming data against existing data. You can make true second-level connections."

"We understand the workings of the positronic brain," Friend Derec," Waldeyer said. "It is the human brain that confounds us."

"Bear with me," Derec said. "I want to pose you a question. Suppose, just suppose, that your basic programming was in error—not just in small ways, but in its most basic assumptions. Suppose every bit of sensory input you received was in total opposition to your basic programming."

"We would spend a great deal of time reasoning erroneously," Wohler said. "But human brains are not at the mercy of programming. You have the freedom to sift through all empirical data and arrive at the truth at all times."

"That's where you are wrong," Derec replied. "The human mind is not a computer with truth as its base. It is merely a collection of ganglia moved by electrical impulses. Truth is not its basis, but rather ego gratification. Truth to the human mind is a shifting thing, a sail billowing on the wind of fear and hope and desire. It has no reality, but rather creates it from moment to moment with that same creative intelligence that you value so highly in us."

"But the base program is available," Euler said. "It is there for the human to use."

"And it is also there for him to reject," Derec countered. "You *must* observe your programming. My mind has no such chains on it. The human mind is painfully mortal. That particular truth in itself is more than most humans can tolerate. We are frail creatures, seeking permanence in an impermanent world. We lie to those around us. We lie to ourselves. We lie in the face of all logic and all reason. We lie because, quite often, the truth would destroy us. We lie without even knowing it."

Avernus spoke. "How do robots that exist with humans on other worlds deal with the deceit?"

"They follow instruction according to the Laws of Robotics," Derec said, quite simply. "They are not autonomous as you are, so they have no choice. The Laws were invented with the salvation of the species in mind. Robots protect humans from their own lies, and honor them because of what's noble in the species. You saw Katherine's grief when she thought I was dead." He reached out and took her hand. "We are fragile creatures capable of great nobility and great ignominy. We make no excuses for ourselves. We are the creators of great good and great evil, and in the creation of robots, we were at the height of our goodness. Our species deserves praise and condemnation, and, in the final analysis, it is beyond rational, positronic explanation."

"You are saying we must take you as you are," Euler said.

"No laws will define us," Derec answered, "no theorem hold us in check. We will amaze and confound you, but I can guarantee you we will never be boring."

"You would tame us with your words," Wohler, the philosopher, said.

"Yes," Derec said, smiling. "I would do exactly that. And I will tell you now that you will let me because the wonders of the universe are contained in my confounding mind, and you can only reach them through me . . . and you desperately want to reach them!"

"But what of the Laws of Humanics?" Rydberg asked.

"Very simple," Katherine added, winking at Derec. "There is only one Law of Humanics: expect the unexpected."

"An oxymoron," Arion said.

"As close as you'll ever get," Derec said. "That's the point. You needn't give up your search for the Laws of Humanics, but you must make them fit us, not try to make us fit them. We can't be anything but what we are, but if you accept us—good and bad—we'll see to it that you reach your full potential."

"Intriguing words," Dante said, "but just words. Where is an example of what you can do with your creative intelligence?"

"If you'll let me," Derec said, "perhaps I can help you save your city."

"All your suggestions so far have tried to force us away from our programming," Euler said.

Derec stood; he thought better on his feet. "That's because until yesterday I never fully realized what was going on and how little control you had over the situation. I'm working on that, too, but I have some other ideas."

Arion and Waldeyer sat side by side, pincers locked together. Derec walked between the two of them, resting his elbows on their shoulders.

"I've watched you digging in the tunnels, trying to siphon off reservoir water to lower the level and avoid a flooding of your underground operations. Has it been successful?"

"To a degree," Rydberg said. "We will break through after our meeting this morning. Unfortunately, we calculate that it will only postpone the inevitable for one more day. We can save our operations through tonight's expected rain, but that's it."

"All right," Derec said. "Let's think about something. I was in the main chamber of one of the quadrants yesterday. Was that chamber dug?"

"No," Avernus said. "Each quadrant Extruder Station is located in a chamber similiar to that one. Our first action in beginning underground operations was to take sonogram readings to determine natural caverns under the surface. The mine tunnels were dug, but the main chambers are natural."

"Has it occurred to you," Derec said, "to take sonograms now, in the present situation?"

"I do not understand," Avernus said.

Derec pounded the tabletop with an index finger. "Find the closest underground cavern to your reservoir, dig a tunnel connecting it to the reservoir, and . . ."

"And drain the reservoir water in there!" Avernus said, standing abruptly and breaking contact with the central core.

"Right!" Derec pointed to him. "Meanwhile, Katherine and I will be working on solving the murder. I'm absolutely convinced that the solution to the murder will also provide the reasons for the state of emergency." He turned to Supervisor Dante. "Is *that* creative enough for you?"

"Happily so," Dante said.

"It seems," Euler said, "that if we are to have the opportunity of putting Friend Derec's suggestions into practice, we should adjourn this meeting and set to work."

The robots stood, Derec wondering if they realized that he had gently manipulated them, for the first time, into including him as a real partner in their planning.

He watched them filing out of the large room, for the first time beginning to feel he was getting a handle on the deviousness of the mind that had brought all of them together. Synnoetics. The worst hills still remained to be scaled toward reaching a truly equal social union of human and robot. Now, if they could only survive the rains, they could perhaps be the trailblazers in the opening of a new era.

As soon as the robots left the room, Katherine hurried to the door and peered out. "They're gone," she said, turning back to Derec.

"Good."

He joined her at the door, Eve and Rec, trailing dutifully. Derec turned to them. "Has either of you ever witnessed within this building before?"

"Yes," Rec said. "Most of this building is given to experimentation on the positronic brain and ways to improve its function. I have witnessed experiments in almost every laboratory in the structure."

"Have you ever seen an office, something that a human might use as his personal quarters?"

"No," the robot answered.

"Are there parts of the building you have never seen?"

"Yes."

"All right, listen carefully," Derec said, shrugging in Katherine's direction. "I want you to take me to all the parts of the building you have never seen."

"I cannot do that."

"Why not?" Katherine asked.

"There is a sector in the Compass Tower that is off-limits to robots. No one goes there."

"Did someone tell you that," Derec asked, "a supervisor?"

"It is part of our programming," Rec said.

Eve agreed. "Not even supervisors are allowed."

Derec shook his head. Just like robots—all duty, no inquisitiveness. "I want you to take us there," he said.

"I already told you it was off-limits," Rec said.

Derec smiled. "I don't mean for you to take me *inside* the off-limits part," he said. "Just take me as close as you can get and point it out to me."

That seemed amenable enough, so the two witnesses led the way, while Derec and Katherine followed closely. They walked the maze-like halls, twisting and turning, but always going higher. An elevator took them six floors up, but that wasn't even the end of it. It was interesting to Derec. The meeting room had been designed to look like it was at the apex of the pyramid, but it was actually only about halfway up the structure, perhaps the illusion being more spiritual in intent than anything else.

The upper levels had begun to get rather small, doorways appearing more sparsely between the gently glowing wall panels, when the robots abruptly stopped. Rec pointed to a door at the end of a short hallway.

"We can go no farther," the robot said. "No one knows where that doorway leads."

"If you want to wait here," Derec said, "we'll be back soon."

"But it is off-limits," Eve said.

"To robots, not humans," Katherine replied.

"But we cannot separate," Rec persisted.

"It is only one door," Derec said. "We'll have to come back through it."

"Our orders..."

"Do what you want," Derec said. "We're going on."

With that, Derec and Katherine continued down the hallway, turning once to see the attentive robots before opening the door and stepping inside.

What they found was a spiral staircase leading up to a door set ten feet above their heads.

"You want to go first?" Derec asked.

"Go ahead," Katherine returned. "I left my courage back in that sealed room."

Derec moved slowly up the stairs, a feeling of expectation rising slowly in his stomach. He connected the word, butterflies, to the feeling, but had no idea of what it meant. He reached the door, and pushed the stud, expecting it to be locked up tight.

It wasn't.

The door slid easily and opened, he thought at first, to the outside. It was as if he were walking onto an open platform set with furniture and a desk, a beautiful, panoramic view of Robot City all around. But there was no feel of the air, no wind, no heat from the mid-morning sun.

"How did we get outside?" Katherine asked, following him in.

"We're not," Derec said, pointing behind her.

The outside view was marred by the still-open doorway, a black maw in the center of downtown. When he pushed the stud to close the door, the full view was restored.

"Viewscreens?" she asked.

"I think so," he replied. "There must be a series of small cameras set around the peak of the pyramid to give the view, which is then put on the screens. Look," he pointed, "even above us."

She looked up to see pinkish-blue sky above. "That would be the view from the platform we materialized on," she said.

"Fascinating," he said softly, knowing they'd finally stumble upon something. "If you were sitting in here, you could watch someone materialize on the platform and they'd never know it."

"Do you think someone watched *us* materialize?" she asked, eyes wide.

He shrugged. "I'd have to think it probable at this point," he said. "We were brought here. We were *meant* to be here. It seems logical that our progress would be measured."

"Have you ever considered the fact, Derec, that *you* were brought here and I'm excess baggage?" she asked.

He walked slowly through the room. It was designed for someone to live in. There were easy chairs and a couch that converted to a bed. Not city-robot material, but real furniture. There was even a plant of some kind under its own growth light. That told Derec that whoever kept this office returned at least often enough to keep the plant watered.

"I've considered a great many things," Derec told her, "including the scenario you've just outlined. But there are several things to consider. I believe our meeting on Aranimas's ship was accidental. The situation was too dangerous and uncontrollable to be otherwise, our injuries too real. But consider the facts that you admit to having known me previously by another name and that that name just happens to belong to someone who looked enough like me to be my twin. It's a large universe, Katherine. That's an awful lot of coincidence. Let me ask you something. Have *you* ever considered the possibility that the David you knew could be the one lying dead in that sealed room, and that I'm somebody else?"

Her face became confused, lips sputtering. "I–I . . ."

Then she started to say something and stopped. Derec would have given a fortune, ten fortunes, to know the thoughts that had been running through her mind that second before she shut herself up.

"What are you hiding from me?" he asked loudly, in frustration.

Her face was a mixture of pain and longing. She responded by solidifying, as she had done so many times since they'd met on Aranimas's ship. "There's nothing up here for me," she said. "I'm going back down with the robots. Join us quickly. We have other work to do."

Then she turned and departed without a backward glance, leaving Derec angry again. He could feel so close to her, and so far away. There was never any mid-point with Katherine; it was all one way or the other.

He decided to inspect the office methodically, rather than simply tearing furiously into things, which had been his strongest desire. Starting on the outer edges of the room, he traversed it slowly, saving the plum of the desk for last.

He found a small, air-tight shelf full of tapes, all marked "Philosophy," then broken down according to planet. Nearly all of the fifty-five Spacer worlds were represented. They weren't of interest to him at the moment, but a perusal in future wasn't out of the question.

He continued his walk of the outer perimeter, his hand finding the ladder where his eyes couldn't. It was a metal ladder, set against the screen and lost in shadows. Even knowing it was there, he still found it difficult to see. It went up from the floor and stopped at the flat ceiling.

He climbed it until he reached the ceiling screen. There was no reason at all for this ladder to exist unless it went somewhere. Gingerly, he reached out and touched the ceiling screen above the ladder. It gave easily on well-oiled hinges, flapping open to reveal real sky.

He moved up through the trap door to find himself standing on the platform where he had materialized. Amazing. He began to put together a theory. Whoever started this civilization, whoever's arm it was that turned on 1-1, with proper use of a Key to Perihelion, could materialize on Robot City at will, move down into the off-limits office and observe his city's progress without ever being seen. When he was through, he could leave by the same means.

So, the city had an overseer, a guardian, who had apparently brought Derec here to sweeten the mix with the human ingredient. Why Derec? That question, he couldn't answer.

He wondered if the overseer had been present during his and Katherine's stay, if he had been watching them, perhaps all the way up to the moment they opened the office door. It would be simple enough for him to get away. All he'd need was the Key and a few seconds' time.

Derec climbed back into the office and closed the trap door behind him, once again sealing in the illusion completely.

He continued his tour of the office by emptying the small trash can that sat by the desk. The trash can held several empty containers that he recognized as standard Spacer survival rations of good-tasting roughage plus supplementary vitamin and protein pills. He torn open one of the roughage containers to find, in the corner, a small glob of the stuff, which hadn't hardened completely. This food had been eaten within the last twenty-four hours. The rest of the trash was comprised of wadded-up pieces of paper containing mathematical equations relating to the geometric progression of the city-building, which seemed to relate to the time it would take to fill the entire planet with city. Others seemed to be directed to the amounts of rainfall and the reservoir size, quick calculations regarding how long it would take an overflow to occur. Derec had the feeling that if he simply sat in the office and waited an indefinite amount of time, he could probably catch the overseer coming back. Unfortunately, he didn't have an indefinite amount of time.

He put the trash back in the can and directed his attention to the desk itself. The top of the iron-alloy desk contained a blotter with paper and two zero-g ink pens. The only personal item on the desk was a holo-cube containing a scene of a very nice looking woman holding a baby. The sight of the cube sent a cold chill down his back.

He turned his attention to the drawers. On his left were several small drawers, which were, for the most part, empty. Only the top drawer contained anything at all, and that was simply more paper and some technical data on the workings of the logic circuits of the positronic brain. On his right, however, he struck gold. As he opened the big well drawer there, a slight motor hum brought a computer terminal up to desktop level, the screen already active, the cursor flashing: READY.

Interestingly enough, the terminal had all the hook-ups and leads for hyperwave transmission and reception. Unfortunately, the power pack and directional hyperwave antenna were missing from the back, taken, no doubt, by the overseer.

He stared at the terminal in disbelief. No blocks, no passwords, no protections on the system at all. He couldn't believe that an entire civilization would open itself up to him just because he'd found an office. Suppose he'd meant to cause it harm?

Cautiously, he slipped into the scheme of things, working his way down to the level of files, then asking to go to the central core. Once reaching that, he asked to open the file marked: CITY DEFENSES.

Within seconds, the READY signal was flashing again. He was in! Rapidly he typed:

LIST CITY DEFENSES.

The computer answered:

```
CITY DEFENSES:  ADVANCE REPLICATION
                SEAL CONTAMINATION
                HALT CENTRAL CORE INPUT
                MOBILATE CENTRAL CORE
                LOCALIZE EMERGENCY
                   TERMINALS
                ISOLATE SUPERVISORY
                   PERSONNEL
```

He sat, shaking, at the typer. This was it. He decided to try his hand at shutting it down. He typed:

CANCEL REPLICATION.

The computer never hesitated.

CITY DEFENSES CANNOT BE CANCELED WITHOUT JUSTIFICATION AND INPUT REGARDING ALIEN THREAT OR CONTAMINATION.

Derec typed:

OVERRIDE ALL PREVIOUS INSTRUCTIONS AND CANCEL REPLICATION.

The computer answered:

OVERRRIDE IMPOSSIBLE UNDER ALL CIRCUMSTANCES. CITY DEFENSES CANNOT BE CANCELED WITHOUT JUSTIFICATION AND INPUT REGARDING ALIEN THREAT OR CONTAMINATION.

It was a lock-out. The computer refused even to talk to him about it unless he could determine the reason for the defensive measures and provide proper rationalization for termination. It seemed etched in granite. He typed:

LIST REASONS FOR CITY DEFENSE ACTIVATION.

The computer answered with a graph of the city, its shape ever changing, turning slowly. A tiny light was flashing in the section marked Quadrant #4. At the bottom of the screen the computer wrote:

ALIEN CONTAMINATION IN QUADRANT #4.

Derec asked:

CITE NATURE OF CONTAMINATION.

The computer answered:

ALIEN CONTAMINATION IN QUADRANT #4.

He sat back and looked at the machine. It was very possible that the flashing light could represent the body of his look-alike. The machine wasn't going to let him off the hook on the murder. He was beginning to see why it was so easy for him to get into the central core from this terminal, and he received his final confirmation quickly, when he typed:

LIST PROCEDURE FOR DEACTIVATION OF CITY DEFENSES.

The machine replied:

DEACTIVATION PROCEDURE:

    ISOLATE CONTAMINATION OR
      PRESENCE
    DEFINE NATURE OF THREAT
    NEUTRALIZE THREAT
    PROVIDE PROOF OF
      NEUTRALIZATION THRU
      PROCEDURE C-15

Derec typed:

LIST PROCEDURE C-15

And was answered:

PROCEDURE C-15: ISOLATE MOBILATED CENTRAL
      CORE
      ENTER CENTRAL CORE

PROVIDE SUPERVISOR
PASSWORD
ENTER PROOF OF
NEUTRALIZATION

Derec just stared at the screen, frustrated and amazed at what he was looking at. Nothing of consequence could be done from this terminal, or from *any* city terminal, for that matter. Input had to come directly at the central core, and unless he misunderstood the word "mobilate," the central core was not stationary. It was mobile, moving. And to round out the entire business philosophically, a supervisor robot was necessary to enter the defensive program.

It was actually the perfect defense. The act of shutting down the defenses had to be deliberate and calculated and agreed to by *both* human and robot supervision. Again, the system was set up synnoetically, and Derec, despite his disappointment, had to admire it. Ultimately, he really didn't know the form of the contamination. The central core was behaving properly by not granting his requests for deactivation until all the facts were in. The problem, of course, was that city could kill itself before the facts came to light.

He was back where he started, with the murder of his twin. There was still much he could learn from the office and the open terminal, but he simply didn't have the time right now. He reluctantly decided that he'd have to close out for now and return when there was more time.

He had reached out to return the terminal to its berth in the drawer when he thought of something. If the overseer were, indeed, keeping track of them, perhaps there was a file extant with that information. Not knowing his own name, he decided to go with another. Bringing the filename menu back on the screen, he typed in the words:

BURGESS, KATHERINE

The machine answered:

BURGESS, KATHERINE, see DAVID.

His mouth was dry, his heart pounding as he typed in the name of the dead man.

The machine answered quickly, in a notation file obviously set in the overseer's own hand:

ASSIMILATION TEST ON DAVID #2 PROCEEDED ON LINE AND WITHOUT MISHAP UNTIL THE TRIGGERING OF THE CITY DEFENSIVE SYSTEM AND THE DEATH OF SUBJECT THROUGH UNKNOWN MEANS.

WITHOUT HUMAN INTERVENTION, ROBOTS ARE UNABLE TO PREVENT VITAL DAMAGE THROUGH OVER-SUCCESS OF CITY PLANNING AND OPERATION WOULD BE TOTAL FAILURE.

DAVID #1 ARRIVED TO INTERVENE IN CITY CATASTROPHE AND PROCEED WITH ORIGINAL OPERATIONAL TESTING OF SYNNOETIC THEORIES. RESULTS YET TO BE SEEN.

UNCONTROLLED FACTOR ARRIVED WITH DAVID #1 IN THE FORM OF A WOMAN. SHE IS NOW CALLING HERSELF KATHERINE BURGESS FOR REASONS UNKNOWN. HER ULTIMATE INFLUENCE OVER OPERATION AND THE EXACT NATURE OF HER AIMS HAVE YET TO BE DETERMINED.

SHE WILL BE WATCHED CAREFULLY.

That was it, the end of the file. Derec stared at the flashing cursor for a moment, his mind whirling with a dozen different thoughts. But one thought overrode everything else, one sentence burned its way into his brain and hurt him more deeply than he thought possible—SHE IS NOW CALLING HERSELF KATHERINE BURGESS FOR REASONS UNKNOWN.

CHAPTER 10

THE SEALED ROOM

Derec had hoped that when he came out of the overseer's office Katherine would have already been gone, but she wasn't. She stood waiting for him with the two witness robots, a smile on her face as if seeing him somehow made her happy. What an actress. He had to wonder now, once again, what it was she wanted out of all this. He'd once again have to pull in and play it by ear where she was concerned. Perhaps she'd say something to give herself away. Meanwhile, she'd get no satisfaction.

"How did it go?" she asked cheerily, but then her face changed, tightened up when she noticed his mood swing. "What's wrong?"

"Nothing . . . Katherine," he said, her phony name sticking in his throat. "I found an exit to the top platform, and a computer, but nothing in it helped any, except to tell me what we already knew—that we'd have to solve the murder."

"Well then, I think we should stop wasting time and get on to that," she said suspiciously, not quite believing his change of attitude. "Are you sure you're okay?"

"Never better," he lied, angry at himself for wanting to be close to her despite what he'd learned. If he had any sense, he'd turn and run as fast and as far as he could from her. Instead, he said, "Let's go."

They moved out of the Compass Tower quickly and quietly, Katherine watching Derec out of the corner of her eye most of the time. He tried to be more nonchalant to keep from arousing her suspicions, but it was difficult for him. He apparently wasn't as schooled in subterfuge as she. As they made their way through the building, robots paid them no attention, already becoming familiar and comfortable with human presence.

When they stepped outside, they found a tram with a utility driver atop it, waving to them. "Friend Derec!" the robot called, and they moved over to the tram.

"What is it?" Derec asked the squat driver.

"Supervisor Euler asked me to be your driver today, honoring an earlier request you made in regard to transportation."

"Well," Derec said, looking at Katherine, "it appears that we're finally being trusted a little bit. Our own tram, eh?"

"It's radio-controlled," the utility robot said.

Derec narrowed his brows. "What's its range?"

"The range of the control is roughly equivalent to the limits of the already extruded city."

"Oh," Derec said quietly. "You mean that the tram won't operate except in city limits?"

"A fair appraisal," the robot said.

Katherine laughed loudly. "Now *that's* what I call trust," she said, and shook her head.

He glared at her and climbed into the tram. "Rec," he told his witness, "why don't you ride up here with me?"

The robot dutifully climbed in beside Derec, leaving Katherine to sit with her witness in the seat behind.

"Where to, sir?" the tram driver asked.

Derec turned to Katherine. "You know where we're going?"

"Quadrant #4," Katherine replied. "Eve will show you from there."

They drove on quickly. Derec, for the first time, took a moment to think about the other things that had happened in the office, things that were pushed out of his mind by his anger toward Katherine. His name, for instance. He was called David #1 on the computer record. Then why did he come *after* David #2? Was it a simple experiment shorthand, or did the name have meaning? It sounded so ... engineered. The thoughts generated by that line of reasoning were more than he could bear. He pushed them away and thought that if his name was, indeed, David, then Katherine *had* told him the truth; at least about that.

There were other concepts implied in those few paragraphs. Whoever the overseer was, he obviously knew David and Katherine, and knew something of their past histories. So whoever had brought him here was someone he'd known before his memory loss, and he couldn't help but consider the possibility that the overseer had had something to do with his memory loss. But the chances were just as good, if not better, that Katherine herself had been connected with his amnesia for her own purposes, whatever they were.

Layers and layers. So much had been implied by the notes on the computer. The city was, indeed, considered an experiment in synnoetics, of that much he could now be certain. But then, when it came time to deal with a reason for the defense system going operational, the overseer seemed just as much in the dark as he, himself, was.

Derec also wasn't sure if he had been deliberately brought here to help the city, or if he had shown up accidentally, the overseer deciding to the use him, as opposed to either stepping in himself or letting the operation shut itself down. The more answers he found, it seemed, the more in the dark he was.

They arrived at quadrant #4 without difficulty. Eve took her triangulation readings to help them find their way back to the house on the pedestal. Derec watched the city developing all around him as they drove, the sight of humans driving the inhabitants into a frenzy of human preparation—the robot equivalent of nesting.

"This is the place," Eve said as the tram stopped in the middle of an ordinary-looking street. The witness looked all around. "It doesn't appear to be here."

"It's moved some, that's all," Katherine said. "We'll go on foot from this point."

They climbed out of the tram and started walking, the tram following close behind them in case they had need of it.

"You sure this is the right direction?" Derec asked, after they had gone a block. "How far could it have moved?"

"Everything looks familiar here," she replied.

"The whole city looks the same," Derec said. "I don't think you . . ."

"There!" She pointed.

Derec needed no pointing finger to tell him they'd arrived. A tall tower stood in the middle of a street, nothing else anywhere near it. Atop the tower was a single room, sealed up except for a circular hole cut out of it.

"Let's leave a witness here with the tram in the case of problems," Derec said. "We'll take Rec up with us."

"Fine," Katherine replied, walking to the pole.

He followed her, watching the spiral staircase reform when she touched the pole with her hand.

"You're not going to believe this," she told him, starting confidently up the stairs. "If this man's not your twin, he went to an awful lot of trouble to look just like you."

Derec smiled weakly in return, wondering, given the fact that he was #4, just who was whose twin.

She reached the top, waiting off to the side for him to join her. "I want you to go in first," she said. "After what happened last time, I'm afraid of my reactions. I may have to work up to it."

"All right," he said, moving around to the cut-out. As he got close to the place, he felt his own insides jumping a bit at the thought of seeing himself dead. He got right up to the cut-out, then quickly ducked his head in before he changed his mind.

It was empty.

He climbed through; there was no sign of a body or anything that resembled a body or anything else for that matter.

"Katherine," he called. "Come around here."

She moved to the cut-out, shyly poking her head inside, her eyes widening when she saw the empty room. "Where is he?" she asked.

"That was my question," Derec replied. "It appears that our corpse has gotten up and walked away.

"Or was taken away," she returned. "Remember what happened when he died? A utility robot had to fight waste control robots for possession of the corpse. Maybe they got him this time."

"Didn't anyone stay behind when you passed out before to keep that from happening?"

"I don't know," Katherine said, and went back out the

cut-out to call down to her witness. "Eve! Did anyone stay behind after I fell unconscious yesterday?"

"No," the robot called back up. "You were our first priority. We all did our parts to get you home safely and to get you medical attention."

Katherine came back into the room. "No one stayed behind," she said.

"I heard," Derec replied. "Pretty convenient."

"Convenient for whom?" she said, eyes flashing. "What are you driving at?"

"Nothing," he replied. "I'm just . . . disappointed."

"*You're* disappointed," she said, sitting on the floor and leaning against the wall. "This was my ticket out of here."

"Just like you," he said, "thinking about yourself while the whole world crumbles around you."

Her eyes were dark fire. "And just who should I think about?" she asked. "The buckets of bolts who run this place, who don't have enough sense to keep from destroying themselves?"

"Like every other human culture that ever lived," he replied. "Yes. Think about them . . ." He pointed at her, then snapped his fingers. "Maybe we don't need a body for this. Maybe we can simply recreate the circumstances."

"You mean try and set it all up just like it happened to the dead man?"

"Sure. The computer in the office told me that there is danger from alien contamination. Let's see if we can bring it out a little."

Katherine stood again, her face uncertain. "Need I remind you that the last man who had to face up to this predicament is dead?"

He walked past her, out onto the now inward-curled disc

that held the room, watching the robots on the streets hurrying to their deadlines through time and space. She joined him within a minute.

"What choice do we have?" he asked.

"None," she answered. "Both of our problems are tied up in the murder. We'll do whatever we have to, to solve it."

"Let's go over everything the witness told you," Derec said. "Look for a loophole."

"It's sparse," Katherine replied. "He was already sealed up, and angry about it, when they arrived to cut him out. He had no idea why he'd been sealed in. When they cut him out, his behavior seemed a bit erratic, he had a headache and a cut on his foot."

"Didn't you have a headache last night?" he asked.

She cocked her head. "I just assumed it had something to do with my passing out," she said.

"Just a thought," Derec replied. "I'm trying everything on for size right now."

"Anyway," she continued, "he went off, against supervisory request, and turned up dead a short time later. When the utility robot tried to turn the body over to take a pulse, another room sealed itself off, and the robot just barely survived the sealing because of his quick reflexes. That's it. The whole story."

He leaned against the curled lip of the disc on stiff arms, trying to reason the way a computer would. "You know," he said after a minute, "the phrase 'alien contamination' could cover a lot of territory. On surface, human beings and their composition are obvious. But, under the surface, on the body's interior, we're all quite a strange collection of 'alien' germs and viruses."

"The bleeding foot," Katherine said. "That thought occurred to me, but I was never able to connect it with the actual murder, so I assumed it to be inconsequential."

"Me too," Derec replied. "But I'm beginning to think that, perhaps, this puzzle works on more than the obvious level." He knelt on the ground, studying the cut-out piece of city-robot that lay on the disc surface.

"What are you doing?" Katherine asked.

"This piece has been taken off stream," he said. "It's not connected to the city anymore, or to its programming source."

"So?"

"So it's dead, it's the only thing around here that isn't going to protect me from its jagged edges."

"You're going to hurt yourself!" she said loudly.

"There's only one way to test our theory," he said, rolling up the sleeve of his one-piece.

Rec poked his head out of the room. "Please, Friend Derec, don't do anything that could cause harm to your body."

Derec ignored both Katherine and Rec, drawing his forearm across a sharp edge of the dead city part, making a five-centimeter gash along his inner arm.

He stood, grimacing with the pain, then watched the dark blood well up from the place.

"Nothing yet," Katherine said.

"Let's try an experiment," Derec said, turning his arm over so the blood could drip on the disc. "The second sealed room didn't develop until the utility robot rolled the body over. Maybe gravity . . ."

"Derec!" Katherine yelled.

No sooner had the blood hit the floor than the curled

lip of the disc began growing, pushing in and up, trying to close them in.

"Let's get out of here!" Derec called, moving toward the stairs, the disc curling up over his head like a cresting wave as he moved.

With Katherine right behind, he reached the stairs leading down, only to have them disappear before he could plant a foot on them. Overhead, the roof of the already existing room was stretching itself out, joining the edge of the disc in a perfect, seamless weld. Where the stairs had been was now a solid wall.

"Keep moving around the disc!" Derec called, breaking into a trot. "Maybe we can beat the enclosure."

He had turned his arm back over now, trying to catch dripping blood on his free hand to keep it off the ground. But it didn't help. The city-robot had isolated him as the alien carrier and was reacting to *him* now, and not his blood.

They went around the perimeter of the room, the roof hurrying to meet the curling disc. It had closed them in completely.

Then, as they watched, the already existing room seemed to melt and combine with the floor, the outer walls straightening and angling to ninety degrees, then pushing in all around.

Within a minute, they found themselves standing in a sealed room, exactly like the one David had been cut out of.

CHAPTER 11

DEADLY AIR

Derec and Katherine sat on the floor of the room, while Rec, who'd been trapped with them, leaned close to Derec, witnessing the boy wrapping his cut arm in a piece of cloth ripped from his one-piece.

"Do you think Eve's called for help?" he asked Rec as he worked.

"No," the witness said. "Eve will not perceive a danger to you. Are you in danger?"

"What about the utility robot?" Katherine asked, ignoring the robot's question. "Will the utility robot summon help?"

"That is within the scope of the utility robot's field prerogatives," Rec replied, straightening as Derec finished. He then wheeled slowly around the room, taking everything in for later recounting. Rec took his job very seriously.

Derec had left two loose ends on the tight bandage, and held his arm out to Katherine to tie them. "Can I trust you to tie a good knot?" he asked.

"What's that supposed to mean?" she asked.

404

"Nothing," he said.

She frowned deeply as she tied. "What happened in that office?" she asked. "You've treated me like your worst enemy ever since you came out of there." She pulled the knot tight, a smile touching her lips when he groaned loudly.

"Look," he said. "You've got secrets, I've got secrets. Why don't we just leave it at that?"

"Fine with me," she said. "All I want is for us to get the rest of this together; then I'll make an emergency hyperwave call and be out of your hair in less than a day. You can rot here for all I care."

"We'll both rot here," he said, wanting to hurt her.

She drew back. "What do you mean?"

"Nothing."

"Damn you!" she yelled. "Tell me what you mean? Why did you say I'd rot here?"

"No reason."

"It's the hyperwave, isn't it?" she asked. "They won't give us access to the hyperwave."

"It's not that, it's . . ."

"It's what? What?"

He leaned his head back and shut his eyes. "There is no hyperwave transmitter," he said softly.

She pulled herself a distance from him and curled into a small ball. "You're lying," she said, but he could tell that she really believed him.

"The robots have no contact with the outside," he said. "They have no spaceport for landing ships. They have no hyperwave, or even the equipment for making one. They've been evasive about the point because of the security alert."

"Why have you waited until now to tell me this?" she asked.

"I told you—you've got secrets, I've got secrets."

"I get it now," she said, her eyes distant. "We're both free agents, looking out for ourselves."

"Something like that," he said, but why did it hurt so bad to say it?

She stood and moved all the way across the room to sit on the wall opposite. "Well, I suppose, at this point, we must work together to solve the murder," she said.

"I suppose," he replied, sorry to have started the whole line of conversation.

Her face was hard. "After that, I will thank you to stay away from me. We'll each take care of our own problems."

"Fair enough."

"So tell me, if it's not a great secret, why the room sealed around us because you cut yourself?"

"I've got a theory, nothing more," he said. "The city-robot is programmed to protect human and robot inhabitants and to defend itself against anything alien . . . foreign to it. Apparently blood inside the body is fine, but once it gets outside the body, its natural microbes register as alien and set off the works. The city program has to be fairly complicated. The omission is obvious, and could either have been a mistake or a deliberate glitch to test the ability of the robots and humans living here to control their own system."

"What do we do now?"

"Well, once we get out, if I can get access to the central core with one of the supervisors, I can reprogram the core to accept human blood as a natural microbe on the body of the city. In this sterile atmosphere, it's perfectly understandable how such a glitch could happen. It could even be a means for the city to protect itself from infection."

"But how did David die?" Katherine asked.

"Could it have been blood loss?" Derec asked.

She shook her head. "No chance," she replied. "There was very little blood. The cut was smaller than yours."

"What's left?" he said. "I have to think that his death is a completely separate incident, unconnected to the blood loss."

She looked skeptical. "Back-to-back coincidences, Derec? Deadly coincidence at that."

He stood. "You're right, of course. It must all tie together . . . but how?" He paced the room. "What other leads do we have? The only other connection is the fact that both of you came away from a sealed room with a headache."

"We have another problem," she replied, watching him moving back and forth in the confined space. "When I came in this room the first time to find the body, it had been sealed up . . . air tight."

He stopped walking and stared at her. "The city would never keep us locked up without air. It would be a violation of the First Law, should we die."

"It happened to David."

"But David was already dead when it happened to him," Derec said. "In fact, this just strengthens my theory. When the utility robot rolled him over to check for signs of life, gravity pulled a little more blood out of an already open wound. The room didn't relate to David as a human, since he was dead. All it fixed its sights on was the 'infection.' We're still alive and the city-robot knows it. Whatever else this crazy place may be, it's run robotically. Ipso facto, we're safe on that account."

"Just the same," she said, "I'll be happier to be out of here."

"Me too."

"You realize, Derec," she said, her voice low and heavy with meaning, "that we are recreating history right now.

We are going through exactly the same progression that David went through before he died."

"I know," Derec replied. "But what else can we do?"

They stared at one another across the space of the room, the witness recording it all, and they may as well have been a million kilometers apart. They sat that way for a long time, far longer than it should have taken for a supervisor to show up.

Derec spent the time alternately trying to think his way out of their dilemma, figure out what was going on with Katherine, and looking at his watch. And the late morning turned to early afternoon, and Derec, who wasn't worried about the air supply in the room, suddenly became very thirsty and began to dwell on the possibility that the robots had either forgotten them or couldn't find them.

"Friend Derec!" came a loud voice from outside the room. "Friend Katherine! It is I, Wohler, the philosopher!"

Derec glanced at his watch. It was nearly five P.M., which meant rain was undoubtedly on the way. "We're in here!" Derec called. "Can you get us free?"

Wohler called back loudly, "An Auroran philosopher once said, 'Freedom is a condition of mind, and the best way to secure it is to breed it.' Ho, Derec. We were held up digging in the mines, but I now have a laser torch to cut you out. I am here on the west wall of this room. I will ask kindly that you move to the east wall to avoid the torch as well as possible!"

Derec was sitting against the west wall. He stood immediately and moved over near Katherine, who looked at him with unreadable eyes.

"Go ahead!" Derec yelled through cupped hands, Rec moving up closer to the west wall to witness the torching from the inside.

Even through the thickness of the wall, they could hear
the hiss of the torch on the other side. Derec slid down the
wall to sit next to Katherine. Their arms accidentally
touched. Both of them pulled away.

"Something's wrong," she said. "Something feels wrong."

"I know," he replied, "but what?"

The inside of the wall began to glow red hot in a small,
circular section. Then the red turned to white, and a rivet-
sized section burned through to reveal the outside through
a quivering haze of heat.

Derec watched the hole expand, his mind racing as the
torch began to etch the beginnings of a human-sized circle in
the side of the room. He thought about headaches, and about
erratic behavior and about blood and its composition—and
then he thought about the nature of the city-robot.

"Stop!" he yelled, jumping to his feet and running as
close to the metal cutting as he dared. "Stop the torch!"

"Derec?" Katherine asked, beginning to stand.

Derec covered his mouth with his hand. "Get on the
floor!" he yelled. "All the way down and cover your
mouth!"

"What's wrong?" came Wohler's voice from outside, the
sound of the laser winding down to nothing. "What is it?"

"We can't use the torch on the wall!" Derec called.

"I don't understand," Wohler said, bending down so
that his eye covered the hole in the wall and he could look
inside.

Derec backed away, getting down close to Katherine on
the floor. "Is there some way to flush oxygen in here?" he
asked loudly.

"We've come in a newly manufactured emergency
truck," Wohler replied. "I believe the emergency equipment
includes oxygen cylinders."

"Get one quickly!"

"The rains are approaching," Wohler said. "We must hurry and get you out."

"Listen," Derec said. "The city material is a kind of metallic skin, an iron/plastic alloy. In the manufacturing process, a great deal of carbon monoxide is used as the reducing agent. I think your torch is liberating the monoxide as a gas into the closed room. By cutting us out, you're gassing us!"

"The utility robot has gone for the oxygen!" Wohler said. "You have my apologies."

"You didn't know," Derec said. He looked at Katherine. "Are you all right?"

"So far," she replied. "Are you sure of what you're saying? David didn't die until later, outside of the room."

"It doesn't matter," he replied. "Carbon monoxide in large doses will simply work its way gradually through the bloodstream, bonding firmly with hemoglobin and starving the tissues of oxygen. His headache and erratic behavior were the first signs of an oxygen narcosis reaction and, unless he was treated to massive doses of oxygen, it would spread throughout his entire body, eventually killing him."

"And *my* headache?"

"You walked into the room with his body just after they had cut through the walls," he said. "You undoubtedly saved your own life by passing out when you did, for they took you out of the room immediately, thus limiting your exposure to the gas. Carbon monoxide is colorless, odorless, and tasteless. You would never have known what hit you."

"The oxygen is here, Derec!" Wohler called, fitting a hissing nozzle up against the hole.

Derec crawled across the floor toward the hole. "Come on," he said, waving her on.

They reached the hole and sat breathing the life-giving oxygen. Derec felt the beginnings of a small headache, but he was sure it would get no worse.

They emptied the cannister of oxygen and began another. When that was finished, Wohler returned to the opening. "Rain is imminent," the robot said. "How do we get you out? We have nothing small to cut through this, and our heavy equipment can't be brought up this high, at least not with the rain coming. Do we leave you for the night?"

"There's no time for that," Derec said. "I must get underground and report this information to the central core."

"The rain is also dangerous for me, Friend Derec," Wohler said. "I must take shelter soon."

"Okay," Derec said. "Stay with me as long as you can. Just let me think for a minute."

"Derec . . ." Katherine began.

"Shhh," Derec said. "Not now."

"Think about your arm," she said. "Think about where you cut it, and how."

"My arm, I . . ." He held his arm up, looking at the blood-soaked bandage and feeling the throb. "I cut it on the dead piece of city-robot," he said.

"Because . . ."

"Because it was the only piece of the city that would *allow* me to cut myself on it!" He put his hands to his head. "That's it! Wohler! Stand back. We're coming through."

With that, he raised his right hand, pushing his pointer finger through the small, burned-out hole. As soon as his finger grazed the jagged edge of the hole, it expanded to allow free passage. Next came his balled-up fist; the hole expanded wide to keep from cutting him. Then his arm went through, followed by head and shoulders. Seconds later, he was standing on the disc, its edges curling up to protect him. Katherine followed him through, and both of them stared into the teeth of a bitter cold wind and a savage vision of blue-purple clouds crackling with lightning.

"We must go now!" Wohler said, his shiny gold body reflecting lightning flashes.

Suddenly, Katherine broke from the group, hurrying to the stairs.

"What are you doing?" Derec called to her, but she ignored him, charging as quickly as she could down the stairs.

"Perhaps she's hurrying to safety," Wohler said, as Rec made it through the hole in the wall.

"Perhaps," Derec said, but as he ran the rest of the disc and began to take the stairs, Katherine had already run to the tram that was still dutifully waiting. She barked some orders to the utility driver, and the unit sped off into the darkening night.

"What is happening?" Wohler called as he followed Derec down the stairs.

"I'm afraid something crazy," the boy answered, remembering a conversation they had had while waiting to be rescued.

They moved to the emergency van that Wohler had brought. "We must get you back to your apartment before the rain comes," the robot said.

"No!" Derec said. "Get me underground. I'll wait out the storm there. Then you've got to go after Katherine. I'm afraid of what she's doing."

A long streak of lightning struck the top of the pedestal right beside them, the metal clanging loudly and smoking.

"But where could she have gone, Friend Derec?" Wohler asked as they all climbed aboard the large, white van.

"The Compass Tower," Derec said, voice heavy with dread. "I'm afraid she's climbing the Compass Tower."

CHAPTER 12

THE THIRD LAW

The Quadrant #4 Extruder Station was less than ten minutes from the sealed room, with Wohler moving the emergency van along at the top speed possible that still allowed a safety margin for his passengers.

Derec watched the city speed past, its full-blown dance of thoughtless progress still continuing despite the gathering darkness, despite the fact that its course was suicidal. He feared for the city; he feared for Katherine, or whatever her name was. She was going for the Key, he was certain of that, trying to take herself out of the situation in the only way she knew how. He didn't expect that the Key would do her much good, but he could hardly blame her for trying. What frightened him was the danger she was exposing herself to by trying for the Key in the rain. He would have gone after her alone, but, having experienced the destructive power of Robot City's weather, he knew he'd be no help at all in a storm. Only a robot would have a chance.

Wohler jerked them to a stop before the Extruder Station entrance, a series of low, wide buildings constructing themselves from ground level. There was no robotic activity here now, no unloading of trucks. All had taken shelter from the impending storm.

"You think she's gone to the Compass Tower?" Wohler asked.

"I'm sure of it."

"She may have time before the storm to get inside to safety."

Derec looked at him, then reached out and put a hand on his shiny gold arm. "She's not going inside," he said. "She'll be trying to climb the pyramid."

"But why?"

"We hid something there, something she's trying to retrieve."

"I must go," Wohler said without hesitation. "She'll be killed."

"What will the rain do to you?" Derec asked as he climbed out of the van.

"Rain in ordinary amounts won't do anything," the robot replied. "City rain could force its way through my plating in a thousand different places and make its way into my electrical system. The limits of the damage at that point are a matter of imaginative speculation."

"I don't know what to tell you," Derec said. "If you don't go . . ."

"Katherine will die," the robot finished. "You can tell me nothing. My duty is self-evident. Good-bye, Derec."

Wohler looked back once to make sure the witnesses were off the van, then hurried off at a pace that didn't include the safety margin he had preserved with Derec in the cab.

"Come with me," Derec told the witnesses, and moved

toward the now-closed entrance to the underground. Despite his fears for Katherine's safety, he had things to do. With his explanation of the murder and its connection to the city defenses, backed up totally by Rec's witness testimony, there was no doubt that he'd at least be able to get into the core and stop the replication. That wouldn't stop tonight's rain, however, or even future rains for a time; but it was a start.

He opened the outside door, then hurried inside, going down the stairs to the now-deserted holding area and its bank of elevators. This wasn't the same Extruder Station he'd been in previously, but it was set up exactly the same.

He walked quickly to the same elevator he had taken with Avernus when he'd gone underground. He got inside with the witnesses and pushed the down arrow. The lift began its long journey to the caverns below.

The elevator opened into the bustling cavern where the work of building Robot City continued unabated. There wasn't a supervisor in sight, however. There seemed to be activity at one of the darkened, unused mine tunnels at the west end of the cavern.

He began to move into the flow, then stopped, steeling himself. Deliberation, Avernus had said. As he stood on the edge of the activity, a long tram sped past him at a hundred kilometers an hour, passing within a few centimeters, his hair being pulled by its suction.

Deliberation. It was the only way.

"Stay with me," he told the witnesses. Then he set his body in line with his goal and shut his eyes, taking a blind step right into the fray.

He walked quickly, without hesitation, trying to direct his mind away from the feel of unrushing robots and vehicles that barely brushed him as they hurried past. Occasionally, he would open his eyes a touch, just to make sure he was still heading in the right direction. Then he'd squeeze them closed again, and keep walking.

He kept this up for nearly ten minutes as he crossed the great chamber without mishap. As he reached the safety of the mine entrance, he released a huge sigh that made him feel as if he'd been holding his breath the whole time.

A utility robot was stationed near the mine entrance, using an overhead pulley system to remove the spent batteries from a fleet of mine trams and replacing them with charged batteries. The trams were parked three deep all around him.

"Robot!" Derec called across the cars to him. "Where can I find Supervisor Avernus?"

The utility robot pointed down the tunnel. "They are releasing some of the reservoir water into the abandoned tunnels. It may be dangerous for humans."

"Thanks," Derec said, then pointed to a tram. "Has this one been recharged?"

"Yes," the robot answered.

"Thanks again," Derec said, and climbed behind the steering mechanism. "Rec, Eve, get in."

As the robots climbed into the back of the tram, the utility called to Derec.

"Did you not hear me? It may be dangerous for humans in there."

"Thanks," Derec said again, waving, then keyed on the electric hum and geared the car down the dark tunnel.

As he sped down the tunnels, marking distance by counting the small, red lights spaced along the length, he passed other trams full of robots going the other way. There were uniformly dirty from digging, many of them dangling shorted-out appendages. Even for robots, they appeared grim. One tram they passed carried a robot shorting from the head, sparks arcing from his photocells and speaker.

He drove for several kilometers, climbing gently upward with the tunnel. Finally, he approached a large egg of light that threw long shadows against the rough-hewn walls. When he reached the place, he found a large number of utility robots, plus six of the seven supervisors, gathered around a drop-off in the tunnel.

He jumped from the tram and pushed his way through the crowd to approach the drop-off. It was the same area in which the robots had been digging the day before, only approached from the other side. A subsidiary tunnel, going upward, had been dug by hand, and it met the existing tunnel, which had been trenched out to carry water. The trench was empty. Euler and Rydberg were leaning out over the trench, looking up the newly dug tunnel, while Avernus sorted out those robots damaged beyond usefulness here, and sent them back down the tunnel.

Derec moved up to Euler. "I've solved the murder," he told the supervisor without preamble.

Both Rydberg and Euler turned to look at him. "What was the cause?" Rydberg asked.

"Carbon monoxide poisoning," Derec said. "When they tried to torch David out of the sealed room, carbon monoxide was released by the heating process into the enclosed space."

"It was our fault, then," Euler said.

"It was an unfortunate accident," Derec replied. "And I have witnesses." Both Eve and Rec hurried to join him.

"Two minutes," Dante called. The small robot was fiddling with a terminal hooked up in the back of a tram, his long digits moving with incredible speed over the keyboard.

"Two minutes until what?" Derec asked.

"Until the charge we placed by the reservoir wall brings the water down," Euler replied.

"I also know why the city is on security alert," Derec said. "It was because of David's blood. When he cut himself, the blood that dropped on the city-robot was mistaken for an alien presence because of the blood organisms. My witnesses will also corroborate that fact."

Euler spoke up. "Then we need to feed this information to the central core and stop the replication, if there's time."

"What do you mean, if there's time?" Derec asked.

Avernus joined the group. "We found a cavern that would hold all the water in the reservoir, thanks to your sonogram. Unfortunately, it will take a great deal of digging to reach it." Avernus pointed to the trench. "This diversion will do no more than put off the inevitable for one more day; then, instead of overflowing above, the water will overflow below, here in the tunnels."

"Where is the central core?" Derec asked. "If we can get to it and stop the replication, then we can use the digging machines to turn the trick before the next day's rain."

Avernus turned to Dante, looking at him over the heads of all the other robots. "Where is the core now?" he called loudly.

The little robot's digits flew over the keys while Euler spoke. "Even with the machines, we'd have to start digging almost immediately to reach the cavern in time."

"The core is in Tunnel J-33 at the moment," Dante called, "moving south by southwest at ten kilometers per hour." He hesitated briefly, then added, "Twenty centads."

Avernus turned abruptly from them all. "That is . . . too bad," he said.

"What do you mean, too bad?" Derec asked.

All at once, there was a rumble that shook the tunnel,

dust and loose pebbles falling atop them. Derec nearly lost his footing on the quaking ground. Within seconds, a low roar filled the mines, growing in intensity with each passing second.

"It is too bad," Euler said loudly above the roar, "because the central core is in Tunnel J-33, on the wrong side of the trench, and the rains are beginning outside."

With that, tons of water came rushing down the new tunnel, slamming in fury into the trench below, churning, forthy white, dangerous and untamed. Derec watched in horrified fascination as his only possible route to the central core disappeared under a raging river that hadn't been there a second before.

Katherine's mind was as dark as the clouds overhead as her tram hurried through the streets of Robot City in the direction of the Compass Tower.

"I fear we won't make the Tower before the rains come," the utility driver told her. "We must take shelter."

"No," she said, determined that she'd keep them from taking away her last ounce of free will. "Go on. Hurry!"

"It is not safe for you out here," the robot insisted. "I cannot in all conscience take you any farther."

Katherine began to respond with anger, but feared it would arouse the robot's suspicions. "All right," she said. "Pull over at the next building."

"Very good," the robot replied, and brought the tram to an immediate stop before a tall building that had the words MUSEUM OF ART embossed in metal above the doors.

The robot got out of the tram and took Katherine by the arm to guide her. "This way, please," he said, and Katherine began to think the robots had been having meetings about human duplicity.

She allowed the robot to lead her into the confines of the building. "This is Supervisor Arion's project," he said, "to please our human inhabitants."

She looked around, taking note that the robot had used the word *inhabitant* instead of visitors. It merely confirmed what she already knew to be the case. They weren't going to let her go. They had no intention of letting her go. The robots needed someone to serve, and they'd keep the masters as slaves just to see that it came to be.

The first floor of the museum was full of geometric sculptures, many of them made from city material that moved through its own sequences, constantly changing shapes in an infinite variety of patterns.

After a moment, she asked, "Please, is it possible to contact Derec and tell him where we are? I'm afraid he'll worry."

"There should be a terminal in the curator's office," the robot replied. "Would you like me to do it for you?"

"Yes, please. I would be most grateful."

The robot hurried off immediately. As soon as he was out of sight at the far end of the building, Katherine turned and ran.

She got quickly out the front doors and down the short walk to the tram, taking the driver's position. It started up easily, and she was off. She had no idea of which streets to take to get to the pyramid, but its size made it a beacon. She simply kept moving toward it.

She concentrated on planning as she drove. The rain was very close now, and she didn't want to get caught in it, but it was worth the try to get out of the city. Derec had said there was a trap door from the office to the platform atop the structure. She'd go through the inside of the pyramid, then, to reach the top. The Key was hidden partway down the outside of the structure, and it would be far easier and faster to climb down from the top than to climb up.

The sky rumbled loudly as she drove; the wind whipped her long hair around her face. She was cold, but put it out of her mind as she concentrated on her objective. Why did he have to do it to her? Why did he have to go over to the other side? The city had become Derec's obsession. He apparently couldn't understand that she had to have freedom, that she couldn't live within its structure forever.

The pyramid loomed large before her. It lit up brightly as a bolt of lightning ran down its face. She skidded to a stop before it and jumped out of the tram, hearing a noise behind her.

There, two blocks distant, the robot that called itself Wohler was hurrying to intercept her. She turned and ran up to the entry. The city material melted away at her approach to allow her inside.

Once inside, she had no idea of where she was going. The only thing she remembered for sure was that she needed to keep going up. She ran the maze-like halls, taking every opportunity to climb stairs or take an elevator that would put her higher. About halfway up the structure, she heard an announcement over unseen loudspeakers that called attention to her flight and gave instructions for her apprehension.

At that, she doubled her pace, going full out. Her only hope of escaping was to reach the safety of the off-limits zone before she was spotted.

She hurried unseen down the now-shortened hallways, reaching the last elevator up. A tech robot with welder arms spotted her as she hurried inside. Heart pounding, she stabbed at the up arrow and the machine sped her quickly to the upper floor.

The doors slid open and she burst through, running immediately. There were voices behind, calling her by name. She turned a corner, ran up a short ramp, and burst into the off-limits hallway just as the robots behind were closing on her.

She ran to the door leading up to the office, her hand going to the power stud.

"Katherine."

She recognized Wohler's voice and turned to face him. He stood, a hallway full of robots behind him, at the edge of the off-limits zone, the same place the witnesses had stopped earlier in the day.

"What do you want?" she asked.

"Come away from there. This place is off-limits."

She smiled. "Not to me," she said. "I'm human, remember? I'm free, and I'm going to be freer."

"Please do not go outside," Wohler said. "The rains are beginning. It could be dangerous for you."

"You're not going to keep me here," she said, opening the door that faced the spiral staircase.

"We would love to have you stay with us," the robot said, "but we would never keep you here against your will."

"Then why don't you have the means on-planet for me to leave or call for help?"

"You act as if we brought you here under false pretenses," Wohler said. "We did nothing. You came here uninvited. Welcome . . . but uninvited. Our civilization has not developed to the point where planetary interaction is possible. You can see that for yourself."

"We're wasting time," Katherine said, and started through the door.

"Please reconsider," the robot called. "Don't put yourself in jeopardy."

She stared hard at him. "I've been in jeopardy every second I've been in this crazy place."

With that, she moved through the door, closing it behind her. She took the stairs quickly and entered the office. The angry clouds rolled up close to the viewers, making it seem as if she were standing in the midst of the gathering storm.

Searching the office, she found the ladder easily enough, climbing it to reach the windy platform above. The wind was so strong that she feared getting to her feet, and crawled to the edge where she and Derec had made their first treacherous descent into the city of robots.

For the first time since being freed from the sealed room, her fears began to overcome her anger at the situation as she turned her body to edge herself off the dizzying height to begin her climb downward. The wind pulled viciously at her like cold, prying hands; her ears and nose went numb, and her fingers tingled with the cold.

Though the pyramid was made from the same material as the rest of the city, it wasn't the same in any other respect. It was rigid and unbending, its face set with patterns of holes that she and Derec had used as hand and footholds previously, and in which they had hidden the Key on their first descent.

Her mind whirled as she climbed, slowly, so slowly. How far down had it been? She had been moving fast, and Derec, carrying the Key, had been unable to keep up. They had stopped for a conference and decided to hide the Key and continue without it. How far down? A fourth of the climb, barely a fourth, in the leftmost hole of the pattern that ran down the center of the structure.

She continued downward, her fingers hurting now, her eyes looking upward, trying to gauge her distance just right.

She began testing the holes in the repeated pattern, to no avail. She still hadn't reached the place. Something wet and cold hit her hard on the back. Her hands almost pulled out of their holds reflexively. It was a raindrop, and it wet the entire back of her one-piece.

She was running out of time.

The pattern of holes repeated again as she inched downward, and when she looked up, squinting against the frigid wind, she *knew* she had reached the place.

Hugging the pyramid face with the last of her strength, she slowly reached out, sticking her hand into the leftmost hole of the pattern.

The Key was gone.

"No!" she screamed loudly into the teeth of the monster, and, as if in response, the rain tore from the heavens in blinding, bludgeoning sheets to silence her protests.

Derec stood at the exit door to the Extruder Station and listened to the rain pounding against the door, and watched the small puddle that had somehow made its way under the sealed entry. Katherine was out there somewhere, and Wohler. Nothing had been heard from either of them since before the start of the rain. Avernus had made contact with the Compass Tower, and though both had been seen there, neither was there now.

With the rain controlling the day, everything had come to a standstill, making searching impossible, making contact with the central core impossible, making everything except the almighty building project slow to nothing. It was maddening.

He pounded the door, his fist sinking in, cushioning. He wanted to open those doors and run into the city and find her for himself—but he knew what that meant. Most likely, nothing would be known until the rain abated the next morning.

He turned from the door and walked down the stairs to the holding area and the six robot supervisors who awaited him there. His mind was awash in anxiety.

"Supervisor Rydberg has proposed a plan, Friend Derec," Euler said. "Perhaps you will comment on it."

Derec looked at Rydberg, trying to bring his mind back to the present. Why did the woman affect him this way? "Let's hear your plan," he said.

"We can go ahead and devise our evacuation schedule for the robots working underground," Rydberg said. "It seems that when morning comes, you will be able to contact the core and halt the replication. It will be too late to dig through to the cavern in time, but at least we will have the opportunity to spare our mine workers before the floods."

"Why do you have to give up like this?" Derec said, exasperated. "You've heard the reasons for the defenses. Can't you just stop them now and use the digging equipment to begin excavating the cavern?"

Waldeyer, the squat, wheeled supervisor, said, "The central core is our master program. We cannot abandon it. Only the central core can judge the veracity of your statements and make the final decision."

"I'm going to reprogram the central core," Derec answered, too loudly. "I'm going to change its definition of 'veracity.' And besides, the Laws of Robotics are your master program, and the Second Law states that you will obey a human command unless it violates the First Law. I'm *commanding* you to halt the mining processes and begin digging through to the drainage cavern."

"The defensive procedures were designed by the central core to protect the city, which is designed to protect human life," Waldeyer replied. "The central core *must* be the determining factor in any decision to abandon the defenses. Though your arguments sound humane, they may, ultimately, be in violation of the First Law; for if the central core determines that your conclusions are erroneous, then shutting down the defenses could be the most dangerous of all possible decisions."

Derec felt as if he were on a treadmill. All argument ultimately led back to the central core. And though he was sure that the central core would back off once he programmed the information about human blood into it, he had no way to prove that to the robots who, in turn, refused to do anything to halt the city's replication until they'd received that confirmation from central.

Then an idea struck him, an idea that was so revisionist in its approach that he was frightened at first even to think out its effects on the robots. What he had in mind would either liberate their thinking or send them into a contradictory mental freeze-up that could destroy them.

"What do you think of Rydberg's plan?" Avernus asked him. "It will save a great many robots."

Avernus—that was it—Avernus the humanitarian. Derec knew that his idea would destroy the other robots, but Avernus, he was different. Avernus leaned toward the humane, a leaning that could just possibly save himself and the rest of Robot City.

"I will comment on the evacuation plan later," Derec said. "First, I'd like to speak with Avernus alone."

"We make decisions together," Euler said.

"Why?" Derec asked.

"We've always done it that way," Rydberg said.

"Not any more," Derec said, his voice hard. "Unless you can give me a sound, First Law reason why I shouldn't speak with Avernus alone, I will then assume you are violating the Laws yourselves."

Euler walked to the center of the room, then turned slowly to look at Avernus. "We've always done it this way," he said.

Avernus, the giant, moved stoically toward Euler, putting a larger pincer on the robot's shoulder. "It won't hurt anything, this once, if we go against our own traditions."

"But traditions are the hallmark of civilization," Euler said.

"Survival is also one of the hallmarks," Derec replied, looking up at Avernus. "Are you willing?"

"Yes," Avernus answered without hesitation. "We will speak alone."

Derec led Avernus to the elevators, then had a thought and returned to Euler. He unwrapped the fabric bandage from his cut arm and handed it to the supervisor. "Have the blood analyzed, the data broken down on disc so I can feed it to the core."

"Yes, Derec," Euler said, and it was the first time the supervisor had addressed him without the formal declaration, Friend. Maybe they were all growing up a little bit.

Derec then joined Avernus in the elevator, pushing the down arrow as the doors slid closed. They only traveled down for a moment before Derec pushed the emergency stop button; the machine jerked to a halt.

"What is this about?" Avernus asked.

"I want to make a deal with you," Derec said.

"What sort of deal?"

"The lives of your robots for one of your digging machines."

Avernus just stared at him. "I do not understand."

"Let's talk about the Third Law of Robotics," Derec said.

"You are obligated by the Third Law to protect your own existence as long as it doesn't interfere with the First or Second Laws. In your case, with your special programming, I can easily extend the Third Law to include the robots under your control."

"Go on."

"My deal is a simple one. Rydberg has suggested an evacuation plan that could save the robots in the mines from the flooding that is sure to occur if the cavern is not excavated. The evacuation plan depends *completely* on my reprogramming the central core to halt the replication. For if I don't, the city will have to keep replicating, even to its own destruction . . . that destruction to include the robots who are working underground."

"I understand that," Avernus said.

"All right." Derec took a deep breath. What he was getting ready to propose would undoubtedly freeze out the positronics of any of the other robots; the contradictions were too great, the choices too impossible to make. But with Avernus . . . maybe, just maybe. "Unless you give me one of the digging machines so I can begin the excavation myself, I will refuse to reprogram the central core, thereby condemning all your robots to stay underground during the flooding."

Avernus red eyes flared brightly. "You would . . . kill so many?"

"I would save your city *and* your robots!" Derec yelled. "It's all or nothing. Give me the machine or suffer the consequences."

"You ask me to deny the central core program that protects the First Law."

"Yes," Derec said simply, his voice quieting. "You have *got* to make the creative leap to save your robots. Somewhere in that brain of yours, you've got to make a value judgment that goes beyond your programming."

Avernus just stood there, quaking slightly, and Derec felt tears welling up in his eyes, knowing the torture he was putting the supervisor through. If this failed, if he, in effect, killing Avernus by killing his mind, he'd never be able to forgive himself.

The big robot's eyes flashed on and off several times, and suddenly his body shuddered violently, then stopped. Derec heard a sob escape his own lips. Avernus bent to him.

"You will have your digging machine," the robot told him, "and me to help you use it."

CHAPTER 13

THE CENTRAL CORE

Even as Katherine clung doggedly to the face of the pyramid, she knew that her ability to hold on could be measured in no more than minutes, as the rain lashed savagely at her and the winds worked to rip her off the patterned facade.

The ground lay several hundred meters below, calling to her. As her body went totally numb in the freezing downpour, her strong survival instinct was the only thing keeping her hanging on.

Her brain whirled, rejecting its own death while trying desperately to prepare for it, and through it all, she could hear the wind calling her name, over and over.

"Katherine!"

Closer now, the sound grew more pronounced. It seemed to come from below.

"Katherine!"

For the first time since she'd begun her climb, she risked a look downward, in the direction of the sound. She blinked through the icy water that streamed down her face only to see an apparition, a gray mass moving quickly up the face below her, proof that her mind was already gone.

"Katherine, hang on! I'm coming!"

In disbelief, she watched the apparition coming closer. And as her arms ached, trying to talk her into letting go and experiencing peace, she saw a golden hand reach from under the gray lump and grasp a handhold in one of the cutouts.

Wohler!

"Please hold on!"

"I can't!" she called back, surprised to hear the hysteria in her own voice. And as if to reinforce the idea, her left hand lost its grip, her arm falling away from the building, the added pressure sending cramping pain through her right arm still lodged in the hole.

The robot below hurried his pace. The wind, getting beneath the tarp he wore to protect himself from the rain, pulled it away from his body to float like a huge, prehistoric bird.

"P-please . . ." she called weakly, her right arm ready to give out.

"Hold on! Please hold on!"

The urgency in his voice astounded her, giving her an extra ounce of courage, a few more seconds when seconds were everything. And as she felt her hand slip away for good and all, his large body had wedged in behind her, holding her up against the facade.

Wohler clamped solidly in hand and footholds just above and below hers and he completely enveloped her, protecting. She let herself relax, all the strength immediately oozing out of her, Wohler supporting her completely.

"Are you unhurt?" the robot asked in her ear.

"I-I think so," she answered in a small voice. "What happens now?"

"We can only wait," Wohler said, his voice sounding somehow ragged. "An old Earth proverb says, 'Patience is a bitter plant but it has sweet fruit.' Survival w-will be our fruit . . . Friend Katherine."

"Friend Wohler," she responded, tears mixing with the cold rain on her face. "I want to th-thank you for coming up here for me."

But Wohler didn't answer.

The supervisors as a group stood behind the gateway excavator that Derec and Avernus operated. Neither helping nor hindering, they simply took it all in, no doubt unable to appreciate the thought processes that had led the big robot to pull the machine away from his mining crews and their replication labors, to put it to work simply clearing a path for something that, at this point, was no more than mere potential.

Derec had seen excavators like these before. On the asteroid where he had first awakened to find he had no identity, the robots had used identical machines to cut out the guts of the asteroid in their search for the Key to Perihelion.

The gateway was a marvel, for it demolished and rebuilt at the same time. Derec sat with Avernus at the two cabin control panels, watching the boom arms cutting into rock face nearly a hundred feet distant. One of the boom arms bore rotary grinders, the other microwave lasers that tore frantically at the core of the planet, chewing it up as it went. There were numerous conveyors and pulleys for the removal and scanning of potential salvage material, but none of these were in use right now. They were simply grinding and compressing the excavated rock and earth, the gateway it-self using the materials to build a strong tunnel behind—smooth rock walls, reinforcing synthemesh, even overhead lamps.

They were creeping toward the cavern, every meter a meter closer to possible salvation. They had been working through the night, Derec desperately trying to let the effort keep his mind off Katherine and Wohler. It wasn't working. There had been no word of them since before the storm had begun nearly ten hours ago. Had they been alive, he would have heard by now.

There was always the chance that Katherine had re-trieved the Key and left, perhaps waiting out the rain in the gray void of Perihelion, or perhaps finding her way to an-other place. But that didn't explain Wohler's absence.

During the grueling hours spent working the gateway, Avernus and Derec had conversed very little, both, appar-ently, lost in their own thoughts. Derec worried for Avernus, who he knew was going through a great many internal re-criminations that could only be resolved with a satisfactory outcome and subsequent vindication of his actions.

"Derec!" came Euler's voice from the newly built tunnel behind; it was the first time the robot had spoken to them since the operation had begun.

Derec looked at his watch. It was nearly five A.M. He shared a glance with Avernus. "Yes!" he called back.

"The rain has abated," Euler returned. "The missing have been located!"

Derec resisted the urge to jump from the controls and charge out of there. He still had work to do. He looked at Avernus. "What now?"

"Now we will see," the robot said. "We must locate the core and reprogram."

"Should I leave you here to continue operations and go with someone else to the core?"

"No," Avernus said with authority. "I am supervisor of the underground and know my way around it. I also... must know the outcome. Can you understand that?"

Derec reached out and punched off the control board, stopping new digging and bringing all operants to the standby position. "You bet I can understand it. Let's go!"

They moved out of the gateweay, squeezing past stacked up cylinders to join the other supervisors in the tunnel behind. It was the first time Derec had looked back at their handiwork. The tunnel he and Avernus had made stretched several hundred yards behind them, nearly as far he could see.

"Where are Katherine and Wohler?" he asked. "Are they all right?"

"No one knows," Rydberg said. "They are clinging to the side of the Compass Tower, nearly a hundred meters above the surface, but they have not responded to voice communication, nor have they attempted to come down."

Derec's heart sank. They'd been out all night in the rain. It looked bad.

"Are rescue operations underway?" he asked.

"Utility robots are now scaling the Tower to determine the extent of the problem for emergency disposition," Euler said.

"The central core," Avernus said to Dante. "Tell me where it is right now."

"Tell me honestly, Euler," Derec said. "Will my presence at the Tower facilitate the rescue operation?"

"Tower rescue has always been part of our basic program, for reasons no one can fathom," the robot said.

"Standard operating procedure has already been initiated. You could only hinder the operation."

"Good," Derec said. Of course Tower rescue was standard. The overseer had worried that, should the trap door to the office below become jammed, he would be caught on the Tower, unable to get down. The almighty overseer didn't mind letting everyone else twist slowly in the wind, but he wasn't going to let himself be uncomfortable on the Tower.

Dante spoke up from the terminal in his tram car. "The central core is in Quadrant 2, Tunnel D-24, moving to the north."

Avernus nodded and looked at Derec. "We must hurry," he said, "lest all our work be in vain."

"Work is already in vain," Waldeyer said to Avernus. "Because of your unauthorized impoundment of the gateway excavator, the on-hand raw iron consignments have dropped dangerously low. Within an hour, replication efforts will begin falling behind schedule."

The big robot simply hung his head, looking at the floor.

"I pose a question to you all," Derec said. "If Avernus and I are able to get to the core and reprogram to halt the replication, will our work already done here enable us to dig the rest of the way through to the cavern before tonight's rain?"

"Barring work stoppage and machinery malfunction," Euler said, "we should just be able to make it. This, of course, is all hypothetical."

Derec just looked at them. There was no satisfaction to be gained from arguing at this point. It was time to deliver the goods. "Where's the data from my blood sample?" he asked.

Arion stepped forward and handed him a mini-disc. "Everything you asked for is in here," he said.

"Thanks," Derec said, taking the disc and putting it in his breast pocket. "Now, listen. We're going to the central core. As soon as we reprogram, we'll need you to begin work here again immediately so that no time is lost."

Arion took a step toward the gateweay. "It is now too late to move the excavator back to the iron mine and pick up our failed operation there, so I see no reason why the digging here shouldn't continue in your absence. There is no longer anything to lose. I will continue to work here, even as you approach the central core."

"No," Euler said. "Will *you* now violate your programming, and perhaps the Laws?"

"The program is already shattered," Arion said, moving into the innards of the gateway. "There is no putting it back together now."

Derec smiled broadly as he heard the standby board being brought to full ready by Arion. He walked over to Dante. "We'll need your tram," he said. "Now."

The fever had come on strong, and along with it, hallucinations. Katherine's world was a nightmare of water, a world of water always threatening to pull her downward, and through it all Derec/David, David/Derec, Derec/David, his face smiling evilly and becoming mechanical even as she watched, metamorphosing from human to robot and back again, over and over. He'd skim the cresting waves to take her in his arms, only to use those arms to pull her underwater—drowning her! Drowning!

"Katherine . . . Katherine. Wake up. Wake up."

Voices intruding in her world of water. She wanted them to go away, to leave her alone. The water was treacherous, but at least it was warm.

"Katherine . . ."

Something was shaking her, pulling her violently from her dream world. She opened her eyes to pain blazing like fire through her head.

It was daytime, early morning. A utility robot was staring at her around the protective branch of Wohler's arm.

"C-cold," she rasped, teeth chattering. "So . . . cold."

A light flared above her and to the left, a light raining sparks. She squinted. Welders were using laser torches to cut Wohler's pincers off the facade where they were locked tight. Above the welder, she could see mechanical pulleys magnetically clamped to the side of the structure, city-material ropes dangling.

"We are cutting you free," the robot said. "A net and stretcher have been strung just below you. You are safe now."

"C-cold," she rasped again.

"We will warm you. We will get you medical attention."

And through the haze that was her mind, she felt the reassuring firmness of Wohler's body protecting her, always protecting her.

"Wohler!" she said loudly. "We're s-safe. Wohler!"

"Supervisor Wohler is . . . nonoperational," the utility said.

Even through the hurt and the delirium, she was wracked by waves of shame. That this robot would give his life for hers, after the way she'd acted, was more than she could bear.

She felt his weight behind her give; then hands were lifting both of them onto the stretchers pulled up tight below. She felt the morning sun on her face, a sun that Wohler would never experience again, and rather than dwell on the unpleasant results of its own selfishness, her mind once more retreated into the blissful haze of unconsciousness.

• • •

"Would you have?" Avernus asked him as they pushed the tram down tunnel D-24, heading north.

"Would I have what?" Derec replied. The tunnel walls rushed past, red lights zipping overhead at two-second intervals.

"Would you have let the robots die if I hadn't agreed to help you dig the tunnel?"

"No," Derec said. "I wouldn't have done anything like that. I just wanted to talk some sense into you."

"You lied to me."

"I lied to save you," Derec said. "Remember our discussion about lying in the Compass Tower? I created a different reality, a hypothetical reality, to force you into a different line of thought."

"You lied to me."

"Yes."

"I do not know if I'll ever really understand that," Avernus said, subtly telling Derec that their relationship would forever be strained.

"I'll have to learn to live with that," Derec replied sadly. "Sometimes the right thing isn't always the best thing. I'm sorry if I hurt you."

"Hurt is not a term that I understand," the robot replied.

"No," Derec said, turning to fiddle with the terminal Dante had left in the back. "It's a term that I relate to."

Derec used the terminal to contact the city's hastily organized medical facility, trying for information on Katherine and Wohler. He and Avernus had left Quadrant #4 and traveled through the city to #2, going underground again at that point. Tunnel D-24 was one of the more distant shafts, drilled as an oil exploration point for the plastics operation. A pipeline churned loudly, attached to the tunnel ceiling above their heads.

"They've gotten Katherine and Wohler down from the Tower!" he said, wishing his fingers moved as well as Dante's over the keyboard.

"Are they well?"

"Katherine is suffering from shock and exposure," Derec said excitedly. "She's being treated now. The prognosis is good. Wohler is ... is ..." He turned sadly to Avernus. "Wohler is dead."

"Look!" the robot called, pointing ahead.

Farther along the tunnel, they were rapidly closing on a moving area of light. It was perhaps six meters long, and just tall enough to miss the overhanging lights.

"The central core!" Avernus said, braking heavily, the tram skidding to a halt.

"What are you doing?" Derec asked. "It's getting away!"

"It will be faster now on foot," Avernus said.

"Not for me," Derec replied. "I can't run fast enough to ..."

"Climb on my back," the robot ordered. "Quickly."

While the huge robot was still sitting, Derec stood and climbed onto his broad back, putting his hands around Avernus's head, the robot locking an arm behind him, holding Derec on tightly.

Then Avernus jumped from the cart and began a headlong charge down the tunnel, moving faster than Derec realized was possible. Tunnel segments flew by in a blur as the moving core grew larger and larger in their vision.

They caught it quickly, and Avernus slowed his pace to match the speed of the core. Its outer surface was transparent plastic of some kind, and very thick. Like a transparent eggshell, it contained the complex workings of a sophisticated, operating machine. In the rear was a platform with steps leading up to a sliding door.

Avernus jumped, catching the stairs and climbing on. He brought his arm around, gently lifting Derec off to stand before the door. "Go on," he said. "Go in. Only one at a time can pass through."

Derec slid open the door by hand and walked in to find himself within the transparent chamber. A red button was set in the plastic before him. He pushed it. Sprayers and heat lamps came on, a full body spray of compressed air traveling the length of his body to remove all traces of dust. There was a loud sound of suction, and then the wall before him slid open and he walked into the beating heart of Robot City.

The core was open, like an exposed brain, its working synapses sparking photons up and down its length, its fluidics a marvel of imaginative engineering. He found a typer halfway down its length and juiced it to life, while hearing Avernus going through the chamber ritual. The robot was doubled over to fit within the "clean room."

The first thing he did was open a file under the heading of HEMOGLOBIN, and enter the disc's-worth of information Arion had procured for him. Then he got into the DEFENSES file again, going as far as he could with the system until it prompted him for the supervisor's password.

He heard a door slide open and turned to see Avernus, still somewhat hunched over, move to stand beside him at the typer.

"It wants your password," Derec said.

Avernus looked at him, not speaking, then reached out and typed on the screen:

AVERNUS—2Q2-1719

PASSWORD:SYNNOETICS

Without a second's hesitation, the computer prompted:

RATIONALIZATION FOR DEACTIVATION OF CITY DEFENSES?

With shaking fingers, Derec typed his rationalization into the machine, dumping, as he did so, all the information from the HEMOGLOBIN file into the CITY DEFENSES file as authoritative backup and information to keep the same thing from ever happening again.

When he was through typing he stood back and took a breath, almost afraid to push the ENTER key.

"We must know now," Avernus said.

Derec nodded, swallowed hard, and entered the information.

The machine churned quietly for a moment that seemed to last an hour. Finally, quite simply and without fanfare, it responded.

RATIONALIZATION ACCEPTED—DEFENSES DEACTIVATED.

They stood for a moment, staring, not quite believing that it could be so easy. Then they felt a noticeable slowing of the core's motion. Within seconds, it had ground to a stop.

It was over.

CHAPTER 14

WORLD PERFECT

Derec walked the corridors of the mostly dark, mostly un-furnished medical facility. It would be a fine building when it was completely finished, a place where the humans who would inhabit Robot City could receive the finest medical care available anywhere in the galaxy under the supervision of the most advanced team of med-bots operational. He knew this would be so because the robots who performed the services would perform them by choice, out of love in-stead of servitude.

He walked the corridors alone—no guides, no keepers, no jailers. He was a free citizen now, a condemned man no longer. And it was good, because now, right now, he pre-ferred being alone.

A room at the end of the corridor was awash with light, and he knew he'd find Katherine there, recovering from her night with the storm. He no longer cared about her subter-fuge or her reasons for being with him on Robot City. For good or ill, he was happy and thankful that she was alive. Nothing else really could, or did, matter.

He was beginning to know why she affected him the way she did—he loved her.

He reached the room and poked his head inside. It was a large room, one that would most likely be a ward at some future time. But right now it was empty, except for Katherine's place at the far end.

She lay in stasis, floating half a meter above a table, bright lights surrounding her completely. She was naked, just as she'd been on Rockliffe Station. This time he didn't turn away, but looked, and her body seemed somehow . . . familiar to him.

A med-bot rolled up to him.

"How is she?" he asked.

"Splendid," the robot replied, "except for her chronic condition . . ."

"I don't want to talk about it," he said, letting her have her secrets. "Other than that?"

"She's sleeping lightly," the med-bot said. "We have rebalanced her chemicals through massive influxes of oxygen and fluids, and warmed her up. She lost a small part of her left ear to the cold, but that has already been adjusted through laser cosmetic surgery. You may visit with her if you wish."

"I'd like that," he said. "But before you wake her up, would you put a robe or something on her?"

"The heat lamps work better if . . ."

"I know," Derec said. "It's a matter of her personal privacy."

"I see," the robot said in its best bedside manner, but Derec could tell that it didn't.

When the med-bot turned and rolled back to Katherine, Derec politely stepped through the doorway and back into the hall.

A moment later, he could hear her talking to the robot, so he walked back in. She was off the table, sitting in a motorized chair, swathed in a bright white bathrobe. Her face was blank as he moved up to her.

"I'm sorry for everything," he said. "I've been suspicious and hard to get along with and . . ."

She smiled slightly, putting up a hand. "No more than I have," she said softly, her voice hoarse. "I guess I've acted pretty stupidly."

"Human prerogative," he said. "You look . . . good."

"They scraped the surface skin off me," she said, "cleared away the dead dermis. I guess I could say you're looking at the new me." She moved her gaze to the floor. "The Key is gone."

"I didn't know," he replied. "I guess we're really stuck."

She nodded. "Did you hear what . . . what Wohler did for me?"

"Yes."

"I never understood your . . . feeling for the robots," she said, eyes welling up with tears. "But his life was as important to him as mine is to me, and he . . . he gave it up . . . so I could live."

"He was burned out completely," Derec said. "They're trying to reconstruct him now."

She looked up at him. "Reconstruct?"

"It won't be the same, of course. We are, all of us, a product of our memories. The Wohler you knew is, for the most part, dead."

"But if they reconstruct," she said, "something of him will remain."

"Yes. Something."

"I want to go there," she said. "I want to go where he is."

She tried to stand, Derec gently pushing her back in the chair. "You're still a sick girl," he said. "You can't be running around doing..."

"No," she said, a spark of the old Katherine already coming back. "He died so that I could live. If there's anything of him left, I want to be there."

Derec drew a long breath. "I'll see what I can do," he said, knowing how stubborn she could be.

And so, thirty minutes later, Katherine, wrapped in a sterile suit, wheeled herself into the dust-free repair chamber where six different robots were working diligently on the body of Wohler, the philosopher. Derec walked with her.

Most of his plating was gone, circuit boards and relays hitting the floor with clockwork regularity, a small robot wheeling silently around and sweeping up the discards.

"Can I get closer?" she asked Derec.

"I don't see why not," he answered.

Just then, Euler came into the chamber and walked directly toward the couple. "Friend Derec," he said. Derec smiled at the reuse of the title before his name. "We are just completing work on the connecting tunnel to the runoff cavern and would very much like you to be present for the opening."

Derec looked down at Katherine. "Well, I'm kind of busy right now, I..."

"Nonsense," Katherine said, reaching out to pat his hand. "I'm just going to stay around here for a while. One of the robots here can get me back to medical."

He smiled broadly. "You sure it's okay?"

She nodded, smiling widely. "I understand completely," she said.

He grinned at Euler. "Let's go," he said, and the two of them moved quickly out of the room.

Katherine listened to their footsteps receding down the hall, then wheeled her chair closer to the work table. Her anger at Derec along with a great many other conflicting emotions, had died along with Wohler on the Compass Tower. Because of her thoughtlessness, a life had been lost. All her other emotions seemed petty in the face of that.

She wheeled up near the golden robot's head. Most of his body was exposed in pieces on the table, but the head and upper torso were intact. The robots working on the body moved around the table to accommodate her presence.

She stared at his head, reaching out a finger to gingerly touch him. "I'm so sorry," she said.

Suddenly, the head turned to her, its photocells glowing brightly. "Were you addressing me?" he asked her.

"Wohler," she said, jumping. "You're alive."

"Do we know one another?" he asked, and she realized that this was a different Wohler, a newly programmed Wohler who knew nothing of their previous experience.

"No," she said, choking back a sob. "My name is Katherine. I'm . . . pleased to make your acquaintance."

"A new friendship is like new wine," Wohler said. "When it has aged, you will drink it with pleasure. Katherine . . . Katherine. Why are you crying?"

Only a small dam held back the waters in the trench from the tunnel that Derec and Avernus had dug to the cavern. The supervisors and as many of the utility robots as could clusters in the opening were there, Derec holding the electronic detonator that would blast away the dam and open up the new waterway.

"This is the first day," Euler told him, "the first day in a truly unified city of humans and robots. The beginning of the perfect world."

"We have reacted synnoetically to make this day happen," Rydberg said. "Working together we can accomplish much."

"While we still have a great deal to learn about one another," Derec said, "I, too, believe that we have proven something of value here today."

"Then open the floodgate, Friend Derec," Euler said, "and make the connection complete."

"With pleasure."

Derec flipped the toggle on the hand control. A small explosion made the wall of dirt and rock jump. Then it crumbled, and rapidly flowing water from the trench finished the job that the explosive had begun.

And as the waters rushed past, he thought of all the things still unresolved, still rushing, like the waters, through his confused brain. Who was he? Who was the dead man? Who put this all together, and why?

And then there was Katherine.

In many ways, he still felt as if his journey had just begun, but he couldn't help but feel he had accomplished something major with the breaking down of the dam. He couldn't help but feel that something good, something positive had been accomplished. And that made him feel just fine. Maybe life was nothing so much as a succession of small battles, small victories to be won.

"Derec," came a voice behind him, and he turned to see Avernus standing there.

"Yes?"

The robot, so large, spoke with a small voice. "I do not know that I can understand why you did what you did to me last night," he said, "but I cannot help but feel that we did the right thing, and that doing the right thing is what is important."

"I couldn't agree more," Derec said, smiling widely. "Friends?"

Avernus nodded solidly. "Friends," he said, as he laid his pincer in Derec's open palm in the universal gesture of peace and good will.

It wasn't going to be such a bad day after all.